Oldearth

ARAM

—ENCOUNTER—

By A.K. Frailey

Hardcover Edition

Copyright 2023 A.K. Frailey

All rights reserved. No portion of this book may be reproduced in any form without permission from the publisher, except as permitted by U.S. copyright law. For permissions, contact akfrailey@yahoo.com.

Cover design: A.K. Frailey and James Hrkach
Photo credit (of man): SensorSpot (Istockphoto)
Photo credit (grass): ThreeJumps (Flickr)

ISBN of Hardcover: 979-8-9861803-6-6

The Writings of A. K. Frailey
Books for the Mind and Spirit

https://akfrailey.com/

Contact

akfrailey@yahoo.com

Historical Science Fiction Novels

OldEarth ARAM Encounter

OldEarth Ishtar Encounter

OldEarth Neb Encounter

OldEarth Georgios Encounter

OldEarth Melchior Encounter

Science Fiction Novels

Homestead

Last of Her Kind

Newearth Justine Awakens

Newearth A Hero's Crime

Short Stories

*It Might Have Been—
And Other Short Stories 2nd Edition*

One Day at a Time and Other Stories

*Encounter Science Fiction
Short Stories & Novella 2nd Edition*

Inspirational Non-Fiction

My Road Goes Ever On—Spiritual Being, Human Journey 2nd Edition

My Road Goes Ever On—A Timeless Journey

The Road Goes Ever On—A Christian Journey Through The Lord of the Rings

Children's Book

The Adventures of Tally-Ho

Poetry

Hope's Embrace & Other Poems 2nd Edition

**Audible Versions Now Available.
Check book details on Amazon
for current listings.**

Dedication

To the human race.

May grace be our guide.

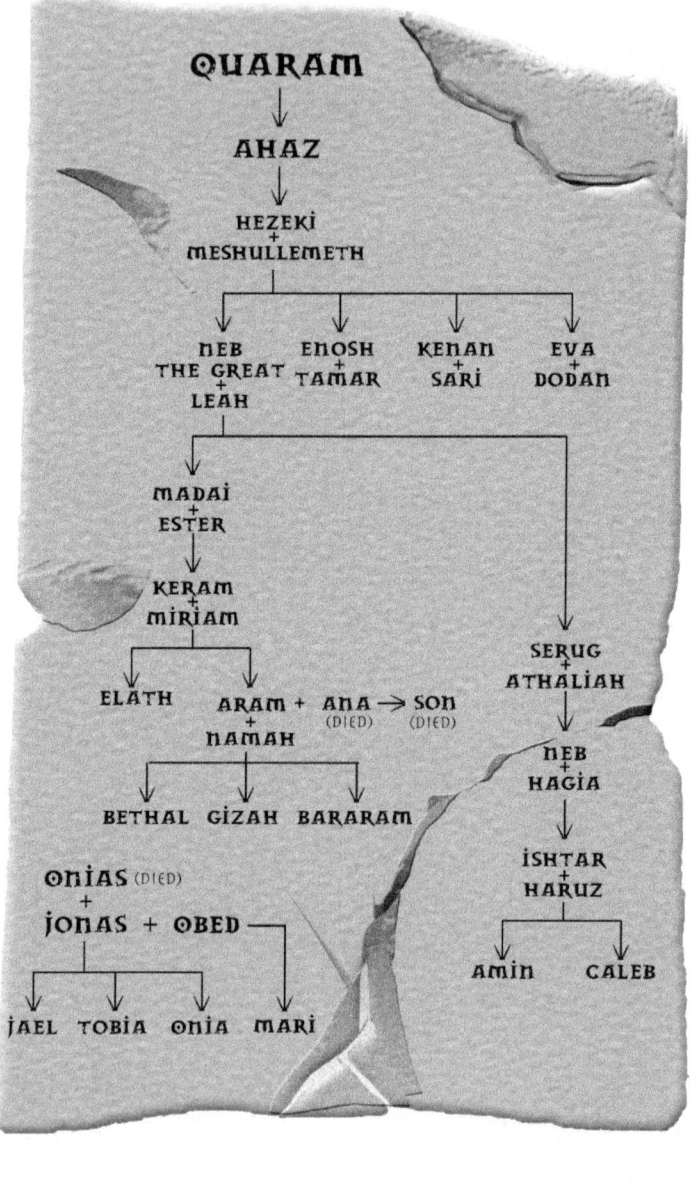

Prologue

—OldEarth—

I Shall Return

Teal exhaled a long breath as he started across the shadowy evening expanse.

The moon, full and bright, wavered among sinewy branches. Light fragments splayed across the forest floor. In his lean, middle-aged human form, Teal stepped sure-footed among the ancient trees. His leather tunic swayed with each step. He stopped and glanced back only once.

A group of men and women huddled around a meager flickering fire. Their drooping heads and muted conversations bespoke mutual exhaustion and despair.

They were not *his* people, yet he cringed at the thought of abandoning these helpless beings to the ravages of an unforgiving wilderness. But his year was up, and he must return to his Luxonian home world. Duty called. The Supreme Council awaited his report.

He lifted his hand in salute. "Stay safe—I shall return." Just before he flashed out of sight, Teal caught the bright eyes of a single human, a brawny man with black hair, who would either lead his people to safety—or die trying.

Chapter One

—Woodland —

The Land Beyond

Aram shivered despite the sweat trickling down his spine. A shower of drops splattered across his face as he beat back the forest's dangling vines and springy saplings. Exhaustion sapped his last bits of energy. With the back of his mud-smeared hand, he wiped his face.

Visions of a warm fire and venison haunches sizzling on a spit caused his heart to momentarily fail. His weary limbs demanded rest, but he only shook his head. Not yet—but soon.

His people staggered in stupefaction. Their flight seemed never-ending, their search futile. Danger lurked in every dark motion of the forest.

As his muscular body plodded through the root-gnarled muck of the late rainy season, a new light grew in his mind. He could still see the tawny-colored fur and glittering eyes of the beast as it snatched its first struggling, screaming victim. When he had heard the throaty growls and the moon's glow had cast uneven shadows on the beast, he had frozen with horror in the face of the cat's great size.

It had struck in twilight when light danced with utter blackness. His wife, Namah, hunch-backed and morose, had been directing the meal preparations. Her orders rang out shrill and abundant—as usual. The other women had obeyed with their typical, sullen compliance.

He had glanced at Namah as the mighty feline landed on its victim, and though her wide-eyed terror had matched his, she had thrown a rock at the retreating creature. Despite her crooked spine, she showed strength of mind—not unlike that of the cat.

Even when he had thrown his spear and others joined in the action with cries of fear and anguish, he knew it was too late. The night was too dark and the cat too mammoth to hunt in the gloomy forest.

Aram had known the youth well and agony had gripped his heart, but his mind would not respond to his grief—only to fear. If he gave his clan time to rest, their anguish might turn to madness. If he kept moving, they might outrun both beast and terror.

A child squalled.

But they were past exhaustion now. The lands of their forefathers lay far behind them. They would soon enter lands unknown to his memory. They had always gained life from familiar trees, made suitable shelters, and found peace beneath their branches. The ancient woods gnarled together in a forest of immeasurable depth. But their frantic travels led them into a foreign land.

"Do you know these trees?" Namah leaned on a staff near his elbow, burdened by the weight of all the earthly treasure she had managed to bundle on her back. No children hindered her grasp. Nearly doubled over, she huffed and her toes squelched, sinking deep into the muck.

Aram surveyed the thinning woods. "Well enough." He swung his oak spear, swatting a sapling out of the way.

"How far have we come?" Namah's unfocused stare feigned calm disinterest, but a weary whine seared her words.

Women swung crying infants over their sagging shoulders, while men grunted in displeasure, adjusting bulky, threadbare packs. An old man groaned as he leaned upon a thin, ragged child's shoulder. A little girl wailed, and a resounding smack bore testimony to raw nerves and worn tempers.

Aram grunted as he considered the woods' strange lighting, the speckled texture of the tree bark, and the warning in his bones.

"Isn't the land different here, Aram? The trees appear more

spaced apart, and the ground lays flat. Where are the hills and ravines?" Namah's gaze flickered to her husband. One inquisitive eyebrow arched.

Aram nodded. He had known land like this—long ago. "We're near the forest edge. It's been a generation since my people passed this way."

From some forgotten abyss, a memory flickered to life. Aram's grandfather had once recounted the story of a huge beast that struck the unwary in the dark of night. The tale had seemed nothing more than the caution of an old man meant to keep the youth from wandering into dark places. Aram swallowed back fear and squared his shoulders.

Two nights ago, the nightmare returned, and the beast had struck again. It had followed them as they edged nearer his grandfather's territory. After the cat struck, they headed straight for the border. Now they had to make a break into the unknown.

"Do you know who lives in the land beyond?" Namah panted and leaned on a shaggy, grey trunk.

"No. I grew up far from here. My father's long dead, though perhaps some of his people still live. I had a brother—" Aram rubbed his chin, his stomach tightening.

Namah shifted her pack.

"He ventured to the high lands. His clan included many women and children—so he favored the safety of mountains. I've not seen him since I was very young."

"And your grandfather—had he no brothers?"

"One, but they disputed over a secret matter and separated. I've no wish to meet my grandfather's brother or any of their kin. They're not to be trusted. We'll do well to keep our distance."

Namah snorted. "Surely, such ancient differences could be put aside at a time like this. Perhaps they know of this beast and could help us defeat it."

Aram scowled. "You know nothing of the matter! We don't need help. We'll keep to ourselves."

Namah bowed her head in servant fashion. She cast her gaze to the broken path behind them and lowered her voice. "Would the beast travel so near the edge of the forest? Wouldn't it fear these strange lands?" Her gaze searched his face as the sun drew level with the horizon.

Tilting his head as he considered it, Aram exhaled and raised his hand. "We'll rest here for the night."

Grunts and sighs issued as bundles slid to the ground and knees sank to the earth in relief.

Studying the landscape, Aram's gaze roved the expanse. The dense woodlands had fallen behind; open space gave way to patches of bare ground covered only by tall, swaying grasses.

Namah's black eyes narrowed.

A voice snapped loud and abrupt. "Aram!" The largest man in the clan, Barak, strode forward; his fur cloak lay slung far over his shoulders and his barrel chest thrust out as if preparing for a weighty pronouncement. His head cocked to one side like a bird intent on its prey. When he came alongside Aram, he folded his arms across his chest. "We're tired of running. The women are beyond their strength, and some of us question the direction you're taking."

With minimal effort, Aram's eyes rolled to the side.

Those looking on frowned in puzzlement.

Aram clasped his hands and faced the assembly. "Tonight we build many fires instead of one. Make a great circle of flame, and we'll sleep inside its protection. Tomorrow we'll travel into the treeless plains." Striding over to an enormous, ancient pine tree, Aram unwound his cape and tossed it upon a bed of dry needles. Leaning against the tree and pillowing his hands behind his head, he closed his eyes.

Namah surveyed the uncertain crowd and masked a wavering smile. Her voice rose in command. "Gather kindling and seek fresh water!"

She gathered ideas as a bird hoarded twigs for a nest. With patience, she would rule—in her own way. Her gaze swung from her husband to Barak. A smile rose up inside as her heart fluttered in excitement.

Chapter Two

—Ingoti Trading Vessel—
—OldEarth—

Intercept Course

Ingoti—large beings that originate from the planet Ingilium, range from six to seven feet tall. Extremely heavy due to their extensive weight and girth, they are also fast and powerful. They are never seen outside of their bulky techno-organic armor, although their faces—typically free of masks—appear quite human.

Like a ship jerked loose from its mooring, an Ingoti trading vessel slipped into Earth's atmosphere...

Zuri, an Ingoti trader renowned for his clever deals, braced for impact, but there was little he could do to protect his co-pilot.
Gem crouched, covering his head with his arms and hoped that the restraints would hold.
The small vessel plowed a deep furrow into the lush dirt and crashed into an earthen hillside.
As the dust settled, Zuri blinked and returned to consciousness. He studied his biomechanical techno-armor. Seeing it intact, he sighed in relief. Hobbling to the main console, he reviewed the status of the ship. Various systems blinked offline, but life support held firm. Glancing back at the cargo hold, he ticked off the needed repairs in his mind and stepped forward.
Gem lay sprawled across the floor unconscious.
Crouching by his side, Zuri made a quick diagnostic review of Gem's bio-suit life signs. With a chuckle, he lightly slapped

Gem's ruddy cheek. "Get up, lazy fool. We're already behind schedule, and Crestas aren't known for their patience."

Rising on one elbow with a groan, Gem shook his head like a confused Ingoti bullock. "I thought I was done for. What happened?"

Zuri stood and rubbed his back. "That replacement Orbital Maintenance you bought blew and sent us spiraling right into the atmosphere. Should've guessed. It was too cheap to be an honest deal."

"Blast! I'll pay them back for this; don't worry." Gem rose and started toward the console. "How long before we're ready to set off again?"

His gaze rising to the ceiling, Zuri crossed his arms. "It'll only take a few hours with both of us working on it. But, I've heard about this planet—how about we take a little tour?"

Gem scowled. "I've heard about humans, too. Primitive and—"

"I didn't say anything about humans. By the Divide, if I wanted to go to the zoo, I'd visit the one on Helm." He stroked his chin. "No, how about scouting around a little? We might find resources we could use. The Ingilium would pay dearly...."

A crooked smile crawled across Gem's face.

~~~

While struggling through dense woodland, Gem wiped his sweaty brow. "How does anyone survive here? It's not fit for habitation!"

Zuri shrugged. "Not where I would've chosen to land—"

A low growl stopped them dead in their tracks.

Slowly, they turned. Zuri raised his Dustbuster and aimed as a tawny, four-legged beast drew near.

Gem swallowed. "That thing's enormous!" Turning at the sound of human voices, he grinned. "Ah, it's tracking *them*." He pointed to a clearing where a large group of humans had settled down for rest.

Crouching low, Zuri peered between the branches and observed the throng.

Men, women, and children crowded around a central figure—a tall, muscled man with long black hair.

Peering back at Gem, Zuri shook his head. "They're practically naked—without any techno-armor at all. Amazing they've survived! They must be brighter than they look." After stepping back, he sent a low-power beam searing through the foliage near the stalking cat, frightening the beast into the thick woods.

Gem scowled. "What'd you do that for? Let the whole planet know we're here, why don't you."

Zuri pointed the Dustbuster at Gem. "Is there anything left of you—on the inside, I mean? We were once naked and helpless too. If the Cresta's hadn't taught us—"

"They *used* us in their studies. They weren't being generous."

"But we *learned* from them! That's what counts."

Gem stared at the Dustbuster in Zuri's hand. "So, what's your point?"

Shoving the weapon into his armor holster, Zuri shrugged. "I'm just giving them a chance to live and learn." He stalked back toward the ship. "It's time we left. I've got enough data to make up for the time we've lost." He grinned as he swiped a branch out of his way. "The Cresta will pay for both the cargo and the information."

Gem marched behind. "And the Ingilium Supreme Command? What'll they say?"

Zuri turned, and, clasping Gem's shoulder, he lifted his eyes to the sky. "Contrary to my expectations, I foresee a day when humans and their primitive world will be quite useful. We're on an intercept course. In any case—information always pays."

Chapter Three

—Grassland—

Veil of Death

Onias gripped his obsidian knife and considered the wooden figure in his grasp. He sighed.

"If your eyes are hurting, go inside and rest. You don't need to sit out here. It's cooler in the shade."

Sitting cross-legged, Onias peered up at his wife, Jonas, and smiled at her mothering tone. He wiped his sweaty brow and laid aside his knife. Blinking, he glanced down at his work. The figure of a boy carved from the root of an old gnarled tree stared up at him.

Wood spoke to him, creating images in his mind. Only recently had he begun to carve bits from broken branches and twigs, enhancing the impression of a face or animal. A shiver sped through his body. Propping his head on his hand, he vaguely wondered if his fever had returned.

Jonas lugged a heavy fur blanket out of their mud-and-straw dwelling into the sun where she strung it up between two stout posts—the same posts that Onias had driven into the ground not long ago when he was still healthy. Rhythmically beating out the dirt and sending billows of dust into the bright sunshine, her face glistened with sweat.

The steady thwacking, in tune to the gentle humming of bees, enchanted Onias. The scent of new life and the whirl of insects responding in ecstasy to all of creation's possibilities widened his eyes as he gazed across the vast, undulating grasslands. He enjoyed the contrast of the fresh green grass against the immense blue sky.

Leaning back against the earthen wall that made their dwelling, he admired their village of neat little one and two room huts laid out in a semicircle formation. A wide oval space dominated the center where the clan gathered in the evenings to share stories and settle disputes. He had always enjoyed listening to his clansmen as they shared their hopes and discussed their fears. His jaw clenched. Before long, he would be too weak to sit and too weary to care.

He peered across to the mountains in the northeast. Fluffy white clouds blew across the wide expanse and dominated the landscape in their own impersonations of mountains. They were but changing things, those clouds. They were pretenders at best and deadly illusions at worst. As a fog that disappears before you can touch it—such is the power of a clan leader.

Onias' eyes followed a young shepherd as he trailed after a flock of goats to a nearby pastureland where they spread out and grazed in placid trust.

Jonas shaded her eyes with her hand and peered across the landscape, mumbling. "Where have Jael and Tobia gone now?"

Returning to the wooden figure in his lap, Onias smiled at the beauty that had flowed from his fingers. What was this magic that entered his hands, allowing him to give new life to old wood? The figure seemed to come alive as he shaped it. As tall as a man's hand, the likeness to a real boy with his arms outstretched in welcome startled him. What god had given his hands this skill? How could he become a creator—even in so small a matter?

Grasping his knife, his hand trembled. He closed his eyes and swallowed back bitterness. Who had the power—and desire—to destroy *him*? This question tormented him even more than the fevers that wracked his body with increasing frequency. What lay beyond the veil of death? In their old age, his mother and a season later, his father had turned cold and their breath ceased in the veil of night. Where had their vital, engaging spirits gone?

Onias leaned his head against the wall and gazed at nothing, his hands still. A vulture circled far above, searching out the weakness of all below. Lowering his gaze, Onias peered at his wife, but he knew better than to ask impossible questions for she would merely peer deep into his eyes, make him swallow bitter medicine, and send him off to bed as if he were a child. He closed his eyes and let the warm sunlight soak into his chilled bones.

Jonas clapped her hands in motherly authority. "I said—go in now. You're tired and need rest."

Rubbing his eyes, Onias hunched forward. There was no use arguing. She was right. It made no difference that his soul cringed at the sight of the dark entrance to their dwelling. Laboring to his feet, he gathered his knife and the boy-figure and limped to the doorway. The cool shade beckoned, but he yearned for the sunshine. He paused on the threshold. His heart pounded. Where would he go when his body went cold? He stumbled backward.

Jonas hurried forward. "Has your headache returned?"

He forced a weary smile. "No, I'm fine." On impulse, he clasped her hand. "But I have a question." He pointed to a shady spot next to their dwelling.

"Oh?" Her steady gaze faltered. She nodded, assisted him to the enveloping shadow, and sat at his side. "What is it?" Her tone reflected practiced cheerfulness.

Peering up at the lowering sun, Onias blinked at the blinding glare. "What will you do when I'm gone? Who will help you with the boys?" He paused and glanced away, his gaze falling to the earth. "Obed is a good man."

Staring wide-eyed, Jonas turned away. "Onias—no."

Running his fingers down her back, Onias stretched out his legs. It wearied him to see how thin they were. No wonder he felt so tired; he was half-dead already. "I was thinking that since Obed is so good to us, and he's here so often, that after I'm gone—"

Jonas clutched Onias' hands and dropped her head to his shoulder. "No! Don't speak of this. Just rest. Wait and see. No one knows the future. Live for today. Don't ask me to think about— I can't!"

He smoothed her long brown hair with the flat of his hand.

His eyes wandered back to the clouds drifting over the horizon. His eyelids closed, and he sighed.

Suddenly, footsteps stopped in front of them.

Onias glanced up.

Jonas sat bolt upright.

Before them stood a thickset man with a full beard and shaggy brown hair loosened from a braid that ran down his back. Everything about him was solid, even the braid. His thick legs were spread far apart to support his massive build. Leather pants and a rough, sleeveless tunic adorned his body. His muscles gleamed in the warm sun. He appeared too massive to be blown by the mightiest wind, yet he swayed with unnatural, punctuated jerks. His grim mouth formed a hard line, though suppressed delight sparkled in his eyes.

Jonas swallowed. "Yes, Eoban?"

Eoban's deep voice boomed. "I suppose these are yours?"

Jonas's gaze fell from his mighty face to the shifting and wiggling cloak as Eoban, with difficulty, managed to expose the hind ends of two small children.

The boys squirmed vigorously in their feeble attempts to kick themselves free. Their muffled cries alternated with moments of quiet as they tried to catch their breaths.

Jonas burst into laughter. She stood and lifted her hands, ready to receive her children. "What have you two been up to now, I wonder? Where did you find them, Eoban?"

"No place special." Eoban's eyebrows rose to dangerous heights. "Just up by the lakeshore. I was coming back from a trip in the north when I decided to stop, and to my surprise, I found not fish but two boys who hoped to grow fins. It was a good thing that I happened along." Without further ceremony, he plopped his captives on the ground where they landed with earthy thuds and cries of anguish.

The taller of the two shook his fist at Eoban. "We're all right. We knew what we were doing."

Jonas frowned in warning. "Jael."

"And you didn't need to pick us up like that just when we

got to the village. We'd have come and told—without your prodding."

His miniature copy, Tobia, frowned as fiercely as his older brother.

Jonas's hand flew into the air in a firm but silent command. Her black eyebrows arched. "I warned you the last time you two went wandering. I hold you, Jael, responsible for your brother. He's too little for such distances."

Jael flushed as he put his arm around his sibling. "He's faster and stronger than you know."

Tobia beamed.

Muted afternoon shadows slanted across the land as clouds gathered.

Jonas wagged a finger at the two boys. "You'll go to bed without your evening meal. That should give you a reason to pause the next time you feel like wandering. You're lucky that Eoban came along." She glanced over. "How many times has this been, Eoban?"

The two vagabonds glowered alternately at their mother and then at Eoban, rubbing their arms to massage the blood back into circulation.

Eoban forced a disapproving scowl into place. "Three times, Jonas. Three times I have caught them. Only the gods know how many times they have wandered far afield."

"That's three times too many! I have been too lenient."

"But Eoban travels!" Jael wailed. "He goes north to trade and learns news from afar. He goes wherever he wants." His eyes flashed angry sparks of resentment.

Onias rose and laid a hand on each of his sons' shoulders. "Your mother is wise. She's seen wild animals attack the unwary and watched loved ones suffer sickness and death. Do as she says. Go in now." He ruffled their heads in gentle reassurance.

With hunched shoulders, the two boys ambled inside their dwelling.

Onias turned to Eoban. "Thank you, friend. You're always good to us. How would this village survive if you weren't here to save our children from their foolish pranks?"

Sucking in a deep contented breath, Eoban shrugged in mock humility.

"For time out of mind, we wandered and endured, and now that we have found peace, our young want to travel to foreign parts." Onias' gaze wandered back to the mounting clouds. "Are we missing something?"

Eoban folded his arms and rocked on his heels. "A boy is not unlike the seed of a great tree. They both must go to a place of their own and push everything out of their way as they stretch toward the sun. They're alive and growing. Someday their daring will come in useful."

Jonas stepped to the dwelling and peered in.

Eoban's voice dropped low as he leaned toward Onias. "I know you don't want to hear it, but it'd be good to have more wanderers who trade and hear the news of the world. We'd do well to prepare ourselves for whatever may come. Besides, I seem to remember a time when you liked to roam far afield."

Having stepped beside her husband, Jonas laughed outright and hugged his arm.

Eoban squared his shoulders. "It's true; the clan depends much on me." He waved this concern aside. "I can stand it for a time, but you must teach your boys to take my place when I've grown old and need a rest. Three or four sons should do the job."

Onias chuckled as Jonas shook her head.

Eoban threaded his way through the village, then turned and called back. "And tell the boys, I'm having roast pig for supper, and I'll have to eat it all by myself since they can't come help me." He turned and was lost from sight behind a dwelling.

A soft smile played on Jonas' lips. "You see? We never know who's looking out for us. Let's see what the future will bring."

Onias peered into the sky as the clouds converged. Soon they would be enveloped in a blanket of night. Only in memory would twinkling stars and a crescent moon speak of a distant, unseen light.

Chapter Four

—The River—

Haunted

Ishtar knew that if it got much darker, he would miss the landing spot. They had to paddle faster. Night was coming on. His mission and three canoes full of his father's warriors depended on him to do his part. The water—still cool from the snow melting off the distant mountains—contrasted sharply with the steam rising from his weary body.

He thought again of his father's directions and his mother's scornful gaze. He was too young for the task, his mother had said, though they both knew this was not strictly true. Other men his age were going on raids, and so far, all but one had been successful.

With a shake, he willed himself to concentrate on the shoreline and to find the exact spot he and his father, Neb, had reconnoitered months ago.

During a long hunting trip in the dry season when the nights were chilly, his father had seen signs of a village to the south. After investigating, Neb had smiled in his grim manner. There before his covetous gaze, a village flourished. The inhabitants appeared strong but not warlike.

Ishtar recognized the gleam in his father's eyes. Their bold warriors would make a surprise attack and take as many prisoners and tools as they pleased. Neb's greedy heart had rejoiced.

As the paddle sliced into the black water, Ishtar set his jaw. He knew his duty and what his father required of him. Neb followed with a larger force. He sent Ishtar ahead to spy out the land and see that all was secure. Ishtar would make his report as soon as his father had landed.

Each warrior had been reared from his early youth to consider it his highest purpose and greatest achievement to be fearsome in battle. Some slaves even acquired their freedom through daring exploits endured for the good of the River Clan.

Ishtar knew that the number of slaves they brought home would determine the success of this raid. They needed healthy young men and women. If he failed, he would be punished.

Swallowing, Ishtar remembered the punishment meted out to Elam when he failed their last campaign. He closed his eyes. Neb was good to those who served him well, but terrible to those who failed. The image still haunted him at night. He could imagine Elam's laughing eyes as they had played in the water as boys. He pictured the pride-filled look of a strong young man with a bronzed body, thick black hair, and the first signs of a man's beard. He thought he could do no wrong. Then came the day of battle when Elam had led his small band of clansmen to the wrong destination. The skirmish had failed, and Elam's eyes filled with shame and anguish.

But Neb's eyes hardened like that of a stalking cat at night, red and glowing like fire, yet cold with no mercy.

Soon after, Elam died from the infliction of too stern a justice. Ishtar did not understand Neb's reasoning. He only knew the sight and sounds of a man in torment before he dies.

Ishtar shook his head to clear away the webs of doubt. His father had not always been so harsh. He had changed, like a tree overgrown with vines that loses its original shape. It was after they had broken ties with the great clan. They crossed vast open plains and finally arrived at the long-sought river lands, which contained everything they needed. Everyone had seemed so happy.

But a silent scourge slowly intruded on their joy, and the clan turned bitter. A few years later, they made their first raid. Ishtar knew little of secret matters, but he did know that he and Elam were like brothers. Neither his mother nor Elam's mother had other sons or daughters. Perhaps more children would have tempered his father's warrior nature. But these thoughts tread dangerously close to questions considered heresy by Neb, and this Ishtar could ill afford. After all, if Elam could be treated in such a manner for a simple failure, what would Neb do if he knew his own son harbored doubts and secret accusations?

Sweating in fear, Ishtar paddled furiously. His brown eyes widened and his long hair sprawled loose across his back. The black water sprayed over his face as his aching arms moved in silent rhythm to the pounding of his heart.

Chapter Five

—Woodland—

The Rising Sun

Aram woke to the sound of discontented murmuring. He sat up, rubbed his eyes, and crawled out of his makeshift tent. As he stood, he reviewed the scene before him. Not far away, Namah pointed into the distance. Others grumbled around her, and she vigorously shook her head.

Shrugging off a weary sigh, Aram rose. A remembered glimpse of his nightmare froze him in place. The monstrous cat had been on his back, biting his skin. He still felt the cold, sharp teeth and smelled the dank odor of wild animal. Shuddering, he rubbed his arms. Glancing about, he reassured himself that the vicious cat was nowhere to be seen. Then he gazed at the crowd. His clan's discontent was not so fierce, but dangerous nonetheless.

"The plains are before us, and we have no shelter there. We need to move back into lands we understand." Barak, a frown mounted across his forehead, waved his arms as if he had said the same thing several times over and no one was listening.

Aram almost felt sympathy for him.

"You fear the open lands too much." Namah hissed her scorn very effectively. She saw Aram and offered one last taunt before she backed away. "What do you fear, Barak—the birds or the grass?"

Chuckles spread through the crowd.

Barak shook his loose arms as if wishing to put them to better use. "We don't know those lands or the people that live there. Warrior clans will enslave and kill us if we're not careful. We're exhausted and with no protection. We need to return to a land where we'll be safe."

Aram strolled to the circle of agitated clansmen. He eyed Namah as she dutifully backed away. He spoke clearly, though not loudly. "Barak is right; we don't know these lands, but we do know what's behind us." He peered at the crowd. "You want to go back to certain danger when we don't know what's before us?"

Aram glared at Barak. "Yes, we're tired, and we need rest. But we may discover a pleasant land not far from here. We'll never know if we perish in the woodlands."

Heated conversation and arguing broke out.

Barak's deep voice rose above the general roar. "Is not a war clan more to be feared than a mere beast?"

Everyone froze.

Aram offered Barak a twisted smile. "You're still young, Barak. I fought in clan wars when I was younger than you. Because I was strong, we've not had to fight for many long years. But I still remember how. You've never tasted battle. I don't fear meeting another clan—warriors or not."

Barak shook his head, his eyes growing wide. "Yet you fear a cat! *I* can defeat the beast, and then we'll live in freedom and not in fear. Later, if need be, you can test your ancient skills against an unknown tribe." Barak's black beard, black eyes, and black hair shone in radiance as the sun streamed over his defiant form.

The clan members shifted nervously, peering from Aram to Barak. Namah backed into the fringes of the gathering. A child wailed, and a mother swung the little one up into her arms, hushing her. Birds twittered in the treetops, then rose and flew like a cloud toward the rising sun.

Aram rubbed his chin as if considering a request. "I give you permission—go and kill the beast, Barak. But we move on after tomorrow, and you're responsible for following our trail and finding us. I'll not send scouts looking for you, for I need everyone to help move this camp. I will, however, allow four men to join you—if any want to."

Aram clamped his jaw tight. He could not speak of his haunting dreams or of his paralyzing fear. The cat was not just looking for prey. It was looking for *him*, and it would not stop until he got clear of the forest.

The clansmen scratched their jaws and leveled their gazes between the two men. In the light of the morning sun, the great cat diminished into nothing more than an insignificant animal. Aram knew that Barak's courage shone brighter than his fear.

Picking up his spear, Aram marched forward. "Go, Barak. Take your weapons and meet your death if you so choose. It's time our people moved out of the dark tree lands." He stopped and peered at the crowd. "You might kill this one beast, but there'll always be more lurking in the depths of the forest. We'll make a new settlement on the plains where no beast or clan can surprise us. You go back. We follow the rising sun."

Flinging his arms wide, Barak thrust out his chest. "I will kill the cat and bring its skin back for—" He hesitated as his gaze searched and found a pair of piercing eyes. "Namah." It was a childish taunt, but he smiled at her blushing grin.

Namah watched Barak stalk into the woods, a grin playing on her face.

Aram's eyes narrowed.

Her gaze dropped to the ground. Limping forward, she tended the campfire. Sharply, she commanded a child to get water.

The little one sped off in fearful obedience.

As Namah's hands bustled in efficient duty, her gaze returned to Aram.

He stood in the middle of the campsite, his eyes fixed on her even still.

With her gaze, compliant and sober, she nodded.

Grunting a command to the air, Aram returned to his tent.

~~~

Eymard sat cross-legged on his pallet, humming tunelessly

to himself. A tiny fire flickered in front of him.

Nearby, a lithe black-haired girl crouched over a worn leather bag and picked out nuts and seeds, which she popped into her mouth and crunched with evident pleasure.

The wizened face nodded, the eyes unfocused, lost in deep thought. "Eh, Milkan, you will see great changes soon. In you runs the blood of a once honorable clan that turned to corruption, but a scion has sprouted anew. This clan may yet rise to greatness."

The girl peered around. Her luminous blue-eyed gaze fell on Aram's retreating figure.

Chapter Six

—River Clan—

Battle Cries

Ishtar's body ached for sleep, but images danced before his haunted eyes. His father had waited to make the attack. When the villagers were sound asleep, they struck. Neb had ordered them to kill as many of the old people as possible and slay all young men who resisted. "Leave the women and children for slaves."

They were practiced warriors. Blind obedience ruled. Shortly before their attack, they had danced around a roaring fire and chanted in unison to Neb's wild battle cries. They had drunk to their satisfaction, and their blood ran hot with the desire to match their strength against the enemy. When they rushed forward into the silent camp, their screams echoed across the vast expanse. The shrieks of terrified women and children and the protests of feeble elders boiled into a melee of madness.

Ishtar had heard vivid accounts of raids before, but nothing compared to the nerve-ripping reality of thrusting his spear into a defenseless old man. Sobbing women and children were dragged from their homes, while fathers and brothers fought in vain to save them. His senses magnified the horror, yet he felt as if he were a mere spectator, even as he committed his knife and spear to the action. No one could question his ability to kill. Blood dripped from his hands and even smeared his bare feet.

As he lay before the fire, he lived the attack over in his mind. Pitiful eyes haunted him. He had been warned that this would happen. Other warriors had returned home after their first raid bearing red-rimmed, grieving eyes and tight lips. But after the slaves had been sorted out and the tools shared to everyone's satisfaction, the village returned to its daily routines. Even the slaves seemed resigned to their fate and did not pine to be returned to ruined homes and disheartened people.

But Ishtar could not close his eyes in peace or ignore the images of the frightened villagers who realized death was upon them. Even the glazed, unseeing gazes of those who had no power to resist rose and spoke as no words could. The children spoke the loudest—though their lips only trembled. A powerful wave of questions crested in Ishtar's mind. Flailing, he thrust them away.

He strained to see through the black night. No stars shone. Even the moon hid from sight. Clouds must have crept up and covered the distant lights that had aided them in their murderous campaign.

The face of an old man Ishtar knew in his early years floated before his eyes. A gentle servant who had no family to speak of would watch over the children. Ishtar would sit with the old man and eat scraps of dried meat and nuts from his bag. He told stories of a great Creator God who formed the lands with His mighty hands and scooped out vast lakes and rivers. He sent rain and storms, pulled up the mighty ball of fire each morning so we would have day, and dragged it back beneath the Earth so we could rest in the coolness of the night. Each story entertained Ishtar and fed the wellspring of his being.

"Oh, my old friend, where are you now? I wish I could sit beside you and listen to your stories once more."

Putting his hands over his mouth in stiff fear, he sat up. A hot sweat broke over his face while a chill ran down his back. Surveying the quiet slumber of the other warriors, he stifled a groan and lay down. A stone pressed into his back. He rolled over, scrambled for the stone, and tossed it aside.

Neb's head popped up from the other side of the sleeping circle. His catlike eyes searched and then rested on his son. Ishtar froze. He could feel his father's burning gaze. He waited. Slowly, Neb's silhouette settled down. Everything was quiet. Ishtar closed his eyes for the hundredth time.

In his mind, a woman with eyes the color of the sky at midday appeared. Her skin glowed like polished copper, and her hair shone as black as the earth near the river. She lifted an admonishing hand, her eyes troubled. "Why do you follow your father into evil?"

Ishtar's throat constricted. An ache built behind his eyes.

"The innocent cry out."

Ishtar's heart pounded as if it would break free from his chest.

"You'll be held accountable for every deed you've done tonight."

As if the ground under him was collapsing, Ishtar gripped his cloak and tried to steady himself.

"But do not despair, for even those guilty of great evil may yet choose another path." The woman faded into the black night.

Ishtar's gaze traveled over the silent camp. He exhaled a long, slow breath and closed his eyes. Someone jerked his arm roughly. His father stood over him.

Neb peered through the darkness. "Wake up! You whimper like a woman!" His voice snapped like dried branches.

"Yes, father." Ishtar clutched his stomach. "I ate too much after so much excitement." He forced a smile to cover his confusion.

Neb peered over the sleeping assembly and then offered a twisted grin. "Go back to sleep. We've got work to do in the morning."

Ishtar rolled onto his side and listened to his father's footsteps pad away. *Evil?* Ishtar pondered the word from every angle. How could everything that he had been reared to think as right be so terribly wrong? Questions flooded his mind.

Maybe this is the beginning of madness! Tears burned in his unblinking eyes. He forced himself to remain still.

Where could he go? To whom could he turn? "Oh, help me, my old friend. Someone—help me." He squeezed his eyes tight as his fists.

A vision of the old man rose before him, his voice gentle as ever. "Evil is not the strongest force in the universe."

The terrible tumult inside Ishtar's head eased and a single tear pursued its course down his face.

Chapter Seven

—Grassland—

Race Against the Wind

Obed sat on a smooth white rock by the stream's edge. The water flowed in bubbling currents over small stones that paved its meandering path from the north hills to some distant, unknown land far south. His gaze roamed lightly over the sparking water.

A slight breeze broke across the plains and stirred the languid grasses. It blew through his hair, which had escaped from a leather tie. He rubbed his short brown beard, which matched the color of his flowing hair.

Holding a gnarled root, he studied it. A few goats and pigs ate this particular root and later grew ill and died. It didn't seem to make them ill every time but only after a prolonged diet of it.

A few days ago while visiting with Onias, Jonas had brought out a meal. Among the dainties sat a dish of this same root, cooked and mashed. When he asked about it, Jonas explained that she had discovered it only recently. Onias loved it, though the children didn't care for it. Jonas was disappointed because she couldn't fix it as her mother had, and it wasn't as good as she remembered.

Could this very root be the cause of Onias' sickness? If he was correct, then he could save Onias' life.

Suddenly, Jael's thin brown body came into view. He ran with his arms outstretched as if to catch the wind in his grasp. The child looked over at Obed. He ran faster, yelling "OOOBBED" into the wind.

Obed peered into the vast blue sky as if to ask the great space above to share its abundant patience.

"Obed, guess what? I know you don't know. It's amazing!" Jael rattled away as he grasped Obed's hand. "You know that little sick goat we found? Well, it's better now, and I made it better all by myself. Don't look at me like that. You know I tell the truth. Remember how it wouldn't eat, and you said it would die? Well, I thought about that owl mess you showed me once, and how owls have to spit things out so they can eat again. I thought to myself, maybe the little goat has something inside he needs to get rid of. So, then I went and got that weed that makes you throw up—the one you told me never to touch. I gave it to the goat. He didn't want to eat, but I made him because I figured he was just going to die if I didn't. Anyway, he did throw up and then lay down and closed his eyes. I thought he was dead, so I ran away, but then I came back, and he wasn't dead. When I took him to pasture, he started eating like all the rest. I did cure him, didn't I?" His dark brown eyes implored Obed.

Obed ran his fingers over the child's thick hair, a smile hovering on his lips. "Yes, certainly. You're quite clever and may have done more good than you realize, Jael."

The child beamed, tugging Obed's hand. "Come on. We'll tell everyone. They'll all be glad I saved a goat, won't they?"

"I'm sure they will." Obed let Jael pull him off the warm rock. He took one last look over the rippling water, then let Jael's hand go as the boy raced against the wind over the swaying grasses toward home.

Chapter Eight

—Planet Lux—

Justify Your Evil

Teal stood holding a drink in one hand, tapping his leg with the other, and a frown building between his eyes.

The brilliantly lit hall filled with trailing green vines, glowing flowers, and an astonishing array of birds, barely scored his conscious mind. He had seen a million such rooms before. The company was different though. Luxonians in their human forms, Ingots, encased in their mechanical exoskeletons, and Crestas, lumbering along in their terrestrial bio-suits mingled in forced diplomacy.

Zuri, back straight, chest out, circulated amid an Ingoti throng across the room, which hummed with the uneasy murmurings of three races attempting to mingle in an uneasy alliance.

Putting his drink aside, Teal's gaze shifted to his superior, Judge Sterling, who looked like he had been chewing glass for breakfast.

Sterling, dressed immaculately in a long, flowing robe and cotton pants, stood square-shouldered as he faced off a leading scientist of Crestar. Sterling's eyes lowered to half-mast.

Boredom or loathing? So hard to tell from this distance.

A hand gripped his shoulder. Teal stiffened as he glanced at the mechanical glove. *How did Zuri manage to sneak around him like that?*

"Teal, correct?"

Clenching his jaw, Teal peered at the Ingoti trader. "You should know my name by now—you've complained about me often enough to the Ingilium—and the Supreme Council."

Zuri's form-fitting techno-armor, a brilliant red for the conference, nearly outshone his wide, practiced smile. "In truth, I'm surprised they let you come. After all, this is where we make agreements to respect each other and—"

"Like you respect the human race?"

Taking two steps into Teal's personal space, Zuri waved a hand that could snap a neck. "Do you see any humans here? And why would that be? Possibly because they're not evolved to the point where they can represent themselves at our level?"

Teal glanced ahead as Sterling wandered in his direction. Teal's frown melted as he lifted his hand in salute.

Zuri backed off.

Sterling offered a slight bow. "Well, what have we here? The most infamous Ingoti trader this side of the Divide?"

Teal's gaze bounced like a ball from Sterling to Zuri.

Flexing his impressive biomechanical exoskeleton, Zuri's chest expanded alarmingly. "Don't get jealous, Judge Sterling. Ingoti trade benefits Ingots, Luxonians, and Crestas—anyone willing to pay a fair price."

Sterling tucked a stray lock of his luminous white hair into perfect place. "Pity, humans keep getting in your way. Teal has reported that humans seem to disappear when they have the unfortunate luck to wander too close to one of your mining operations."

Zuri's hands clenched. "I've taken plenty of native-sensitive precautions. I introduced three kinds of protective repellants and made bloody well sure that they appeared to be right out of one of their superstitious belief systems. I did my research!"

A bell toned.

The two Luxonians glanced at the Ingoti representative beckoning them to their next meeting.

Zuri kept his glare plastered on Sterling.

Teal glowered. "Like it or not, we need stronger non-interference regulations for undeveloped planets. You're already exploiting their natural resources, and humanity will suffer from your greed."

The tone repeated—louder.

Judge Sterling tugged Teal toward the conference door. "We'll handle this issue in the proper setting."

Zuri smacked his metallic fists together. "You think humans don't exploit each other? What about that creature called Neb? And his son—Ishtar? Don't tell me that *their* noble hearts will win out over generations of greed. I'm just doing to humans what they'll do to each other given time."

Teal pulled away from Sterling's grasp and stared deep into Zuri's narrowed eyes. "You don't know who Ishtar might become or what'll happen to Neb. Don't justify your evil by insisting everyone is evil. It's too simplistic—even for an Ingot."

Chapter Nine

—Great Lake—

Joy

Aram marched ahead and studied his new world. Each day grew longer and warmer, and the dim forests were not so longingly remembered. This fresh open land, with its immense sky, invigorated his soul. In the north, low hills rose as if hulking moles had dug up mounds of earth in the imagined distance, and beyond those hills stretched colossal mountains.

Namah carried her bundles silently, occasionally nodding to the other clanswomen near her, her gaze most often downcast and serious.

Toward evening after an uneventful day of slow traveling, they climbed a low rise where a few trees spread freely in the open spaces. After they climbed the incline, they stopped in wide-eyed joy. An enormous lake of sparkling water shimmered before them in the slanting rays of the setting sun. Green grass rippled in the south and a rocky shore led to a high cliff on the north. The low west bank curved back, covered with pebbles and sand. The eastern shore leveled out with the grassy land.

As the clan edged closer, several trees, old leafy friends, met them with outstretched arms. There were not so many trees as in the forest, but their very presence spoke of welcome and good fortune. Children tried to scamper toward the bright water but worried mothers stopped them in mid run.

"Do you think it's safe?" Namah slipped up behind Aram and placed her hand on his arm.

Aram gazed across the glorious expanse and sighed. He

tilted his head toward her. "What are you afraid of—the water or the sunshine?"

She grimaced and glanced away. They stood in silence while the clan gathered around, peering at the panoramic view. Like proud eagles, they savored the breathtaking view.

Namah clasped her hands together. "Some might wish to stop here for a long time."

A smile wandered across Aram's face. "That's putting it mildly." He inhaled a deep breath. "Yes." He squared his shoulders. "We could know peace here. From this vantage, we could see an enemy approach from every side. We have the comfort of many old and familiar friends among the trees. And from the lake, we can draw water and food."

He nodded. *Yes.* Now that he saw this glory, he could only think that some Great Force beyond his reckoning had sent the cat and forced him out of the woods into this new land—like a child led home.

Barak could go off on a wild hunt, and Aram could almost wish him well. He would merely return with a cat skin and speak of noble adventures. But they would be peacefully settled in a new and better homeland.

Suddenly, his eye caught the movement of an old man leading a young girl to the water's edge. They attempted to climb down the steep embankment. Aram stepped forward and called out, "Careful, old man! That dirt is loose, and the slope is steep."

Eymard looked up with a cheerful gleam in his ancient eyes. "Milkan has never seen so much water. She thinks it is a dream. She wants to touch the water to see if it's real."

Grinning, Aram jogged forward. "Come then; I'll lead the child." Aram took the child's willing hand into his own strong grasp.

Milkan, caught between childhood and womanhood, blinked at Aram bashfully.

Eymard started to follow, so Aram stopped and grasped the old man by the arm.

Once they reached the bottom of the slope, Milkan dashed ahead. She ran thrashing into the clear water. Her skin shone in the warm sun, and her blue eyes sparkled. "Come, Eymard. Isn't it wonderful?"

Eymard cupped water in his hands and drank. He smiled. "It is good, child. May it always be so!"

As if in response to an unspoken command, the entire clan broke loose and ran, splashing into the water. The children screamed and laughed no more than the mothers and fathers, old women and men alike.

Aram stood back and marveled, for he had never seen his people like this. They were like birds escaped from a net. Their faces worn with anxiety broke into grins of delight. Shouts of laughter and yelps of mirth sent birds scattering from the trees. Men jostled with boys, and women bathed their babies. His eyes feasted on the sight.

Aram glanced at the girl with the old man again. "How do you like being a caretaker, old man? Are you strong enough?"

Eymard waded out of the water and meandered next to him, letting the water drip from his tunic. The old man lifted his wrinkled hand to his chin and mused. "Oh, it's true. I'm older than the hills, but that makes me no less fit to be a guardian. Though she's not flesh of my flesh, still, she carries my heart with her wherever she goes."

Aram nodded. The same sickness that came through the clan twelve years before and carried off his first wife, Anna, and their newborn son had taken Milkan's parents. Aram pointed at the laughing child as she splashed and played with the other children.

"It is good she found you, old man. She grows in strength and beauty." His gaze glanced off Namah who stood on the water's edge with an uncertain, dour expression. "I could use a bright smiling face around me once in a while."

Eymard's gaze found Namah, and he sighed.

Splashing droplets as she ran, Milkan shrieked in glee and grabbed Eymard's hand, tugging him back to the water.

Aram laughed and lifted his heart in praise of he knew not whom. For though men could do many things, he could never create a blue sky, a sparkling lake, or a land such as this. The power that created such things must be thanked. Surely, joy was the purest response of a grateful heart.

Chapter Ten

—Grassland—

Shadow of Fear

Onias studied the small, wooden figure before him. He swallowed a lump in his throat. It was truly some other power at work, for it was beyond his skill to create such a thing. The small figure stood with ears pointed, bright alert eyes, tail up and legs caught as if in mid-motion. It was the perfect image of a baby goat. It looked so lifelike—yet he had created it from his own hands. He marveled. *I now know how a woman must feel looking down at her infant for the first time. Did I form you? How could it be? I may have helped fashion it, but surely there is more at work here.*

He stood and stretched, as if reaching for the bright sun overhead. He had changed so dramatically these past few weeks that he wondered no less at the power that had restored flesh to his wasted limbs. A smile crossed his face as he thought back to the doubt with which he had first received Obed's ideas.

Obed had come to him in early spring and explained that he thought his sickness was due to a root he'd been eating. He believed a form of purging would make him better. He continued to explain—despite Onias' protest—that he had been studying the matter and believed that if Onias came with him, ate only what he told him to, laid in the hot sun and bathed often, drinking great quantities of fresh water, that he would grow stronger. He told him of all the things he had seen in nature that led him to consider this solution. He even shared Jael's feat in saving the goat and how that had helped him to think things through. Onias questioned the reasonableness of a starving man purging himself to good health. But Obed had insisted.

After a time, Onias decided to take the risk and trust his friend's judgment. He didn't explain the matter to Jonas, for he knew her protests combined with his lingering doubts would cancel his faint resolution. He simply mentioned that he and Obed were going on a short expedition. She protested briefly, but sensing his determination, she let him have his way.

Onias ceased smiling when he recalled, with a blush, the doubts and accusations he flung at Obed as the cure began. He started to believe that Obed was trying to kill him so he could take over as clan leader.

Obed quietly accepted these insults, and because Onias was too weak to go anywhere or do anything without Obed's help, it did not change his treatment. Obed simply treated Onias as a very sick child having a tantrum. He remained gentle but firm.

Finally, when Obed declared he would take the cure too—eat only what Onias ate and drink as much as he drank—Onias calmed down and began to hope for a real cure.

Within a week, they both felt healthy and refreshed. Onias ate better and enjoyed calm, dreamless sleeps. After a few days, they decided that they had done so well they ought to return to the village.

Jonas met them with narrowed eyes, but when she saw Onias' clear eyes and ruddy cheeks, she smiled. Onias stood straight again and held his head high. A sparkle danced in his eyes, replacing the shadow of fear.

When Jonas learned that the root she had prepared might have been poisoning him, she wailed in horror, but Onias was quick to assure her that he didn't know exactly what had made him sick and only suspected the root. In any case, the purging had ended the cycle of fevers. His body was returning to health and vigor, and he blamed no one for his illness.

Studying the wooden goat, Onias mused. "You understand, don't you? We're like brothers who faced a similar enemy. Jael had to force open your mouth to receive bitter medicine while Obed had to force open my mind to get me to take my cure."

"Father?" Tobia meandered to his side. "Who're you talking to?"

Onias grinned and ruffled the small boy's hair. "No one. Tell me, where is Jael? I have something for him."

"Only for Jael?" The little boy's eyes glimmered wistfully.

"Yes, for Jael, but if you like it, I will make something for you another time. Now tell me, where is he?"

"He is with Mother in the field. I'll show you." Tobia ran off shouting. "Come here, Jael! Father's got something for you."

Onias followed, swinging the little figure in his hand. He glanced over the field.

Jonas bundled sheaves of wheat into neat piles. The summer sun was falling toward the western horizon and a slight breeze had begun to stir. Jonas's hair, golden in the slanting light, blew every which way. She wiped sweat from her brow.

Onias stared at her and murmured, "Who has the skill to make such a woman?"

Jael jogged forward. "Are you going to help with the harvest, father?"

Onias shook his head. The smile playing on his lips faded as he stared at his wife.

Jonas frowned as she worked.

Onias pulled his gaze back to his first son. "I have something for you, Jael, something to always remember your little friend by."

Jael's mouth fell open, his eyes wide and unblinking.

Onias lifted his open palm. There stood the little figure of the baby goat.

Jael accepted the goat and caressed it, his eyes sparkling. "Oh, thank you, Father. Thank you very much!" He showed it to Tobia at his insistence. Then he peered at his father in wonder. "You carved this?"

"Yes, I shaped the figure, but how I did it is beyond my understanding. It was a gift to me that I pass on to you."

"Can you teach me, Father? Could I learn to carve too?" Jael's eyes glowed like bright stars.

Tobia tugged on Onias' left arm, hopping up and down in excitement. "Me too, father, me too. I want to make all kinds of things. Can I learn to make birds? Will you teach me?"

Onias laughed at his sons' exuberance. His eyes roamed back to Jonas, and his smile faded.

Jonas stopped working, her face dark with smeared sweat and furrowed brows. Her mouth clamped tight in a straight, unbending line.

Onias called to her. "What's wrong, Jonas? Take a rest and share the children's fun." He smiled through building irritation. He, too, worked much of each day in the hot sun. But he had not forgotten the time of wonder when he had realized he could carve figures from wood. There was more to life than work. He would not sacrifice his second chance at life to nothing but work. "Jonas, you look tired. Let's take a rest in the shade. The sun is almost down—you've worked long enough for today." He held out his hand.

Jonas shook her head and turned away.

Chapter Eleven

—River Clan—

Cursed

Ishtar sat against a small fruit tree by the water's edge. The bright sun streamed down on his still form. On the horizon, a light blue sky met green-blue water. The steady current flowed past him as if a gentle hand directed it. He turned at the sound of an angry voice.

Neb's long, slim form hunched forward as he sat amid the council members.

Ishtar knew he was not wanted in that inner circle of serious faces and bent figures. He had not been able to hide his anxiety from his father. Hesitations in his voice and the confusion in his eyes must have given him away. His father knew.

How can he judge me harshly when I have behaved exactly as before? I have maintained my loyalty and murmured not a word of protest. He looked back at the water as the sun sparkled on the ripples at the surface. *If anything, I've been more dutiful and I've tried harder to please him, though the effort has nearly killed me.* He groaned. *But I'd do anything to—*

"Ishtar, come here! Can't you hear me calling?"

Ishtar jerked to his feet. His face flushed.

As he approached the circle of old men, all eyes focused on him and narrowed in displeasure.

Ishtar set his face and squared his shoulders. "Yes, father?"

"Ishtar, we need your service." Neb's voice was as neutral as a snake's hiss.

They wore only the short tunics and wrapped armbands of

their clan and glared at him through doubt-filled eyes. The heavy scent of fish and unwashed bodies pervaded the air.

Ishtar stood with his naked brown arms limp at his side, his long hair tied tight in back. His leather skirt waved to the motion of his nervous legs. His restlessness grew under their unflinching gazes.

Neb enunciated each word methodically. "We want you to go west and scout out a people who live this side of a great lake. A stream runs north, and the land all around is grassland. We've heard from travelers that they grow their own grains and keep goats and sheep. We want to know more. How many of them are there? How many are warriors? Could they resist an attack? Go among them and find out all you can. Learn their ways, but don't let them know where you've come from. You understand?"

Ishtar's heart leaped with the possibility of getting away from his father. He could leave on good terms and accomplish an important task without battle. He suppressed a smile. "Yes, father. I understand. When should I leave?"

Neb peered at his son, and the furrows on his forehead faded. "As soon as you can. Get food together and your best weapons. Leave by the break of day." He tapped his fingers together. "Say that you have traveled far and that your clan is looking to find a new settlement. Tell them anything, but never tell the truth." Neb's gaze bore into Ishtar's.

"Yes, father." Ishtar had said that phrase so often he wondered whether it had lost its meaning.

With a grunt, Neb returned his attention to the council members. Their near-naked, bent forms chattered in serious consultation.

Ishtar bowed his head and backed away.

As he strode to his tent, his mind raced. The first thing he needed to do was tell his mother, Hagia. He found her shaping a large basket.

Her quick hands braided the fibers while her eyes peered into an unseen distance. At the sound of his footsteps, she lifted her eyes and raised her hand in defense of the sunlight, low on the horizon. Her face appeared worn as her dark brows creased, and her golden eyes squinted in the light. "Ishtar, you need something?" Her brows furrowed. "Neb is not planning another raid, is he? You look worried."

Ishtar forced a smile and cleared his throat. "No. Father is sending me west to a grassland clan. I'll travel and bring back news."

Hagia frowned, sullen, and returned to her work. "So, your father has found a way to make you useful without testing your bravery in battle."

Ishtar winced. "But I've done nothing wrong." His shoulders sagged.

"Your father says he can smell your fear and see questions behind your eyes. He reported that you were unmanned the night of the battle and cried in your sleep." Hagia shook her head. "You've always been different from the others. You and Elam." She stiffened and blinked as if in pain. Clearing her throat, she bent over her work as if to shut him out.

Ishtar stared off into the glowing horizon, chewing his lip. Finally, his gaze returned to his mother. "Before I go, I need supplies to take with me. I leave at the break of day." He shifted and his gaze fled to the sky again. "But I want to ask you something first."

Hagia's eyes narrowed. "Yes, what is it?"

"It's that—" He coughed and started again. "I remember stories of the Great Clan. It's said that there were a great many children at that time. But now, there are hardly any." He shifted, his legs itching to move. "It seems only the slaves have children. Where have all the babies gone?"

Hagia's shoulders slumped, while her gnarled hands flew to her face. "Get away!" She choked. "No woman in this cursed clan knows! You're a fool to ask. Gather your own food and leave me alone."

Seeing tears glimmering in his mother's eyes, Ishtar swallowed back his pity. Part of him wanted to comfort her, but a larger part of him was trained to obey. He bowed and backed away.

"Ishtar!" Hagia rose, grunting to her feet, and wiped her face with the back of her hand. "I'm the fool. I shouldn't get angry with you. It is natural to wonder. But it's a painful thing and no one can speak of it without suffering. You're all I have—come back quickly." Tears spilled down her cheeks.

Ishtar embraced her—his forehead touching hers. He peered into her grieving eyes. "I'm your son. I'll not abandon you. My journey won't be complete until I see you again." A gentle smile hovered over his lips.

Hagia stifled a sob.

After taking a step back, Ishtar nodded and strode away.

Hagia stared at his departing figure until he was swallowed up in the labyrinth of the camp. Her tears flowed freely. "Oh, my son." She rocked on her heels, wiped her face, and then turned around. Glancing at the empty council spot, she frowned. She hurried to the riverbank and found Neb by the river's edge.

"Neb, I must speak with you." She ran forward and stopped before him.

Neb didn't move a muscle.

"Send someone with Ishtar. He can't go alone. Something could happen, and he'll need help." She towered above her husband's slim, still figure.

Slowly, Neb peered up at Hagia. "Do you think so little of your son? You think he can't manage this small task?"

Hagia raised herself to her full height over Neb's cross-legged form.

"What do you call a small task? This journey could take weeks. Are there no wild animals in the grasslands? Can men ever walk alone in this world and not be attacked? Do you want him to fail? I am no fool! I remember Elam well, and I will speak his name. Ishtar will serve this clan as he has always served you faithfully. You must do what is right and protect him."

Rising slowly, Neb showed little sign of his age. His tall, slim form with catlike green eyes appeared more powerful than any ordinary mortal. He wore his black hair pulled tight in a leather thong at the back of his head, while his bare chest and feet were as golden as the late summer grasses. The knife at his side was ornamented with a series of s-shapes, which were also worked into the leather armband on his upper arm. He raised his hand.

Hagia refused to flinch, though her gaze darted to another figure picking his way along the water's edge.

Neb lowered his arm and watched the approaching man.

Joash, older than Ishtar but slightly smaller, sparked a gleam in Neb's eyes. A perfect warrior—a perfect son. Neb had watched him grow and had found his own son wanting in comparison. This one would never fail in battle, no matter how bloody the field.

Joash stopped before the two tense figures. He nodded, his gaze fixed on Neb.

Hagia folded her arms across her chest, her lips pursed tight.

Neb nodded back; a glint of a smile crept into his eyes. "Yes, Joash, what do you seek?"

Joash clasped his hands behind his back. "My father, as a council member, suggests that I accompany Ishtar on his journey. He thinks that two men would have a much better chance of gathering information than one. Also, it would be safer."

Hagia grinned in triumph.

With his eyes cloaked in a dark shadow, Neb's jawline tensed. He glanced aside. "It seems you've won approval from Hagia. I rarely see her so happy. So be it. You may go with Ishtar. But I'll speak to each of you privately when you return, do you understand?"

Joash's face remained impassive. "As you wish. I'll get ready now."

Hagia stood silent as Joash backed away, her joy fading, her whole body deflating.

Neb murmured as though to himself. "I didn't kill Elam. I'm not sending Ishtar to his death. We must have discipline, or all will perish."

Hagia peered at the river as the sun dipped into the water, wavelets of shining sparkles dancing before her eyes. Orange and pink rays paled into blue and purple shadows. "I'm sure you think that's true." She dropped her hands to her sides, her shoulders sagging. "Ishtar asked where all the babies have gone. Before leaving on this journey, he risked my anger to learn the answer. But I have no answer."

Neb continued to gaze toward the disappearing sun as the burning globe faded in the shimmering river. "You should've told him the truth. We're cursed."

Chapter Twelve

—Woodland—

Betrayal

Barak bent down gripping his spear and, with his other hand, stirring the dark green foliage on the ground. He scowled. The cat had left prints in the mud, and remains of its victims were clear, but it had moved in a random fashion, crisscrossing its own path, making it impossible to discern its current direction.

Barak glanced over his shoulder. He had a strong conviction that the cat stalked near. Though he had thought this before, only to be wearied by hours of fruitless searching.

Four other men accompanied him: Shem, Anikar, Lamech, and Irad. Shem leaned on a thick cudgel, his short, heavy stature accentuating his boulder-like build. His puffy eyes glared over his red-cheeked face, while his straggly brown hair and bushy beard bespoke an unkempt air of dissolution. "She'll hear us long before we see her—you can be certain of that. Useless venture—trying to catch her. Might as well try to pull a full-grown tree from the ground."

Barak bit his lip and concentrated on the broken stem before his eyes.

Anikar, who could hardly be more different from Shem, shivered, his eyes widening and hands twitching. His shimmering shoulder-length black hair and beardless face reminded Barak of a young maiden. While Shem's gaze bore into everyone, Anikar's brown eyes shifted in perpetual, nervous anxiety. Like a bird that darts from perch to perch, he exuded high-strung fear from the time he awoke until the moment he fell into an exhausted sleep at night. Clutching a spear, he reared on his heel and turned completely around.

"Did you hear that? Are those eyes glowing over there?"

Shem smacked Anikar on the shoulder. "Settle down! You'll have us as nervous as rodents before long."

Lamech rarely spoke, preferring to listen and smile. He appeared to enjoy Barak's company, offering constant, gentle reassurances with agreeable nods and murmurs of content. He gazed in sympathy at Anikar.

Irad, the most intelligent man of the group, always seemed to be at the right place at the right time. Slim and quick, he could stand as still as a rock and then capture a bird with his own two hands, amazing the others. Stepping up to Barak, Irad nudged him. "She's right ahead of us, biding her time—watching us."

Barak raised his eyebrows and stood to his full height.

Irad shifted, a broad smile flitting over his face. "We need bait to bring her in." He raised his brows. "She seems to have a taste for man flesh. Perhaps one of us should sleep outside the circle of fire tonight."

Barak jerked around to face him, his voice rising thick and furious. "We've lost more than enough men to her already!"

Irad laughed. "No, I don't mean to offer her anything more than a quick death. First, we lay a bundle of clothes and food outside the circle of fire. Then, we cover ourselves with ashes and watch throughout the night. When she pounces, she becomes the victim and we the predators."

With a grin hovering on his face, Barak patted Irad on the back and called to the others. In haste, they made everything ready.

In the flickering light of three small campfires, Barak wiped his mouth and straightened. After finishing off the hindquarters of a large, succulent rabbit, he wrapped the bones inside his blanket outside the circle of light. He stamped down leaves and twigs and then lay on the ground and rolled over several times. Then he backed away into the darkness. The others moved into the shadows and waited.

After the moon rose, a predatory yowl sent shivers down

their backs.
Irad nudged Barak. "You forgot your ashes."
Barak ignored him. *Too late to think of that now. The only thing that cat will want is what it sees on the ground.* He peered into the black tree line, willing the cat to appear.
The fires died down, and his spear grew heavy in his hands. Two of the ash-covered men drooped in drowsiness.
Irad kept his head up. He grinned, and his brown eyes glowed as he swept his gaze across the scene.
Barak stood silent and tense, waiting and watching. As he stood in the darkness, the image of his father's face appeared before him, and he wondered why he had never spent much time with the old man. He remembered his father's joy at his return each day and felt a pang of guilt that he had never cared as much for his father as his father had clearly cared for him.
Glancing around, he noticed that two figures hunched forward and quietly snored. A hot flush crept up his neck. His gaze searched for Irad, but he couldn't see him. Turning, he stepped aside and a stick snapped.
The loud crack surprised him, but a greater shock hit him when a sudden force knocked him to the hard ground. He fell on his back, his knife flying out of his grasp. Great paws clutched his chest. He tried to gasp for air but found it impossible. The sharp claws of the mammoth cat dug into his flesh. Hot breath wafted across his face and a low snarl sent tingles down his arms. The heavy, dark scent of wild animal filled his nose. His mind went numb.
Barak scrambled for his knife. Snatching it, he jabbed at the beast from the underside, giving her a nasty slice in the belly.
She yelped and jumped to the side.
Barak rolled and crawled to the fire. Grabbing a smoldering stick, he started to rise when a sudden weight landed on his back. He fell forward and caught himself. Twisting around, he swung the red-hot brand into the cat's face, forcing her aside again. He regained his footing. With his knife in one hand and the burning brand in the other, exhilaration spread through his

body.

She hunched, poised to pounce, but suddenly, she screamed in a high-pitched howl of pain and staggered. A spear stuck in her side. She struggled to stay on her paws.

Irad stepped into the flickering firelight and thrust another spear into her chest.

The great cat flopped silently to the ground. Her glittering eyes glazed and soon stared sightlessly into the black night.

Striding to Barak, Irad offered his hand.

After being pulled to his feet, Barak propped his hands on his thighs and panted. "It all happened so fast. I never heard her coming." Grasping Irad's arm, he choked a ragged laugh. "Thank you. I don't know how long I would've lasted."

Irad grinned, his eyes dancing in merriment.

Barak straightened and shook his head. "But how'd you know she'd come for me and not the bundle?"

Irad waved a finger in chastisement. "You forgot to cover yourself with ashes. It seemed to me that such an intelligent beast might know the difference between a man and a blanket."

Barak stared at the cat, frozen. With a blink, he forced his gaze to Irad. "Since you killed her, the hide, in all rights, must be yours. I'm only grateful I didn't lose mine."

Irad laughed along with the other men. "The cat's skin will be a trophy to show off for the rest of our lives." He paused. "But I think you should take it. You're our leader, after all."

Nudging the cat's great jaw with his toe, Barak heaved a deep sigh. "Time to go home—wherever that may be."

Shem crouched and slapped the beast's rump. "By the gods, I'm ready."

Only Irad betrayed a flicker of discontent. "Since we've managed so well, why not rest a few days? Let's have a feast before we return to the clan."

All smiles faded.

Running his fingers through his disheveled hair, Barak shrugged. "I think we'd all like to leave as fast as our legs will carry us. After all, we only came for the cat. It'll be good to see our families again."

Every head nodded except Irad's.

Shem, as an expert skinner, pulled out his knife and set to work. He was loud and exact in his cuts, and whenever he came to a tricky spot, he let them all know. "It'll be a miracle if I get this beast's skin off in one piece! By the gods, this cat is beyond anything I've ever seen." When the job was complete, he lifted the mammoth skin and let loose a long series of oaths. "The demon gods surely make such monsters for their own employment. Undoubtedly, we've destroyed the servant of a cruel master. Tales will be told of this adventure for generations." He stroked his chin. "Though, there may be ill repercussions—the gods might exact a price for the slaying of such a mighty servant."

Anikar shivered and glanced around, wrapping his arms around his thin waist.

Lamech patted the youth's shoulder and gave him a grin.

~~~

Barak rose early. As soon as the cat skin was rolled into a tight bundle and the carcass disposed of, he led his men through the woods. Shem, Anikar, and Lamech followed Barak in single file, while Irad trailed along well behind.

The feeling of the great claws on his chest plagued Barak even as he trudged through the woods. Raucous birds cawed in the distance, sending a thrill through his body. Wiping his face, he tried to erase the cat's hot breath from his memory.

He could hardly blame Irad for saving him, but part of him wished he had been able to finish the fight. With the glowing brand of fire and his knife—and perhaps if he had been able to reach his spear—he could have killed her himself. But shaking his head, he'd bite his lip. There was no disputing the fact; Irad had saved him.

Thoughts continued to haunt him as he led his men through

the deep woods. He could be dead right now and few would miss him—except for his father. It began to irritate him that Irad made so little of the event—as if he had saved no one of importance. As the days wore on and they tramped over fallen logs and through old forest glades, he began to wonder at Irad's new silent, secret disposition. It was almost as if Irad had repented of his heroic rescue.

The trees spread further apart, the grass grew thicker, the sky brightened, and the sun warmed their skin.

Anikar had appeared ever more nervous during their adventure. He swiveled in every direction like a leaf twirling in an everlasting breeze.

Lamech kept in step with Barak. He wiped the sweat from his brow and ran his fingers along his shaggy beard. "I wish I'd been the one to save you, friend. If only I had stayed alert, I'd have killed her quickly and not watched and waited."

In wide-eyed surprise, Barak faced Lamech, but a shout turned his gaze.

Anikar pointed to a shaft of sun breaking through the trees and the glimmer of open land ahead. "We're almost there! See?"

Barak picked up his weary feet, hustling faster. The joy of being in the open lands drew him.

Suddenly and silently, Irad was at his side. "Would you mind if we stopped for the night and continued tomorrow, Barak?"

Barak stumbled, righted himself, and faced Irad. A burning flush crept up his face. "Why? We're within sight of the grasslands."

Irad's lips twitched and a grin hovered as if he had to explain a difficult lesson to a moody child. "Yes, that's my point. We should hunt tonight and eat well. Once we're in the grasslands, we don't know what we'll find."

Barak thrust his misgivings aside in the face of Irad's winning smile and signaled the men to stop. It was a reasonable plan. Besides, the heavy skin he carried on his back wearied him.

Barak grimaced and poked the skin as it thudded to the ground. "At least I won't have to worry about you creeping up on me in the middle of the night." He leaned against a tree. Soon, he would present the skin to Namah as a sort of—what? Why, under the great sky, had he offered the skin to her? Would she appreciate what he had done to get it? What would Aram think? Suddenly, the insult seemed childish and petty. Why had he ever held Aram in such contempt? Was it simply because Aram was the leader and must make decisions for them all? Barak squeezed his eyes shut, his stomach churned. Taking long deep breaths, he settled his nerves.

As Shem, Anikar, and Lamech searched for game, Barak built a small fire. Irad crossed his path, making a wide arc as if to avoid coming too near. Watching Irad out of the corner of his eye, it struck Barak as odd that Irad refused to take the cat skin—even to touch it. When Irad had insisted that Barak take the skin, he had felt grateful. The idea of returning to camp without it on his own shoulders humiliated him. But something in Irad's eyes said he feared the skin. Barak scowled.

Irad called from a distant shadow. "I'm not feeling well. I'll come back later."

The evening passed quietly. Before long, Shem carried a small hog into camp, and Lamech cleaned it and set it roasting over the fire. As the smell of cooking meat wafted through the woods, Irad sauntered back looking happier than when he had left. No one asked any questions.

The moon rose like a white orb in the star-studded sky. They sat around the sizzling meat and enjoyed the cooling night air. When the meat was barely cooked, they began to slice off hunks and eat.

Shem, a wreath of a smile on his face, chewed and pointed his knife at the roast. "On my first hunt, I speared a tree and the deer got clean away."

Lamech laughed and patted Shem's arm. "Better than me. I nearly killed my brother by mistake." He rubbed his face. "Father wouldn't take me hunting for many moons after that."

After the meal, the men relaxed and settled on their blankets. Barak grabbed his roll and pulled it near the fire.

Irad's eyes glowed in the firelight. "I bet that skin makes a nice place to rest your head. Of course, I wouldn't get too close to the fire—it could catch. Cats are afraid of fire for good reason."

Barak nodded and pulled the skin away from the fire and finally lay down with a contented sigh.

Anikar stretched out and stared at the sky. "My little girl rolls over three times on her bed each night before she closes her eyes." He exhaled. "So like her mother."

Flopping onto the ground, Shem grunted in satisfaction. "My boys couldn't care less where they sleep. The eldest fell asleep in a tree once, and we couldn't find him until morning."

Lamech propped his head on his arm. "No one can sleep like the young."

Irad's shoulders shook with suppressed laughter. "Oh, I don't know. You two slept soundly the night of the cat attack."

Anikar and Barak froze. Lamech's shoulders slumped. He lay down and closed his eyes. Shem opened and closed his mouth several times but said nothing.

Barak watched them all slip into morose introspection as the flickering fire burned into mere embers.

Irad sat close to the fire pit. A strange odor followed him all afternoon.

Barak shuddered. He could see his own selfish motives all too clearly now, but he couldn't fathom the depths of Irad's mind.

After staring into the fading embers, he rubbed his fingers deep into the thick fur. No, this would not be for Namah—this skin would be a warm blanket for his father. He didn't want to insult Aram any more. He knew the price of leadership, and it was a role he no longer coveted. This skin would not enkindle his pride but rather keep an old man warm on cold nights. Only to that purpose did this long, perilous journey have meaning. A soft smile settled on Barak's face as he slipped into a dreamless sleep.

Thud! His teeth knocked together, and he wondered briefly if he had cracked his jaw. His numbed brain gathered strange and scattered images together in his mind. Huge claws dug into his chest. Hot breath seared his face. A low snarl vibrated at his throat. The cat's face glowed in the dim light before his eyes. It could not be! The great cat was dead. Yet here, with claws extended, it pinned to the ground.

Where is Irad? Where are the others? Why is no one helping me?

Without an organized thought, Barak reached for anything at hand. His fingers closed over a rock. He brought his arm around and down. Surprised, the animal reeled off to the side long enough to give Barak the chance to scramble to his feet. He stared at the mammoth male cat before him. So, there had been two—a pair of great cats! He faced the furious beast. His spear and knife lay on the ground near the cat's heavy paws.

Where are the other men? He looked around and saw no one. As though he heard the words whispered in his ears, he knew that Irad had foreseen this, and he had planned his own escape. The male cat had come back for its mate—that's why Irad would not touch the skin.

The skin lay strewn on the ground near at hand. Barak grabbed it and ran at the cat. Blanketing the cat's head, he scooped up his knife from near his pallet.

The great animal squirmed and yowled and sprang forward, forcing Barak's knife into its chest. In its desperate thrashing, it knocked Barak to the ground. While it writhed and clawed at Barak, he struggled to cut deeper. Blood poured down his arm, searing pain shot through his body. As one great claw racked across his face, his head smacked the ground. The dying beast fell across his chest. Horror and exhaustion took Barak's mind and forced a merciful darkness to cover his eyes.

When his mind woke to the sound of voices, Barak realized that he couldn't move. The cat's lifeless body pinned him to the ground. His whole body burned in a feverous flame, and his face hurt so badly he could not open his eyes.

Irad murmured something, and then he laughed. "I told you how it'd be. A cat that big must have a mate—he came to seek his revenge."

Footsteps shuffled toward Barak, and Irad called out sharply. "Don't touch! Other beasts will gather shortly to get their fill of this feast. We must leave quickly."

Lamech's voice rose in a wail. "Why didn't you warn him?"

"Warn him? How could I warn him? No one would've believed me. Only when the cat struck, and we all ran that it occurred to me that I must be right. That's why I had you all wait a safe distance away. There could've been a whole pride of cats, and we'd all have been devoured."

Shuffling of feet and thumping of weapons and gear hoisted onto backs sounded in Barak's ears.

"Come along. Hurry! I've been right once this night; I don't want to be right again."

The tromping of footsteps receded into the distance. Barak fell back into a pit of black dreams.

~~~

Barak awoke to the realization that he couldn't feel his legs. With a grunt and great exertion, he roused himself and forced the dead cat off to the side. Then he pushed himself up, groaning at the pain. Gingerly, he felt his face. It was swollen and tender. He rubbed his legs and brought the feeling back slowly and painfully. Terrified at the idea of another beast catching him off guard, he peered around for a weapon and found his knife in the belly of the great cat. When he pulled, it slipped out easier than he thought, and he fell backwards.

The moon hung low on the western sky, providing a glimmer of light on the horizon.

Remembering a nearby stream, he gingerly shuffled his way to it. Falling on his knees, he scooped water onto his bleeding face. It stung fearfully, but he could see better. He gave himself a long drink of the clear, cool water. Then sitting by the water's edge, he surveyed the scene before him.

Alone, injured, and unable to trust his friends, Barak cursed the day that brought him to such a place. "Why is it taking you so long to rise?" The bitterness of loneliness and betrayal stank like the smell of the cat.

Only when the image of his father's wrinkled face floated in the darkness before him did he cease to berate the world for his ill fortune. He would not stay and be conquered by whatever came next. No, this time he had killed the beast, and he would take the skin too. When he imagined himself walking into Aram's camp, it would not be with someone else's trophy on his back.

He checked himself over and discovered to his relief that none of his injuries were deadly. After he skinned the cat, he gathered his things. He would follow Aram north and hopefully find the clan before Irad and the rest.

With Aram's impartial judgment to guide him, he would set things to rights when he was in the presence of the clan. The truth would come out, for it was not in Shem, Anikar, or Lamech to lie. In time, justice would be served. But, in the meantime, he had an overpowering need to be out of the forest and safe under an open sky.

Chapter Thirteen

—Lakeland—

Prophesy

Aram watched Milkan play with her friends and smiled at the children's innocent games. His tribe was content, he had no fearsome dreams, and Namah finally seemed satisfied to do her work and little else. The land lay glorious before him in its natural beauty. The sky turned various shades of blue and white during the day, and in the evening, he could watch the play of purples, reds and oranges until they blurred into the black of night.

Aram watched Milkan play with her friends, the land stretching out behind her in all its natural beauty. A flock of birds soared above them in a cloudless sky, squawking and chirping to each other in eternal freedom.

Inhaling a deep breath of fresh air, Aram let his gaze drift to the lake, to where wild game drank at the water's edge. In the evening, he liked to sit against an immense, gnarled tree and watch the children play in the open field. He would delight in their childish chatter. If someone wished to speak with him, they'd find him in a congenial mood, and he'd listen with benign interest. His words began to resonate with the wisdom of peace, and he repeatedly suggested an attitude of tolerance and forbearance that he had failed to encourage in earlier seasons. Healing beauty benefited the whole clan.

As he watched the children, his vision blurred. Blinking back tears, he realized how much he missed his first wife and the son he had lost. He once met travelers who spoke of a creator God who formed all life and then took all life home to Himself when their time on earth was finished.

Aram had never taken much interest in gods, as he saw in them nothing more than the leaning posts of anxious women and old men. Yet, when the travelers spoke of their God, his heart had leapt like a child into its mother's arms. It comforted him to consider that perhaps his first wife now rested under the protection of a generous Creator spirit.

Milkan ran across the field with her arms stretched out like a little bird, skimming the grasses as she bent her body to the wind. She was as free as the wild animals and as innocent. Aram turned to the old man next to him, who sat weaving a basket. "Eymard, do you know anything of the land where our loved ones go when their journey here is finished?"

Eymard's fingers froze, and he peered into Aram's questioning eyes. With a shrug, he swallowed. "Yes, I've heard of stories about the land beyond."

Aram leaned in. "Tell me, what do you believe?"

Eymard pursed his lips, his fingers hovering over the basket. "Do you want to know what I believe, or do you want to know what beliefs your people carry around in secret?"

Aram shook his head. "I want to know what *I* believe, but I can't decide."

Eymard's gaze lifted to the sky. "God is holy and one. He is good and great—the foundation of the Earth and the sparkle in every star. He forms each living being from His hands, and He takes those whom He loves back to His home at the end of their time."

"Where is He? Why can't I see him?"

"You see Him in the life all around. His presence is manifested in every leaf and twig, every newborn babe, and every bird that knows how to make a nest. But I, too, yearn to see his face."

"Can you speak to Him? Does He answer?"

Eymard paused and chewed his lip. "Anyone might speak to Him, but whether He answers is not for me to say. I have prayed to Him, and I feel that He does hear me, but I can't fathom His mind."

"But have you ever heard His voice?"

Eymard's gaze shifted to the children. "I heard His voice when Milkan's mother died. The gentle woman begged me to look after her baby. As I held her hand and she waited for my response, I heard a voice say, 'I will be with you.'"

Aram's eyes wandered over the horizon. The beauty before him opened the way for an avalanche of hope. "Did He help you? I mean in some extraordinary way?"

Returning to his work, Eymard's fingers weaved in perfect rhythm. "Once, when Milkan became very ill, I feared she'd die. So, I called to God and reminded Him of His promise. Very soon, she became better, as if she had never been sick at all. God had heard me and fulfilled His word."

Aram tapped his fingers together as he studied the old man. "Has He ever spoken to you again?"

A stem snapped in Eymard's fingers and he fished through the strands at his side, his gaze averted. "It's not always easy to understand what He says. I might not have heard correctly."

"What did He say?" Aram stared through penetrating eyes.

Eymard shook his head and rested his hands in his lap. "I'm not sure I should tell you."

Aram frowned. "Why?" He straightened, his throat tightening. "He didn't speak of me—did He?"

Eymard's shoulders slumped. "When Barak told you that he wanted to hunt the great cat, I heard the voice say, 'I will draw that man to Myself, and generations of his seed will serve Me well. Milkan shall be his wife.'"

Aram's face drained of color. "Me?"

Eymard closed his eyes. "It's hard to say. It was either you or that young bull, Barak—and I can't see him begetting anything but more fools like himself."

Aram leaned back against the tree trunk. The evening sky blended into swirls of pink, orange and blue.

Milkan stood off in the distance—only a child. Aram stroked his chin. "Many men take young brides, and when a man is successful, he may have more than one wife." He sighed. *How could I start again? Namah would never accept a second wife, and few would willingly share her company.*

Eymard returned to his work in silence.

Milkan ran in a wide circle with her friends as the light faded. Namah's shrill voice rose in the distance.

Aram's eyes roamed over the burgeoning village and came to rest on a group of women. Namah sat among them. Some sewed and others worked with clay. Two women squeezed juice from berries. Everyone did something useful—except Namah. She was talking, making a pretense of picking berries from a basket. He could clearly see the averted bodies, the sidelong glances. Even from this distance, he felt the animosity. Her scraggily and unkempt hair fell across her face, and her back rounded in an unnatural hump. *An ugly woman.* Aram sighed.

As if becoming conscious of his gaze and the quiet around her, Namah glanced up and saw Aram's eyes fixed on her.

Though he averted his eyes, Aram could still see her out of the corner of his eye.

Namah thrust her basket on another woman's lap and stood. She stretched, grimaced, and wandered to where Aram sat with Eymard. Peering at the old man as he continued to weave his basket, she tapped her fingers together. "What're you making, old man?"

Eymard's face lit up. He lifted the basket for inspection. "A basket for my Milkan. She goes to gather each day, and she needs a new one."

Wagging her head, Namah wrinkled her nose. "Oh, yes, a beautiful basket will help a child gather many things. She'll fill the basket full of flowers rather than berries."

Eymard's smile twitched. "Yes, she might do that. And the flowers would be as welcome as the berries. One must feed the soul as well as the body."

Namah snorted, and she knelt by the old man. "The soul? The gods have souls, but we have stomachs that must be filled, and berries will do that better than flowers. I am surprised you'd encourage a child in foolish nonsense."

His gaze dropping to his work, Eymard continued weaving.

Aram frowned in irritation.

Though Eymard's gaze remained on the basket, his voice lifted. "Tell me child, can you see the wind?"

Rolling her eyes, Namah curled her legs to one side. "No, though I can see the leaves move and the water ripple, so I know there is a wind."

Eymard raised his eyes and peered at her with calm patience. "Thus it is with a soul. A man thinks, loves, or hates with his soul. One does not need to see it to know it is there."

Namah waved his words away. Her gaze followed the women as they gathered their things and headed to their separate tents. "I know nothing of such things. I only know that a man must fight to survive. Life is a battle won by the strong. Souls do not put food in the stomach."

Aram cleared his throat. "Eymard believes in a compassionate God."

After gathering the scattered fronds, Eymard tucked them into the basket.

Namah tilted her head, her gaze fixed on Eymard. "It makes no difference to me." She stood and peered into the now dim-lighted east.

The sun hovered on the horizon, and a gentle mist rose from the lake. The figure of a man hovered in the distant southwest.

Namah frowned. "Supper'll be ready soon, Aram. I'll see that it's as you like it." She shuffled toward a large campfire encircled by several women hovering over a large pot.

Aram swallowed as tantalizing smells of stewed meat wafted to his nose.

Eymard wrapped his arm around the basket and wearily climbed to his feet. Lifting his chin, his eyes found Milkan. "Come, child. Help an old man to rest."

Milkan ran to his side.

Aram stood and rubbed his stiff back. He smiled at the girl as if a fresh wind had blown away the confusion of his thought.

His eyes twinkled. "You must take this old man home to eat. He's been working hard for you." He pointed to the basket.

Eymard handed the basket to the child. "Gather food—for body and soul."

A smile radiated through Milkan's body as she wrapped her arms around the gift. Propping her hand on his arm and standing on tiptoes, she kissed Eymard on the cheek.

Eymard squeezed Aram's shoulder. "In your hope for something beyond the sight of men, you'll find peace."

"If I could think as you do, I'd know peace, but that's not my gift."

Milkan took Eymard's hand and led him to the cooking fire. As she nodded goodbye to Aram, her gaze strayed toward the field beyond. She gasped. "Eymard, someone's coming!"

Framed against the glowing sky, a lone figure—a hunch-shouldered man—made his way toward them.

Aram scowled. "Who'd be traveling at this time of the evening?"

The figure lifted his head and stared directly at Aram.

Aram stared back. His mouth fell open, and his shoulders straightened.

Barak had returned—alone.

Aram scratched his jaw.

And he seemed to be carrying a heavy weight.

Chapter Fourteen

—OldEarth–

They Are Not Pets

Teal stomped his foot. "Bloody hell!"

In a wooded glade, Teal paced in front of a body sprawled on the ground before him. Four more bodies lay in a shallow grave. Freshly turned earth formed a mound behind him. After slipping a datapad out of a deep pocket, he tapped the panel. Sucking in a deep breath, he ran his fingers through his hair.

"For official Luxonian record, Teal reporting from Earth, subject—Alien Abuse. I just discovered five human bodies in a shallow grave on continent four, central basin. Cause of death unknown, but the lesions on their faces and bodies suggest Cresta experimentation."

—Planet Lux—

Sterling grinned. In a gloriously bright room filled with glowing foliage and comfortable furniture, he poured a mug of thick, honey-sweetened brew and laid it on an ebony table before Teal. The table contrasted sharply with his white flowing robe, but Sterling always enjoyed contrasts. He grinned at Teal's petulant expression. "Please, be kind. I ordered this especially for you."

With a wave of acquiescence, Teal lifted the mug and sipped. He licked his lips and leaned back in his chair. "It's better than I expected."

Sterling's eyes glittered. "I read your reports. Even the

recipes."

Shoving the mug to the side, Teal, dressed in a brown tunic, loose pants, and sandals, leaned forward and clasped his hands on the tabletop. "Did you read about the Cresta incursions?"

Sterling poured a second cup, took a tentative sip, and shivered. "Ugh!" he set the cup on a side counter.

Teal scraped his throat clear. "Sir?"

Clapping his hands, Sterling turned to the arched doorway.

A young woman, about twenty in human years, approached with a tray piled high with assorted sweets.

Sterling's gaze shifted from the woman to Teal. "Sienna has a great future in Earth studies. She's practiced maintaining their form for extended periods and even eats their food.

Teal frowned at the tray of neat confections. "These look like Bhuaci—"

Sterling waved the woman away. "You don't expect me to sacrifice my health? I note your recipes. I don't actually try them." He scowled at the mug. "Except occasionally."

After Sienna's figure sashayed out of the room, Teal rose and strode to the open window. He gazed over the bustling cityscape filled with glowing beings in a variety of shapes and forms. "You should spend time on Earth—then you'd understand."

Strolling over to the window, Sterling rested his hand on Teal's shoulder. "We've known each other for a long time— you were my best student. Have you ever seen me accept any level of discomfort willingly?"

Teal's gaze remained fixed on the bustling throng below. "You're a judge now—you have new responsibilities."

Sterling's hand fell to the side. "You're a guardian. You can relate the news in your reports. Lovely reports by the way. Though, I must say, you could go into a little more detail about the planet itself." He shrugged. "I have to find out about their mineral deposits from the Ingots." One eyebrow rose. "You know how that makes me feel?"

Teal turned and frowned, his gaze fixed on his superior.

"And do you learn about human physiology from Cresta dissection reports?"

Sterling spread his hands wide. "Naturally."

Folding his arms over his chest, Teal's body glowed in rising heat. "You don't care about alien life forms at all?"

Sterling slapped the window frame. "Why should I care? We study them to protect ourselves—they're not pets." He glared at Teal, his own body glowing at the edges. "Do you care about Ingots? The Crestas?" He wagged a finger. "How about the Bhuacs?"

Flaming through a long intense stare, Teal's gaze zeroed in on Sterling.

Sterling closed his eyes and leaned against the window frame. A breeze blew in, ruffling his white hair. His glow faded. "You do."

After pacing across the room, Teal's heat receded to normal. He stopped in front of Sterling. "I always have. And you're right—they're not pets." He turned sharply and marched toward the doorway.

Sterling opened his eyes and lifted one hand. "All right! I'll go with you—I'll visit the planet." He exhaled a long breath. "But none of that horrible brew!"

Chapter Fifteen

—Grassland—

When Evil Comes Upon You

Onias stopped outside his dwelling and met his wife's angry gaze.

"Two new men arrived in the village, Onias, and I'm worried." Jonas thrust her hands on her hips, facing him with a sweaty, furrowed brow.

Onias lifted one eyebrow and led Jonas to a shady spot near their dwelling. As they sat on the soft earth, he took her hand and coaxed her good humor. "What's really bothering you? Are you working too hard? Perhaps it's my turn to remind you to get out of the sun."

Jonas took a deep breath. "I am tired, but that's not what's upsetting me. You are."

Onias scratched his head. "I've missed something."

Rolling her eyes, Jonas rose and padded over to a blanket that had fallen in the dirt. She shook it and threw it over a pole. "Yes, my dear. Every free moment, your eyes glaze over and you start shaping something in your mind. You hardly notice anything beyond the sunrise and the sunset."

Onias grinned. "I see your beauty as well."

Jonas blushed. Glancing beyond him, her smile vanished. "But there's a great deal that you do not see." Snatching a broom from the corner of their dwelling, she swept the front area clear. "Our visitors have been with us for over a week now."

Rising, Onias gripped a pole and gazed at the field. "I'd have to be blind and deaf not to know that. I've seen them but haven't spoken to them yet."

"There lies my point, Onias. You're our leader. These travelers should have spoken with you right away. But you were always too busy, and now they've made themselves at home." Jonas scowled. "They're not civilized. The older one, Joash, looks to impress us. He speaks fine words; but I don't trust him. The younger one, Ishtar, carries a terrible secret. I can see it in his eyes. They bring trouble—you should speak with them."

Onias frowned. "Are you sure you're not imagining troubles? We're strong, and they haven't done anything wrong, have they?"

"They ask too many questions." Her frown morphed into a beseeching pout. "Why do they want to know so much about us?"

Pulling her close, Onias' shrugged. "It's natural for travelers to be curious. Remember, they're just boys—not warriors." He nuzzled her hair with his chin. "I'll talk with them, but if I see no harm—" He gazed into her eyes. "You must accept my judgment and let your anxiety go, all right?"

Jonas leaned into his embrace and nodded. After a moment, she stepped back and called to the boys. "Gather the tools—night's falling fast." Clapping her hands, she traipsed after her sons into their dwelling.

Onias stretched and ambled to the center of the village. The sweltering air hung thick and heavy, though a cooler breeze rose from the north. His gaze wandered from the darkening sky to the villagers assembled around the central fire.

Soft murmurs of men and women and the occasional shrill yelp of a child filtered across the land.

Onias smiled. As he strolled, he greeted various families. He praised new additions to homes and laughed at the antics of the children. He asked about those who had not been feeling well, and he sympathized with those who had an ache or a bruise to show for the day's toil. He teased one lazy fellow and the nearest villagers laughed good-naturedly.

As he passed a large dwelling on his right, he saw the

silhouetted figures of many men sitting around a fire. Some sat cross-legged, while others squatted some distance away. A few stars twinkled overhead, and for a brief moment, a soft, cool breeze blew through his hair and against his back, sending a shiver of delight through his body. He drank in the soothing freshness.

Voices murmured softly as Onias ambled closer, but stopped abruptly when the evening fire illuminated his figure.

He smiled as he scanned the faces in the crowd, but his eyebrows rose at the sight of two strangers in the inner circle.

"Good evening, Onias," A voice boomed from the darkness. Onias glanced over.

Jerah, the owner of the dwelling, waved him closer. "Come, sit with us. It's a beautiful night."

A loud clamor inside the dwelling attested to an evening struggle between children and their bedtime.

"Good evening, Jerah. How are your many offspring?"

"All doing well. Growing like mighty cedars. Ah, such is the fate of health and good living." He put out his hand palm up, offering a seat in the circle. "We're just speaking with our guests. Won't you sit with us?"

Onias nodded and perched on the edge of a log.

Two youths moved to a spot further away, giving Onias room.

Onias' gaze roamed about the circle until he settled on the two newcomers. The first, he noticed, was still quite young—only about sixteen, though tall and strong. He appeared all over dark—hair, eyes, and skin. He wore only a leather skirt tied about the waist with an obsidian knife stuck in a belt. The other youth was smaller, but clearly older, and sat straighter, with a more determined pose. He stared at the second youth for a moment longer than was polite.

The younger one flicked a gaze over Onias and scowled.

Jerah pointed to the youths. "Let me introduce to you our guests. This young man—" pointing to the first, "—is Ishtar, and his companion is Joash. They've come a long way, traveling as a part of their journey to manhood, they say. They've enjoyed meeting us, though they just told me that they'll return home in the morning. I'd hoped they'd stay longer, but it's not to be."

The fire had died down to a mound of glowing coals. The cool breeze that Onias had felt earlier returned, but now the chill was not as welcome. The night darkened and the twinkling stars hid under wispy clouds. The moon climbed from the east, but it remained only a sliver of faint light.

Onias heard his voice before he had determined what he was going to say. "Ishtar and Joash, you're welcome in our village. I'm sorry I've been been so remiss that I haven't met you until now. I am from the family of Jabal. My people settled this land long ago—many generations past. We're a peaceful people and welcome strangers into our midst. We enjoy the exchange of new ideas. It's through invention that our people have prospered. I would enjoy hearing your travels—and especially about your people. Share your story with me. I very much enjoy hearing about other clans."

Joash cast a sidelong glance at Ishtar, who stared moodily into the fire. Joash shifted and then glanced around with a practiced smile. "I'm glad to meet you, Onias, of the family of Jabal. We did try to make your acquaintance, but you were busy at the time."

Ishtar coughed and grunted, but his gaze remained fixed on the glowing embers.

Joash lifted his hands as if in rehearsed oration. "We've enjoyed our visit, and we're impressed with everything you've accomplished here. Our people won't understand, of course, as they are but a simple people. You'd find us a dull community. You must be a great leader indeed." Joash's smile stayed fixed, though his glance slid over to Ishtar.

Ishtar didn't move a muscle.

Onias' gaze darted to Ishtar, who, though he hadn't spoken a word, seemed to be saying more than any of them. "And you, Ishtar, how did you enjoy your stay?"

Ishtar raised his head enough to show his furrowed brows and pursed mouth. "Your village is fine. Your people are kind, and we've been treated generously." He choked on his next words. "But I see no warriors, no guards—no defenses at all. This I do not understand."

Joash's head snapped up.

Onias stiffened.

A mummer swept through the watching crowd.

Joash stumbled into the breach. "Yes, I meant to ask too. You see we've visited other warrior clans. Since we don't know of such things, we were afraid to ask. But perhaps you could explain this mystery. We'd like to share news with our village." His smile remained wide and adamant, though his eyes burned in fury.

Ishtar gazed more deeply into the glowing embers.

Onias lightened his tone, though his eyes bored into the two youths. "I wish I could tell you more, but we're not warriors. We're just a humble village and have no desire to take what is not ours, so we have not become a conquering people. I've heard of tribes who raid. But I always hoped such clans would stay far from us. If you want to know about warriors, you must ask a warrior—we've none here."

Ishtar's voice rose from the gloom of his thoughts. "There'll be none to defend you when evil does comes."

Onias met the hardened gaze of Joash. He spoke quietly. "We'll continue our peaceful ways and endure trial—if it comes."

Jerah shifted and lifted his voice. "What Onias says is true. A warrior can take tools, food, and even members of a family, but no warrior can take the traditions built by generations. We're builders and creators and will long remain so, while a warrior's days will last only the length of his spear."

Joash stretched and patted Ishtar on the back in an over hearty manner. "We have a long journey tomorrow."

Ishtar stood with his back bowed by an invisible weight.

Joash nodded his good night.

Onias and Jerah nodded back.

The two youths turned and walked into the black night.

Onias stood and glanced at Jerah. "We'll speak again in the morning."

Jerah nodded in agreement.

In a few minutes, Onias stepped into the large front room of his dwelling.

The two boys lay sleeping by the back wall.

After laying blankets over the children, Jonas glanced up and pointed to a tray with food laid out.

Onias lifted a bowl of broiled goat meat garnished with leeks. A dish with beans, goat cheese, and several small, thin round flat breads lay to the side. He sat on a pillow, made himself comfortable, and began to pick at the meat and bread thoughtfully.

Jonas knelt by his side. "Did you see the boys?"

Onias looked out of the depths of his thoughts and smiled. He patted the ground next to him.

Pulling a dish of figs, grapes, and dates nearer, she sat at his side.

"Yes, I spoke with them. The one called Joash is quick-witted and speaks to please his audience, but the younger one, Ishtar, bears a sad burden. They're angry and carry a secret. They may be spies. Ishtar even complained about our lack of warriors, and Joash was furious. Perhaps Ishtar feels guilty because he knows of an agreement Joash made with a clan that wants to attack us." He rubbed his chin. "I'll hold a council with our men tomorrow."

Jonas' profile flickered in the light of the flame from a wick soaked in oil. She gazed upon the two sleeping figures in the darkness.

~~~

Onias strolled across the village the next morning. Ishtar and Joash had left before the break of day. Having taken them at their word, he expected to find them preparing to leave, not already gone. He shook his head in wonder and hoped that they were gone for good and wouldn't return with an ill wind at their back.

Jonas gathered dirty clothes for a long day of washing. When Onias returned, she motioned for him to come closer. "There's trouble ahead, Onias. I can feel it."

Onias smiled and wrapped his arm around her waist. The troubles of the two boys seemed remote in the light of a new day. Embracing her warmly, he tilted her chin so she could look him in the eye.

"Perhaps. I'll speak to the men at a council meeting at Jerah's today. But the threat is a distant one. We don't even know if there's cause for alarm. I don't want our people to fear every stranger that comes through. In any case, I don't want you to worry."

~~~

Eoban awoke with a strange foreboding in his heart. He went out before sunrise and heard the two youths as they prepared for the return journey.

He watched them as they scattered the remaining embers of the fire they had built the night before. They moved with sharp, decisive actions as if motivated by fear or urgency. His distrust of their prodding questions and their lack of openness about their people had made him uneasy.

Eoban knew that not every clan was as peaceable as his own. He had seen villages after an attack. Such a defeat could destroy a clan. He had seen the remains of horrors that had seared his heart and burned the ignorance of evil away.

His own clan had been decimated. Images of his older brother and father being struck down still haunted his dreams. Fortunately, his mother had been quick-witted and strong enough to lead him and his brothers to this village. She made herself useful, married again, and raised her three sons and, later, three daughters in the peace and security of a new home.

After the death of his brother in a hunting accident, Eoban took over as head of his family and found himself as an uncle to every child in the village. But in his heart, he considered his first role to be that of the clan's only warrior—no one else seemed much interested in the position.

As the moon settled into the horizon, Eoban watched the two strange youths throwing their bags over their shoulders and begin their trek. They trudged off silently with their spears in hand, heading east.

Eoban jogged north steadily and quietly, as his years of successful hunting had taught him. He shook his head in frustration. He wished he knew more of all the lands around here, but the Earth was so great and clans moved. He was only one man, and the land was broad.

He knew of a small clan of hill dwellers to the north, so he swung himself up further north, staying low to avoid calling attention to his presence. He ran until he was just north of them.

The sun spread its glorious rays over the horizon. Red and orange hues seeped into the whiteness of the sky.

Suddenly, Eoban's gaze was wrenched from the beauty of the sky to the surprising sight of Ishtar and Joash on the ground among the swirling grasses in a tumult of rolling fury. Arms and legs flailed as each tried to get the advantage of the other. But Joash was clearly the superior fighter.

Eoban frowned. Of the two, he would rather Ishtar best his opponent as it seemed that he was not as bold a liar as his companion. He stood watching, unsure what to do, when Joash unsheathed his knife and leapt onto Ishtar. The younger boy twisted to keep the knife at bay, but he was unable to either break free or knock the knife from Joash's hand.

Eoban edged closer.

Joash spat his words at Ishtar. "You're a disgrace to your father. He'd want you dead if he knew you betrayed his orders."

Sweat beaded on Ishtar's face. His long brown hair flew wildly across his face as he tried to keep the knife from his throat.

Joash raised his arms high, and with a mighty yell, he threw the weight of his body behind the knife.

Eoban bounded through the tall grass and thrust himself on the outstretched form of Joash.

Joash flew forward, falling to the ground. He twisted around, stunned, and furious. Scrambling to his feet, he glared at Eoban. "Who are you to interfere in a fair fight?"

Eoban snorted and stepped closer to Joash, screening Ishtar who still lay sprawled and panting in the grass. "A fair fight, you call it? I'd call it a few things but fair wouldn't be one of them. I'm Eoban—from the clan you recently visited. I was returning home, when I saw such a sight as to make my blood run cold. Now, tell me, where do you come from, and why are you trying to kill this boy?"

Ishtar struggled to his feet, rubbing his arms and neck.

Joash glowered as he slipped his knife into its sheath. "I've nothing to tell you, old man. We're on our way home. Nothing more." He glared at Ishtar. "Let's go."

Eoban pointed to Ishtar. "And how is he going to survive such a journey, I wonder?"

Joash snorted, "That's no concern of yours. Come, Ishtar. Your *father* is waiting."

Eoban faced Ishtar, putting his hand on the boy's shoulder. "You realize—he must finish you? He cannot let you arrive home with this tale on your lips or the look of truth in your eyes every time you meet. You'll never be safe with him."

Ishtar nodded. His hair blew in all directions, falling over his face.

The sun had risen, glowing golden in the pink and blue sky.

Eoban frowned at the despair in Ishtar's eyes.

Ishtar's voice hovered at a whisper. "I must return."

Clenching his jaw, Eoban glanced from Joash to Ishtar. "Be that as it may, I'm going to detain you for a while so your friend can go on his way. You and I can follow in due course and return you to your family. I've no desire to separate a boy from his family, but I can't entrust you into this one's care." He thrust out his massive hand in a gesture of dismissal.

Joash stood his ground, glaring at Ishtar.

Eoban repeated the gesture as if shooing a pesky fly. Gripping Ishtar's shoulders, he turned him back toward the southwest. Keeping one hand on his back, Eoban directed Ishtar through the open grasses. His ears were tuned for any sudden movement even as Ishtar marched stiffly at his side.

When he peered back, Joash lifted his spear and yelled in a taunting voice. "Ishtar, your mother will be waiting for you, but I'll tell her your decision." Screaming a war cry, he swung around and ran eastward through the undulating grasses.

Ishtar watched as Joash disappeared into the swaying mass of gold that separated them. "Thank you for your kindness, but Joash knows I must return. He knows what awaits me. He probably thought he offered mercy by ending my life before I had to stand before my father. It'd be better for everyone if I never make it home." He started to shuffle after Joash.

Eoban flushed and thrust his hands on his hips. "Now wait a moment. I didn't save your life so you could offer it up again to that nasty little vermin. Do you mean to tell me that your father would condemn you because of what Joash says? If that's so, then you'll come home with me. You have no future with such a family. In truth, I don't think you're fit to judge what should be done at this moment."

Ishtar sighed and leaned on his spear.

Eoban took Ishtar by the arm. "I know of a stream near here that joins the one that goes through our village. It won't take us much out of the way, and it'll give you a needed rest and time to think."

A look of resignation passed over Ishtar's face. He stumbled along at Eoban's side. In a matter of moments, they both drank thirstily from a clear, shallow stream that meandered over a rocky field.

The undulating grass rustled around them, and the sky

seemed larger than ever.

Ishtar sank down on a grey rock half buried in the sand by the water's edge.

When Eoban settled himself on the green lawn, he leaned back and waited.

Ishtar leaned forward, perched his elbows on his knees, and began to speak of his father. He told about his clan's passion for raids and his father's obsessive demand for perfection. His voice remained calm and dispassionate, even when he told of his friend's death.

A sharp pain grew behind Eoban's eyes as he imagined the scenes Ishtar described.

Ishtar's voice quivered at the mention of the part he played in the last raid. "I vowed after that last mission, that I would never go on another raid. I thought this trip would spare me—but it won't spare anyone."

Eoban kept his gaze fixed on Ishtar, but he didn't interrupt.

"I thought that once Joash met you, he would change his mind." Ishtar shook his head. "But instead, he made plans for who would become his slave." Ishtar's eyes glimmered. "He can't wait to return and tell Neb how best to attack your people."

"So you confronted him?"

Ishtar shook his head. "No, he accused me of trying to get us killed. I was sure he would kill me, and I was glad—my only hope is the black night of a forever sleep."

"Why didn't you try to fight back? You're strong enough. You should've pushed your advantage."

Ishtar shook his head. "Joash spoke the truth. If my father knew I wouldn't fight for him, he'd want me dead. He has killed other men who failed him. He'll always claim it's for the good of the clan. All the while our people are dying—" Ishtar let his voice trail off as he stared over the bubbling stream.

Eoban sighed. "And your mother? Will she understand?"

Ishtar bowed his head. "She believes, as does the whole clan, that we are abandoned by the gods because we are not a worthy race of men. That's why my father is so determined to make his people a clan of conquerors. Then perhaps the gods will once again give new life to our women."

Eoban shook his head. "Worse and worse it is. I've never heard the like of this in all my days." He continued to sit hunch-shouldered for a moment and then slowly rose and stretched.

He beckoned to Ishtar. "Well, one thing's for certain—you can't return home now. Joash will surely get there first, and I'm sure he won't speak of you in glowing terms. Your mother is undoubtedly a wiser woman than you realize, and she'll think the best of you despite that snake's venom. She, more than anyone, wouldn't want your untimely return. Now, let's be off. We have much to discuss with Onias. Maybe you can open his sleepy eyes to the dangers that lurk outside his pleasant village."

Chapter Sixteen

—Lakeland—

After a Hard Journey

Barak trudged slowly up the steep slope. Though his head hung down, he had no doubt that his people were directly in front of him. He had found their unmistakable tracks hours ago and shuffled over the final distance in expectant hope that he would soon rest. The silhouettes of several figures shone against the evening twilight. Tree branches loomed starkly across the sky as he labored toward the watching group. He lifted his weary head and slowed his step as he peered at the faces.

Recognition fluttered from face to startled face.
"It's Barak!"
"Barak has come back!"
Then a note of worry crept in.
"But where are the rest?"
"Where's my husband?"
"Where's my brother?"
The voices grew clamorous.

Barak took a step backwards and lifted a limp hand. "Calm down! It's all right. I was injured. They probably thought I was dead, so they left without me. I must have passed them in the night. They'll be here soon enough, I assure you. Now, tell me, where's Aram?"

Aram stepped into the firelight and folded his arms over his chest. "You've found us, Barak." As he gazed at Barak, the anger in his eyes melted. "You look like a weary man after a hard journey. Here, come to my tent."

Aram glanced around. Namah stood by, staring at Barak. Aram waved his hand and frowned. "Namah, get him something to eat."

Barak heaved a sigh as he shouldered his burden and pushed the last few steps to Aram's dwelling, using his spear as support.

Aram leaned Barak's spear against a tree by his tent. Then he helped Barak release the mighty burden from his back. Aram huffed. "Your cat must've been larger than I ever imagined to wear so much skin."

Barak merely nodded as he allowed himself to be led to a woven mat. He sat down with a sigh and smiled weakly as Namah brought him a bowl of hot stew. He blew on the steam as it rose into the cooling air. As others were served, Barak ate hungrily.

Suddenly, as if waking from a stupor, he stopped and searched the small crowd of watchers.

An old man peered at him from the edge of the crowd.

Laying the bowl aside, Barak grinned and stumbled to his father.

The old man stared at his son as gleaming tears tumbled down his cheeks.

Wrapping his arms around the stooped shoulders, Barak embraced him.

Aram watched, his mouth open, his eyes wide with surprise.

Taking a step back, Barak led his father to the mat and offered him his bowl of stew. The old man refused, but Barak, insisted. Someone passed another bowl to Barak, and the two began to eat.

Barak finished two bowls of stew, several flat cakes of bread, and a dish of nuts and raisins to appease his appetite. He lay back comfortably, his gaze darting to his father.

After finishing his meal, Aram dismissed Namah with a wave of the hand. A number of clan members paid their respects to welcome Barak home and ask questions about his adventure.

Barak sipped his mead and told what he could without going into too much detail. He spoke quietly as if telling of another man's adventure. The fact that there had been two cats drew a crowd of hungry listeners and eager exclamations of surprise. Everyone was well pleased that both cats had been killed, and they were troubled that the other clan members had mistook him for dead and left him to fend for himself. But it was a wonderful thing that he had been returned to them and that the cat skins could now be put to good use.

One man slapped Barak's knee. "We'll have a feast to celebrate your safe return."

Aram nodded agreeably at the glad faces bunched at the entrance of his tent.

As the moon reached its zenith, Aram clapped his hands. "Time to settle down and let this weary man rest. You can pester him again tomorrow.

Before the crowd dispersed, a woman called out. "What're you going to do with the skins, Barak?"

All eyes focused on Barak as he rose and lumbered to the roll. Pulling the tie loose, he stretched one skin out for everyone to see. Then, hobbling on his sore feet, he dragged the thick fur to his father and laid it over the old man's thin shoulders. "You deserve this more than anyone for putting up with me, old man."

Tears filled the women's eyes and murmurs of approval filled the air. Only Namah frowned and folded her arms in reproachful anger.

Within moments, the clan shuffled to their homes. A few babies awakened and had to be hushed back to sleep. Few night sounds broke the silence, and the sky glowed clear with the distant points of bright specks.

Barak sat up and clasped his arms around his knees.

Aram sat to the side, his gaze fixed on the starry sky.

Clearing his throat, Barak leaned forward. "Aram, there's something I need to tell you. I couldn't speak freely before because I'm confused, and I don't want others to decide they know what happened better than I do." He drew a long breath. "I think Irad wanted me dead."

Aram turned and regarded Barak. His eyebrows rose as he motioned for him to continue speaking.

"Irad did save me the first time, though he seemed to wait until he was certain that I was getting the better of the cat before he acted. I began to wonder if he was disappointed that I survived. I know what you're thinking, and I was thinking the same. I'm being unfair. Irad did save me, and that's all that counts. But then I recalled how he killed animals, not for their meat, but for the sport of it. I began to wonder where his loyalties lie. He liked adventure, but to what end? Would he set the cat on me for pure excitement?"

Aram interrupted, "But didn't you admit that it was you who had forgotten the ashes and that it was your smell that must have attracted the cat?"

Barak nodded. "Yes, that's true, and so at first I could not reconcile my feelings with the possibility that I was simply embarrassed by my failure. But then I remembered—he made the ash mixture himself. When it was my turn, he ran out and said he'd make more, but we forgot. Doubt had crept into my mind when I pondered all these things. He wouldn't even touch the cat skin. He encouraged me to take it. When the second cat attacked, every man ran for his life. I suppose that was natural enough, but surely there was time enough for someone to have come to my aid. Someone could have shouted or thrown something. But I was all alone."

Aram rubbed his jaw. "Fear can make a man to run farther than you might think. Remember, they didn't expect a second cat. They might have thought it was the spirit of the first cat come back to haunt them." His eyes glowed softly as he offered a compassionate smile.

"But afterward—" Barak hesitated. "I probably looked dead, it's true, but they should've checked. When they came back, I was too stunned to open my eyes, but I heard them talking.

Irad even laughed. He said he had expected the mate to come." Barak paused, clasping and unclasping his hands. "It was as if he wanted to see me die—something he arranged for his pleasure."

Aram tapped his fingers together in front of his face in a poise of contemplation. "Are you sure you heard a laugh? I've heard sounds similar to laughter, but they spring from overwhelming grief."

Barak shook his head. "I heard the laughter of mirth. Irad found the situation amusing."

Aram took a deep breath. "Once during a hunt, Irad had an opportunity to kill a large buck while a doe and a fawn stood in the background. Irad shot the fawn. When asked why, he said that he liked to do the unexpected." Aram raked his fingers through his hair.

Barak snorted. "Sounds like Irad." He sucked in a long breath. "I waited, but they never returned. I skinned the second cat myself and began the long journey to find you. I'm almost afraid to meet Irad again. It's been a nightmare. It seems odd even now that no one checked on me. They all took Irad's word for it that I was dead."

Aram looked up sharply, "Are you positive that no one did anything to help you? Perhaps you fainted and don't remember."

Barak shook his head. His voice lowered with little emotion. "No one did anything for me. I was abandoned." With a stifled groan, he rose and made ready to go. "I've told you what happened. It's your choice to believe me or not."

Rising, Aram followed Barak out the doorway into the cool night. "I'm glad you told me." He gripped Barak's shoulder. "I'll ponder what you said. When Irad and the others return, I'll speak to them and see what I can discover." He pointed to a makeshift tent on the left. "Your father sleeps there."

Barak nodded, his head, drooping in exhaustion.

Aram patted Barak's back. "I'm glad you made it home—alive."

Tears welled in Barak's eyes. "Thank you." He lumbered toward his father's tent. The faint moonlight shone down on new homes of mud and stone. A pleasant thrill spread through his body. Taking a deep breath, his smile widened as he saw his old father sitting outside his shabby tent, waiting for him.

Barak shuffled closer and crouched down to look his faithful father in the eye. "I'll start a new house tomorrow. A house to stand through the ages.

The old man's toothless grin reached out to his son.

Namah thrashed about on her pallet like a strong wind in the treetops. Her mind would not rest. *Aram pays no attention to me. Barak forgot his promise. Everyone is jealous of my position and probably laughing behind their hands. Aram used to need me, but now he hardly looks my way.*

She turned again. *He's an ugly, stupid man.* She paused. *Why the council with Barak? What happened to the other men? He mentioned Irad's name. What will Irad say when he finds out that secret words are whispered in Aram's ears about him? Perhaps he'll appreciate the advice of a faithful woman.* Namah settled back on the pallet, a smug smile dancing on her lips.

Aram entered the tent, stretched out at her side, and was soon snoring.

She turned her back to him. She felt her heavy body relax and allowed sleep to take her.

Chapter Seventeen

—River Clan—

Sky Warrior

Joash marched home pondering how to best present himself before Neb and the council. It must be very clear that he had not failed but rather that he had succeeded despite everything Ishtar had done to hinder him. Ishtar would not return anytime soon. Perhaps he would never return.

Standing before the council in the open air, Joash had told the truth. He did not volunteer any information but allowed the story to unfold through their eager questions. Dismay clouded their eyes, and their hands clenched in anger. He recounted Ishtar's refusal to ask questions or even make any attempt to learn about the Grassland People. Joash stoically repeated Ishtar's comment, "But I see no warriors, no guards—no defenses at all."

Neb snorted in disgust.

Joash described the final parting, embellishing his story with images of his grim determination to bring Ishtar safely home despite the interference of a stranger. He could only assume that Ishtar had returned to the Grassland Clan and told all he knew.

Disapproving grunts issued from the council.

"I'm grieved that I could not force Ishtar to return home, but I'm grateful to be back, certain that we can conquer this new clan, with or without Ishtar's help."

Neb merely nodded, his mouth straight and his eyes fixed ahead.

One elderly member pointed across the way. "You've been given a slave girl as a reward, and since Ishtar has not returned, you might as well take the boy that would've been offered to him."

Joash held his smile in check and bowed his way gratefully out of the meeting.

Hagia bustled to his side as she scooted around a campfire. "Where's my son, Joash? What's happened?"

As his gaze searched the compound for his new slaves, Joash brushed the old woman aside. "Ishtar stayed behind. He's chosen his own path."

"What do you mean? Was he hurt or—"

Joash quickened his steps. "The less you know, the better you'll feel." Leaving Hagia wringing her hands, Joash returned to his dwelling.

Two children sat hunchbacked outside his tent near a pathetic fire. He scowled as he strode before the two crouched figures. They were skinny and dirty and much younger than he had hoped. He kicked the boy.

The child scampered backward, out of reach.

Joash shrugged. This would raise his status in the clan. They were his to command—or kill—as he saw fit. His scowl deepened. "I'm hungry—can you cook?"

They stared at him, shivering despite the fire.

"Stand up!"

The girl rose and held her head high, her gaze wandering to the bright sky.

The boy, younger and thinner, with a tear-stained face, stared at the ground as he climbed to his feet.

"You, boy, what's your name, and where are you from?"

The boy kept his gaze lowered. "My name's Lud. I'm from the clan of Tiras. You came through and destroyed my village two years ago. We're a North Hills—"

Joash blushed and slapped the boy. "Your people were conquered. They're weak and they—" He lifted his hand again.

The girl stepped forward, her gaze shifting from the sky to focus on Joash.

His hand dropping to his side, Joash pursed his lips as he considered the girl. "What's your name? Where're you from?"

The girl's brow furrowed. "My name is Pele, but I don't remember my people or where I'm from. I've worked for many people."

Joash rotated his neck to relax his neck muscles. The weight of slave holding was not settling easily on his shoulders. "You're both weak and stupid."

Pele's gaze drifted to the sky again.

Joash squeezed his eyes shut. He took a deep breath, opened his eyes, and spoke more softly. "It doesn't matter. I'm your master now, and you'll do what I say. You understand?"

Lud nodded while his gaze darted across the ground like a bird searching for escape.

Pele's eyes rose to the blue sky.

Joash slapped Pele's arm. "You, girl, will take care of the meals." He turned to Lud. "You—make some kind of shelter for yourself and the girl. If you need something, go to my mother, and she'll get what you require." He waved an admonishing finger. "When I call, come quickly. I hate disobedient slaves." He glared at them a moment as if to make his meaning abundantly clear.

Lud nodded.

Pele gazed solemnly at her master.

They'll learn. He stared down at their filthy faces. They were like beasts of the field. No use smiling at them. He inhaled a long breath and stalked away.

Lud lifted his head warily and watched his master shout greetings to friends—his proud head up, swaggering with confidence.

Lud's gaze slid toward the girl at his side.

Pele's eyes had returned to the sky once again, her lips drawn into a thin line of quiet determination.

Lud peered into the clear, blue sky. A few green tips of

leaves framed the sky in the north and east near the river's edge. Birds flew from trees into the open space overhead.

Lud inched closer. "Do you wish you were free—like the birds?"

Pele's lips moved as if she were whispering to someone beyond his sight. A smile washed over her face, and her whole being radiated joy.

Lud swallowed back fear. What could she see that he could not? He screwed his brows together and concentrated, trying to see what she saw, but found nothing but the sky overhead. He tapped her shoulder.

Pele dropped her gaze and peered at him, a glad smile twinkling in her eyes.

Confused, Lud stepped backward. He pointed up gingerly. "What do you see?"

"You saw nothing?"

He shrugged. "Only the sky and a few birds."

Her smile faded into peaceful acceptance.

"Tell me—what did you see?"

Pele took Lud's hand and led him to the clearing near the entrance of Joash's dwelling. She sat down and patted the ground, inviting him to sit next to her. Folding her hands in her lap, she bent forward. "I saw a great warrior—wondrous to behold."

Lud's mouth fell open. A shiver ran over his body. "A warrior—in the sky? Like the warriors of our master's clan?"

As if swallowing a bad taste, Pele grimaced. "Nothing like that. He's greater than any man—a sky warrior."

Lud dropped his voice. "Does he have weapons?"

Pele nodded vigorously. "Of course! He carries a shining spear. He's young and strong with gleaming muscles. His skin is bronze and he wears a brilliant white tunic. Yet he smiles so gently, that I'm filled with hope." Her eyes glimmered even as she returned her gaze to the sky.

Lud looked up.

Nothing.

She seems sane. Perhaps her vision is keener than mine. His heart began to pound. "Will he help us escape?" He held his breath—waiting.

Pele's smile faded. "He speaks of hope, not of escape. But someday—we'll be free."

"When?" Lud clasped his hands together so tightly the knuckles turned white.

Pele dusted her hands free of dirt. "In trust, we'll find our hope." She stood and began to make preparations for the midday meal. Stoking the small fire, her eyes no longer wandered. Only a gentle smile hinted of her secret.

Lud shook his head in disgust. A lump formed in his throat and scalding tears burned his eyes. His village had been destroyed, his people were dead, he was a slave, and nothing would change that.

Joash called from across the village. "Lud, wake up and come here!

Must he let the whole village know he has slaves to command? Lud padded toward him, his shoulders slumped.

Pele's confident eyes seemed to speak clearer than her words. "Don't be afraid. We're not alone."

Lud froze and stared at her. With an unexpected burst of comfort, he knew she was not mad. Squaring his shoulders, he strode across the compound to Joash.

The scowl on Joash's face smoothed out. He peered at the boy. "Go to my mother and get fish for our noon meal."

Lud nodded and strode forward. His gaze wandered to the sky.

Chapter Eighteen

—Grassland—

Be Prepared

Eoban and Obed sat together. Each sharpened his weapon. Other clansmen worked at similar tasks, turning their hunting weapons into tools of war. No one smiled.

The noonday sun no longer glared in the heat of high summer. The grass had turned golden brown, and late-season flowers bloomed in muted orange, faded yellow, and scarlet. The buzzing insects, as if aware of the shortness of their lifespans, fluttered about in a final rush of activity. Bees hurried from flower to flower, ignoring the tramping of distracted, dusty feet. Grasshoppers leapt from grass blades, spilling brown juice when crushed underfoot. Every living thing bustled in autumn intensity.

Eoban craned his neck and peered through the village pathways, his gaze sweeping from side to side. He grunted.

Obed looked up. "What is wrong?"

Continuing to survey the horizon, Eoban growled, "Where are Ishtar and those two scoundrels, Jael and Tobia?"

Obed shrugged. "Probably exploring. You know how they use Ishtar to get out of work."

With a snort, Eoban returned to the task at hand. "They don't much care for work, those two, and Ishtar will do anything to please them. Onias pities him and lets the boys entertain him. Still, I told Ishtar to keep the boys close to home. He, better than anyone, knows what danger we face. Our days of peace will soon be over, and we'll have no second chance."

Obed shaved the handle of his knife so that it fit his hand

exactly. His spear with a sharp stone tip strapped tight with double ties lay next to him. He tested the weight and feel of the long obsidian knife. "You're right. Ishtar should be here. And Jael and Tobia should be helping their mother."

He stood and peered at a figure stuffed with dried grass some distance away. After swinging the knife in an arc, he threw with a terrific force.

Eoban glanced up—eyebrows rising.

The knife tore through the figure's middle.

"That's fine—if your opponent is made of grass. I'm afraid the men we will meet won't stand for such treatment."

Obed scowled and strode off to dig his knife from the haystack behind the figure. As he walked, a shout broke the silence. He felt himself thrust forward as a small body clung to his back like an oversized bat, its arms wrapped around his neck.

"If warriors come, I'll save you, Obed!"

Obed turned first to the right and then to the left, his arms flapping helplessly as if he could not understand who was speaking to him. He faced Eoban, his eyes wide and innocent.

Fighting manfully, Eoban conquered a grin.

Tapping his chin thoughtfully, Obed's eyebrows furrowed. "I thought I heard a voice, but I can't see anyone."

Tobia climbed further up Obed's back.

Reaching back, Obed flung the child over his shoulder, and landed the boy softly on the ground, tickling him.

Tobia laughed in gulping gasps.

Obed tapped his foot on the child's tummy. "You'll get them, little one. Just don't kill me first—all right?" With a grimace, Obed rubbed his neck.

Eoban burst out laughing. He grasped his spear and passed it to the child.

Intercepting Eoban, Jael ran forward and grabbed the heavy weapon. He hoisted it clumsily to his shoulder. "Here, little brother, let me take it. I'm older, and I really can fight the enemy to the death." Jael attempted a thrust and staggered with the weight of the massive spear. He reached out to save himself.

Running forward, Ishtar snatched the spear from the boy's grasp and nailed the point into the ground. He heaved a deep breath. "Boys are not warriors." He scowled. "At least they shouldn't be. Men and war are constant companions. Enjoy your youth while you can."

Eoban stood and pulled the spear from the ground. He held it lightly and then handed it back to Jael. "It's best to be prepared."

Chapter Nineteen

—Lake Clan—

Love in Agony

Irad scanned the horizon. Fresh mud dried on his legs and arms. He ran his fingers through his hair and rubbed vigorously. Scratching at a couple of recent cuts, he let them bleed afresh. His clan lay directly ahead. As the sun's rays stretched their first morning light over the land, he smiled grimly and made sure he was ready for his homecoming.

Standing alone, his heart beat in fierce exultation. Still savoring his recent adventures, he was only sorry that he didn't have one of the great skins to add glory to his story. Still, as he was the only one left to tell his story, no qualms dampened his spirit. Aram would look small indeed after his glorious deeds of triumph and survival had been told.

After Barak's death, each of the other men met a strange fate. A deadly snake had bitten Shem, Anikar had fallen off a cliff and broken his neck, and an unfriendly clan had murdered Lamech. Irad retold his story over in his mind until it seemed as true as the sun rising in the east.

Songs of his marvelous daring would be sung around evening fires for generations to come. The clan might acclaim him leader, for even in his quiet authority, Aram could never compete with his daring deeds in overcoming the evils that had destroyed each of his companions. After smearing his face with dirt, he ascended the hill toward the welcoming trees and the bright sun.

Aram lifted a stout pole into place while two men braced it in position. They grunted and sweat poured off their faces despite the mild temperature.

As one man wiped his brow, he froze in mid motion, "Look! Someone's approaching from the west."

Aram fitted the log in its hole securely and turned around. Wiping his brow, he peered into the distance at the rise of land in the west.

The familiar figure shone clearly in the bright morning light.

Aram drew a long breath. Relief swept over him at the thought that he had sent Barak fishing with a couple of men this morning.

The man trudging up the hill had no companions.

Aram's brow furrowed as uneasiness crept into his heart.

His companion shouted and pointed. "It's Irad! But where're the others? There should be three more."

Aram ran his hand across his mouth. "Wait. Don't get excited. Let's hear what he has to say first." He stood with one hand resting on the pole.

Aram and his companions watched Irad make his way up the incline. Soon, he saw the dirt and blood on his face. A rush of sympathy increased his growing anxiety.

Irad stumbled and then caught himself handily. His hair stood at odd angles, matted with dirt. Trickles of blood had dried in smears across his arms and legs. His gaze swept the ground like a man bowed with grief. When Irad glanced up, his eyes widened and a crease of a smile formed on his lips, though haunted fear peered through his eyes.

A woman spied him coming and called to others. A crowd gathered as he staggered toward them. Children ran around, yelling in surprise and delight. Women sprang forward, begging questions. As Irad neared, an eager woman grabbed his hand and pulled him toward the village. The whole village sprang in an uproar.

"Where're the others?"

"Where's my husband?"
"Where's my brother?"
"Where's my father?"
Irad covered his tear-stained face with his hands.
Groans and gasps issued from lips like lava frothing out of a volcano.
Aram watched his clan spin into an uproar of fear and grief. Quietly striding forward, he raised his hands and barked a command. "Quiet now! We can all see that Irad has returned from a difficult journey. I'll talk to him. The rest of you, wait until I give word that he's ready to tell his story." He peered at a little girl standing near. "Maie, tell your mother to bring food and fresh water."
The girl stood transfixed, staring at Irad.
Aram frowned and nudged her along. "Hurry, and do as I say."
With a yelp, she rushed off.
Aram spied Eymard standing near. He beckoned the old man closer as he led Irad to the entrance of his dwelling. He waved Irad inside, and then laid a hand on Eymard's shoulder dropping his voice low. "Stay here, and see that no one enters until I give word. Bring in the food and water when it's ready."
Eymard nodded and crouched by the entrance.
As Aram crossed out of the light into the dark, Irad staggered forward. "I'll do better in the fresh air. I know they're anxious to hear my story."
Aram pursed his lips. "Not in your condition. Rest and have something to eat. You can tell me your tale if that would ease your mind, but don't let the others worry you just yet. There'll be time enough for that later."
Irad let himself be led inside to a pallet where he dropped down heavily.
Namah bustled in hastily. "Irad, it's good to see you. We wondered—"
Aram gripped her arm and ushered her out the doorway. He glared at Eymard, who shrugged and lifted his hands in silent

surrender. Aram's jaw clenched. "No one! You hear me?" He darted inside and then returned, thrusting a spear into the old man's gnarled arms. "Use this if need be!" He retreated inside again leaving the flap open.

Irad glanced out.

Namah stood outside, her hands on her hips, her lips pursed, and her eyes sparking with indignation. After a moment of sterile fury, she shrugged and stumped away.

When the food arrived, Eymard laid the spear aside and brought the tray to Aram who sat next to Irad.

Irad half reclined on Aram's bed, moaning softly.

Aram accepted the tray and laid it near at hand. He motioned Eymard off to the side. "Would you look at his wounds and tell me how serious they are and what can be done? I'm not as skilled a healer as you."

Eymard nodded and padded to the reclining figure. He poured water into a clay bowl and with a piece of softened leather gently washed the wounds on Irad's body.

Irad opened his eyes and sat up. "Aram, is that you?" He trembled like a man waking from a nightmare.

Aram crouched at his side. "I'm here. You're safe. Just rest." Aram's gaze wandered over Irad's stricken face. "Were you attacked by another clan?"

Irad stared fixedly ahead, his eyes unnaturally wide, as if reliving a terror. His voice wavered. "Not a clan, but evil forces worked against us. It took every skill I have just to survive." Leaning back, he laced his fingers behind his head.

A nagging irritation rose in Aram's mind. He sat cross-legged, and his gaze fell to the ground.

"Barak and I managed to track down the great cat, and when it attacked, I killed it. But a few days later, another cat—the mate—attacked and killed Barak. I destroyed the beast, but there was nothing we could do to help Barak, so we gave him a decent burial and began our weary journey home."

Aram's head jerked up, his eyes wide, a frown cresting low over his brow.

Undeterred, Irad sighed. "That evening, when we were just getting ready to settle in for the night, Shem decided to go hunting. I tried to persuade him to stay and be content until morning, but he would not rest. He went off by himself, and when it grew dark, I went in search of him. After searching in vain, I tripped over his body. He'd been bitten by a poisonous snake and died in my arms."

As bile rose in his throat, Aram swallowed and rubbed his temple.

"As soon as the sun rose, we continued our journey, but evil followed us. Anikar, already half-crazed with fear, stumbled upon a wild boar. In his frantic haste, he climbed a rock ledge. I called out a warning, but he didn't hear me. He fell the length of the ledge and broke his neck." Irad wrung his hands together. "At least his death was quick."

Aram choked back a groan, holding his head in his hands.

"Lamech went mad with grief. I tried to reason with him, but he screamed at the gods. He cursed the sky and the Earth, and I was afraid that he'd do himself harm. I spoke gently, but it was of no avail. He ran north, and though I pursued him for a long time, and as fate would have it, he was not far ahead. He lay dead in an open field, his body pierced by a single spear."

Clasping his hands, Aram shook his head. "Impossible. How could this happen?"

Irad straightened and his voice grew stronger. "Evil haunted us—but I refused to succumb. On my way home, I met vicious attacks by wild animals and wild men, but I let nothing stop me from returning to my people."

Aram rose and paced across the dark room. "What men? What animals attacked you?"

Slumping back on his pillows, Irad's shoulders sagged. "It doesn't matter now. The powers spared my life so I could accomplish whatever destiny has planned for me." Irad closed his eyes, apparently exhausted by his horrific tale.

Eymard dabbed at a last bit of blood on Irad's arm.

In a flash of irritation, Irad opened his eyes and brushed the old man away. "I don't need your help. I've endured too much to be bothered by these trifles. Leave off."

Eymard nodded and backed away, carrying the bowl of water.

Aram glanced from Eymard to the doorway and waved at Irad. "Rest now. I'll check on you again soon."

Once outside, Eymard poured the water on the ground and draped the cloth on a stout pole. Stepping away from the dwelling, he wiped his hands on his tunic.

Aram followed, blinking in the bright sun. "Was anything he said true?"

Eymard lifted his hands, his gaze clear and serious. "The marks on his body do not lie. He was neither attacked by an animal nor cut by a knife or spear. I saw no mark on his body suggesting anything more than struggles with brambles and bushes."

"What then caused all the wounds? He was covered with blood."

A hawk soared high above and cawed a warning.

Eymard's gaze lifted and followed the bird's flight. "Scratches bleed heavily if rubbed. The blood was smeared—but not because there was a quantity. Rather, I would say, it was because there was not enough. I saw the wounds and scabs on Barak's body, and they were—as he said—deep wounds inflicted by the teeth and claws of an animal."

Clenching his hands against rising fury, Aram hissed his words. "What am I to do with Irad? Barak told me that Irad left him to die—he knew the cat's mate would attack and laughed at the result. Irad certainly did not bury Barak's body as he claimed. Do I pit one against the other and let the clan decide? Three men have disappeared. I must know the truth!"

A few curious heads turned his way. Aram closed his eyes. Finally, he rubbed his face in utter vexation and motioned to Eymard to find a place to sit out of the sun. "Keep everyone away while I think this out."

Aram marched back inside the dwelling, but Irad lay sound

asleep. Crouching, he reached out to shake Irad but changed his mind. Rising, he stroked his chin, his gaze roaming over his dwelling. He froze. The tunic he wore on special occasions was hanging crooked, and his wine skin lay on the ground. Smacking one fist into his hand, he pounded back out into the sunshine.

Eymard stood and gripped Aram's shoulder. "You'll be interested in something one of the men just found. Come to Lamech's dwelling."

Aram frowned but followed the old man. He stopped. "I shouldn't leave Irad alone. There's so much—"

Namah stood at the central fire, staring at him.

"Namah! Come, I need your help."

With a sullen expression and half-lidded eyes, Namah shuffled forward.

"Irad's sleeping. Stay here and see that no one bothers him."

She nodded, shrugged her shoulders in acquiescence, and edged closer.

Aram traipsed at Eymard's side.

Moving at a quick pace, Eymard gripped Aram's arm. "Jethro just came and told me the most extraordinary tale. He went out early to the northwest with one of his friends to see if they could find some game. Surprised, he saw a figure in the distance limping toward our village. The figure fell, too weak to finish the journey, so Jethro and his friend lent assistance."

Eymard stopped as he reached Lamech's dwelling, a primitive tent with a long loose flap of tough hide hanging at the entrance.

Aram snorted. "I am assuming you've found Lamech. Why not just say so?"

"Sometimes it's better not to say too much at once." He bent closer and spoke low. "Yes, it was Lamech they brought in—more dead than alive. They called his mother and father and wife, and they've just come."

Aram scowled. "Why wasn't I told first?"

"Calm yourself." Eymard rubbed his temple. "I just found

out a few moments ago. They feared he would die, and they thought of his parents and wife first. Was that wrong? They meant no disrespect to you."

Aram gritted hi teeth. "Before I go in there—tell me—is he still alive?"

"I don't know." Eymard lifted his hands in surrender. "There's nothing more anyone could do. Jethro said that he'd been stabbed in the gut. It's a wonder he made it this far and lived to speak at all."

Aram's head jerked up, and his eyes grew wide. "He spoke? What did he say? By the great sky above, I must know what is going on!" Aram stormed forward and threw back the stiff door flap. He froze immediately.

Lamech's wife and parents crouched over a prone figure, sobbing.

Aram peered past them to the body laid out on a pallet on the floor.

Lamech lay pale and lifeless with a heavy fur blanket over his torso.

Aram's heart clenched. A wave of nausea passed through him. He grabbed the blanket and flung it to the side.

A gasp of surprise and stifled wails broke forth like waves upon rocks during a storm.

Lamech had indeed been stabbed in the stomach—but not by any spear. A great number of deep gashes marred his body, made most certainly by a short knife held by a determined hand. A wide red stain covered Lamech's middle, his face frozen forever in a mask of taut suffering.

Aram stared utterly aghast. As his rage reached the boiling point, he let loose a howl.

Lamech's parents joined the lamentation, and soon the room filled with the sounds of love in agony.

～～

Aram marched to the cliffs and stared over the lake's blue expanse. As the sun began its descent, he returned to Lamech's dwelling and found the place quiet with Eymard inside nibbling off the end of a hunk of goat cheese and washing it down with small sips of water from a skin bag. Lamech's body was now covered with the heavy blanket. Lamech's wife sat next to the body, staring into the past.

Eymard peered at Aram as he entered, speaking softly. "It's good you've returned. They want to bury the body this evening."

Aram nodded absently, his shoulders sagging. He sat beside Eymard near the back of the dimly lit dwelling and dropped his hands into his lap.

Eymard handed him a piece of goat cheese.

Aram took it unseeing and chewed while his eyes stared blankly ahead.

"His parents and wife cleaned the body and prepared him for burial. His children came and said their goodbyes." Eymard's voice trembled. "That was hard to watch."

Aram's voice dropped to a whisper. "He was a loving father and husband. A friend to everyone."

"Yes, a simple man with a simple heart. His death is a grief to us all."

Aram leaned in, his voice cracking. "Now, I must face Irad and question him. He lied to me, and Lamech's death must be at least partially his fault. Either he killed him directly or he let him be killed in some cowardice—why else did he lie? Once the clan learns of Irad's part, they'll want a public execution. I'm too grieved to seek vengeance. It's as if Irad has died also. I don't know the man who lies sleeping in my tent."

A voice spoke from behind.

Eymard and Aram turned, their heads up, their eyes wide.

Lamech's father strode to them. "If Irad had anything to do with Lamech's death, I will know of it." He stared hard at Aram who stood up and faced him.

Aram motioned to the entrance, so they stepped outside.

After marching some distance from Lamech's dwelling, Aram stopped and faced the old man. "You can speak to Irad yourself—he'll have to explain what's happened. He told me that an enemy killed Lamech. But a spear did not cause Lamech's wound." His gaze roved to the cliff. "I've spent hours considering the matter, but I can only ask that you be willing to listen to Irad—let him defend himself. The truth will be plain in time."

They continued walking and arrived at Aram's dwelling. All was silent. Aram strode inside and called Namah's name. The room was empty. Ready to rush outside, he turned and saw Lamech's father and Eymard crossing over the threshold.

Lamech's father raised his hand in an oath. "Promise me, Aram, when Irad is found, I'll be given the right of the first throw."

Aram shook his head wildly. "But Namah was here, and Irad was injured. He must be nearby."

A voice called from outside.

Aram hustled past the two and out the doorway.

Jethro panted, his hands on his knees. "Aram, the whole clan is up in arms, for Barak learned about Irad and Lamech, and he told a terrible tale." He straightened and pointed at Aram's home. "When we came to find Irad, he was gone. Namah's gone too. They're saying that he's heading north, afraid of receiving the just punishment for his wickedness."

Aram glanced at Eymard and clenched his hands in frustration. "Where's Barak then?"

The youth caught his breath. "Once he discovered that Irad and Namah were gone, he went to look for Irad himself. He said that no one is to follow him."

Men, women, and children gathered around.

Irad's mother bustled forward, wringing her hands. "Where's my son, Aram? I was away in the south, gathering, and I didn't even know he had returned until noon. When I got here, he was gone. Now they're saying evil things of him. You won't let anyone hurt my son. He's a good man. He was always your friend."

Lamech's father spat on the ground. "An uncertain friend is he who tells tales instead of the truth when it comes to injury and death."

The old woman moaned, anxious lines creasing her eyes into worried slits.

Others began to shout their opinions.

Aram patted Irad's mother's shoulder. "Cry, old woman, for this has been a bitter day."

He turned to Eymard. "Stay here and comfort those you can. I must find Irad before Barak does." He hesitated. "Or perhaps it's the other way around."

Chapter Twenty

—OldEarth—

We All Have Our Burdens

Teal rubbed his chin and surveyed the landscape.

The sun shone in brilliant splendor as five vultures circled overhead. The brassy sky, free of clouds, stretched from one side of the horizon to the other. Weathered grasses drooped like weary soldiers no longer able to stay erect.

Standing several feet away from Sterling, Teal motioned ahead. "You can't see them, but there's an artisan clan that way." He turned and flicked a finger in the opposite direction. "And a lake clan this way." He pulled his lip. "And Neb and his warriors are on the move."

Sterling swayed on his feet.

Clicking his tongue, Teal strode over and gripped Sterling's arm. "You all right, sir?"

Sterling smoothed his rough brown tunic. "Adjustment fever. I'll be fine." He pursed his lips. "There's a reason I never wanted to be a guardian. Too much bloody traveling."

Teal flung his hands on his hips, his own tunic grey and patched. "You travel all over the region—Ingot Magisterium Assemblies, Sectine Ultra Command Accords, Cresta Science Reveals. You even attend Bhuaci music festivals."

Sterling plucked a grass stem and studied it. "In each case, I'm treated with high regard and fed extremely well." His gaze rose and followed the vultures. "I suspect they'll feast more to their liking this day than I shall."

Clenching his jaw, Teal swiveled on his heel and started to pound away. "First, we'll visit Aram, then take a glance at Onias, and finally—if we're lucky—we'll observe Neb."

Sterling groaned. "*Then* will you show me the mineral deposits?"

Stumbling over a tuft of grass, Teal caught himself and cleared his throat. "That'll be our last stop—before returning home."

~~~

Aram strolled through the village, appraising the new homes and the layout of the village. He gestured to a youth.

The young man trotted near.

"Tell your father to spread out a little more; there's plenty of room. We're not hemmed in anymore—are we?"

"No." The boy gazed at the landscape. "We have the whole world before us."

Aram chuckled and patted the youth on the arm. "Well, not the whole world, but enough." His gaze locked on a man. "I need to attend to business—remind everyone to keep the space between structures wide, so that even on a dark night a drunken man can find his way home."

Grinning, the youth ambled off.

Aram sucked in a deep breath and marched across the village.

~~~

Teal hid in the shadow of a large spreading tree and rested his hand on Sterling's arm. His voice dropped to a whisper. "You see how he cares for his people." He frowned. "But he seems agitated. Something must've happened while I was away."

"By the Divide, these are primitives. Of course, something happened. Weren't they outrunning a vicious mammal last time you were here?"

Teal gestured to the lake shimmering against the bright sky. "Yet, they've outsmarted evil fate and found a new home.

Impressive, don't you think?"

A cluster of children scrambled into camp, followed by a large man with a huge grin. The children ran into their mothers' arms, and laughter broke out all over camp.

Sterling blinked. "Wonder what that's all about."

Teal chuckled. "Children like to play, and fathers like to tease." His chest tightened. "Something we rarely experience." Turning abruptly, he pointed toward the sun. "Let's go."

Smothering a suffering sigh, Sterling nodded. They blinked away.

~~~

Teal rubbed his hands together like a man well pleased with a hard day's work. "We've seen Onias assisting in the harvest and Neb marching across the plains—now let's head west."

In a hilly region, they stood on the edge of a crater and peered down.

Teal gestured into the pit. "Cresta investigators said it looks natural, but the telltale signs are obvious. Ingots have been mining and, fortunately, they didn't find what they wanted."

Sterling shrugged. "They covered it up, so humans won't be the wiser. What are you worried about? A little foreign mining won't hurt anyone."

Teal clumped back down the crumbling dirt. "No?" He plodded to a sheltered spot between two large boulders.

Sterling joined him, standing shoulder to shoulder, staring at a small black mound. "What are we staring at?"

Without breaking his gaze, Teal remained fixed on the mound. "A grave. There are five human beings buried here. A hunting party that strayed too far and paid for it with their lives."

With a weary harrumph, Sterling flapped his arms against his body like a guilty child about to explain away his misdeed. "It could happen anywhere—to anyone. Humans kill each other all the time." He faced Teal. "You saw Neb. We both know what he's planning—"

Pounding his fist into his hand, Teal's colors blazed. "It's their fight—they're humans. It's not right that a race with superior advantages comes in and steals—"

"You've become such a blasted moralist. What's wrong with a little innocent skimming off the planet?" His gaze flittered over the mound. "I'll admit—the deaths are unfortunate."

"They had families—their people will suffer because Ingoti incursions rape the land, and Crestas experiment on their people."

Sterling clapped his hands together. "You're hysterical. And, frankly, vulgarity disgusts me."

Teal shimmered. "Vulgarity? But murder is acceptable." Gripping Sterling's arm, Teal glowed like a furnace. "What're the Cresta offering you?"

Shaking Teal's hand off, Sterling stomped to an open space. "You've just crossed a serious boundary! I'm a judge—and your superior. Just because I was your favorite teacher, don't assume you can take liberties." Scowling, he shook a finger at Teal. "I'd hate to accuse you of treason before the council."

Teal's colors simmered as his human form solidified. His voice dropped to a stiff, formal tone. "Judge Sterling, I must inform you that Cresta incursions will likely alter the balance of power in this region."

With a snort, Sterling waved at the mound. "How?"

"The Cresta will use any race they deem fit to further their scientific ends. If they find this planet resourceful, they might influence the inhabitants to protect their interests against the Ingots—and everyone else. Nothing works so well as using the natives to fight your battles."

"They'd have to manage a whole planet! Cresta aren't that stupid."

"They wouldn't see it that way. They'd simply see an easy profit and an expendable life form."

Rubbing his hands together, Sterling trod back to the mound and stared at the gravesite. "As I ponder the ramifications, I believe that the Supreme Judges need to consider this situation more carefully."

Teal's head dropped to his chest, and he exhaled slowly.

As the pink horizon signaled the end of the day, Sterling sniffed the air. "Someone's built a fire."

"Probably making dinner."

"Yes. Well, I suspect I'll be dining with the Cresta Ingal in the near future." Grimacing, he appeared to swallow back a bad taste. "I hate their before-dinner delicacies. But their vegetable dishes are quite good."

Raking his fingers through his hair to control his temper, Teal forced a placid expression. "You know what's in them?"

Sterling waved off the thought. "It's best not to ask." Placing a hand on Teal's shoulder, he sighed. "We all have our burdens."

Teal tipped his head at the obvious.

Looking askance, Sterling waved goodbye and flickered out of sight.

Teal's gaze returned to the shallow grave.

Chapter Twenty-One

—River Clan—

Endure

Joash remained impassive as Neb stared deeply into his eyes. Neither man blinked.

"Now that we're only a day from the Grassland Village, we'll make camp. You and two others will leave tonight and reconnoiter the village. If there are guards and clear preparations for battle, bring back a full report as quickly as possible. In the meantime, I'll make preparations."

Joash stood with his hands clasped behind his back, unblinking.

"We'll move closer before we strike." Neb's eyes narrowed. "Do not seek out Ishtar. He'd likely raise an alarm."

Joash nodded, bowed, and returned to his dwelling. "Lud! Pele! Get my things ready."

The two children responded obediently in swift silence. Pele kept her eyes on her task. Lud no longer watched Pele as if he were looking for some secret sign of hope. He looked neither to the right nor the left. They both obeyed in meek obedience to the will of their master.

Joash grinned. He turned his back on them, his gaze straying back to the council setting.

Neb stalked away and entered his tent.

Hagia's hands were covered in wet clay. She glanced up, startled.

Neb scowled and folded his arms across his hairless chest.

Kneeling before a figure of her god, she pressed fresh clay over a crack. The creature, with its large head, lumpy body, and tiny arms and legs, looked more like a misshapen animal than a god. She frowned.

Neb snarled. "The ruling spirits of the invisible world are well known to me. I bow before them each day and pray for their assistance to emerge victorious. The coming battle will be the greatest we've ever fought. The Grassland people are well advanced. If I'm strong, we'll take this clan and claim authority even over those the gods have favored." His mouth curled into a line of sneering disgust.

Hagia trembled. She turned her back on Neb and fought with the only weapon she had—her prayers to a god she made with her hands. Her shoulders slumped. It was no use asking those blank eyes to see her tears or that cold heart to feel her pain. If only her prayers could reach a god bigger than her hands could make, and he would save her son.

At least, have him die quickly in battle. Anything but torture and death at Neb's hands.

Her tears blurred her sight as she stared at the silent figure she had made. It had wolf-like ears to hear her whispered prayers, a wide chest to enclose a large heart to understand her worries, and a broad head to discover a solution to her impossible problems. As tears coursed down her cheeks, despair flowed through her body. The clay had cracked in multiple places, and she feared he might dry up and fall to pieces before the battle even began.

Without looking at Neb, she rubbed the figure to erase the cracks.

Neb strode over and wagged his finger. "Crazy woman!"

Hagia froze.

"That's no good." He kicked the clay figure.

It sailed to the back of the tent, hit the weathered hide with a thud, and fell to the earth. Its head fell from the body.

Neb grunted in satisfaction. "Ha, you see! It can't even withstand a man's foot."

Hagia crumpled but quickly righted herself. She would not break like her small god. She would weather the storm of his scorn.

"See that my things are ready. I want to move camp today. Joash will meet us tomorrow. Get up and get to work!"

Hagia shuffled, slowly straightening until she stood next to Neb, who peered at her through narrowed eyes. She lowered her gaze.

Ishtar wouldn't be the only one sacrificed if she crossed his will. She must endure.

Chapter Twenty-Two

—Grassland—

Spark of Hope

Eoban peered at Onias as he sat in a circle with his clansmen. Ishtar perched on a log near at hand.

Obed sat off to the side with his shoulders bent over, clasped hands in an attitude of concentration.

Jonas and the boys worked in the field, gathering the harvest.

Onias clasped his hands together, like a man in prayer. "Above all, we must stay calm. When the enemy is seen, I'll meet with their leader and offer terms of peace that no one could refuse." His gaze roamed over the assembly. "We may have to offer a large part of our stored grain and half our animals to appease the enemy's greed, but it'd be better to lose goods than lives." His eyes glowed. "We can even offer to help them set up their own village—send laborers to teach them how to plant and build as we've done."

A fanatical spark of hope glimmered in Onias' eyes. "We'll keep no secrets and hold nothing back. When they see that we offer no resistance, they'll choose our friendship."

Most were lulled by Onias' assured attitude—except Ishtar. Obed did not appear to hear anything except the thoughts that raced through his own mind.

Ishtar rocked on his haunches, his eyes over bright and darting, as if seeking an escape. His brows knit together. Finally, he burst from his internal restraint and sprang to his feet. "I can't stand any more of this! You don't understand your enemy. Neb is not interested in your village or taking what he wants. That comes after the battle. Neb must *conquer*. He must destroy this village and make the survivors his slaves.

He'll please his gods by his might—not his mercy. He'll see you as a weak child and enjoy killing you and raising your head on the point of a spear!"

Eoban stood with his spear gripped in his right hand. He let the butt end thud on the earth. "Ishtar is right. All respect due to you, Onias, as a leader—" He bowed and looked Onias full in the face. "But you're no warrior. You don't think as warriors do. Ishtar understands the mind of a conquering clan. They care not for reason and words. They're men of action and brave deeds. They'll come to kill, and if we're not ready, they'll kill many of us and take your wives and children as slaves to do with as they please. We must do more than sharpen our spears and make a few more weapons. Our enemy may be here before daybreak!"

Eoban plunked down, a sour feeling in his stomach set his lips into a hard line. His frown deepened as he glanced around and expressions of anxious hesitation met his eye.

From the far side of the circle, Obed's voice rose. "Is there a way that we can make ourselves impossible to attack successfully?" He lifted his head from his clasped hands.

Rows of staring eyes fixed upon him.

Obed cleared his throat and sat straighter. "We're vulnerable here—out in the open. But in only a morning's walk, we can reach the big lake. We have a few fishing boats—boats large enough to carry our women and children to the other side. The high cliff and trees would offer us a defensible position and screen us from the enemy's gaze. We'd be in a position to fight them as they advance across the grassland."

Smiles broke over the assembly.

"We should send the women and children away with a few men to make a temporary camp. We don't want to alarm the enemy and hasten their approach. Eoban and I could scout to the east and see if the River Clan has entered our land. In just a few days' time, we'll present them with an empty camp and no one to conquer."

Onias, Eoban, and the rest of the clansmen considered

Obed's words.

Relieved grins, relaxed shoulders, and grunts of approval spread around the circle.

Only Obed's gaze remained distant and dreaming.

Eoban read his friend's mind and shook his head. His gaze grew dim with grief.

Chapter Twenty-Three

—Lake Clan–

This Bodes Ill

Namah leaned over Irad's sleeping form. As she stared at his cuts and mud-splattered hair and clothes, she tried to imagine his struggle to return to the clan. But she had also seen her neighbors carry Lamech to his dwelling. *Why did they arrive separately?*

A shout sent her to the doorway, where she peered at Aram marching away. A pout lifted her lip in disdain. Dropping the flap, she returned to Irad and pulled back the blanket.

He didn't stir.

She prodded him and whispered his name. "Irad, wake up. You must flee for your life. They're coming to question you soon."

Irad's head turned as he lay on his back, his eyes blinking open. His gaze roamed over the dwelling and then settled on the rounded figure of Namah as she knelt beside him. His nose wrinkled and his eyes grew hard. He turned over and closed his eyes, grunting with a wave of dismissal.

Namah's eyes glittered in the dim light. Gripping his shoulder, she shook him hard. "Irad, you know our people. They'll not wait; they want answers now. Barak told of strange adventures, and you're no hero in his eyes. Lamech returned grievously injured and—"

Irad stiffened and sat bolt upright. He grabbed her arm roughly and spat his words. "Barak is alive? And Lamech also?" His eyes glazed over. "It's hardly possible. Barak was as dead as the cat that lay with him." He yanked her dress and pulled her close. "Lamech has returned? No one could've survived—"

Namah yanked her dress free. "I know what my eyes saw. You'll see for yourself. Aram will tell you everything."

Irad's eyes narrowed. He scrambled to his feet.

Namah tilted her head as she considered his obvious surprise and anxiety. "They will come and—"

Irad gripped her arm, pulling her close with a smile. "So, Barak is telling tales, is he? Well, that can't be helped. And Lamech has returned from the dead?"

"Not for long. He's dead now."

Irad gazed into Namah's eyes. "Lucky I have a friend who believes in me." Jerking her to the doorway, he lifted the flap a sliver and peered out.

The village bustled in everyday activity.

"It's possible there might be a misunderstanding. Perhaps I should leave and learn from a safe distance what's being said about me."

He's a sly one, with secrets and distant plans. She grinned and shrugged her shoulders. "I heard that before Lamech died, he claimed that you tried to kill him." She bowed her head in mock sorrow.

A jolt shivered through Irad's body, but he composed himself with a stiff jerk.

Namah traced Irad's strong jaw with the tip of her finger. "Lamech's story told of deceit and treachery. His family wants to question you." Padding to the back of the dwelling, she lifted the bottom edge, creating a man-sized gap. "You won't have a chance to argue your innocence. Their spears will do all the talking."

Irad strode over and whispered in her ear as he caressed the back of her neck. "See who's near."

Namah peeked out. Several men milled about. She ducked back in and faced him. "A few men, nothing more."

Irad rubbed his chin. "Step out front and hesitate. Look around as if you'd like to talk. Draw the men to you. Say you must get water and lead them away. I'll climb out back."

A grin wavered on Namah's lips. "I'll meet you at the north end of the lake. There'll be no one there this time of day. Most go south to fish at the sandy bank. Few travel to the high ground."

Irad nodded, a glint in his eye that sent shivers through Namah's misshapen body. "You'll come with me, Namah? I can trust—?"

A shout turned their attention. Irad pushed her gently towards the door.

Namah stepped into the late afternoon sun, blinked, and glanced at the long shadows.

Her clansmen peered at her, searching for answers.

Namah smiled and hesitated. A trio of men meandered to her side.

The shuffle of footsteps treading into the distance brought a smile to her face.

~~~

Namah strolled like a woman in a dream as the sun glowed pink and orange on the western horizon. She swung a bag of dried fruit and nuts in her hand, and her eyes roamed the hillside.

Irad waited at a rocky promontory.

With a distant, dreamy look in her eyes, Namah joined him and marched at his side.

With each pounding step, Irad quickened his pace. Pebbles scattered under his feet.

Soon, Namah's shoulders sagged. She tossed a few nuts into her mouth and chewed, but her stomach growled for the evening meal.

Even as they climbed higher, the sun sank lower and an evening gloom descended. Namah stumbled. She wiped her face with the back of her dirty hand, leaving a dirty smear. Her hair had slipped into a tangle, and she drooped in weariness.

"Irad?"

Irad continued forward, his gaze fixed ahead and his steps pounding the ground as determined as ever.

Namah scowled and halted. "IRRAAD!"

Irad stopped in mid-motion and turned on his heel. He peered at Namah through squinting eyes.

In nervous haste, she spoke too quickly as she hastened up to him. "What're we doing? Are we going to join with another clan?" Plopping down on the rocky soil, she sighed in relief. "I'm too tired for a long march. Let's stop and eat and sleep. We can start again in the morning."

Without warning, Irad gripped her arm and dragged her closer to the edge of the cliff. Just as suddenly, he dropped her arm.

Gasping and groaning in pain, Namah glared at him. "Why'd you do that?"

Irad tilted his head and wandered to the cliff. He peered over the edge to the lake view below. A smudge of smoke rose in the distance. He scowled at Namah, who had followed him. "There's a clan in the east?"

Namah brushed dirt off her clothes. "You've not been here long. There was no occasion to speak of it. Yes, there's a clan, but we don't know anything about them. You want to go there?"

Irad rubbed his hands together as the cool evening breeze wafted over the grass. The sunlight gleamed in golden rays as it settled on the water's edge. His eyes glittered. "Namah, why are you following me?"

Namah's head jerked. She stepped back, fear clenching her stomach. "That's a strange question—you asked me to help you."

Irad crossed his arms, and his voice dropped low, devoid of all emotion. *"Did I?"*

Swallowing, Namah shook her head and pursed her lips in disapproval. "Irad, it's growing dark, and I'm hungry and tired. This is a good place to rest. No one will follow us up here in the dark for fear of falling. Tomorrow we can join the clan in the east there, or we can find another clan that'd suit you better." With her hands perched on her hips, and her tone reasonable, she hinted an invitation with a provocative smile.

A teasing grin flittered over Irad's face. "You know, Namah, I didn't tell you what happened while I was away on the cat hunt. Perhaps you'd like to hear the story now."

Stretching out her legs, Namah yawned. "No, that's not necessary. I'll be content with food and rest. Maybe you can start a fire?"

Irad's gaze returned to the lake. He appeared deaf as well as blind to her.

A boat bobbed on the water. A slight gasp slipped from Irad's lips.

Namah scrambled to her feet and stood beside him. "I wonder where they're going."

Irad's eyes narrowed in concentration. "There're more women than men." He chuckled. "It seems your mystery clan will pay a visit to Aram before we get a chance to visit. Why are they leaving their village in the cloak of twilight?"

"Maybe they're running from something."

He nodded. "From what?"

Namah gazed across the water. Three more boats followed the first, all filled to capacity with women and children. "This bodes ill. My heart tells me there's danger near. Perhaps we should go back and face the false accusations rather than—"

Irad continued to stare at the boats. "They're not false accusations. I did try to kill Lamech. I'm only surprised I didn't succeed." He turned to Namah in the growing darkness.

Namah backed away toward the cliff's edge.

"He saw me run Anikar off a cliff. Anikar saw me put a snake under Shem's blanket. Shem realized that I didn't even try to save Barak. None of them understood."

Namah groaned, clutching her hands together, beseeching his mercy or a prayer, she didn't know.

Irad stepped closer. "They believed the cat hunt was important. But it takes little skill to kill an animal. However, to kill a man—"

Gasping, Namah took another step back and realized with stiff shock that she stood at the edge.

"Or a woman."

She reached out and clasped his tunic, pulling him with her. As she fell, she screamed. "Aram!"

Chapter Twenty-Four

—Lake Clan—

Troubles of Our Own

Milkan's small feet pounded the earth as she ran. Dust flew up in swirling puffs where the dirt in the village had been pounded into fine silt. Towering clouds piled in the west, and a faint breeze swept through, sending a chill through the air. She skimmed around a half-finished dwelling as she glanced wildly about.

Eymard stood next to Aram, talking with Jethro who gestured with his hands in wide, circling arches.

Milkan trotted toward Eymard and Aram, gritting her teeth, her shoulders tight, anxiety bubbling in her stomach.

Eymard had sent her down the slope toward the south end of the lake to join the women washing clothes. She had joined the children splashing in the water.

Barak had run north, followed by several young men. The women had called after them, but they only answered a single word—a name—and they sped off in greater haste. In consternation, the woman piled their laundry, clean and dirty, together and started home.

Before they reached the grassy edge, a child pelted toward them yelling that boats were crossing the lake. Milkan had peered across the lake until her eyes alighted on the boats in the distance. Her mouth had opened in surprise, and nameless dread sent shivers down her spine.

An old woman called to her, waving in urgency. "Run quickly—tell Aram—boats are coming to our shore."

As Milkan raced away, she looked back only once to see all the women scrambling up the slope. No one wanted to be left behind.

Milkan ran to the familiar safety of Eymard and threw her arms around his waist. She gasped, attempting to catch her breath. A blur of scenes—the cat attacks, the scars on Barak's body, Lamech carried into camp—sent shudders through her slender body. A sob strangled her throat. "Oh, Eymard, we're going to die. Strangers are landing on our shore."

A puzzled frown creased Eymard's face. "This is not a good time, child. I told you to go play on the shore while the women do the washing."

Stepping forward, Aram smoothed Milkan's hair back in gentle reassurance. "What's this, child?"

Jethro called to the women lumbering back into the village. "What stories have you been telling the children today?"

Milkan peered into Aram's face, her jaw set and her tears forgotten. "It's true! I was sent to tell you—boats are arriving on our south shore. I saw them myself." Milkan pointed to her witnesses as they climbed the slope. "See! They're afraid too."

Aram and Eymard followed the point of her finger.

Indeed, grim-faced women struggled with children and baskets of wet clothes. One woman strode to Aram and brushing a few strands of hair away, she glowered. "Well, what're you going to do now? Word is that Irad has run away, Lamech's dead, and Barak's planning revenge. Now strangers come to our shore. Perhaps it would have been simpler to face the cat."

Aram closed his eyes. After a deep breath, he opened them and glanced around the assembling crowd. "I was just setting out after Barak and Irad when this child arrived with the news."

The woman flung a hand on her hip. "Well, I've no desire to meet strangers, though I don't think they're warriors. I saw women carrying children." An eyebrow rose knowingly. "Still, whether it's sickness or threat of war that sends them, I've no wish to get involved. We've troubles enough of our own." After shifting her bundle, she padded away.

Eymard studied Aram, stroking his chin. "An ill wind brings

fear and misfortune."

Milkan peered from Aram to Eymard. "Don't worry, Aram's strong. He'll protect us."

Aram snorted a choked laugh.

Eymard patted her head. "Yes, we're safe. Don't worry."

Refocusing his attention, Aram signaled to his men. "We'll go north and watch them disembark from the top of the cliff." He turned to his friend. "Eymard, stay here and keep alert. If there's any trouble, send for me." A tired smile broke the hard line of his lips has he pressed the old man's shoulder. "Now'd be a good time to speak to that God of yours."

Eymard's wrinkled face broke into a wide grin. "I'll speak to Him, but I don't know what He'll say."

As Aram marched north with three men, the last rays of day waned into evening.

~~~

Barak edged his way across the crest of the cliff. He peered at the boats landing on the western shore a little south of his position. Women and children huddled together. Shoving his anger aside, he frowned. *Who are these people, and why are they landing here?*

One tall, slender woman left the safety of the boat and directed the others.

Barak sighed. *Not another Namah!* He studied their jerked, uneasy motions and their tight grips on their children. They were afraid and probably needed help. With a rough shake, Barak scampered down the high embankment and jogged along the shore to meet them. As he drew near, he slowed and called out a greeting.

Suddenly, two men skirted around the women and took defensive positions. The women and children hung back, eyes wide with alarm.

Barak tried to think of what to say, but in the face of their stark fear, his mind clouded with uncertainty.

The tall woman stepped forward. Two boys called after her, but she squared her shoulders and strode forward undeterred. As she came face to face with Barak, she stopped. "I am Jonas, the wife of Onias, the leader of our people. We live in the grasslands but have been warned of an attack and are fleeing. Is your clan near?"

Rubbing his chin, Barak grinned. This was no Namah. This woman's eyes engaged him; her beauty set his heart racing, and her clear, calm voice filled his heart with gladness.

"I am Barak of Aram's clan. My people live on the crest overlooking this lake. I saw you from above and came to greet you. You're welcome here. Aram will want to speak with you, so I'll take you to him."

Jonas nodded and beckoned the others to follow.

As Barak strode toward the sandy shore, a small group of men intercepted him. "Here, he's coming to meet you."

Aram approached and Barak stepped out of the way.

Aram bowed with his hands clasped over his chest. "My name is Aram. My people live on the cliff above this lake. How can we assist you?"

The woman returned the bow. "My name is Jonas, wife of Onias. Our people live in the grasslands east of here. We've learned of a threat coming our way—so I've been sent to secure safety for the women and children.

Aram frowned, his gazed rising to the high cliffs. "We've had our own troubles, but—" He forced a smile. "Please, feel free to stay with us. What provisions we have, we'll gladly share."

Jonas eyed Aram carefully. After a private discussion with others, they agreed to go to the village. The women carried babies on their hips, little ones toddled behind, and boys and girls stayed close as they wound their way up the incline toward the village.

The two clans met like strange dogs circling and taking each other's measure. Aram's clan clustered together, a stocky and copper-skinned people, while the Grassland People stood tall, their fair skin clear and unblemished.

Jonas and her women stared at the primitive tents and half-finished dwellings, frowns and subtle sneers replacing their wide-eyed fear. Refuse stank from open pits, and sewer water ran throughout the village. Some of the newcomers covered their faces in disgust. Jonas held her head high, undisturbed.

Aram stood apart and appraised the newcomers. They wore clothes made of soft material, their hair was pulled back out of their faces, and their skin seemed as smooth as polished stones. They must have been fleeing an enemy, but they walked as proud as peacocks.

He gestured for the men to sit with him outside his dwelling. The strange man who strode at Jonas' side pressed her to sit with them and to speak for the clan.

She settled on a bench with the two men on either side of her. "I am Jonas, the wife of Onias, the leader of our clan. These men, Obed and Eoban, are my friends and protectors. They've come to see the women safely settled before they go back and help others to cross the lake and gather on the shore."

She frowned as if at a memory. "A clan member who broke away from a River Clan has warned us of an impending attack. Obed scouted to the east and has determined that the enemy is on our very doorstep. We do not mean to become a burden to you, we only wish to take temporary shelter until the threat has passed."

Aram sat with his hands clasped under his chin. When he peered up, he glanced at Obed rather than Jonas. "Thank you, Jonas, for your explanation, but I'm used to taking council with men. Please take no offense, but is there a man here who might speak for your clan? I would like to hear the story of how you came to know of this threat from beginning to end."

Jonas bowed her head and motioned to Obed.

Clearing his throat, Obed shifted uneasily. "I'm not a good speaker, but I'll try to tell you our recent history, so you'll understand why we came upon you so suddenly." Quickly, Obed recounted Ishtar's story.

Aram massaged his chin in weariness. He considered the people before him, waiting in expectancy, tightening the nerves of everyone in both clans.

He straightened. "You're welcome here, and we'll do all we can to help you. We don't have much, but we will gladly share what we can. Barak here will direct you to a sheltered place nearby, and you can make provisions for yourself as you may. If you need something, ask Barak and he'll do what he can. When the threat has passed, you can return to your clan knowing that you have allies ready to serve."

Aram shifted and glanced into the dark sky. "In the meantime, I must attend to an urgent matter. I'll be honest; we've had troubles of our own, but I'll explain at a more suitable time."

Barak glared at Aram in unspoken fury. He stood and pointed north. "I, too, have unfinished business."

Rising, Aram lifted his hand in a silent command. "I'll attend to it in the morning."

Chapter Twenty-Five

—Grasslands—Lake Clan—

Believe Me

Onias strolled through the undulating grass. As the sun crested the horizon, he looked back. His wife and sons were safe. His trusted friend, Obed, was seeing to their care and to the care of the other women and children. He had been told about the clan on the other side of the lake and of their friendly reception. He smiled as his gaze swept over their sturdy, well-built homes with cleared land and neat gardens. The odor of goats and sheep carried on a gentle breeze. Their bleating filled the air as they clamored over the trail toward the green fields.

Only the men of his clan remained. One of the neighboring clansmen, Barak, had arrived to offer his assistance. Pink and golden sunlight illuminated the clay rooftops. The thatched buildings had weathered to a soft grey, and the mud brick walls glistened like burnished gold. The world appeared fresh and indescribably beautiful.

His hand went to his pocket, and he felt the shape of a figure he had been carving for Jonas. Now that she was expecting again, he wanted to give her something to take her mind off their troubles. If he failed in his secret mission, it would be up to the clan to prove their worth as warriors. But he could not imagine failing. He had never met a man who was not willing to accept such an offer as he was willing to make. He would offer their crops, tools and whatever goods the invaders wanted. They would be stripped, but they would live and build again, and their women would not mourn the death of sons and husbands in battle.

Blinking, he faced east again. His resolve strengthened, and his pace quickened. A sound echoed over the open land. Onias frowned and halted mid-step.

Eoban pounded through the waving grass. "Onias, stop! Wait!"

With his hand tapping his thigh, Onias stood. His scowl deepened, shadowing his face.

Gasping his words, Eoban floundered to a halt. "Onias, you can't do this." He grabbed Onias' shoulder for support and sucked in deep breaths.

Pulling away, Onias started east. "I can and I must. Go home and wait for me."

Eoban circled in front of him. "If you get too close to the enemy, you'll never return home."

"The enemy is in your own mind, Eoban. I am going to meet a man like myself—a man who wants what I have and who'll be surprised and pleased by my offer."

With pounding feet, Eoban ran after him. "You're a fool! You think that because you don't understand evil—it doesn't exist, but it does. These men will destroy you because they like the feel of the act. They don't care. Their evil is stronger than your good."

Stopping once more, Onias stared at Eoban for a long moment. "If I'm a fool, at least I'm an honest fool. I've already faced death. It doesn't scare me. If I die doing what I know is right, I'll be better off than those chained by fear. Now, return to the warriors. You can prepare for battle if it makes you feel better. I'll face the enemy alone."

Eoban stood with his arms limp at his side.

Onias wandered away as if he were taking an early morning stroll.

Eoban cursed under his breath. Propping his hands on his hips, he stood and raged. Suddenly, fear gripped his heart and his eyes widened.

Two figures ran toward Onias.

A scream caught in Eoban's throat as he sprinted forward. *Joash!*

Joash plowed into Onias and threw him to the ground

Onias struggled to his feet, talking, gesturing—to no avail. "Listen to me! We'll surrender. My clan will give you whatever you want. Let me talk to your leader—"

Holding his spear aloft, Joash sneered as the other man held Onias on the ground.

Onias squirmed. "Don't you understand? You can have the food, the animals, everything. Just—"

Joash sucked in a deep breath. "We don't make treaties. We conquer." With the full force of his strength, he thrust the spear into Onias.

Eoban charged, barreling in and grabbed both warriors about the middle. Puffing hard, he wrestled the spear from the silent warrior and struck him on the head with a crushing blow.

Joash wrestled his spear out of Onias' limp body.

Eoban turned his spear on Joash.

His grin twisting grotesquely, Joash spat his words. "You have a choice. Waste your time trying to kill me—or save your friend."

Swallowing back bile, Eoban glanced from Onias' body to Joash. "Start running. But some day, I will find you and take your head from your shoulders." He lunged forward.

Joash jumped back.

Swerving on his heel, Eoban pelted to Onias' side.

Regaining his sneer, Joash dashed to a safe distance, turned, and shouted. "He's a fool. He deserved to die." His laughter drifted to the horizon.

Eoban bent over Onias, peering into his fluttering eyes.

Onias clutched Eoban's tunic. "A fool, yes. But I still believe—" His head fell back, and his sightless eyes gazed up into the brilliant sky. His hands slipped off Eoban's chest. Out of Onias's grip dropped the small, carved figure of a woman and child.

Eoban barely noticed the weight of the lifeless body he carried. His tears, like a burning fire, seared his face. Joash's final thrust replayed in his mind. Eoban hastened to a jog. Onias' head bobbed mercilessly. Eoban hefted his friend's body over his shoulder and hurried on.

As he strode into the village, everyone poured out to meet him. No words were spoken. Eyes spoke louder than any voice.

Two men ran forward and threw cloaks and blankets in the place where Onias would often hold council in the center of the village. Eoban gently laid his body down, folding Onias' arms across his chest.

Clansmen gathered weapons, stripped off unnecessary garments, and prepared their bodies for battle.

Like thunder, so Eoban roared. "Onias died trying to save us. His sacrifice will not be in vain. We will fight!"

"We fight!" Echoed throughout the village as the lust for blood engulfed them.

The chant had hardly begun when a new shout rang out. "They're coming! Look east!"

Eoban lined the men in battle array, striding from man to man, assigning fighting instructions. He stopped before the blazing eyes of Ishtar.

He clasped the youth on the shoulder. "Ishtar, do you mean to fight against your own clan? Against your own father? No one expects it of you. Retreat to the other side of the lake. You'll be of better service there than here."

Ishtar's lips drew into a tight line. "I accept my fate. My father thinks I am a coward. I think he is evil. We shall see who's right."

With a weary grunt, Eoban shook his head and moved on.

Suddenly, Ishtar's head jerked up in recognition.

Neb's taunting call bellowed over the grassland. Hundreds of feet pounded closer.

Ishtar's voice dropped to a husky whisper. "They're here."

From that moment on, few words were spoken. Every action proclaimed both conviction and ability. After the first volley of spears, opposing warriors rushed upon each other in hand-to-hand combat.

Neb and Joash lead the way as their clansmen fanned out and encircled the village.

Eoban and his men knew the lay of the village and drew from scores of weapons close at hand. They had the advantage of fighting on known territory and dodging behind familiar walls. But the enemy was well trained and relentless. The villagers had more men, but it took almost two of them to make a well-coordinated effort to take down one of Neb's warriors.

As the struggle went on, the sun crossed its zenith and began to drop down from the heights. Eoban peered at his panting, exhausted men. Scowling and wiping sweat from his filthy brow, he fought his way through a melee of advancing warriors. Searching frantically for some way to lead a retreat to the lake, he scrambled up the side of a storage hut.

Suddenly, the air was rent with a series of battle cries unlike any he had ever heard. His blood froze. Sliding to the ground, he saw men with leather skirts similar to those of the enemy smeared with red paint over their bodies. They advanced with howling cries of murderous rage, and they wielded weapons larger and fiercer than any he had yet seen. They were coming from the west—the very direction he had wanted to send his men. His heart sank. A groan caught in his throat at the sight of Obed. He was not painted as the others, but he was clearly leading the charge.

The new clan of warriors clashed with Neb's men.

Eoban's eyes widened in shock. A delighted grin spread across his face.

Ishtar froze at the sound of his father's voice lifted above the melee. Turning slowly, he saw his father only a few feet from him.

For the first time, Neb hesitated. He raised his spear high in the air, calling for retreat. As he scanned the battle, his gaze fell upon his son. Neb's eyes narrowed, and he dropped his arm. With a mighty effort, he threw his spear at Ishtar.

Ishtar did not flinch. He watched as the deadly point embedded in the earth before him. He stared at his father as if in a trance.

As his men fell in line behind him, Neb backed away. He turned, and he and his warriors retreated.

Plucking the spear from the ground, Ishtar cried out. "After them!" Surprised, the villagers paused, sucking in deep, relieved breaths.

Eoban echoed the cry. "After them!"

Seeing an opportunity, Obed raised his voice. "Let us end this madness. Give chase!"

A bellowing cry rose from a myriad of voices. "Kill the invaders!" "After them!" "Kill them!"

The chase lasted into the evening. Neb's men turned several times to fight their pursuers, but they lacked confidence. They had never fled before. Only Neb's cool thinking took them out of reach as they climbed north and hid in the hills.

As darkness descended, Obed and Eoban called their men home.

The moon rose, and Eoban, Obed, Ishtar, and Barak sprawled around a fire with their spears still close at hand. Two goats had been hurriedly slaughtered and their meat roasted over a dancing fire. The fallen were laid aside for burial. Men skilled in the art of healing herbs tended the injured.

"Will they come again?" Eoban peered through the flickering light.

Ishtar hunched with his arms wrapped around his legs, chewing on a handful of dried fruit. "Yes, they'll come again—and again—as along as my father leads them. They've never tasted defeat, and they'll never accept such a fate. Next time, they'll come with a better plan. My father may have an evil heart, but he also has a clever mind."

Obed stretched out with a groan.

Eoban nudged him with his toe. "What? You sleepy?"

"I prefer to use my mind more than my body. This is not the way I like to spend my day."

Eoban tossed a stick hitting him on the forehead. "Well then, think up a way we can win our next battle."

Obed looked momentarily ruffled as he picked up the stick and threatened to throw it back, but heaving a sigh, he tossed it away.

With a snort, Ishtar pointed to the spot where his father had stood. "I wish I could've seen my father's face when he first saw the red clan descending upon him.

Obed grinned. "Aram is their leader. I don't know much about him, but from the way his clan fights, I can't help but think that he must be a formidable man. I'm glad he decided to be our friend."

His eyes sparkling, Ishtar leaned forward. "You think he'd help in the next battle? Such a man might humble my father's proud spirit. He's never retreated before and has certainly never been pursued by his victims. If Aram would come to our aid, we'd have a chance—a very good chance."

Barak struggled to sit up and rubbed his eyes. "He said he'd come. He has important matters to see to first. Though, he said he'd enjoy ending a reign of terror." Barak scratched his jaw. "He seems to know something about your people—but he won't talk of it."

Ishtar leaned back and closed his eyes. "The next battle will be fought among equals, warrior to warrior."

~~~

Aram and his men followed dusty footprints, scanning broken stems of grass and twigs crushed under hurried feet. The trail was so obvious—neither Namah nor Irad had taken much care. At one point, they found a crushed spot where one of them had fallen and the other had dragged the companion a short way. Aram's eyes squinted. Surely, Namah could not drag Irad. But why would Irad drag Namah? If she were sick or exhausted, he could carry her. Sweat trickled down the inside of his tunic.

Who was Irad? The question came sudden and unbidden. *Or rather,* he clarified his thought, *who had Irad become?* Evil possesses the man, directing his actions. This was not the man he knew. Or had Irad always been different than he had imagined? Aram's mind floundered on questions he could not answer.

When he came upon the footprints at the edge of the cliff, he peered around. No one—no body—was there. Then he glanced down.

A solitary figure crouched by the shore. Something floated in the water.

Scampering down a craggy pass, Aram let his men follow in due course and jumped from ledge to ledge. Finally, he slid to the shore. As he ran, sand flew in a backward spray. His gaze locked on his wife, and he came to an abrupt halt.

Namah crouched, huddled over, rocking and moaning.

Irad, his clothes billowing in the water, floated face down.

Clenching his jaw against tearing pain in his middle, Aram lifted his head and strode to his wife. Crouching at her side, he laid a hand on her shoulder.

Namah continued to rock, shaking and groaning.

Lifting her chin, Aram peered into haunted eyes. Her face, streaked with mud and blood, held shock and grief so deeply etched that words failed. Aram wrapped his arms around her, and held her, rocking and groaning with her.

With a scream, Namah pulled away. She hesitated, her words dropped to a mere whisper. "It wasn't my fault." Swallowing, she cried. She gripped her leg in agony but still stared at body. "He's crazy—evil! You didn't know him, Aram. But I did!"

Aram rubbed away the tears coursing down her face. He surveyed her body. Her leg lay twisted at an odd angle. Bile rose in his throat.

Gripping her thigh, Namah sobbed. "He tried to kill me, but I killed him. He killed Lamech—Shem—Anikar. Now he knows what it feels like." Shivering through a feverous tremor, she clawed at her leg. "I'll die too."

Rising, Aram whistled to his men who scrambled to the shore. With quick instructions, they tore off their outer tunics and formed a soft cradle to carry Namah between them.

Holding her steady, Aram helped to carry her past the body of his one-time friend. He kept his eyes averted. They negotiated Namah up a gentle incline and started the journey home.

Namah whimpered, clutching at Aram's arm. "You'd have killed him yourself. He's an animal—a dangerous animal." Her head sank back, and, covering her face, she sobbed.

Without willing it, Aram looked back. The floating body rocked with the ebb of the morning tide.

~~~

Aram leaned against a tree with his hands spread on his lap and mused on the strangeness of recent days. He stretched his legs and closed his eyes, letting the sun warm his face.

Upon their arrival, Jonas took charge of Namah. No one else claimed the honor, and he was grateful to be relieved of the burden.

His bones ached in weariness. Images flashed before his eyes: Eymard's pleased expression as he observed Jonas apply healing poultices to Namah's broken leg, Barak's grim expression, Lamech's wailing wife, and Irad's floating body.

After a long nap, Aram rose, ate with Eymard, and watched Milkan play with Jonas' sons.

They were handsome youths with quick and ready smiles. Big for their ages, with fair skin and bright eyes, Jael and Tobia pattered about trying to keep Milkan's attention fixed on them. In oblivious innocence, she showed them around the village.

Eymard stepped near, blocking the bright sun. He nudged Aram. "Your wife is well cared for."

Aram nodded. Rising, he sucked in a deep breath, exhaled, and padded home.

Jonas stooped over Namah, wiping her sweating brow. A cup of steaming brew sat on a stand next to her, and a wet cloth hung from a peg on the wall.

Namah lay sound asleep, her body straight and a woven blanket lay over her legs.

Aram stepped forward, wringing his hands. "How—?" His throat tightened, choking off his words.

With two fingers, Jonas waved him back. Her voice never rose above a whisper. "It was a challenge, but we've learned the art of setting bones." Glancing at Namah, she winced. "Sometimes it works—"

Aram blinked back sudden tears. "Sometimes?"

With a gentle squeeze, Jonas gripped Aram's arm. "She's lucky to be alive."

Shuddering, Aram scraped his courage together and braved a smile. "We thank you for that. You're very kind—and brave."

Jonas waved his gratitude away. "You took us in at our hour of need—and sent warriors to assist our men. I'm still very much in your debt."

Pulling his gaze from Namah, Aram's eyes glistened as he gazed at the beautiful woman before him. "I'm sure my men have had the time of their lives. Warriors—like boys—need a good fight now and again."

Namah stirred, groaning pitifully.

Jonas waved Aram to the door. "I'll keep watch tonight. There's nothing you can do."

The sunlight made him blink as he stepped into the bright day. The entire clan bustled with activity. Aram wandered to Lamech's grave. His head fell to his chest, and he squeezed his eyes shut.

Where are you now, Lamech? Can you see my wife, Ana, and our son?

With a groan, Aram fell to his knees.

Irad is dead—buried near the sea. God! He deserves to rot and be eaten by carrion—but his family would not have it so. He can do no more harm. Yet—

Suddenly a child fell into his lap. Aram's eyes snapped open, and he toppled backward.

The boy grappled furiously to sit upright.

In surprise and relief, Aram chuckled. "Careful, son, you could've crushed me in your fall."

Jael jumped to his feet. "So sorry! I didn't mean to—" He glanced into Aram's sparkling eyes and grinned bravely. "Are you Aram—the leader? Milkan told me that you're a great man." He pointed at a group of boys, shuffling their feet. "We're just playing."

Attempting to leap upright, Aram jerked forward and yelped in pain. He rubbed the small of his back, wincing.

Jael's eyes rounded. He flung his arms out, braced Aram, and helped him stand, as he had often done for his father in his illness. "Can you walk?"

Smothering a grunt, Aram pried himself free. "Fine. Just not as young as I used to be."

Pointing to center of the village Jael talked fast. "So sorry. I'll get mother. She is a healer—she'll help. Just wait, I'll be right back."

Before Aram could protest, the boy flew away as if he had wings instead of feet.

Jonas stood outside the dwelling, wringing out a cloth when her son skidded to her side in a cloud of dust and gestured his frenzied message.

Jonas jogged to Aram. "My son tells me that he hurt you and you're having trouble standing. May I—"

Aram smiled bravely, his cheeks flushing. *Here's a woman a man could cherish forever—and beyond.*

"Thank you, but I'm fine. Your boy merely fell on me and I—" He chuckled. "I jumped up too quickly for an old man."

Her lips quirking, Jonas clasped her hands. "You're hardly an old man. And my son is rather large to be landing in people's laps." Her gaze softened. "I know you've had troubles of your own. Your wife told me—things. She's sick at heart for the part she's played."

Aram blinked. *She's sick at heart?* He nodded slowly, uncertainly. "You've done what few could. Made friends with Namah." Rubbing a hand over his chin, he paused and glanced around helplessly. "Have you eaten yet?"

"Oh, yes. In the early morning, I pray, then I eat and go about my duties."

Aram strolled alongside her to his dwelling, his gaze fixed ahead. "You speak to the One God?"

"That's how I begin my day."

Jael tugged her sleeve. "I prayed for father this morning."

A shadow rippled over Jonas' face. She stopped. "We're concerned—" Her voice trailed away.

Ruffling the boy's hair, Aram chuckled. "Don't worry. I'll go over this morning. I'll meet your father and fight alongside him if need be. I sent men yesterday—all warriors at heart—and they were well dressed for battle. Didn't you see them?"

The boy nodded emphatically. "They scared me."

"You see? They'll scare away the enemy before a spear is thrown. Besides, that God you speak of will protect his own." His gaze slipped to Jonas. "You believe me?"

Jonas nodded, but her gaze strayed over the lake.

Chapter Twenty-Six

—OldEarth—

A Hostile World

Teal led the young Luxonian, Sienna, to the far side of the lake and perched on the edge of a boulder.

A creak tripped over an embankment and illuminated a rainbow in a shower spray.

Enchanted, Teal turned from one glory to another and grinned. "So, you want to become a healer?"

Dressed in a rough brown tunic with a thin shawl thrown over her shoulders, Sienna navigated the swirling creek bed and perched on another rock, dipping her toes in the rushing water. "Yes." Her arched brows bespoke a serious nature, while her soft tone beguiled unwary hearts. "Luxonians serve in many capacities—I'm drawn to the healing arts. My father and grandmother were healers in their own time."

Slipping out of his sandals, Teal splashed in the water, his grin tightening as the cold rippled over his body. "Why Earth? These people have nothing like our physiology or skills. What do you hope to—?"

A falcon flew overhead and landed in a tree. It turned its head, peering at them through one piercing eye.

Sienna's gaze swept the area. A lizard sat sunning itself on a rock a few feet away. Snatching the reptile by the tail, she flung it into the tall grass.

The hawk squawked and flapped its wings.

Glancing up, Sienna blushed. "Innocent creatures shouldn't suffer just for being at the wrong place at the wrong time."

A pigeon fluttered into the air. In an instant, the falcon soared in hot pursuit.

Teal winced as the falcon plucked its dinner from the sky. He glanced at Sienna.

Unperturbed, Sienna bent over and splashed water on her arms. "Though humans are not very advanced, they do have a keen eye for detail and an amazing depth of insight. In your reports, you mentioned purges, herb drinks, and poultices, which humans use to heal their sick and wounded."

Teal nodded. "True. Both the Lake Clan and the Grassland Clan have healers." He squinted. "I don't know about the River Clan. Neb appears bent on hurting more than healing."

"It's in war that the greatest cures are found—when they are most needed."

"That hardly justifies war."

With a nod, Sienna tiptoed to a distant perch. "Yet you have set the Supreme Council on the brink of war with both the Cresta and the Ingoti."

Jerking to his feet, Teal's face flushed. "Why are you really here?"

Leaning back on a rock and lacing her fingers together, Sienna shook her head. "Isn't it obvious? I want to learn. I've read every one of your reports. Fifth years are allowed access to planet documents—when it bears on our studies."

Like the falcon, Teal turned his head and stared out of one bright eye. "And what—exactly—are you studying here? Certainly, Luxonians don't need human poultices and herb drinks."

Leaving the stream, Sienna wandered to the grassy bank and plucked a wildflower. She held it before her like a shield. "Some Luxonians look to a brighter, broader future, where we will interact with other beings more freely."

Teal plodded out of the water, water dripping down his legs. He glanced at the perimeter. "There's plenty of interaction between the Supreme Council and other—"

"That's my point!" Sienna flung her flower to the ground.

"The Supreme Council shrouds us in darkness. We know little beyond what we read in the guardian reports. They insist that they shield us from a hostile world—but do they?"

A murmur of voices rose in the distance. Teal sucked in a breath; alarm bells rang in his mind. "Neb's closer than I thought. We need to move on." He glanced around.

Scurrying across the distance, Sienna arrived at Teal's side. "Would they hurt us?"

Peering into Sienna's bright eyes, Teal scowled. "Neb would attempt to kill me—certainly. What he'd do with you—I don't dare think about."

"I'd flash away."

"He'd remember you. You'd become the stuff of legends—and nightmares." Taking her arm, he pointed to a high embankment. "We'll hide over there. Lizard?"

"I'd rather be a rock."

"Not a good choice."

Sienna squinted, confused.

"If you need to move, it'll look odd."

Glancing to the sky, she pointed. "A falcon then."

"Fine. Just remember, the Supreme Council does shield us from a hostile world, even when we'd rather they didn't."

"And the Cresta and Ingoti?"

The murmurs grow closer. Teal frowned, lifting his hand like a man taking an oath. "I'll fight that war myself."

Sienna gripped his arm. "And I'll heal you—if need be." She blinked away.

A gorgeous Peregrine Falcon swooped overhead.

Teal stared—fascinated—and then blinked away just as Neb and his men pounded into view.

Chapter Twenty-Seven

—Grassland—

A Daring Plan

Aram arrived at the grassland village and frowned at all the sober faces. Everyone bore marks of their recent struggle—bruises, scratches, nasty cuts, bandaged arms...and several men limped.

Obed and Eoban jogged forward. Obed extended his hand. "Our success was due to your warriors. We'd not have survived on our own."

Eoban slapped his thigh. "Such warriors! The gods be praised for your men!"

Later that same afternoon, Eoban, Obed, Ishtar, Barak, Aram and the rest of the valiant warriors stood silently at the trench-like grave mound.

As the glinting rays sent long shadows across the land, Obed lifted his voice. "God of all that is good, deliver these souls to their appointed place of honor. May they be welcomed with joy."

As the assembly broke up, Obed turned to his companions. "Who'll tell Jonas? We must prepare for the next battle soon. The enemy could return at any time."

Closing his eyes, Eoban cleared his throat, like stone scraping over stone. "I'll go." He swallowed hard and opened his eyes, his face setting into a flint mask. "...though I'd rather face ten of the enemy single-handed. Still, I'd better hurry before some fool babbles it without thinking." Glancing around, he raised his arm in salute. "I'll return soon. I've not finished my revenge."

Obed and Ishtar nodded and strode away.

With a deep sigh, Aram caught up with Eoban as he started away. "Eoban, may I speak with you?"

Eoban halted and met Aram, their gazes appraising each other.

"I've heard a great deal about you from your friends."

Eoban blushed. "I'm not nearly as bad as my reputation—"

Aram chuckled. "On the contrary. You have many admirers. Both Obed and Jonas spoke high words of praise—though her sons begged me to remind you that they're to learn the warrior craft at your hands. Any hero of old would be proud of their esteem."

Grinning, Eoban shook his head. "Their words speak more about their noble hearts than any good deeds of mine."

The two men clasped hands as friends.

~~~

Eoban made his way across the lake and met a gathering of clansmen who, after questioning, pointed to a distant dwelling.

Sitting outside his home, Eymard graciously welcomed his guest, offering him food and drink.

Only accepting water, Eoban clenched the offered cup and looked away. "May I speak with Jonas and her sons?"

Eymard sent Milkan to the task. She bounded away like a yearling at his command.

After a few awkward moments of silence, Jonas strolled toward Eoban with the boys trailing behind. They each saw Eoban at the same moment, and their faces broke into happy grins.

The two boys cried out his name and ran pell-mell across the encampment, skidding to his side. They grabbed his arms and shouted questions in a mad rush to know everything at once.

"Did we win yet?"

"Did any warriors come?"

"Did father fight?"

"Did anyone get hurt?"

"Stop, stop!" Eoban lifted his hands in surrender. "Wait for your mother, and I'll tell you everything." Peering into their eager faces, he tousled their hair. "I see how well you two are doing. Well fed—as usual."

Jonas strode forward, her stately bearing as composed as ever. Only when her piercing gaze searched his eyes did her lips quiver and her shoulders slump.

Eoban blinked rapidly, his jaw tightening. He struggled to find his voice.

Jonas waved to the boys. "Go and play. You can speak to Eoban later."

"No, the sons of Onias need to know the truth."

Eymard inched near. "Please, come and sit in the shade where you can speak comfortably."

Grimacing, Eoban settled down near Jonas and the boys. He told of Onias' plan to save the clan from bloodshed. He explained that Onias could not believe in the evil of others because he had no evil in himself. "It was best that the burial was quick and that you remain hidden in safety." He dropped his head to his chest. "Though you were not there, we did him all the homage we could."

Tears streamed from Jonas and her sons' eyes when Eoban repeated Onias' last words. "I still believe." After wiping his own eyes, he handed Jonas the carved figure that Onias had made. She clutched it to her breast, sobbing and gripping her grief-stricken sons.

After a few minutes, Eymard crouched near and wrapped his arm around her shoulders. "As long as you have his sons, you'll always have him."

Jonas nodded mutely while her tears flowed.

Clenching his teeth, Eoban rose. "Jonas, I have no desire to burden you with any greater sorrow, but you must know. The enemy has attacked once and, were it not for the warriors that Aram sent, we'd have been defeated. The enemy was driven back but not crushed. Neb will return, and unless he's stopped, he will come here. I must leave immediately and rejoin the warriors. We'll have no peace until Neb is dead."

Jonas wiped her face and hugged her sons tighter, squeezing her eyes shut. "We await news of your victory."

Bowing, Eoban clasped the boys' shoulders, retrieved his spear, and strode away.

~~~

Barak stood straight as a cedar tree, facing Aram. He folded his arms across his barrel chest. Obed stood next to him, his lanky form leaning on his spear, his eyes almost closed as if in contemplation.

Dropping his load of spears on the ground, Aram thrust his hands on his hips. His dark eyes squinted in the bright sun light. "Go on then, say what's on your mind. Is there a problem?"

Barak glanced from Obed back to Aram. "We have a plan. If it works, we'll beat Neb's clan before they arrive for their next attack."

Aram's eyes widened, his brows arching. He rotated his wrist. "Continue."

Barak glanced at Obed and nudged him.

Obed shrugged. "It is simply this—" He outlined his plan step by step.

Aram's eyes narrowed while he massaged his jaw. When Obed was through, he nodded. "A daring plan. Where're you going to find men swift and cunning enough to complete such a difficult task?"

Obed and Barak grinned at each other.

Aram picked up his load. "So, when will you leave?"

Barak glanced at the sun still high in the sky. "Immediately."

Lifting his voice, Aram turned to his next duty. "I suggest you take Ishtar with you. He'll be of great service."

As the two men strode away, Aram stopped and watched them. His gaze turned inward. He almost wished their plan would fail—he greatly desired to meet Neb in battle. Still, he would gladly accept peace if it were possible. He had no desire to hear the wailing of any more widows.

Chapter Twenty-Eight

—River Clan—

Lift a Curse

Joash clenched his jaw as he stood waiting. They were camped a day-and-a-half's march north of the Grassland's Village.

The old men rose and directed their steps toward the evening meal and a rest from the strain of constant duty. After the council, only Joash remained standing, his service that of an errand boy, not advisor.

Neb padded away, muttering to himself. "Not the time to guess what went wrong, but time to make new plans. Fools discuss failure!"

After peering around, he gestured to Joash. "There are so few I trust." Poking Joash in the shoulder, he scowled. "Go back to the enemy's village tonight and see what preparations they've made. Very likely the new warriors won't stay. When they leave, that's our chance." He peered into the distance as if seeing a future glory.

After a moment, he refocused on Joash. "Get your things and leave tonight." As Joash began to speed away, Neb shouted. "Joash—return quickly. We'll not wait for you."

As he stalked away, Joash thought over Neb's snappish words. *He will not wait for me? When he knows that only I can get the knowledge he needs? Neb is losing his mind. One day I'll choose the council members, and there won't be an old man among them.*

Seeing Lud, he called to the boy. "Get me food for a two-days' journey, and sharpen my blade."

Lud turned and sprinted away.

Joash gathered his materials. When Lud returned, he grabbed the boy's arm and stared deeply into his eyes. "Do exactly as I say, or I'll gut you like a pig. Go back home—tell everyone that Neb stupidly attacked without forethought and he's been killed, but I'm going to save the clan. Say that—but nothing more. You understand?"

Lud maintained unflinching eye contact. His voice dropped to a whisper. "Yes."

Joash thrust him away in angry satisfaction. "All right then! Go! And remember to give my message and nothing more." He lifted his hand in warning. "Don't make any mistakes!"

Lud nodded and gathered his things.

~~~

Lud left in the early morning after Joash had gone. He knew the direction he needed to go, and he carried a spear and tucked a knife in his belt in case any wild animals lurked in his path. His mind raced with the fear not only of the long, lonely distance he must cover but also with the great lie he must tell.

He had never been very good at telling stories, and he could see in his mind's eye the suspicious glare of the elders as he passed on Joash's words. The women would ask questions he couldn't answer, and everyone would demand details that he couldn't invent. Someday, Neb would hear of this misadventure and would demand an account. Joash would kill him to keep him from telling the truth, or Neb would do the unimaginable and make him tell.

Nausea rose from his middle. After walking for several hours in the morning light, he collapsed on the grass and watched as sunbeams highlighted the long stems of waving grass. His mind stilled into peaceful observation.

Then, without warning, a bird cawed and soared into the sky, sending a chill over his body. A sob welled in his chest. Wrapping his arms around his bare, dirt-streaked legs, he laid his head on his arms. A vast, unfeeling sky loomed over his shaking form.

Swallowing back the last of his misery, he peered into the clear blue expanse. Three birds soared in circles high above him. In his mind, he pictured Pele and as she had gazed into the same vastness. Yet Pele could see something that he never could. Her face radiated visions as real as the sun itself.

"I can't see you, but Pele tells me that you're great and powerful. Please help me, or surely I'll die."

Nothing. As he waited, a fresh wave of grief poured over him. He closed his eyes and tried to regain his calm, but new sobs wracked his shoulders.

Without warning, a hand gripped his shoulder. Lud froze. If it was Joash, he was as good as dead.

"It's all right, boy. Don't be afraid. Are you injured? We'd like to help if we can."

Slowly raising his head, Lud saw three figures towering over him. The first two he could not recognize, but the other was someone he knew—Ishtar—the son of Neb. He shuddered.

"Take my hand and stand up. Let me look at you. My name is Obed. This is Barak, and over there is Ishtar. We're traveling to the river. You going that way?"

Lud swallowed back the last of his tears, too frightened to speak above a whisper. "I know Ishtar. He went on a mission with my master, Joash, but—" Lud's words trailed off as he shuffled his feet.

Ishtar clapped the boy on the back. "Yes, I remember you." He frowned. "But Joash had no slave."

"I was given as a reward for his success."

"Oh, I see." Ishtar grimaced. "Would I have gained a slave if I had returned?" he spat on the ground.

Silence and the hum of insects filled the warm air.

Tapping his foot, Barak waved the others forward. "We'll talk as we walk. We need to keep moving."

Obed patted Lud's shoulder. "Can you walk? Here, step between us—tell us where you're going."

Lud pointed east. "I'm returning to the village. I'm on a

mission—but not of my own choosing. I'll probably fail, and then I'll be killed for my efforts."

Ishtar, Barak, and Obed exchanged glances. Flinging his arm about Lud's shoulder, Obed grinned. "As we're going the same way, perhaps we can walk with you. You may live yet to tell of your travels. Besides, four is greater protection than three."

Lud peered at the men who strode so easily at his side. "I'd like to walk with you, for four is greater protection than one." As if the sun had broken through a dark cloud, Lud's face brightened.

A strong wind screamed, rippling the grass in waves. White clouds mounted across the vast blue expanse.

The small group quickened their pace.

Ishtar questioned Lud, who would have to raise his voice against the rising wind. Soon, Joash's plan was made known to them.

Lud told stories of his family and the home he had been pulled away from as he struggled against the rising wind. "Do any of you know any clans in the north hills? That's where I lived." Lud swallowed hard, not daring to hope.

Shrugging, Ishtar shook his head. "The only clans I've known were destroyed by our warriors. Don't ask me about living clans."

Obed wiped loose strands of hair from his face and bent into the wind. "I don't know much about other clans, but there is one among my people who travels—Eoban had family in the north hills. He might know something of your people or what remains of your clan." He leaned closer. "Listen to me, Lud. It's my clan that Neb plans to attack. We'd like to stop him. Would you help us? We don't hold slaves, so all those held by Neb's clan would be free."

Lud's neck muscles strained as he bent into the wind. A flush worked up his face. "If you'd take me in until I find my family, I'd gladly serve you."

Obed patted the boy's arm and even Barak grinned.

"But, there's a girl—I couldn't leave her behind. She's not very strong. She needs my help."

An eyebrow rising, Obed glanced at Ishtar and back at Lud. "How old are you, boy?"

Lud shrugged. "Don't know. Does it matter?"

Ishtar waved Obed's concern aside. "Bring the girl with you. We may collect a whole family before we're through."

Lud grinned, jutting his chin in defiance of the wind. "I knew he'd help me. Pele said he would."

Obed leaned closer. "What?"

"The Sky-Warrior helped me—like Pele said."

Obed and Ishtar's gazes lifted searching the stormy clouds as they filled the wide expanse. They both frowned.

They all leaned into the impending storm and marched faster.

~~~

Lud led Obed and Barak directly into Neb's village, while Ishtar hid in the north. A crowd came out to meet the newcomers. Lud explained that he had met the two men on his journey home and had offered them hospitality. The matter was accepted as custom.

Suspicious old men and curious women asked questions, but Obed explained that they were simply traveling through from the south. In a short time, the villagers grew bored and returned to their duties.

That night as Obed sat at one of the community fires and shared roasted pork with them, he asked questions about the absence of their warriors. They told him that they were off on a hunt.

After a full meal and pleasant—though decidedly boring—conversation, Obed and Barak slipped into Lud's tent. Obed ran his fingers through his hair. "How can they be so kind yet send warriors off to pillage another village?"

Putting his fingers to his lips, Barak shushed Obed's

questions.

When Lud slipped in, Obed cornered him, his voice a harsh whisper. "I don't see any great farms or multitudes of cattle that need attendants. These people are backward and simple. Why do they need slaves at all?"

Scowling in the dim light, Lud peered from Obed to Barak. "I don't know. They don't have enough people."

"What do you mean? Do they lose so many warriors to battle? Surely it'd make more sense to stop going to war."

Hunching closer, Lud's tone dropped to a rasp. "I've heard that Neb is trying to lift a curse. He believes there are so few healthy babies because the gods are angry. Neb must please them by becoming a great warrior and dominate the land."

Barak nudged Obed. "What's wrong with their babies?"

A rustling noise froze them in place.

Pele poked her head into the tent. "Lud? Are you all right?"

Lud tapped Obed's arm. "It's Pele, the girl I told you about. She can help us."

Obed nodded, and Lud opened the flap further and drew Pele inside. He introduced Obed and Barak and recounted his return journey.

Crouching, Pele listened and peered at the shadowed figures. "How can I help?"

Obed nudged Barak with a grin. "Once everyone is asleep, Ishtar will join us. We'll wake every slave and offer them freedom if they help us fight Neb. We'll take such weapons as we find and return home during the night."

Lud gripped Pele's hand, his eyes glowing with delight.

Chapter Twenty-Nine

—Grasslands—

I Won't Go Alone

Neb's eyes flashed open. Darkness lay like a blanket. Through sheer force of will, he stilled his shaken senses, though his heart pounded, and his skin crawled in the damp night air. A gusting wind howled outside his tent. Listening intently, he pictured a woman wailing in pain. He had heard such cries when he committed husbands, sons, and brothers to the blade.

Straining, he tried to pierce the blackness before him, but glimpsed nothing to grab onto—no spark of light to illuminate any shape or form. His sinewy hands gripped the bearskin covering his body. After smoothing the soft fur, he dug his fingers deep into the thick hairs. This blanket had accompanied him on many journeys. His grandfather, Neb the Great, had bestowed it upon him, along with other unspoken gifts.

Old Neb had been like a god and ruled his people with absolute authority. His first son, Madai, had been a severe disappointment, but his second son, Serug, became like his second self—in looks as well as desires. When Serug was blessed with a son, Old Neb intervened and trained the youth himself. When his grandfather passed to the other side, young Neb knew he'd joined the gods of their heritage—the gods that ruled them still.

The howling wind ravaged the tent, the cloth straining to break free from the wooden pegs holding it in place.

A voice called through the wind. "N-N-Neb."

Neb's eyes flicked open.
The voice wailed his name again. "N-N-Neb."
He bolted upright.
The voice screamed again, angry. "N-Neb!"
Neb lurched onto his knees and clutched at the air, trying to grab the flap of the tent. As he finally flipped it open, the wind tore it from his grasp. Pitch-black night showed through the opening, not a fire in sight. He could see no man or beast or even the other tents, though they could not be more than a few footsteps from his own. He crouched alone in a black wilderness.

Trembling, he lifted his head. "Joa—" He frowned remembering that he had sent Joash away.

Checking his fear, he crawled backward inside his tent. Just as he settled down, he heard his name again.

"N-N-Neb."

Scrambling outside, he thrust out his chest, opposing the wind and the terror that clutched at his mind. With a chill, he heard his name once more directly behind him. He turned. The grotesque figure of his grandfather floated above him. The face was too familiar to doubt. Shock stole his breath.

"Neb—My own."

Neb straightened his shoulders, forcing himself to face the apparition. "I'm here. Why do you seek me, grandfather?"

The emaciated vision pointed with a stick-like finger. "Your time allotted is soon fulfilled. You must not allow the weak to succeed the strong."

The form paled as the wind shredded it to pieces.

Neb lifted his arms. "I need more time!"

The wisps of vision faded into the night. "Time is our enemy."

The ache in his feet awoke Neb to the biting wind. He yanked the tent flap and crawled inside. After rubbing his feet and massaging his chilled arms, he arranged the fur blanket around his body. Though he lay down, his eyes would not close. *My appointed hour is at hand? Will I be called to give an*

account—to the gods?
Neb turned on his side. *But who will follow in my place?* Joash's face rose in his mind's eye. His lips curled in disgust. If time were his enemy, then deceit would be his friend. He would conquer his enemies—then choose his fate. When he was finished, even his grandfather's spirit would be amazed.
He murmured to the air above. "I won't go alone."

Chapter Thirty

—Grassland—Lake Clan—

A Curse You Share

Lud grinned. The sight of so many ragged slaves marching resolutely across the plains would make anyone stop for a second look. It was just as well that no one saw them.

Obed, Ishtar, and Barak marched at the head.

Lud tugged Pele's hand to keep her close. "It was so easy! I can't think why we never tried it before. What can they do? There isn't one leader among them. All this time that Neb and his warriors have been gone, we could've walked away free, if only we'd realized it!"

Pele panted as she kept the hurried pace. "But where would we've gone? That was always the problem. Neb would've hunted us down, and it would've been worse than before. If it wasn't for your friends and Ishtar, we'd never have made this escape."

His gaze falling, Lud bit his lip. Then a smile broke through. "But we're free now, and maybe we can search for our homes or make new ones. Your faith is rewarded, Pele. We're a free people again."

Gripping her side, Pele stopped to catch her breath. "Go on, I'll catch up later. I am not strong enough to keep this pace."

Lud frowned and clasped her hand like a frightened child.

Pele laughed. "Don't worry so! Go on—catch up with the others. I know you'd rather be with the men. I'll stay in the back with the women and children. It'll be better for us both."

After a brief inner struggle, Lud nodded. "I'll check on you later. Stay close to the women—you hear me? Don't get left behind."

Pele smiled and waved him on.

He turned and ran. After maneuvering his way through the throng, he caught up to Ishtar.

Talking to Obed and Barak, Ishtar recounted Neb's family history.

Ishtar's description of his grandfather sent a chill over Lud's body. He tugged at Ishtar's sleeve. "Could our Neb die and turn into a god too?"

Ishtar peered at the young, ruddy face. "Which do you fear more? Neb alive—or dead?"

Lud's eyes grew wide and round. "Both!"

Barak and Obed laughed.

As a sharp wind beat against their bodies, Ishtar peered into the distance. "It's time my father learned what fear feels like."

~~~

Barak stared at the glorious sunset but did not see it. He marched up to Ishtar and Obed. "I'd like to run ahead, circle around Neb, and arrive at the Grassland Village in time to tell Aram our success and make further plans."

Ishtar opened his mouth, but Obed spoke first. "It's a good plan. One man will travel faster, and Aram must be prepared."

As Barak took his leave, he patted Lud's shoulder. "Don't be afraid. We will prevail."

~~~

Barak gloried in his lone run through the cool winds. All the pent-up emotions of his recent experiences released untold energy, and he relished the peace of the open land. The sun poured its radiant heat on his body, while the breeze swept the sweat away.

Only when the picture of Lud's tear-strewn face entered his

mind did a searing fire cut through his gut. Then all peace fled, and he yearned to cut Neb's head from his body.

~~~

Neb peered through sunken eyes at Joash, his hands clasped before him. His men completed their morning duties behind him.

Joash stood tall with his shoulders squared and his eyes flashing. He gave a clear, succinct report.

Neb continued to stare without any further questions.

Shifting from one foot to another, Joash swallowed and gripped his spear. Neb's piercing eyes stabbed him like a sharp knife. Joash's gaze flickered away.

Finally, lifting his eyes to the sky, Neb took a step away. "Joash, you will take me to the Grassland People, and you'll inform them that we want the peace that they offered through their leader, Onias."

He stopped and peered back, glaring into Joash's eyes. "You'll also inform them that you murdered Onias. You'll explain that you acted on your own and that I was never told of the situation until recently."

Joash choked. His spear slipped from his hand. "They'll kill me."

"You'll be a sacrificial peace offering." Neb titled his head. "A small price to pay." He stepped away. "We'll leave now. You don't need to bring anything. I'll dispose of your slaves for you."

Frozen, Joash's face blanched. He clenched and unclenched his hands. His jaw clamped and the skin on his face grew tight. Finally, he croaked a few words. "How do you know—?"

"Stupid! Were you alone when you did your deed? Did I not send you to keep an eye on Ishtar? Do you think I'd trust you more than my own son?"

Joash saw in his mind's eye the face of his silent companion—the one who helped him kill Onias. Now his greatest wish was that the message he sent with Lud would not be a lie. His hands stopped twitching, and his eyes narrowed. His gaze swept over Neb's thin elderly frame. Flexing his fingers, Joash bent to grasp his fallen spear.

Neb turned away and threw his cloak about his shoulders. He called to his men. "Follow my orders. We leave now." Staring straight ahead, he marched into the grasslands.

Joash strode silently at Neb's side, his heart pounding in his chest. As the sun climbed high, Joash peered around, his eyes narrowed at the open land without a human in sight. Without warning, he swung his spear butt around and thrust a direct hit at Neb's unprotected head.

Neb leaped quicker than Joash thought possible, and swung his staff around. Before Joash could react, Neb's staff cracked down on his shoulder and he slipped in the tall grass.

Joash knocked Neb's staff to the side and swung again.

Neb dove to the ground and grabbed his ankle, thrusting upward with all his might.

Losing his balance, Joash toppled onto his back with a smothered thud.

Neb grabbed his fallen spear.

Joash pushed himself up, prepared to lunge.

Neb cracked Joash on the side of the head.

Grimacing and his legs crumpling under him, Joash fell to his knees.

Neb's foot slammed into his chest, knocking him flat on his back again and pressed his foot to Joash's throat. He prodded his chest with his spear. "Never underestimate an old man!" Neb's eyes gloated.

Joash squirmed as Neb applied pressure with the heel of his foot.

Neb whispered. "Was it like this for Onias when he offered you peace?"

Joash glared, his lips tight.

Neb increased the pressure

Joash's arms flailed. "Yes!"

Neb grinned. "You see—I know many things. You called

Onias a fool for offering peace, but I call you a fool for offering me lies. It all depends on who is standing and who is on the ground."

He lifted his spear and gestured with a sharp wave. "Get up! Your end is coming soon enough. Don't shorten the little time you have left." Before Joash had a chance to retrieve his spear, Neb threw it into the wide expanse. He prodded Joash before him with the tip of his spear.

When they came in sight of the village, a man standing near a dwelling called out. "Who are you? Why've you come?"

Hunching his shoulders, Neb waved his staff feebly. He responded in a tremulous voice. "We've come to make peace. Please send someone to speak with us."

Only the buzzing insects and murmurs could be heard as the message was relayed.

A new voice spoke. "You come to us. We've no desire to play games, old man."

Joash peered at Neb out of the corner of his eye.

Neb nodded with a glint in his eyes. He gave Joash a hearty shove from behind. They shuffled into the bustling village.

Dwellings in various stages of development were arranged around the compound. Stubborn grass beaten to thick rounded humps tripped the unwary. Ancient trees with moss covered limbs stretched over the village and offered welcome shade.

Aram stood with arms crossed, silent and frowning. Two warriors flanked him, standing with similar grim expressions and spears in their hands.

Neb halted, like a weary wanderer, in front of Aram. He raised his staff in formal salute and waved to Joash.

Joash stepped forward and looked Aram in the eye. "I killed Onias. Neb didn't know of the message of peace he offered. I acted alone." His gaze did not flicker, though his hands remained clenched.

Neb dropped his gaze, his eyes hooded.

Aram looked from Neb to Joash and back to Neb. He stepped aside and indicated that two warriors were to take Joash away.

The warriors grabbed Joash by the arms and thrust him into the village.

Aram turned his palms up in a gesture of welcome. He gestured for the old man to walk ahead.

Neb tottered forward as if ready to collapse.

Aram stepped behind him but peered over his shoulder and waved a new warrior to stand guard. Inside the large council dwelling, Aram faced Neb.

The flap rustled, and Jonas stepped in and sat down a little distance away.

Aram frowned.

Neb ignored the woman and seemed to withdraw into an inner world.

Eymard offered food and water, and then gamely positioned himself as an assistant.

Aram scratched his head and leaned toward Eymard. "I'm surprised Namah hasn't made it inside."

Eymard's eyes widened, clearly horrified.

Shifting into a comfortable position, Aram cleared his throat. "You're welcome as a messenger of peace. As you know, Onias sacrificed his life to bring such a message to you. But before we speak of peace, I'd like to know more about you and your people. It's always best to know exactly who we're dealing with."

Neb acquiesced, lifting up his trembling hands. "I am Neb, son of Serug and grandson of Neb the Great. Our home is on the shore of the Great Eastern River. Long ago, we lived among the trees in the far western lands south of the mountains. When my father moved from my grandfather's clan, we traveled north to the hills and east through grasslands very much like those we crossed coming here."

His shoulders slumping in apparent misery, Neb clasped his hands together. "We've been attacked so many times—we see enemies everywhere. A mistaken report warned our council that you had prepared an attack on our people. Only lately have we learned that your messenger of peace had been killed." He sighed.

"It was a terrible mistake, and the guilty should pay with his life. It'll be my greatest joy to assure my people that we have established a peaceful treaty with you."

Aram's face flushed. His gaze dropped to his hands and he forced himself to stop clasping and unclasping them. Sweat broke over his forehead. He called to one of his men and whispered in his ear.

Straightening, he met Neb's steady gaze. He spoke slowly—each word emphasized with deliberate force. "Tell me—do your women—bear many children?"

For the first time, Neb's demeanor cracked. He frowned. "I don't know why you ask, but the answer is a painful one. No, our women do not carry many babies, and even when they do, the babies come too soon and die quickly. It's a miserable fate. Who told you? My son, Ishtar?"

Aram shook his head. "Not Ishtar."

Neb's eyes glanced aside, as if searching for his son. "Even if a son lives, yet he may be as good as dead."

Aram observed his clan members shifting in unease, murmuring aside to each other. Some men's eyes were wide and sympathetic, while Obed and Eoban frowned in confusion. Barak maintained a stony silence. Only Eymard, sitting in the shadows, leaned forward, a knowing gleam in his eyes.

Aram folded his hands in his lap. He lowered his voice. "I'd like to tell you, Neb, son of Serug, who I am, so that we may see eye to eye in all things."

His gaze returning inward, glassy-eyed and bored, Neb nodded.

"My name is a common one. I am Aram, and my father was Elath. My grandfather was Madai—and my great-grandfather was Neb the Great."

Gasps bounced around the council chamber.

Neb's knuckles whitened as he clasped them, his shoulders

stiffened, and his head bowed.

Unperturbed, Aram continued. "Neb was considered evil among my father's people. They lived in the southern hills for generations, but when my grandfather and his brother disagreed, our clan traveled into the forests while his brother settled in the grasslands. A pair of wild cats recently forced us from our land, and we've made a new home not far from here. The Grassland People sent their women and children across the lake to seek safety from your invasion. Seeing the threat to an innocent people, we gave aid. I didn't know until a few moments ago that I'd find a lost kinsman in such a conflict."

The entire assembly murmured, everyone speaking at once.

Neb remained still and silent, his head bowed.

Rising to his knees, Aram stared at Neb's immovable form. "We do not speak of our history—it's been lost to all but a few elders who hold the truth deep inside. But as leader, I learned our history well, and I remember the tales told about your father. I know what forces formed you. I know why your women are barren. You accuse the gods in vain."

Aram stood and called several men to his side. After giving curt, whispered commands, he returned to Neb. "Because it is the cause of so much torment, I'll explain why your women suffer so." He lifted his hands and turned to the assembly. "There is a plant that, when eaten, will kill the baby in the mother."

His glare swung back to Neb. "Do you tell them that this toxic plant is good for them—or insist that the gods require them to eat it? What lies do you spread to achieve your ends? My grandfather never used this plant, and when my father learned of it, he would not allow it."

Neb lifted his head, his gaze locking on Aram, a hint of a smile playing on his lips.

Aram spat to the side. "I see in your eyes that you have used it knowingly—as your father did." Aram stomped away. "I was only a child when my Grandfather died. I'm only sorry he didn't end your evil line long ago."

A warning shout rang through the air. "Attack! Fire!"

With a look of mad glee, Neb leapt to his feet. He shrugged as in helpless innocence.

A frightened youth scampered into the tent. "Warriors have come! They're setting fire to everything."

Eoban and Obed rushed outside.

Aram poked Neb in the chest. "You will inform your warriors that the battle is over—the curse has been lifted. You can go home and dispel the darkness caused by your terrible lie."

With a stubborn purse of the lips, Neb shook his head as if he were a petulant child who would not mind his parent.

Gripping Neb by the shoulder, Aram shoved him toward the opening, but Neb wrenched free.

Aram stood back and allowed his enemy to walk outside into the bright sunlight. Three huts smoldered in smoke and flames. Aram growled. "Call your men! Tell them the curse has been lifted, and there's no need to battle for slaves. If not, you'll die at my hand right now, and utter darkness will consume you."

Neb raised his hands in a dramatic gesture and called out in an alarmingly strong voice. "River Clan! I am Neb. You know my voice! Listen to me!"

The shouts and yells quieted to murmurs and a sporadic scream.

"I command! Kill them all! Leave no man alive!"

Aram grabbed Neb around the neck and threw him to the ground.

Neb's unnatural smirk of satisfaction froze Aram in place. With a gasp, he shook his head as if to release himself from an evil spell.

Leaping like a yearling lamb, Neb sprang at Aram and wrapped his fingers around his throat.

In turn, Aram locked his powerful hands around Neb's neck. His eyes widened in horror at the strength of his opponent. He pictured Onias's burial mound. The man died because he underestimated his enemy.

Eymard hustled behind Neb, a cudgel in his wrinkled, shaking hands.

Cold horror shivered over Aram as he thought of what Neb would do to the old men and the children. *God Almighty! Give me strength!*

Suddenly, a tremendous force bowled the two men over. Two young men landed on them at the same time. Barak and Ishtar grabbed Neb's claw-like fingers and pried them away from Aram's neck.

Aram rolled to the side as Ishtar grabbed his knife and held it against his father's throat. He looked into Neb's glaring eyes and whispered. "The only curse on our people was you!"

Neb cackled, his face breaking into a monstrous grin. "It's a curse you share, my son!" Gripping Ishtar's hands, he redirected the knife and thrust it into his own heart. Neb grunted on impact and his blood spurted.

With a strangled yelp, Ishtar sprang to his feet.

Exhaling a hissing breath, Neb's head turned to the side. He shook one feeble finger at his son. His eyes glazed over and saw no more.

Ishtar stood rooted to the ground, blood splattered on his hands.

Barak gripped Ishtar's shoulders and pulled him away. "It's not your fault. The man was mad. Perhaps—it's better this way."

Falling to his knees, Ishtar's gaze traveled from his father to his bloody hands. "A curse I share." He howled like a wounded animal and crumpled, covering his head with his arms.

Still rubbing his neck, Aram stood by Ishtar's prostrate form and surveyed the tail end of the battle. Neb's warriors were being rounded up. The freed slaves had arrived, and the combined forces had made their victory inevitable.

Tears welled, blurring Aram's vision. He spoke to no one in particular. "It didn't have to end this way."

Aram crouched next to Ishtar and gripped the young man's shoulder. "Your men need you, Ishtar. You're their only hope now."

Swallowing back a shuddering sob, Ishtar rose and threw back his shoulders. He appraised the confused warriors as they assembled before him.

Stepping forward, Aram lifted his arms. "Neb is dead! The battle is over. Ishtar is the leader of the River People now."

All eyes turned to Ishtar.

Ishtar sucked in a deep breath and his narrowed eyes swept over the vanquished warriors. His hands unclenched. "I offer peace."

A mixture of cheers, angry grunts, and taunting yells met Ishtar's words. Neb's warriors, collected into a surly mob, stood huddled together, surrounded by warriors and freed slaves. Joash, with a bloody nose and a bruised face, stood among them. He cradled an arm hanging at an odd angle, his jaw clenched against the pain.

Aram passed his gaze over the sullen and defeated throng. A spark of familiarity stirred in his gut. These were his people by blood. Had it not been for Neb's lies and threats, these men might never have chosen this violent path. Now, like craven wolves, they needed a leader.

Rising from his stupor at the sight of his defeated clansmen, Ishtar paced before the assembly.

Aram led Barak, Eoban, Obed, and the others to the side.

Sucking in a deep breath, Ishtar threw back his shoulders and raised his voice. "My father was your leader, but he did not serve you well."

Sneers and grunts challenged him. "Neb ruled like a man! He never ran—"

He flung a hand up. "Listen to me and learn the truth! We never suffered from a curse. The plant Neb used in his ceremonies weakened our women and killed our unborn children. No woman can eat that plant and carry a healthy child. The Lake People know this to be true. Aram is related to our clan, and his people broke away over the use of this plant generations ago. Neb lied to us. Our battles did not lift a curse. They *were* the curse—meant to keep us enslaved to Neb's will and the will of the evil spirits he followed."

A voice rang out. "Neb was a god!"

"A god who kills his women and children? Is that the god you wish to follow?"

Silence.

"Let our women grow strong and our babies healthy. We can live in peace."

Confusion replaced fury and several warriors' gazes dropped, blinking in confusion.

"I will lead you home, and we'll build homes and raise our children without the threat of constant battle upon us. Surely, there is a God who creates rather than destroys. That is the God I wish to follow."

After an uneasy silence, Joash stumbled forward. "And how can we trust you?" He turned to the warriors, wincing as he moved. "This story could be a creation of Ishtar's demented mind to appease his guilt for running away and betraying us to the enemy." Swinging back on Ishtar, his voice rose to a pain-filled shriek. "You freed our slaves and turned against us. If it were not for you, Neb would be alive, and we'd be going home in victory."

Shouts and accusations flew through the air.

Then Jonas, covered with a long scarf, stepped forward. As the scarf fell from her face, the evening light slanted across her glossy hair.

The angry voices ceased as wide-eyed gazes considered her in wonder.

"I am the wife of Onias—the one Joash killed when he offered peace. Ishtar tells the truth. We, too, had to learn through sorrow about the toxic plant Neb used. Aram is your kin, and he knows too well the lies that ensorcelled your people. You've been forced into a slavery no better than those you conquered."

She glanced at Ishtar. "Ishtar rejected his father's lies because he could not endure the evil reasoning of Neb's mind. He now stands before you—victorious. He could leave, but he has decided not to abandon you."

Her voice hardened. "It is your choice. Live with the truth and grow strong and healthy—or die with a lie."

Jonas stepped back into the shadow. A hushed silence fell over the entire village.

Then a single, plaintive voice rose from the defeated throng. "I'd like a son." Nods and whispers echoed this sentiment.

Aram stepped forward and gestured to his men. "Set guards around the perimeter and arrange care for the wounded."

A group of his men marched away. Others herded the conquered warriors to a separate location.

Only Joash remained standing, alone, staring at an empty sky, and hugging his broken arm.

Obed clapped Eoban on the shoulder. "Now, don't you feel silly for worrying?"

Eoban's return glance spoke volumes.

Obed turned to Aram and jerked his thumb at Joash. "So, what do we do with him?"

Ishtar snorted. "Put him out of his misery."

Jonas stepped forward, her jaw set in a firm line. "He killed my husband, so he's mine. I've decided that he shall be spared. You two—" She pointed from Obed and Eoban to a nearby hut. "Bring him to that shelter."

Stunned silence filled the air. Then, with a long-suffering sigh, Obed nudged Eoban. "Or we could give him to Jonas—to heal or hurt—as she sees fit."

As Ishtar watched in glowering fury, Eoban and Obed obeyed Jonas' command.

Aram gripped Ishtar's shoulder. "A woman's cure is not always easy to bear—especially a woman like Jonas. She may dig deeper than we dare to imagine. You should pity the wretch."

Ishtar's gaze rolled to the bloody body of his father.

~~~

Aram stepped to a mound of dead bodies and crossed his arms, his gaze hard and his throat dry. He looked at the men gathered around the remains of their slain enemies. "We'll burn them. They sacrificed themselves in the fire of Neb's evil. It's only just."

The slain warriors were laid out with quiet ceremony on a pyre of wood. The spark was about to be struck, when out of the assembly a medium-built man with piercing black eyes stepped forward. He stood before the pyre, his hands clasped beseechingly.

"My brother was young and only did as he was told. He came to me with doubts, but I pushed his fears aside. He was never Neb's follower—not in his heart, and I'll not have him joined with Neb in death. I'm the eldest of my family, and I have my rights. I'll bury him myself—that he may know some measure of peace."

No one made any objection. The boy's body was collected and taken away.

As the funeral pyre sent sparks twirling into the sky, Ishtar stared into the flames, silent and mesmerized.

~~~

Aram strode to Ishtar's side in the evening twilight, after the flames had died and clasped his arm around the young man's shoulders. He pointed to the glowing red and white mound. "We all become dust in time. Many paths lead to the same end."

His voice empty and hollow, Ishtar clenched his hands together. "Is our end then? Only this?"

Aram glanced up at the first stars twinkling in the darkening sky. "I do not believe so."

"What do you believe?"

"We are spirit, and our spirits live on."
"To what purpose?"
"Only God knows."
The two men stood as still as stones, staring at the mound of crumbling dust.

Chapter Thirty-One

—Lake Clan—
—Three years later—

Our Weakness

Aram strode along the beach, rubbing his temple where a headache threatened. Stopping short, he stared at the familiar expanse of clear, blue water. He smiled—but then the memory of why he was pacing rushed back to his mind with an urgency he could not dismiss. He hurried on in exasperated helplessness.

Will she be all right? She suffered so much with the last one.

A shout turned his attention.

Barak hurtled down the incline, a grin spread wide across his face. "Another girl, Aram, strong and healthy! She's as beautiful as all creation—if you can believe Jonas!" He pounded Aram on the back. "Jonas thinks every baby is as beautiful as all creation. As she's expecting her fourth, she thinks she's an expert."

Aram's shoulders relaxed, and the knot in his stomach unclenched as he headed back up the incline toward their dwellings. "An expert indeed. Our people learned more from her these last few years than we could've learned on our own in three lifetimes."

Barak grunted and smiled. "Motherhood is a great teacher, they say. Namah is certainly a different woman since she became a mother, and your Bethal is a joy."

Aram flushed. "I'd do anything for that child—and she knows it, too. Now will come the test!" He tapped Barak's arm. "Bethal has never had a rival."

As they strode into the village, Aram scratched his chin. "Namah imitates Jonas in every detail, and the result is remarkable—" He left his unfinished thought and charged into his thatch hut.

Sitting on a thick pallet with pillows strewn around, Namah cradled her baby in her arms, her eyes beaming with joy.

Aram's eye twinkled as he crouched at her side.

A sudden anxiety shadowed her face as she peered at her baby.

With a gentle hug, Aram whispered in her ear. "Thank you." Then, like a child unwrapping a gift, he peeked into the bundle she pressed close to her chest.

The baby's pink face, eyes closed, rested against Namah's warm breast.

"She's lovely. What shall we call her?"

Startled from her sleep, the infant raised her sleepy hands in protest before folding up again in contented slumber.

Aram stiffened with shock. One of the baby's hands was misshapen. He glared a silent question at his wife.

Jonas hustled forward. "I thought Barak told you."

Swallowing his bitterness, Aram shook his head. "He only said she was beautiful."

Namah's voice rose plaintively. "Isn't she beautiful to her father?"

Clenching his jaw, Aram closed his eyes and stomped out the doorway.

Jonas turned to Namah as tears filled the mother's eyes. "Don't worry! How can he know the worth of a baby he's not carried inside himself?"

"No! If this were a boy, he'd accept him despite his imperfection. Or at least if she were a well-formed girl, she'd be desirable. But now—he'll want to destroy her."

Jonas clutched her chest. "Your clan doesn't do such things!"

Tears meandered down Namah's face. "It happened in the past. Many questioned why I, with my hunched back, was allowed to live. But my mother threatened anyone who tried to harm me. Even my father became afraid of her. But I've always been an outcast." She caught Jonas' eye. "Until recently."

Jonas thrust her hands on her hips. "Well, the rest of the world can do as it wishes. Our job is to love this baby."

The bright and forceful smile seemed to cheer Namah, who returned it as weakly as a moon tries to shine at the sun.

As Jonas wiped a bowl, she muttered. "But if a certain someone doesn't love this baby—I'll make threats of my own!"

~~~

Eoban sat with little Onia, Onias' last child—the one he never had a chance to know—wiggling in his lap.

Jonas and Obed, carrying empty baskets, headed to the field.

They make a beautiful couple. And no, I'm not jealous in the least.

Onia squirmed. At two, he could already toddle about in competent authority over his environment, and he seemed to want to do so now.

Eoban did his mighty best to slip a tunic onto the slippery little body. Jonas had asked him to dress the little one—if Obed forgot. Of course, Obed forgot.

Eoban loved children, and he usually had great success with them. But this morning had been a series of misadventures. This little one with light brown eyes and brown hair had a mind of his own. He did not talk much, but he would not be forced to do something he did not want to do. He did not want to put on a tunic at this time.

Eoban was determined. He was a strong man in his prime and had both patience and kindness. But patience and kindness were of no avail in this quest to dress a squirming baby. He slipped one arm in the armhole, and the other arm would slip out as if greased. The child smiled up winningly at undoing what Eoban had just painstakingly accomplished.

He had been struggling with this task for far too long, and yet he still held a loose tunic and a naked child in his arms. He managed to put the child's head through an armhole, but Onia gleefully saw the mishap and pulled it off, waving the garment in triumph. As grunts and sighs mingled with smothered oaths, Eoban slapped the tunic to the ground.

Returning with a load of wheat berries, Obed passed by and paused. "Having trouble mastering your opponent?"

Eoban peered up with one arched eyebrow. "You could do better?"

Laying the basket aside, Obed knelt in the dust and opened his arms to the baby who came toddling over joyfully.

Eoban tossed him the tunic with a shake of his head.

Obed caught it handily and dangled it temptingly over the child's head. He teased. "Sorry, baby, you can't wear this today. It's too hot. You go naked, all right?"

At this, the little one gleefully grabbed at the tunic and dexterously pulled his head and arms through the proper holes and stood triumphantly in his gay apparel.

Obed laughed, hugging the child.

Eoban stroked his chin. "It's good you're the married man—not I."

Obed patted the child who wiggled free and toddled off to his brothers, who played nearby.

"Oh, but I hear that is to change shortly."

Eoban cleared his throat. He glanced around. "What do you mean? I've said nothing."

With a wicked grin and a twinkle in his eyes, Obed shrugged. "Well, perhaps your eyes have been talking, because word in the Lake Clan is that you plan to take a wife from one of their own."

Eoban grunted and leapt to his feet. "They like to talk. So many silly women! But I've heard that Aram just had a second daughter."

Obed's face clouded over. He picked up his basket. "Yes, I've heard the same, though he's not happy—the child is not perfect."

Eoban nudged Obed. "Neither are you, but it hasn't hurt you any."

Obed flicked a broken stem at Eoban. "I've heard that the Lake Clan has a tradition of disposing of misshapen babies."

Eoban grunted as he strode across the village. "Aram hardly seems capable of such a deed. Someone must be speaking of a time long past."

Obed shook his head. "We all have our weaknesses."

Eoban peered over his shoulder at a group of women. "Or fears."

Obed turned sharply, glancing from Eoban to the women. "Of marriage, perhaps?"

Eoban stared at the children playing in wild abandon.

Little Onia stood in the midst of them, naked as a newly hatched bird. His tunic lay in the dust off.

"Ay!" Eoban sighed.

Chapter Thirty-Two

—Lux—

Allies and Enemies

Teal sat in an oval-shaped room draped with thriving vines and flowering plants. A central holographic image of the universe rotated in colorful splendor. Seated around the perimeter in chairs adapted to each species, an assembly of Luxonians, Crestas, and Ingoti contemplated the magnified sector—focused on planet Earth.

Dressed in a short white tunic and leggings, Teal, in his human form, sat with his arms crossed and glowered in mute objection to the proceedings.

Judge Sterling sat at his right.

On his left, Sienna perched on the edge of her chair, apparently ready to leap into action at a moment's notice.

The judge, draped in voluminous robes, leaned back in a padded chair and clasped his hands in serene authority.

The three Cresta representatives with their bio-suits adjusted to Luxonian settings, lounged in mock comfort. Occasional bubbles rose in their breather helms while they exhaled the soupy liquids that offered their only nutrition and comfort on this alien world.

A triplet of Ingots, all decked out in their bio-armor, sat ramrod straight with their legs firmly set on the marble floor. Zuri's mechanically gloved hands gleamed in the sunshine streaming through the skylight. His sneer flickered from Teal, skimmed over Sterling, and landed on Sienna. With a barely perceptible twitch, he nudged the Ingot next to him. The Ingot, older, bulkier, and slightly more worn around the edges, glanced over. He focused on Sienna and his eyebrows rose.

A matronly Bhuaci in elven-style clutched a bell in her petite hand and slid behind a console. After tapping the data-recorder to life, she peered at Judge Sterling.

The judge nodded.

The Bhuaci secretary shook the bell, sending a stream of tinkles across the chamber.

Judge Sterling leaned forward. "On this date 24,354.78, we will open these proceedings with the formal complaints made against both Crestar and Ingilium by—"

The central Cresta representative rose and waved a tentacle dismissively. "State the full truth—that these trifles arise from only one source and bear little weight on—"

Judge Sterling rose, his height lengthening by meters. "These proceedings will not be interrupted by an under-member of the Ingal!" Straightening his robes, Judge Sterling glared at each Cresta representative. "You have your opinions, but you will not voice them until you are given leave." His gaze traveled around the room. "This is an investigative report only. After we discuss the facts, then details will be sent to the proper authorities and a mutually satisfactory decision will be made."

The Cresta plunked down, his mouth puckering and his brow furrowing.

Teal lifted a hand. "Permission to speak?"

Sterling pursed his lips, halted an eye-roll, and nodded.

Standing, Teal turned to the assembly. "I'd like to make it clear that I did not request this hearing. I presented my facts to the Supreme Council, and *they* deemed it beneficial to all that we clarify certain boundaries before something unfortunate occurs." He cleared his throat and sat down. "*More* unfortunate, I should say."

Zuri jumped to his feet, waving his hand. "Permission?" Without waiting, he leaned toward Teal four seats away. "You've complained about Ingot mining on Earth for as long as I can remember. But we've been very sensitive to humankind. We shouldn't be called to account as if we've committed a crime." He pointed to the central Cresta across the room. "It's Ark you're angry at. He's the one who killed the five humans and tried to cover his tracks."

Ark jerked to his feet. "By the Divide! You make accusations you can't substan—"

Sterling slapped his armchair. "I will charge you both with crimes against this proceeding if you continue!"

With shy hesitation, Sienna rose and caught Judge Sterling's attention with a beckoning finger. "I have an idea—to end this confusion and the accusations."

All heads turned toward the young Luxonian.

Judge Sterling rubbed his temple. "Pray—do tell."

With light steps, Sienna bounded from her chair to the center arena. She twirled before the Holographic image of Earth and neatly bowed to the assembly, crossing hands like a dancer introducing the main event.

Teal stiffened, his eyes narrowing.

Apparently charmed, Ark grinned.

Zuri clenched his jaw against all efforts to entice him into a better mood.

Sweeping a languid hand across the universe, Sienna pointed to the swirling blue and white ball. "It's beautiful, don't you think? And we—each of us—have a stake in Earth's future. That means that we have a stake in each other." Her eyes widened as a grin breached her lips. "So why don't we work as a team—a unit? One representative from each race will always travel with the others to Earth—never alone." She clapped her hands like a child winning a game. "We'll learn so much more this way."

Teal fell back against his chair.

Ark's twinkling eyes narrowed.

Spluttering, Zuri nearly exploded.

Judge Sterling laughed. "It's brilliant!" His lighted gaze appeared to savor Sienna. "I see you're ready to move on. Your sixth year?"

Abashed, Sienna bowed her head.

Teal gripped the armchair and pulled himself to his feet. "I can barely get my work done now. What will Ark and Zuri do to my schedule—my priorities?"

Ark shuffled to his feet. "I could ask the same question, but I'm not going to make waves in an already murky sea." He glanced at Sienna. "She has a future, Judge Sterling. If you ever decide to export your students, please send this one my way."

Teal ripped his hands from the chair and waved them at Ark. "This means no more experimentation on humans? You realize that I'll watch your every step!" He turned to Zuri. "No more mining? You'll stick within legal inter-alien agreements?"

Zuri shook his head. "This whole idea is ludicrous. We'll kill each other before sunset."

Judge Sterling peered at Ark and then swiveled his gaze to Teal. "This way, you will keep each other in line. No more infractions—or accusations." He clasped his hands together and nodded. "I'll send a formal proposal for approval to the Supreme Council, the Cresta Ingal, The Ultra High Command, and the Ingoti Magisterium." A light glinted in his eyes. "I'm quite sure they'll be very pleased."

~~~

Teal marched at Sterling's side along a well-lit white corridor. He paused before an entranceway. "Before I leave, just tell me one thing."

Sterling yawned. "Make it short. I'm exhausted. Arbitration always wears me out."

Slapping his hand on the wall, Teal braced himself. "You didn't arbitrate anything! You never even addressed the murder of innocent men." He glanced at Sterling. "If I didn't know better, I'd think you and Sienna orchestrated the whole thing. Or rather, you did, and she accepted the opportunity to graduate to sixth year."

Sterling frowned, stroking his face. "I'm going to

disintegrate soon, but I must say—before I fall apart—you have a vivid imagination."

"You didn't set the whole thing up?"

"It is a brilliant idea, and—by the Divide—I wish I could claim it as my own." He patted Teal on the shoulder. "Don't fret. You'll protect your precious humankind better this way. It's what you really wanted—if you could just see it that way."

"How can I protect anyone—?"

Sterling clasped his hands and stared into Teal's eyes. "You're a guardian. I am a Judge. Remember that."

Teal straightened and stepped back. "I'll make every effort to fulfill my duty to the Supreme Council and to Lux. Sir."

Sterling smiled. "As I knew you would." Sterling dissolved into a million shining sparkles and floated into his room.

Teal turned on his heel and jogged along the corridor. As he neared the chamber, he peeked through the entranceway.

No one.

The council chamber stood dim and silent. All the chairs were now lined up in neat rows with two pastoral paintings hanging slightly askew on the back wall.

He turned and wandered down the corridor.

~~~

The two paintings vibrated, morphing into two females: the Bhuaci clerk and Sienna.

The clerk gripped Sienna's arm. "Just remember, he must not go alone. Determined as he is, the Cresta will beat him at his own game."

"The Ingot'll probably kill him."

"Just so."

"Then why have me suggest the plan in the first place?"

Using the tip of her finger, the clerk drew Sienna closer. "We're never safer than when our enemies are obsessed with each other."

"How will I follow?"

"You like to fly. So fly as a falcon."

"And if I need to catch prey to keep the illusion?"

The clerk grinned. "It's not hard. You saw me do it." She glanced around the room. "It's time I sent in my report." The two hustled out the doorway and along the corridor.

After a moment of silence, Teal stepped out of a shadow and watched until they turned the corner.

Chapter Thirty-Three

—River Clan—Lake Clan—

Deep Learning

Pele peered at Ishtar out of the corner of her eye and smiled. Her heart beat with a gentle rhythm. She no longer searched the sky.

Ishtar's bronze skin shone golden in the sun. With his shoulders thrown back in confidence and the easy way he chatted with various clansmen, he was a new man.

Her eyes welled, and she sighed with a nameless longing.

Hagia gently pressed the girl's shoulder. "You look tired. Come into the shade and help me." A half-formed pot stood to her left. "My hands hurt, and I need another pot. My busy son didn't see what he was doing this morning and knocked one off the shelf. Ruler, yes, but still a bumbling boy." She grinned slyly at Pele.

Pele kept her mouth closed and sat before the pot, though she bowed her head to hide a smile, while she worked.

Hagia leaned against a wall and plated grass stems. A scowl crept over her face. "Do you believe the reports that invaders from the north hills are attacking small tribes near here?"

Pele smoothed the surface of the pot gracefully. "We shouldn't be surprised that others want to profit from raiding as our own tribe did not long ago. It's justice come to visit us."

With a snort, Hagia thrust her mat aside. "Hardly that. We were forced into evil by lies and treachery. If we hadn't been deceived, we'd have been a peaceful people all along."

Pele told her opinion with a humble shrug.

"Anyway—" Hagia rubbed her hands together. "It's good that Ishtar has had time to grow into a leader. The clan respects him, and the council heeds his advice. Ishtar thinks carefully and acts cautiously. Those are the marks of greatness." She nodded knowingly. "Trust me."

Pele smiled. "Your wisdom grows with your son."

After a sidelong glance, Hagia returned to her work. "I only wish that the gods would grant him a good wife, someone with a noble heart and intelligent mind." She sighed. "Too bad the women in this clan are so dull."

Pele flushed.

Hagia waved a finger in her face. "You seem to have good luck with that God of yours. Talk to Him. Ask for a bride for my son. And while you are at it, ask for many healthy grandsons too." She grinned as her fingers picked up speed. "Yes, many grandsons."

With her head lowered, Pele nodded in mute agreement. The pot seemed to fashion itself.

~~~

Eymard sidled up to Barak, who sat on a bench admiring his handiwork—a new home for his father.

"You've done good work. The whole village looks beautiful." He glanced at Barak's sweaty brow. "You should be very proud of your efforts."

Barak wiped his forehead. "I've nothing to be proud of really. Most of what I've done, I learned from Obed's clan."

"You worked hard for them. It's only right that they share their secrets with you."

Barak sorted. "I shared my muscles. They shared their minds. It worked out well for both of us."

Eymard gazed into the distance. A green hill rose up to meet the blue sky. "I hear there are new adventures on the horizon."

Barak peered up and followed Eymard's gaze. "So they tell me. Obed has a wonderful new scheme to pen in prime animals for breeding. So guess who's going to build fences?" A wide, ironic smile told his opinion of the matter.

Eymard's frail hand packed a sturdy wallop as he thumped Barak on the shoulder. "It's good for young men to try new things. Grow and learn!"

Heaving himself to his feet, Barak rubbed the small of his back. "I'm happy to learn. And Obed is happy to offer advice. And Aram is happy to lend my hands to whoever needs them." He grimaced as he started away. "Everybody's happy!"

Long shadows stretched over the ground as Eymard followed Barak. "Before you go—I have a question."

Barak stopped. "Sure, ask. Just let me get a drink. I'm dying of thirst." He shuffled to a water jug outside his father's house, poured a measure into a cup, and took a long draught. Water dribbled down his chin as he groaned in base pleasure. "Oh, I needed that."

Milkan crossed in front of the two men. She tossed a shy glance in Barak's direction, dipped her head, and hurried on.

The last drops dripped from Barak's cup as his arms fell to his side and his gaze followed her. He swallowed another low groan.

Eymard tapped him on the shoulder.

Shaking himself, Barak frowned and poured another measure of water. "Yes, Eymard, what do you want?" He scowled like a petulant child. "Build something? Pen up something? What?" He took another long drink.

"Would you marry my Milkan?"

Barak choked, spluttering his water. "Say again?"

A chuckle rose inside Eymard, joy flowing over his entire body. "I've been waiting months for you to ask, but I see I must take matters into my own hands. Listen to me, son. I'm an old man, and my Creator will call me home soon. I want Milkan settled before I take that journey. So, I ask you—in all earnestness—will you marry my Milkan?"

Barak's eyes widened. He glanced around as if seeking a place to hide.

Milkan strolled forward, smiling innocently. "Grandfather,

supper is hot. You ready?"

Glancing from Barak to Milkan, Eymard pursed his lips. "Not now, child. You go ahead. I'll be with you shortly. I must get an answer from Barak, or I'll not rest easy tonight."

Milkan's smile vanished as she turned her luminous eyes on Barak. "I'm sure he'll do whatever you ask, Grandfather."

Turning like a man in a trance, Barak faced Eymard. "In that case, yes, old man, I will take Milkan for my wife."

Milkan dropped her gaze and flushed. "Oh!" She turned on her heels, her black hair swishing across her back as she scurried to her dwelling.

Eymard chuckled. "She's surprised but pleased. Like you—she sees much but speaks little." Eymard sighed deeply. "You're a lucky man, Barak. And I'm content, for I believe she is a lucky girl."

~~~

Aram strode out of his house on a bright sunny afternoon and scowled. When he had heard that Barak would take Milkan for his wife, his mood had darkened. Had not Eymard once hinted that he would be the father of a great nation and that the beautiful young woman would be his wife? Though Namah had improved, she was still just Namah and had only given him two daughters—one with a deformed hand. Nothing great could come from such seed. His weary heart hardened into a tight knot.

When Barak suggested a hunt, Aram's spirits rekindled. He always enjoyed the hunt, and wild pigs were a special challenge.

A thickset young man ran panting to Aram, struggling to catch his breath. "They're drinking by the stream...near the lake. Barak says hurry...or you'll miss your chance."

Aram grabbed his spear and rushed forward, his dark thoughts scattering.

The passel of wild hogs bunched together in a thicket where

low bushes and saplings grew near the water's edge. A meandering stream flowed from the northern tree lands and spilled into the lake. The hogs jostled one another in their eager thirst.

As Aram approached, an over-hasty youth let loose a spear, setting off fierce squealing and fighting as some hogs tried to force their way back toward safety and others tried to get to the water.

As the turmoil at the water's edge increased, Barak urged everyone away. His eyebrows knit in frustration.

When Aram thrashed through the thicket, the hogs grew more frenzied.

Barak nudged Eoban as Aram strode forward. He held up his hand in warning. "Careful, Aram! It's slippery—"

Seeing Barak's retraining gesture, Aram's scowl deepened. He thrust his spear forward and jutted his jaw. "I've been hunting longer than you've been—"

Suddenly, his foot slid out from under him. Stomach leaping, he tried to regain his balance but jerked too far forward. Unable to stop the momentum, he slipped into cold, muddy water.

The now furious hogs found in Aram a source on which to vent their confusion and anger.

Horrified calls rose from the watching crowd, some running back while others surged forward for a better look.

Barak leaped into the mass of writhing bodies while a few of the heartiest men followed behind. Several hogs were dispatched quickly, but too many were still intent on their personal mission of destruction. Barak waded up and began slamming against them with the full weight of his body and stabbing them with his spear. When he reached Aram, he reached through the mass of furious pigs into the murky water and grabbed his arm, screaming lustily for assistance. With Eoban's help, they pulled Aram from the slippery bank onto safe ground.

The passel of pigs scattered into the safety of the woods while the hunters stood around their fallen leader.

Sucking in deep breaths, Barak gripped his stomach, a retching wave of nausea rising to his throat. Lifting his hands, he gagged. Two fingers on his right hand had been bitten off. Blood poured down his arm as he stared transfixed at his mangled hand. He fell stonily to the ground next to Aram. With a moan, he passed out.

~~~

Barak sat in the shade of an oak tree, which overhung the great lake, cradling his bandaged hand. He stared blankly ahead.

Eymard strolled nearby, gazing at the calm blue water.

Evening clouds of orange, pink, and purple glowed in a glorious arrangement.

Eymard absorbed the scene in a long breath. "Even after a great loss, the Creator comforts us with natural beauty."

Barak sat in stony silence, staring at nothing.

Laying his staff down, Eymard settled close at hand.

Averting his gaze, Barak blinked back tears and shifted his damaged hand. "So good—yet your Creator allows so much suffering." He bent his head. "Not just mine—but Aram's. He'll never be the same."

Eymard clasped his hands in his lap and lifted his gaze to the first star. "Aram bears many scars. He'll recover from this adventure too. And when he does, he'll have a new story to tell his daughters. In time, bitter memories fade, and new joys replace old sorrow."

Brooding over the water, Barak's voice dropped to a growl. "Will a tragedy be less a tragedy because time has passed?"

Eymard merely folded his arms around his skinny knees. He inhaled a deep breath. "Truth remains true into eternity. But one understands truth better in the passing of time." He paused, peering at Barak. "In deep suffering, deep learning takes place."

Barak shook his head. "What in this great world am I supposed to learn from this?" He lifted his thickly bound, damaged hand.

Eymard whispered as if not to frighten away the last rays of light still peeking over the edge of the earth. "Your loss will teach you many things, but perhaps it will be your response to your loss that will teach you the most."

A tear slipped down Barak's face.

Eymard stood. "I'll leave you for now, but Milkan will call you to supper soon." He paused as he passed. "The sun has set, but the Creator will raise it again, and we shall meet another day."

Barak still sat, staring at nothing, when Milkan called him for supper.

Laying her hand on his shoulder, she knelt beside him. "Are you in pain?"

He turned and peered through the darkness at her shadowy form outlined by the evening starlight. "Do you really want to marry a man with only three fingers on his right hand?"

Milkan lifted the bandaged hand to her face and kissed it. "It will be my honor."

Barak trembled in cold and confusion. "There's no honor in being stupid. I didn't even save Aram. Surely, you'd do better to marry a man with two good hands."

Milkan tipped her head, peering into his eyes. "You risked yourself to help a friend. The deed was a valiant one! Could I love you less for your injury?" She kissed his cheek. "I'd be missing more than you if I did not value your worth."

Leaning forward, Barak kissed her forehead. "I don't have to wait for morning to see the sunrise."

Chapter Thirty-Four

—Grassland—

Resolve

Eoban stood outside Obed's house under the hot sun and observed his friend's face. He folded his arms high over his chest and tapped the ground with his foot.

Obed leaned on the doorpost, a mallet dangling by the tie in his hand. "Eoban, you're sure these aren't rumors spread through idle tongues and imaginative minds?"

Grunting, Eoban stomped a few feet away. "Would I come to you with a story? I went to see for myself." He turned on his heel and faced Obed, slapping his fist into his hand. "I know looted homes and burned crops when I see them! I saw the battleground where the few and valiant stood to defend their wives and children. I heard the wails of widows and orphans. These attackers are swift and vicious. I could almost wish that Neb were here to face them."

His gaze sweeping the ground, Obed placed the mallet on the bench. He shook his head, looking weary and perplexed. "That would not do." Glancing up, he rubbed his forehead. "I need time to think."

Eoban stomped forward. "There's nothing to think about. We must prepare for battle. We don't know when we'll be attacked, but with our wealth of animals and crops, it won't take long."

Obed waved to the broad expanse. "And how do we battle the whole world? We know nothing about the men we'd face or the weapons they'd use. Tell me something for certain!"

Jabbing Obed's shoulder, Eoban glowered. "I don't know who will attack or where they'll come from—I only know that if these invaders find us unprepared, they will kill us. We must do something!"

Frowning, Obed jabbed back. "Do not forget—I'm your leader. You're supposed to show respect."

Closing his eyes, Eoban waved the comment away with a snort. He began pacing before the house.

"But I do agree." Obed slid his knife from his belt and studied the blade. "Sharpening our weapons isn't enough. We need to make ourselves so strong that hardened warriors will tremble at the thought of fighting us."

Peering at Obed, Eoban paused. "What do you have in mind?"

"An idea. Bring Ishtar. I'll send word to Aram that we need his counsel."

Resuming his pacing, Eoban grimaced. "Aram is still recovering from his wounds. We shouldn't bother him."

"Aram may not look the same, but Jonas says he is healthy—at least on the outside. His spirit may be as dark as a moonless night, but he has a worthy friend in Barak—though he doesn't see it." He slid the blade back into his belt. "Aram is not the man he was."

"If so, why call him to a council?"

"We must. He's still the leader of a large and vibrant clan, and as you said, we must act quickly. We can't wait for him to appoint a new leader. Perhaps the threat of war will draw out the noble spirit hiding inside."

Eoban tightened his belt and adjusted his tunic. "I hope so. I'll leave the calling forth spirits to you. I'll see Ishtar. Surely, he'll come to our aid. He knows all too well the threat that hangs over us."

"He may be more prepared than we are." Obed perched on the edge of a bench and faced the distant hills.

A lone hawk swooped across the sky, cawing as it flew.

Eoban wiped his sweaty brow and watched the bird soar

away. "It's hot for this time of the year. Wish it would rain."

"We never know when—or if—the rains will come again."

"And I have the reputation for being the gloomy one! I'll tell Jonas to store half the harvest in my house, so I'll be ready for whatever happens."

"If you'd just get yourself a wife, you'd never need to worry." A smile flooded Obed's face as Jonas strolled toward him.

Lifting his spear from where it rested against the house, Eoban nodded. "That's fine for you to say! There's only one woman like Jonas, and she's yours. I'm too spoiled by her perfection to accept a lesser woman. So I'll have to live out my lonely years—"

Laughing, Jonas tweaked Eoban's ear as she passed and strode to Obed's side. "I saw you playing with Onia today, and I also noticed the way Obal watches at you. She's a good girl with a large heart. You might give her a chance to make you happy."

Pounding the butt of his spear into the dirt, Eoban turned away. "Yes, a large heart and large feet, large hands—a large body. The girl is almost as big as me! I'd fear for my life if I crossed her." He strode away, calling back. "After playing with your little ones, I always give them back!" As Eoban sauntered on, children tagged behind, grabbing his tunic and calling his name.

Obed chuckled and encircled Jonas in an embrace. "He's jealous, you know. He really loves you."

Jonas slapped Obed's hand. "Eoban's my friend. He's just afraid."

Choking back laughter, Obed stared after his friend. "Eoban, afraid? The man is afraid of nothing! If ever there was a man looking for a battle, it's Eoban. He can't even wait for the next battle; he has to bring it to our door."

Jonas' eyes widened and her grip on his arm tightened.

"Why? What do you mean?"

Obed pulled her closer, his gaze rising over the bustling village. "Probably nothing. But Eoban is right. The more prosperous we are, the more likely someone will want to take what we have."

"Who now?"

"Clans have been attacked by men from the north. They looted and burned the way the River Clan used to do, but this sounds more organized—bigger. We might find ourselves fighting not just one enemy but many."

Jonas laid her head on Obed's chest. "We have the children, the babies." One hand curved around her expanded middle. "This one is due any time."

"Don't worry. I've been thinking. And if my idea works, few marauders will venture to attack us."

Pulling away, Jonas peered into his eyes. "What? Tell me. I need to know."

"Have you ever heard of a nation?"

"A nation? Like a gathering of clans?"

"Yes, exactly. We'll form treaties with the Lake Clan and the River Clan—band together as brothers—and whenever there is trouble, we'll come to each other's aid as only brothers can. Word will spread of our agreement and few will want to test our combined strength."

Jonas passed her hand over her belly. "The baby's kicking." She closed her eyes with a sigh. "A nation. We've been so in spirit these past years."

Obed nodded, his jaw firm. "Let's share our resolve with the world. It's good to be strong—but it's even better to let our enemies know it."

Chapter Thirty-Five

—River Clan—

Haunted

Pele's hand fell to her side as Ishtar slouched across the village. She furrowed her brow, blinking in the strong light. She glanced aside.

Hagia only shrugged with her palms up, helpless. Returning to her work, she squinted as she cut and cleaned the fresh fish for their midday meal.

Pele gripped her paddle and beat the worn hides hanging in the warm sunshine. Her eyes followed Ishtar's every move as he meandered through the village, his face a mask, while Eoban strode at his side.

Looking over, Eoban patted Ishtar's arm and casually sauntered her way.

Ishtar wandered out of sight.

Eoban stopped between Pele and Hagia.

Each woman continued her work, watching him from the corners of their eyes.

Glancing from Pele to Hagia, Eoban grinned. "It's good to see such devoted industry." His stomach growled. Flushing, he rubbed his stomach and leaned toward Hagia. "Could you spare a bit of fish for a hungry traveler?"

Her eyes shining, Hagia bowed. "I'm the best cook in the clan if the truth be known. Please, sit. I'll fix you something hot and delicious." Before she bustled into her house, Hagia gestured for Pele to make Eoban comfortable.

Scrambling to her feet, Pele pulled a rush mat aside and

placed it in the shade, motioning for Eoban to sit comfortably. Eoban shuffled over and plunked down on the ground. "Whew, what a hot day!"

With trembling hands, Pele poured water from a jug and set a bowl and cloth by his side.

Absently, Eoban dipped his fingers and sprinkled water on his face.

Pele frowned and handed him the cloth.

After wiping his face, Eoban cleared his throat and leaned closer. "Pele, what's happened to Ishtar to make him act like he has had a knock on the head? I have been here all day, and he'll not speak clearly. Everything is a riddle. I should've sent Obed to figure out his secrets."

Glancing around, Pele lowered her voice and wrung her hands. "He'll speak to no one—not even Hagia. She says that he should marry—he'd feel better—but he's not interested."

"You've no idea what is bothering him? Surely, if a wife were the problem, he could have his choice. There must be something—"

Squaring her shoulders, Pele straightened. "His father's spirit haunts him."

Eoban's mouth fell open and he jerked back.

"It's true! I hear him cry at night. Hagia hears nothing, but I've heard Ishtar call his father's name…and speak as if he were talking to him."

Eoban's lips turned down like a man who's swallowed a bitter draught. "I don't believe such nonsense. Death is death. Once gone, we're not allowed to return."

Pele knelt at his side, clenching her hands, as she implored him. "But you must believe me. There is a spirit world, and spirits can bring either good or evil."

Eoban, unblinking, draped his arms over his bent knees. "How do you know?"

"I've seen them."

Eoban rubbed his jaw. "Well—if he *thinks* he's talking with spirits, this could be the answer to the riddle. But we need leaders who can see and think clearly!" He sighed and squeezed his eyes shut. "It's best I know the truth."

Pele bit her lip. "It's not his fault—Ishtar can't help himself." She settled back on her haunches. "And neither can you."

Hagia toddled forward bearing a heavy-laden tray.

Eoban rose and opened his hands to accept the tray, his eyes glittering with hungry anticipation.

Pele climbed to her feet and stepped back. Her gaze turned to Ishtar, who paced across the village with his head down and his eyes haunted. Her voice dropped to a whisper. "But I can."

Chapter Thirty-Six

—Lake Clan—

Thinking Like a Man

Aram stepped into his dwelling, letting the heavy door flap close behind him. He leaned his staff against the wall and untied his belt. His tunic, free from constraints, hung loosely on his body. With a sigh, he plunked down onto his mat.

In the corner, Namah nursed the baby while Bethal slumbered on a fur blanket next to her.

Pulling a water flask off a low shelf, he took a long drink and gazed at his wife and children. He never mentioned Gizah's disfigured hand, and as far as he knew, no one dared to voice the ancient custom of killing undesirable babies.

If anyone mentioned Gizah's hand in her presence, Namah glared at the speaker into silence. The only exception Namah made was when a little child would ask about it. Then Namah would lift the hand and smile. "My daughter is special. The Creator set her apart. She'll have special gifts to make up for this small loss."

Aram watched her as she hummed softly and lay down. He rubbed his chin as the shadows from the fire flickered against the dark walls. His gaze traveled from her curving hips to her rounded breasts and lingered on her face.

Glancing up, her eyes met his. She grinned.

A tingle ran down his arms. Aram grinned back.

Unlatching the baby from her breast, Namah laid the contented infant next to her sister and shuffled over to her husband.

His arms folded around his bent knees, Aram shivered and

scooted aside.

After tugging a blanket from the corner, Namah settled it around his shoulders. "Are you hungry?"

Aram shook his head and massaged his damaged leg. "Just the evening chill—it bothers my leg."

Namah retreated to the back of the room and returned with a clay dish. She dipped her finger in an oily mixture and crouched at his side. "Where?"

He rubbed his calf.

Settling on the ground before him, Namah massaged the ointment on his leg. "Jonas said this helps with deep wounds, stops the cramping." She bent her head, her fingers gently circling up and down his leg, her long dark hair falling loose over her shoulders.

Caressing her head with his hand, Aram studied his wife in the dim light as if he had never seen her before. "Namah?"

Glancing up, her eyebrows rose. "Yes?"

Swallowing, Aram leaned back and rested his full weight on the wall. "You're a different woman. From the time of Irad's death to now, you've changed so much. I don't know you anymore. Are you one woman or two?"

Beginning work on the other leg, Namah pulled his tunic up his thigh and slathered on the ointment, massaging his leg in caressing circles. "I've changed. It's true. I've traveled on a long journey with many twists and turns."

Keeping her head bent to her task, her hair fell like a curtain before her face. "I've always been uncomfortable with the world. Maybe because I'm ugly, I don't know. After Ana died, you chose me as your wife, and I was happy to please you. I scolded and demanded that everyone obey your slightest wish, not realizing how it made me repugnant to everyone. Soon, I dreamed of an escape, of becoming great like the cat through cunning and fearlessness. But they were foolish dreams. I'm no cat, and I have no taste for murder."

Namah exhaled a long breath. "When Irad offered escape, I thought perhaps I could become great through him. I was stupid…and lucky to live to repent my mistake."

Pulling his tunic into place, she laid the ointment aside and snuggled up to him, wrapping the blanket around her shoulders too. "Jonas told me wonderful stories and said that I could do noble deeds and be welcomed as a sister—not an enemy. She lived her friendship, and I envied her. But after a time, I realized that it was her smile as much as her deeds that drew people to her."

Chuckling, Namah rested her head against Aram's shoulder.

"I copied her every move and expression. But Jonas is kind. She told me I had worth of my own, that I was not supposed to be exactly like her." She glanced at Aram, who stared straight ahead.

"I speak to her Creator now, and though He does not use words, I feel I understand, and I'm drawn to Him. To everyone."

Her gaze drifted across the room. "Our children have been the answer to a desire I didn't even know I had. Now I understand who I'm meant to be—and it's made all the difference."

Aram rested his head on hers and sighed. A tear trickled down his face. He shuddered.

Namah jerked forward and peered into his face. "What's wrong?"

Thrusting out his scarred hands, Aram's voice trembled. "Who am I supposed to be, now?"

Clasping his hands, Namah crouched before him. "You are Aram, my husband, the leader of this clan—a man made on purpose by our Creator."

"Once, I believed that, but now—"

Though you have been badly injured, still, you're alive! I love you. Our daughters will love you, and the scars will be nothing to them."

Pulling Namah back under his arm, Aram embraced her and sighed. "I'm a tired, bitter old man." He kissed her forehead. "You should rest now. The little ones will give you no rest in the morning."

Namah leaned in and kissed Aram, caressing his chest.

The baby sniffled a weak cry.

Tucking Namah's hair behind her ear, Aram jutted his chin in the direction of the children. "Go and take care of them." He eased himself up to his feet. "I need a bit of air before I sleep."

The baby's crying rose to a wail.

Namah scurried over and scooped the bundle into her arms. She glanced at Aram as he stood at the door. "I'm here, Aram."

With a nod, he stepped out into the cool night air. He peered across the moonlit village.

Suddenly, a soft voice spoke off to the side. Eymard tottered over and perched on a log bench.

Aram glanced over. "What're you doing wandering about so late, old man? Don't you have dreams to dream like the rest of us?"

A soft chuckle wafted up into the star-studded sky. "Oh, I dreamed enough in my youth for many lifetimes. I don't need sleep as I used to." He clasped his hands and peered into the vast universe. "You're feeling stronger now?"

Aram shook his head. "Not strong enough to claim Milkan as my wife—if that's what you mean." He turned and looked Eymard full in the face, his voice dropping low. "Why did you tell me that the Creator ordained me to become the leader of a great nation when it's clear He planned no such thing?"

"Me? You think this old body capable of offering nations and making prophecies? I'm no such man." He raised his hands in protest. "Yes, it's as you say. I did say that a voice puts words into my mind. But I told you at the time, I didn't know for certain whom He meant."

"You said it must be either Barak or—" His voice trembled. "You led me to believe a fantastic story about great things to come. Instead of greatness, I'm the father of a misshapen girl and misshapen myself. The blessings of God, I suppose!"

Eymard raised his hands as if in supplication. "I heard a voice speak. But I was wrong to speak of what I could not comprehend. In the end, it only made sense to marry Milkan to the man she loves."

"Milkan loves Barak?"

Eymard nodded his head slowly. "And he loves her. Barak has suffered too. It is no small thing to lose two fingers. It seems the Creator wished to test you both. Perhaps He trains His great ones with great trials. He asks things of us we would never ask of ourselves. He forces us to take the shape He intends for us as a stone is molded to fit the building it'll belong to. He can make us greater than we are."

Staring at his damaged hands, Aram blew air between his lips. "Surely, the God who carved the moon and the stars could've shaped me better than this?"

"Surely, you are thinking like a man—not as God."

Aram dropped his hands to his sides. "Barak lost fingers and gained a wife. How does he take the exchange?"

"He adjusts well, though he carries the burden of your anger. He thinks you aimed your spear at him."

Aram dropped his head to his chest. "Anger darkened my mind."

"I pray your mind grows clear once more, for this clan needs you and Barak in full fighting form once again." He tipped his head, peering at Aram. "Your courage is still intact?"

With a jerk, Aram straightened.

"That's why I've come tonight. Obed sent a man with a message, but you kept him waiting so long, he left."

Aram frowned. "Was he a messenger? My mind's been confused."

Eymard nodded. "But now is a time for clear thought and decisive action. Are you ready?"

Rubbing his sore leg, Aram's gaze wandered to his doorway. He stood and straightened his shoulders. "Could Barak row me over to the Grasslands?"

With a twinkle in his eye, Eymard raised his skinny arms. "If he's unable, I'll be glad to do the job."

For the first time in months, joy spread from Aram's middle and reached his eyes.

Chapter Thirty-Seven

—River Clan—

Proof of the Need

Pele woke with a start, her dwelling shrouded in the black night.

No moon brightened the trees, and no night animals broke the silence. A faint breeze blew, but the grass hardly moved in the heavy air.

She sat up and sensed a storm drawing near. Memories of Ishtar's anguished cries and a strange dream sent shivers down her back. She wrapped a thin blanket around her shoulders and crept to the doorway. A stronger, howling wind aroused the night from its slumber. The dull thuds of pots falling over sounded in the distance, and the lines of hanging fish swung madly.

Rushing forward, a blast of cool air filled her lungs and tingled over her arms and legs. She gasped. Her blanket flapped wildly, wrapping itself like a scared child around her legs. In frustration, she tossed it aside and raced back to the tangling fish lines. She grunted, vexed, as one fell to the dusty ground.

Struggling with an end of the sinewy rope, she pulled at the tie. Her fingers slipped and a fingernail tore. Her long, black hair flew into her face. She spluttered, shaking her head in fury to match the storm. "Of all the ridiculous things! I can't even—"

From behind, a familiar voice and large, strong hands

grasped the lines. "Here, let me." Eoban grasped the lines firmly, allowing her to work the knot as he struggled to free the week's worth of dried fish. "These fish won't be dry much longer." He pulled out his knife, cut the other end of the coil, and together they rolled up the lines and bundled them into a storage hut.

Rain pelted their backs as they rushed for the shelter of Pele's dwelling.

Eoban ushered her forward. "Go in now before you're soaked."

In the doorway, Pele turned and wiped back her rain-soaked hair as water streamed down her face. "Thank—"

Eoban pressed her shoulder, interrupting. "Pele, do me a favor?"

"Of course." She peered at his kind, strong face.

"Tell Ishtar that I returned home. I've had a strange dream, and I'm uneasy. He must forget about his father and join us in council tomorrow. Will you tell him, Pele?"

Dropping her gaze, she whispered. "Yes, Eoban, I'll tell him, though I doubt he'll listen to you—or me."

Large drops of water dripped off Eoban's beard. Clasping his spear, he appeared like a rock in a mighty stream with water pouring swiftly over him.

Pele's eyes widened. "You're not going to cross the lake in this storm, are you? Surely, you'll wait for morning and speak to him once more?"

Eoban shook his head vigorously, sending a shower of spray all around. "I dare not wait. Though I don't believe in the unseen, I've had a dream that sent my heart leaping, and my limbs will not be stilled. I must go. And you must convince Ishtar that danger approaches."

Pele touched his arm gently. "I'll do as you ask. Ishtar shall know the truth before the sun sets tomorrow."

Eoban smiled with an approving grunt and turned to go. He mumbled. "Now, if the gods will just calm this storm a bit."

Pele smiled at his contradiction and watched him hustle into the murky night. Breathing through a silent prayer, she turned to her mat.

The raindrops diminished. The stillness of the night returned, and the stars reappeared in the night sky.

She tugged her blanket around her wet shoulders and settled on her mat. The dream returned to her mind. She could see herself climbing a steep cliff with a bundle on her back.

The rain stopped, the wind calmed, and a bird chirped in the distance.

A voice rang in Pele's ears. *Night must give way to day.*

Stiffening, she glanced around. All quiet. Resettling, she pulled the blanket tighter. She knew the cliff in her dream. A tableland sat at the top of that same cliff directly north. But how could she climb it and return home again before sunset?

She rose, wrapped a belt around her shift and tucked a small knife into a safe fold. Exchanging the blanket for a wrap, she swept it over her head and shoulders and slipped her feet into her sandals.

Stepping outside, she glimpsed the stars sparkling overhead and the clean, fresh smell of wet earth and green grass filled her lungs. She imagined Eoban trudging through the tall grasses toward his home. They were both taking risks. They were both fulfilling destinies allotted to them. She grinned in the darkness, her eyes on the faint light that highlighted the hills in the distance. Courage was not new to him, but a steadfast spirit gladdened her heart. Wrapping the shawl tight around her, she scurried through the village, toward the hills.

The moon edged its way down the western sky. Pele trudged over wet grass and brushed past saplings that had ancestors by the river. Her gaze fixed on the hills in the distance. Owls hooted, and night animals called to one another.

She stumbled in weariness, her shoulders drooped, and her mind grew dim, disordering her thoughts as they flickered from one image to another.

Lud's face floated before her mind's eye. She smiled wistfully at the image of his parents welcoming him home. A shudder wrenched her from the pleasant images. What if no one was left? Waving this thought from her mind, she kicked stones from the rocky path. He had said that if he found no sign of his family, he would return quickly. Surely, he had met with good fortune. The last echo of a wolf's cry drifted into the distance. The image of him lying dead beneath the paw of a vicious animal widened her eyes in horror. She waved that thought away too.

It was near-dawn when she realized that her aching feet had begun to climb. She slid on the rubble-strewn foothills. Light brightened the horizon. It grew rockier. She looked up and blinked at the tableland looming just above her. How was she going to climb to the top? Her feet did not share her indecision but simply kept moving.

Clinging to handholds, she pulled her body upward. At the top, she thrust her body over the edge and rolled onto the grassy pasture. Inhaling deep breaths, she let the new day's sun soak into her exhausted limbs. New life filtered through her.

She peered northeast. By the river's edge lay what she had hoped and feared to see—the enemy's camp. She sucked in a breath. Even from this distance, the men appeared much too large. Spears and huge shields leaned in piles against towering trees. Over smoky fires, enormous black kettles bubbled. Surely, they must eat twice what a normal man would need.

As one giant turned in her direction, fear shot through her body, dropping her to the ground in a shivering heap. Her heart pounded as her promise to Eoban echoed in her mind.

Clenching her jaw, she scurried down the enemy hillside, crouching as she ran toward the camp. Clusters of trees and bushes grew all around the mountains. Scampering from one hiding place to another, she finally stopped just outside a group of four tents.

Giant warriors with small heads and oversized jaws grunted and gestured as they sharpened their massive weapons. She shuddered, her breath quickening. A pile of weapons with

sharp cunning blades shimmered in the morning sunlight.
Sliding to damp and musty ground, she closed her eyes. A sudden commotion, an argument, broke out near her. She squeezed her eyes tighter, awaiting the climax, but the sound of a drum broke the tension and all arguments faded. The warriors hustled away.
Opening her eyes, she peeked around the tree. She was alone. A large gathering congregated near the river's edge. *Are they holding council? Eating?* She shook her head. This was no festival. Her eyes strayed to the pile of weapons. They were so large that there would be no swift getaway. With a deep breath, she trotted over and seized the smallest spear and a long obsidian knife, which she stuffed into her belt. Half-dragging the spear, she scuttled back to her hiding place.
The rumble of voices and padding footsteps drew near. They began muttering—arguing.
Pele did not think, she simply stepped away, slowly, step by weary step. She never looked back.
When she reached the summit once again, she lay still and chuckled at her own foolish bravery.
As the sun climbed into the sky, she realized that her entire body ached with exhaustion. Closing her eyes, she tried to imagine her Sky Warrior. Lud's face floated before her instead. With a weary sigh, she rolled onto her elbow and pushed herself upright.
The warriors bunched into large clusters.
Frowning, Pele stared at the fresh green grass and muttered to herself. "They haven't been here long—and it looks like they're planning to leave soon." Fear gripped her heart.
She tripped as she scampered down the far side of the hills, trying to balance the heavy spear in her arms. Closing her eyes, she prayed for strength and jogged faster.

~~~

Hagia stopped Ishtar in his tracks.
Ishtar sat against a tree and glanced at his mother in dumb

surprise. "I haven't seen Pele or Eoban. I don't know where they've gone."

"Perhaps they were injured in the storm or—"

Ishtar's eyes rolled skyward. "Eoban is a man, and Pele is a woman. Perhaps Eoban has finally found his match. It's time for him to marry and settle down. Unfortunately, this will give him another reason to come here and annoy me."

Hagia peered doubtfully at her son.

Ishtar's hair hung loose and tangled. Dust and grim covered his face. Even his tunic looked ragged.

Hagia wrinkled her nose. "Son, it's been too long since you've refreshed yourself in the river. Take a swim while I get you something to eat."

Ishtar sat with his arms hanging loose at his sides and his legs stretched out across the dust in front of his dwelling. He stared into the distance, unconcerned.

Wringing her hands, Hagia followed her son's gaze. "Where is she?" Pele might not have answers, but at least she always listened sympathetically.

Slipping inside her dwelling, Hagia pulled her clay god off the shelf. His arms snapped. Swallowing back a gasp, she hastily put it back and returned outside.

Her hands on her hips, she appraised her son. "Ishtar, you must tell me what weighs on your mind. Pele says she hears you cry out at night, as if you're doing battle with some terrible foe. Tell me..." She knelt at his side. "Has Neb's spirit returned to trouble you?"

Turning eyes of pity on his mother, Ishtar shook his head in wide-eyed wonder. "Neb? He has no strength now. All his actions were directed by his elders in spirit as was Grandfather and his father before him." He leaned over and whispered in a rough unnatural voice. "But there are spirits that have never known a mortal life...never suffered the loss of blood or the pain of flesh. They live like the wind but have wills of their own. They're cunning."

Hagia cowered and moaned, her hands shielding her head. "How can a man fight such an enemy?" She gripped his shoulder. "Why do they strike at you? You're not like your father."

"I don't consent to their will as Neb did, but I can be tempted. Still, they have no hold over me. I've become more powerful than they ever were."

Hagia tugged her hair like a woman half mad. "He has appeared to you, then?"

"Only as a shadow. I'd pity him, but he has chosen his fate."

Hagia muffled a sob. "I'd never survive an apparition. Can't you send him back to the netherworld, so he'll pay no more visitations?"

Ishtar straightened his shoulders. "I'm tested. All worthy of greatness are tested."

Hagia shrugged. "To what end? Do we all die and turn into horrors?"

"No! Our fates accord to our deeds." His eyes softened. "You've always been a woman of service. You have nothing to fear." Rising, Ishtar stared off into the distance.

Climbing to her feet, Hagia brushed the dust from her dress, a glimmer of a smile wavering. "I wish I had no fear." Her eyes strayed to the horizon, her brow furrowed.

A small figure swayed in the distance.

Hagia squinted and clasped her hands, her smile growing into full flower. "Well, it seems there are others this day will speak of visions, for I cannot but think that it was a vision that sent Pele out so early. She must be exhausted."

Ishtar's eyes narrowed.

The figure stumbled.

Ishtar's brows knit in confusion.

The figure stooped low, nearly doubled over. She stumbled again.

Hagia's smile faded, her hands twitching with anxiety. She jogged forward and stopped.

Pele's dirty clothes, disheveled hair and sweating face came into focus. In her arms, she bore the weight of a massive spear.

Ishtar sprinted ahead to intercept her.

Hagia's rushed forward with her arms out.

Pele halted, leaning on the massive spear, sucking in shuddering breaths. Her head dropped to her chest.

Hagia screamed. "Pele!"

Ishtar outdistanced his mother and reached Pele as she fell to her knees.

Hagia knelt at the girl's side. "Pele! What's happened? Where've you been?"

Ishtar stared at the massive spear that spoke louder than any human voice.

"Carry her, Ishtar. She's too weak to walk another step."

He swiveled toward his mother, glanced at Pele, and scooped her into his arms.

Pele relinquished the spear into Hagia's arms but met Ishtar's gaze. "A message from Eoban. You must go to a council meeting. I brought proof of the need." Her eyes closed, and her head fell on his shoulder.

With his head high but his eyes troubled, Ishtar carried the bone-thin, exhausted girl home.

Hagia settled Pele on a fresh blanket with water and food near at hand.

A fever rising, Pele tossed and turned in restlessness. By mid-afternoon, she awoke from a tormented sleep, rubbed her sunken eyes, and begged to see Ishtar.

Hagia shook her head and tried to get the trembling girl to eat and drink. Laying a damp cloth on Pele's head, she wagged her finger in admonition. "Lie still and rest. Such a foolish thing to do. Traveling all that way—to prove what rumors always say—an enemy waits at the door."

Pele nodded dumbly, but her gaze searched the doorway.

Hagia bustled off.

When Ishtar entered, Pele's eyes shone unnaturally bright at the massive spear in his hand.

"Pele, tell me, where did you get this? It's not from the clans around here."

Pele shivered. "Giants from the north. They're coming."

An eyebrow rose, and Ishtar pursed his lips in a low whistle. "From the north? What caused you to wander so far—how did you manage to come away with this trinket? Was it given to you?"

Struggling to sit up, Pele fell back against a pillow. "Not given, but stolen. I took it when the warriors quarreled. Now you know…you'll be prepared."

Titling his head, Ishtar lifted the spear and gestured to the door. "Did Eoban send you to get this?"

Pele's eyes rolled up as she convulsed in a violent shudder. She gasped. "Eoban's your friend. You wouldn't listen. I got proof." Her body clenched, and she fell back in exhaustion.

Hagia wrung her hands. Tears trailed down her face. "Such a journey with no guide to protect her. It's a wonder she survived to tell us."

Stepping outside, Ishtar leaned the spear against the wall. Returning, he strode to Pele and knelt on her pallet, taking her hand in his own. "Pele?"

She stirred, her eyes straining to open.

"Who were these warriors? What were they like? I must know."

Pele smiled and reached for his face, but her hand fell limp at her side. "Giants."

Ishtar stared, his hand holding hers. His gaze rose to the door and seemed to travel over the horizon to the mountains.

Hagia pressed Ishtar's shoulder. "You can do nothing for her now. Go and do as she says—seek the company of the council."

Rising, Ishtar clasped a knife and stuck it in his belt. "It's time. I'm ready to leave the mists behind and face the challenge of bone and flesh." He strode to the doorway. Looking back, he dropped his voice to a whisper. "Take care of her, but do not grieve if she passes. She has accomplished a mighty task."

"You'll go to Eoban and Obed?"

"First I need to speak to Joash."

"Joash?" Hagia spat her words. "He's a defeated fool who means you no good. Even Jonas with all her kindness could not turn his heart to goodness. He'll do you no service."

"If I leave this clan unattended, I'll return to a divided clan."

"The council chose you—the clan is yours. Why speak with Joash?"

"Because Joash has a determined spirit. That's more dangerous than the mightiest weapon."

Stepping outside, Ishtar called to a young man sitting near an open fire.

Hagia followed her son.

The youth looked up and trotted over to Ishtar.

"Tell Joash to meet me here. We're going on a journey."

The youth bounded away.

Ishtar strode toward the river.

Hagia hovered in the doorway. "Where are you going now?"

"I believe you hinted of my need to wash this morning." Ishtar waved as he strolled away. "I'll need a clean tunic and food for the journey. I'll leave as soon as possible."

"You're not taking Joash with you? You can't trust that man!"

Ishtar disappeared down a slope.

Hagia turned at the sound of a moan from inside. She started forward but stopped at the sight of Joash approaching.

As he grew close, Joash bowed in greeting, but his eyes held no warmth.

Hagia stiffened. "My son will be here shortly. He wants you for some service."

Joash stared at her as if inspecting some strange breed of animal. When he did speak, his words were heavy with boredom. "Where is young Ishtar today? Risen from his bed yet?"

She frowned and pointed to the river. "He's swimming but will return shortly. He has an important mission."

Joash's gaze strayed from Hagia to the side of her dwelling and the giant spear. His eyes widened as a new light entered.

He strode to the spear and lifted it. "Where did this come from?"

Hagia shrugged.

Joash flushed and stepped toward her. "Old woman, where did you get this?"

Hagia stepped out the doorway and planted her feet on the ground like roots of a mighty oak. "Tell me why it interests you so much! What do you know of such things?"

Joash glanced around and back at Hagia. He stepped closer and pointed the tip at her middle. "Tell me where this came from, or your fleshy carcass will join Neb's."

Moaning and swaying on her feet, Pele groped at the entrance of the dwelling. "Hagia!"

Turning, Joash pounded to Pele. "What do you know about this spear, girl?" Joash thrust the spear in Pele's face.

Pele tottered, stumbling backward.

Hagia rushed ahead and caught Pele as she collapsed in her arms.

Joash jabbed the spear at them. "Tell me!"

Hagia spat at his feet. "From the north. Giant men, Pele said. She's near death with exhaustion. Now leave us alone!"

Joash's eyes shone unnaturally bright. "Did she bring anything else back?"

Hagia glanced up and grinned.

"Only this!" Ishtar jabbed Pele's obsidian knife in Joash's back.

Joash turned his head. "You would attack from behind."

"I should kill you now and simplify my life." Ishtar pressed the knife a little harder.

Joash stiffened, flushing with rage.

Hagia nodded in angry satisfaction. "You're a dangerous beast who can't be trusted."

Flinging his arms wide, Joash raged. "As if I could ever trust you!"

Ishtar pressed his advantage, nicking Joash's flesh with the tip of the knife. Then he relaxed, releasing Joash. "You don't deserve to live, but I don't like the feel of blood on my hands. I'll let you go, but you'll leave here and never return."

Joash rubbed his back. "Since Neb's death, nothing's been the same." His eyes swiveled to Pele. "She's my slave. I ought to have her back before I go."

Ruffling like an angry hen, Hagia squawked. "She is no one's slave! Now go your way before my son changes his mind."

Suppressing a bitter smirk, Joash sauntered away.

Ishtar watched him a moment and then settled Pele inside the dwelling. Hagia busied herself preparing food and muttering. "Ishtar's leaving. It's about to rain, and you're sick with a fever. That stupid Joash still lives. I'm worn out. Haven't had a bite to eat all day, and giant men plan to attack us."

Pele's head swam with images.
Eoban standing in the pouring rain.
Lud's wistful face staring at the sky.
Hagia's fingers smoothing a clay pot.

Pele opened her eyes, but she did not see Hagia though she heard her shuffling about the room. A gleaming figure stood before her—not a warrior—a being of might and glory.

She reached high into the air—

Hagia turned and watched astonished.

A happy sigh broke forth from Pele's lips, her hand dropped to her side, and she laid still.

Hagia knelt beside the girl, her hands clasped over Pele's. Tears coursed down her face. "To think you were once merely a slave. Now you're as my own flesh. Don't go where I cannot follow!"

Ishtar stepped in, his gaze taking in the scene. He bowed his head.

Striding over, he caressed his mother's hair and closed Pele's eyes. "Don't feel bad, mother. Even now, she has better vision than we ever did."

Chapter Thirty-Eight

—OldEarth—

Exhilarating

Zuri stood behind a storage shed, propped his hands on his hips, and glared at his two companions. "Well, that was a complete waste of time."

Rolling his eyes, Teal leaned against a wall, while Ark wrapped his tentacles around his middle and huddled in the shade.

Their elongated shadows frothed in a background sea of tall grass. Large boulders marked the edge of the grassland beside the tree-lined stream. A small rodent scampered near, lifted its head in inspection, and then scurried away.

Ark shuffled closer, keeping his tentacles tight about his body. His gaze swiveled right to left and stopped on Teal. "You're sure you can get us out of here? What if someone arrives unexp—"

A ball rolled against Ark's Cresta boots. His eyes widened, horror blanching his mottled pink skin to bleached white.

A child scampered near, calling back to his friends. "It's over here! I'll get it."

Teal kicked the ball in the child's direction, morphed into a thick, hairy spider, and scampered after the ball.

The little boy scooped up the ball, saw the spider, and shrieked. Turning, he pelted away as fast as his legs would carry him.

Scuttling back to Zuri and Ark, Teal returned to his former human shape, sweating and panting. He leaned against the wall, sucking in deep breaths. "Normally, it doesn't take so much out of me—"

Glowering, Ark wagged a tentacle in the direction of the boy. "He could've squashed you with his foot."

Teal straightened, a frown building between his eyes. "No one squashes a poisonous spider with their bare foot—unless they have a death wish." His eyes narrowed. "Have you learned so little about humans?"

Swooshing one tentacle before him, Ark shuddered. "That child will bring his whole family to see the—the—giant arachnid."

Zuri tapped his foot. "Can we move on? Ark is right. We've over-stayed out time here. I can't see why we bothered to watch that stupid little interlude. It's not like we learned anything."

Frowning, Teal pointed to the largest boulder. "If we move beyond that rock and get behind the trees, we'll be out of their line of vision. Besides—" He pointed to the pink and purple horizon. "The sun's almost set. No one'll see us in the dark."

Without another word, Zuri plodded around the boulder to the copse of trees. Ark and Teal followed. Stopping on the bank, Zuri lifted his hand. "Now it's my turn. I want to get a series of proper samples. I've heard that there're valuable deposits not far from here."

Teal glanced at Ark. "You comfortable with going last?"

Ark shrugged. "I'm always accommodating. Besides, it's not like my mission has a deadline. Ha!" His face lighted up in a wide grin. "Private joke."

His eyelids dropping to half-mast, Teal turned to Zuri and waved him forward. "Then take the lead. As long as you don't blast a crater—or kill anyone—"

Zuri plowed into the water, his arms arched like a swimmer. "Stop with the accusations! I've never killed anyone." He glanced back at Teal, his gaze swiveling to Ark. "You should keep your eye on that one." He shrugged as he negotiated his way up the far bank. "Besides, you saw that girl die just a bit ago—it didn't seem to break any of your synapses."

Wading into the river, Teal's tunic darkened as it wicked up water. He threw his arms wide for balance, keeping his gaze fixed on the shoreline. "Pele is a perfect example of what I've been saying all along—humans are remarkable. She offered her life for her clan."

Ark stood on the far bank, his tentacles hanging limply at his side and staring at the foaming water. "Uh—Zuri?"

Stepping clear of the water, Zuri wiped drops off his mechanical bio-suit and laughed. "The child was besotted by the leader, that Ishtar. She'd have done anything to please him. But sad fact—he didn't even notice her."

Ark waved a tentacle. "Oh—Teal?"

Teal wrung the edge of his tunic dry. "Don't they teach you anything before they send you out?" He straightened and ran his fingers through his hair. "Ishtar saw Pele's sacrifice, and he cared deeply. But he has a job to do, so he must stay focused. Besides, he knows there's more to life than—"

Ark clapped his tentacles together. "Idiots!"

Teal glanced up. "Ark? What're you doing? Hurry up. We're on a schedule."

Murky liquid swirled in Ark's breathing helm. He harrumphed, sending boiling bubbles to the surface. "Normally, I'd be pleased as a Salean seal to jump into water, but unfortunately, the creator of these terrestrial bio-suits made them with one purpose in mind—to walk on *land*!" He lifted a soft booted foot and shook it in emphasis.

"Zuri smirked. "What? Will it dissolve…leaving you naked?"

Tight lipped, Teal shot Zuri a swift glance. "Come on. We'll carry him over."

Zuri clenched his hands into fists. "You're joking!"

Teal splashed into the stream. "Do you want your samples or not?"

Thrashing his way forward, Zuri passed Teal and gripped Ark by a tentacle. "Hurry up."

Ark shook his tentacle free. "On your shoulders. I'll be safer. And have a better view." He grinned benignly as Teal reached his side.

With a clenched jaw and tight lips, Teal lifted Ark. Zuri cursed under his breath in every foreign tongue he knew. Hoisting Ark between them, they carried the bulky Cresta to the opposite bank and dropped him unceremoniously.

Ark clapped his tentacles together, a smile drifting over his face. "I must admit—that was rather exhilarating."

Zuri slapped his head and groaned. "Oh blast!"

In unison, Teal and Ark turned and stared at the Ingot.

Zuri pointed across the stream. "I left my sample kit on the ship."

Chapter Thirty-Nine

—Grassland—

Come What May

Obed raised his hand, and the angry voices gradually lowered to a simmering rumble. In the late afternoon sunshine, Aram sat on his left while Ishtar sat cross-legged on his right. Barak and Eoban sat hunched across from him. Men from each clan circled around, some standing, some sitting.

Aram caressed a small stone. "It'd be best if both of your clans migrate over the water and settle on the northern shore. That's the place of greatest defense. Ishtar, your people are used to traveling. Surely it won't distress them to move again."

Ishtar shook his head, his hands balling into fists. "We should meet our enemy in battle—not run like rabbits. Our warriors will doubt their strength, and doubt leads to defeat."

Obed lifted his hands. "You're the source of their strength and inspiration. Demand their trust, and they'll follow you—no matter where you lead." He sighed. "But I, too, am reluctant to leave home. We have a great deal to lose." He glanced aside. "Aram, have you considered the possibility that they might come from the forest and force you back to the lake?"

Aram sniffed. "There's an unpleasant thought."

Obed rubbed his jaw. "Our clan has the largest supply of crops and livestock, and we're in a central location. Perhaps, all three clans should gather around our village. If the enemy approaches, we'll move in closer. And when the threat is driven off, everyone can return to their homes."

"What's left of them." Ishtar's jaw clenched as he rose to his feet. "If we are not going to force their hand, then it makes sense that my people gather near yours. We'll form a mighty chain of warriors less than a day's march from one another."

Aram tossed the stone aside and nodded. "Now there's a plan I can agree to. Our clans will be close yet remain independent. We'll gain strength but maintain our own identities."

Obed stood and turned to Ishtar. "How soon can you get everyone moving?"

Ishtar pointed to a dish of bread, cheese, and minced meat set to the side. "As soon as I've had something to eat."

Eoban grunted. "Thinking of food before duty!" He climbed to his feet. "In my time as a young warrior, I'd go for days without eating when necessary."

Rising, Barak tapped Eoban's girth. "It's been a long while since that occurred, warrior."

Obed chuckled.

Using his staff to keep his balance, Aram pointed to well-organized stack of weapons. "I want a better look at that great spear."

With a handful of nuts, Eoban stopped mid-motion. "There's nothing more to learn beyond what I told you. These are men great in size but small in imagination. A heavy spear makes a formidable weapon, but everything depends on the mind of the man who aims and throws."

Aram bit into a piece of thin bread wrapped over minced meat, and talked around his chews. "It'd be best to have both great weapons *and* great minds. Encourage the men to make their own great spears—anything the enemy can do, we can do better. After all, we have some giants among us, do we not?"

As the throng milled around the food platters, all heads nodded in agreement.

Obed glanced over. "Ishtar will see to the migration of his people while Aram—"

"I am afraid these legs of mine would only slow you down. Still—" Aram met Barak's gaze. "I'll send Barak in my stead."

Barak nodded at Aram, exchanging a silent understanding.

Obed clasped his hands together. "Then we all have our tasks before us, and we'll make ready. Be quick, Ishtar, lest the enemy find you in the middle of your migration when they attack."

Scowling, Aram lifted his hand. "That's a worthy fear. Barak, take twenty strong men to help guard the migration, especially when they travel across the open lands."

A tingling of relief and excitement spreading through him, Obed stepped forward. "Good thought. Send runners ahead, Ishtar, and when you're in the clearing, we'll join you to offer safe passage."

Grasping his spear, Ishtar stood tall, youthful, and proud. "My people will make a new beginning. Storytellers will sing of our great march in triumph—even in the face of danger. We'll make a new home and forge a better life. Sons will be named after the warriors of these days."

Aram lifted his hand in a salute. "We shall become one—united—like brothers."

Ishtar raised his head. A smile spread across his face. "Brothers!"

Obed nodded solemnly. "Come what may."

Chapter Forty

—Lake Clan—

We All Lost

Jonas settled her boys in front of wooden bowls filled with a mixture of fruits, nuts, seeds, and dark grains sweetened with honey. A carafe of fresh water sat on the shelf. As the boys ate, they poked each other and chattered more like cubs than boys. Jonas laughed at their antics until a shadow crossed Jael's face.

He raised his hand, stopping Tobia's antics, who turned to his younger brother, Onia, and tickled him until he fell over. Jael spoke over the ruckus. "Mother, how big are these giants? Eoban told me that they're as hairy as beasts, and they howl like wolves. Do they bite, you think?"

Tobia jumped to his feet. "They wouldn't bother me! Once they saw my spear and the anger in my eyes, they'd run away!"

Jael pushed his little brother to the ground with one hand. "Are they men at all?"

Jonas sipped her water and leaned back. She folded her dress of dark cloth about her. "There've been clans in the high mountains for as long as memory goes back. They're not like our people—or the Lake Clan—or even like the River Clan. These are wild, barbaric people with no love for the stories of the past or plans for the future. My grandfather once met travelers who lived in the low hills, and they'd seen these mountain men. He said that they were like slinking foxes, for they shied away from other men."

A frown creased Jael's forehead. "But why have they come out of the mountains now? And why do they want to attack us?

We've done them no harm."

"I don't know. Perhaps there's been famine that we've not experienced in our fertile lands. If Eoban hadn't seen the destroyed villages, I'd think it was merely a story to frighten the young."

Jael's eyes glinted in the dim light. "I'm making a spear of my own. When they come, I'll lay their leader in the dust."

Her gaze dropping, Jonas heaved a sigh. "Your father would've chosen a different way."

"And he died for doing so! He should've thought of his sons first and lived. If I'd been a man, I would've gone with him, and he would've returned home alive."

Her stomach churning, Jonas tried to embrace her son, but he jerked away.

"I am not a child looking for comfort. Eoban is teaching me the ways of a warrior." His lips curled. "Obed would rather think his enemy away. It was such foolishness that cost my father his life. I'll not fail to fight, for I'm the next in line to rule."

Jonas closed her eyes and clasped her hands before her lips. After a brief silence, she opened her eyes. "You're not a man yet, Jael. You have years of training and preparation before you can rightfully make that claim. Obed will agree with me—you must stay home and help the women and children." Her eyebrows arched. "You'd not abandon us when the warriors go off, would you?"

His scowl deepening, Jael pursed his lips and clenched his hands. "The women and children will only be safe if the men succeed. They'll need every spear—that includes mine. What use will I be if the enemy defeats our warriors? Besides—" He glanced at Tobia who stared at his brother wide-eyed. "You have Tobia to help you. Is that not so, Tobia?"

Tobia nodded, but as his eyes widened, his nod turned into vigorous head shaking.

Obviously impatient with the arguing, Onia picked up his bowl and threw it, hitting Tobia on the head.

Like a fallen warrior, Tobia fell backward.

Jael glanced from his brother to his mother. "Well, it's clear he's not ready for battle!"

Jonas scooped Onia into her arms and shooed her other two sons to the door. "Perhaps when these Mountain Men hear of our united clans, they'll grow shy once again and return to their homes. But in the meantime—"

A cacophony of voices rose outside. Men and women called to each other in urgent tones.

Frowning, Jonas scurried outside.

Jael followed and sprinted over to Obed.

Breathless, Jonas caught up with Jael and gripped Obed's sleeve. "What's happened? Where is everyone going?"

Obed took his wife by the arm and led her out of the way of the panicked crowd. "The enemy attacked Ishtar and his people as they traveled. They're trying to outrun them, but they're in no position to fight. The enemy will be here at any moment." He glanced up at the sound of a woman's scream. Heaving a deep sigh, he peered at Jonas. "Take the boys to the lake."

Her heart racing, Jonas swallowed and wrapped her arms around Onia. "They're coming this way? I thought they were going to the river?"

"There is no time to discuss this. Take the boys and go! Hurry!"

Jael gripped Obed's arm. "I want to fight, Obed. You'll need every spear and able hand. I'm no use if I run away."

Obed turned, his face red and his eyes wide. "Go with Jonas and take your little brothers! You'll defend them with your life. You're a warrior already. Now obey me!"

Tears welled in Jael's eyes as Obed turned and directed his men to move ahead.

Tobia gripped his mother's skirt, hugging her leg.

Jonas stared at Obed as if wanting to carve his face into her memory. Sudden shrieks and men's curses jerked her from her stupor. She hurried away, clutching Onia while Jael and Tobia jogged along on either side.

Aram trotted forward as men lined up facing east.

A herd of goats gamboled into the hills, distancing themselves from the noise and confusion.

A slight breeze stirred the dust, in contrast to the still form of Obed, who stood like a man carved from stone, his jaws clenched and his hand gripping his spear.

Aram marched up to Obed and stood shoulder-to-shoulder with him. He surveyed the beardless faces of the Grassland People and shook his head. "Your men were made to create—not to kill."

Obed grunted. "No men were made to kill."

Tipping his head, Aram shrugged. "Could've fooled me."

Aram assembled his men in the forefront so they would receive the first blow of the enemy's assault. He glanced aside when Obed gave new directions to his own men, moving them around to the side and further back. He caught Obed's eye.

With a snort, Obed's eyes glinted. "I have a plan."

Glimpsing at the men's furrowed brows and confused expressions, Aram sighed. He stepped forward, facing the assembly. "Men of the Grassland, Men of the Lake!" He lifted his arms. "Not for the first time do we face battle together. But today—" He gestured to Ishtar and his warriors. "—We include our brothers of the River Clan." He turned, his arms wide. "A united people, we will help one another as kinsmen have done from the beginning of time." He grabbed his spear and lifted it high. "We'll conquer the enemy and bring our families home again."

Aram stepped back. The assembled warriors glanced aside, shifting in uncertainty.

Leaping forward, a blazing light in his eyes, Eoban raised his arm. He held the figure of a woman and child that Onias had carved. "For our women! Our children!" He pumped his arm higher. "For Onias!"

As if a volcano exploded, the deep-throated roars of the hundreds of men responded. "For our women! Our children! For Onias!"

The shouting stopped almost as quickly as it had begun. All eyes turned to the dirt-streaked form of Ishtar as he bolted through the throng of bustling women ushering young children and babies toward the lake. Skidding to a halt in front of Aram and Obed, Ishtar heaved a deep, shuddering breath. "They're upon us!"

Aram braced himself. The onslaught was sudden and fierce. Spears, longer than any the warriors had ever seen, soared like swift eagles over defensive mud walls and into homes and yards and through open windows. Huge men with thick beards hurtled upon the unwary like wild boars. Once inside the village, they fought hand-to-hand with long knives and great clubs, which they swung with easy triumph.

Gripping his own formidable spear, Obed thrust forward, tripping an oncoming enemy. Without warning, he found himself drawn into the grasp of a fierce warrior who looked like a monster intent on eating his prey.

Standing in one place and spearing or stabbing the giants as they ran, Eoban dropped three of the enemy before him. He glanced at Obed. "They may be big, but they're not too bright!"

Locked in the grip of a massive arm, Obed threw a half-exasperated look at Eoban and then elbowed his opponent in the face. Regaining his footing, he knocked the giant senseless with a blow to the head with his spear. He raced over to Eoban, threw his whole weight against his friend's shoulder, and knocked him aside.

A spear flew by and thudded to the ground.

Eoban peered at Obed through narrowed eyes. "I was planning on catching that and sending it back!"

Aram fought shoulder-to-shoulder with Barak, who held his own against a giant of giants.

The brute swiped at Barak's throat.

Aram threw his spear, hitting the giant in the shoulder.

Knocking the spear aside, the giant turned his narrowed,

glittering eyes on Aram.

Aram backed up, but his weak leg faltered, and he fell. Grasping a club from a fallen warrior, he swung it over his head.

As the giant took aim, he grinned and grunted.

Swiveling to his side, Aram rolled out of the way.

Suddenly, the giant fell forward with a spear sticking from his neck.

Barak stood behind him, huffing. He offered his hand and pulled Aram to his feet.

Aram grinned. "I was going to save you—I thought."

Barak stiffened with a jerk and groaned as he slumped into Aram's arms. Another enemy had come up behind and stabbed Barak in the back. Letting Barak slip to the ground, Aram's wrath blazed. He gripped his club.

The brute took slow aim with his spear, a malicious smile playing on his lips.

Rather than swinging, Aram threw the club with both arms in an overhead swing. It maneuvered wildly, and to the attacker's wide-eyed surprise, found its mark as he stupidly stood there and received its full thrust.

Aram did not watch him fall but turned to Barak and covered him with his own body. Another hulking warrior shadowed him, but Aram spied help close at hand. "Ishtar!"

Pelting full tilt, Ishtar plowed into the giant and stabbed him in the chest. Sucking in deep breaths, he skirted aside and pulled the enemy's knife from Barak's back and dragged him to a sheltered corner away from the central fight.

Aram, sinking once again under the combined effort of two advancing enemies called for help.

Grabbing a spear, Ishtar dispatched one man with a quick thrust. Coming up from behind the other, he swung his knife in a perfect arc, dropping the giant to his knees. Ishtar pulled Aram away from his attacker and dragged him over to Barak.

Barak's eyes remained closed, but his breathing remained steady. Swallowing, he grasped Aram's arm. "Take care of

Milkan."

Aram shook his head as the battle swarmed around them. He leaned against the shed wall with sweat pouring off his dirt-streaked face. "She's your wife—you take care of her. If anyone's going to join their ancestors this day, it'll be me."

Two warriors sped by and another fell in front of them with spear sticking out of his limp body.

A giant lumbered forward, toed his dead enemy, saw the two men against the wall and lifted a war club.

Grabbing the spear from the fallen warrior, Aram rose shakily to his feet. He used his last bits of energy to shield himself and Barak from this newest attack, but his arms and legs trembled. In some part of his mind, he traveled back to the days of the cat when he had first seen a clansman being dragged away, and he had realized his own helplessness. Then he saw the body of his wife as she lay in death's slumber. Death stalked him. He shook his head to dissolve the evil visions clouding his mind.

Scrambling forward, Obed positioned himself between Aram and the giant.

As the attacker swung his club, Aram threw his spear, which pierced the giant's side.

Like a battering ram, Obed charged with his knife and ended the struggle. When the enemy's head fell to the side, eyes open and sightless, Obed heaved and retched into the dirt. Straining to control himself, he glanced from Aram to Barak. His voice was low, his speech thick. "How is he?"

Bent over, his hands braced on his knees as he regained his breath, Aram shook his head. "He might live. He might not."

Frowning, Obed wiped his mouth, but his attention was jerked away by yet another foe, this one with an enormous black beard. He grabbed a fallen spear and lifted it.

The enemy backed away.

Obed snorted as he lowered his spear. He turned to Aram.

Suddenly the black bearded warrior snuck up from behind, swinging an enormous red-stained club. The blow sent Obed sprawling to the ground in a heap.

Aram stiffened, horror flooding his mind.

Black Beard stood before the sun and blocked the light. His toothy necklace hung low over his chest. Though not the biggest warrior, he was the nimblest and appeared invincible. He advanced slowly, a smug look of satisfaction lighting up his face.

Aram shifted his gaze from Obed's crumpled body on one side to Barak's groaning figure on the other. He glanced around but Ishtar was nowhere to be seen. Eoban fought across the village, too far to hear a call above the tumult of battle. Suddenly, Ishtar joined Eoban, and the two fought back-to-back as a tandem pair. Aram's attention was jerked back to his foe.

Black Beard lifted his arms. "Ready to die?" Spittle spewed over blackened teeth.

Nausea rose from Aram's middle. His gaze strayed back to the swift moving Ishtar, and a hint of a smile wavered on his lips.

Staring across the village, directly at the black-bearded warrior, Ishtar swung a loaded leather strap high over his head.

At the same time, Obed's fresh warriors arrived, surrounding the giant men.

Black Beard took a step closer, his eyes fixed on Aram. "Ready?"

Holding his enemy's gaze steady, Aram grinned. "You?" he leapt forward.

Ishtar's rock found its mark, and the giant stumbled backward, but before he fell, he grabbed Aram around the neck.

Aram's eyes bulged as he stared into the brute's face. He found no mercy in those eyes. With a flash, he pictured his baby daughter with the withered hand. "No!" Using his forehead as a battering ram, he slammed the giant's nose.

The giant yelped, loosening of his grip.

Aram swung free. He grabbed a short knife from his belt and

thrust the point into the giant's neck. Both men fell in a heap.

Black Beard rolled to the side, his arms limp and his gaze sightless.

Aram lay flat on his back in the bloody dust. He closed his eyes and answered his enemy's question. "Not today."

The tumult died as the battle ended.

When Aram opened his eyes, Obed stood over him, his chest heaving as he sucked in deep breaths. "You all right?"

Struggling to sit up, Aram blinked. "I could ask the same of you."

Obed rubbed an ugly scratch on his face. "I may not be as handsome as I once was, but no one will question my skill as a warrior. We may be beardless, but we can fight!"

With a weary laugh, Aram rubbed his face. "You've proved your worth indeed." He glanced at the fallen giant. "Did you happen to notice—I took down the worst monster of all? No need to thank me, happy to do it."

Grinning weakly, Obed pulled a groaning Aram to his feet. They surveyed the field in sickening horror.

Covered with splatters of dirt and blood, warriors lay in gruesome glory. Those left alive shifted among the bodies, searching for survivors.

Ishtar jogged to Barak's side. He lifted Barak's eyelids and peered into his eye. With a curt nod, he bent over his chest as if listening for a heartbeat.

With a moan, Barak lifted a limp arm. "If you're my wife, continue; if not—get off me!" His eyes fluttered open.

Ishtar's eyebrows rose. "You're still with us, stubborn one."

"Yes, and I'd thank you to help me to my feet so no one feels the need to put their head on my chest again."

Ishtar pulled him to a sitting position."

Barak clenched his teeth and groaned. His gaze swept across the battlefield. "I did all this before I fell?"

Ishtar slapped his shoulder sending Barak into another gritted groan. "You fell early in battle. We won't tell. Your valor is safe with us."

Eoban strode over, peered at the slice in Barak's back, and pursed his lips. "My grandmother met more serious injury with her sewing needle."

Barak bowed his head, while Ishtar and Aram grinned at Eoban.

A loud, tormented scream turned every head.

Obed raced toward the scream, and Eoban followed. Ishtar and Aram assisted Barak to the shed doorway where they helped him lean against the wall in the shade.

Obed's anguished cry froze them in their tracks. They turned as one.

On his knees, his clenched fists raised to the sky, Obed screamed again.

Grimacing, Aram gripped Ishtar's shoulder. "Find out what's happened."

Ishtar's feet swept clouds of dust into the air as he ran.

Barak locked his gaze with Aram. They were silent in mutual understanding.

A breeze stirred the air. A dark bank of clouds billowed and thunder rumbled.

Wincing, Barak groaned and slid onto his side.

Aram stared stoically into the distance.

Ishtar marched toward them, his hands and jaw clenched.

Barak closed his eyes.

Ishtar stopped in front of Aram and spoke only one word. "Jael."

Aram dropped his head to his chest, tears filling his eyes. "Obed and Jonas will suffer more over this than over the whole of the battle."

Ishtar folded his arms over his chest, his eyes haunted. "It feels like—we all lost."

Chapter Forty-One

—Grassland—

Spirits Above

Obed sat on a boulder beside Jael's grave. Dozens of stones pocked the earth with their unspoken messages. He held a crudely made figure of a boy with the head and legs a little too big and the arms straight out.

The bright sun shone, but a cool breeze tossed the grass like undulating waves.

Obed stared at the figure.

Eoban strode up behind and laid his hand on his shoulder. "What's that you're studying?"

Obed lifted the figure into the sunlight. "Tobia made it for me. He's becoming quite a carver. He'll become a master—like his father. He said it was to remind me of Jael, so that I wouldn't forget him." He swallowed hard. "As if I ever could."

Lifting the figure from Obed's hand, Eoban nodded. "It's good work—the like of which I could not do. I have neither the skill nor the patience." He handed back the figure and nudged Obed. "Jonas is looking for you. She is fretting over the baby and wants you home. Calm her fears, would you?"

Obed shrugged. "I can't."

"Don't be a fool. Only you can make her feel better, and well you know it."

"Not this time." Obed shifted and glanced up at Eoban, shielding his eyes against the glare of the sun. "When Onias died, I married his widow and supported his sons. I've solved many problems by thinking out a solution. But when I looked down at Jael in a pool of blood, I could do nothing. There's no replacing a first son. I cannot heal her."

Eoban stood solemn as the wind ruffled his hair. He cleared his throat. "I'm no wise man, but like you, I want to stop the suffering of those I care for. I have pondered Jael's death, and I believe that he did not die in vain. Onias was no less honorable for refusing to fight than Jael was for insisting on fighting."

Eoban's gaze rose to the sky. "I understand the need to belong to something that is better and bigger than self. It's like a friend calling you to adventure over deep waters and high mountains. Onias and Jael answered the call with all their hearts. We weep for our loss, but we should not weep for them. I feel certain that someday, we'll meet again." Eoban stared off into the limitless horizon.

Caressing the figure between his fingers, Obed shared Eoban's view. "For a man of few words, you speak fairly well when you've a mind to."

Eoban folded his arms and tapped his foot. "Will you come along then and see to your family? No one expects you to bring life back from where it has fled. The clan needs you as their leader. No one asks for more."

Obed stood, clutching the figure. "You're right." His eyes swiveled over Eoban. One eyebrow rose in teasing mockery. "I think I'll call you Wise Warrior from now on."

With a sharp turn, Eoban jogged away. "Do that, and you'll join the spirits above sooner than you think."

Chapter Forty-Two

—Lake Clan—
—Two years later—

Fever

Aram patted Gizah's hand. She had fallen over a sharp stone, and, at almost three years of age, seemed to find the blow to her slight body only a little less hard to accept than the blow to her pride. She had been walking for almost two years now and apparently felt that she was mistress of open spaces. The red-tinged scrapes on her knees and palms had needed less attention than she believed. Her insistence that Aram look, see, and do something was met with a gentle hug and much head patting.

Aram loved his children more than he had ever imagined possible. It was as if the sun rose and set when they did. Gizah could transfix him with a cold stare one moment and send him into smothered fits of laughter the next. He hardly noticed her deformed hand. Nature had made up for her imperfection by giving her a will and a mind beyond that of most children.

Gizah had learned to speak early and was forever demanding things that challenged her mother and stymied Aram's imagination. Only yesterday, she insisted on fishing for dinner by herself. After being given a small net, the child had toddled off and caught a fish from the stream. It was quite small, but that hardly mattered.

Aram hugged her again and smiled in distraction as he wiped his brow.

The rains were late and the crops suffered. The hunting had

been poor. Men, women, and children plodded in weary exertion while the land withered. Even the lake had shrunk.

Gizah contented herself by nestling in the crook of her father's arm while fading hiccups rocked her to sleep.

Aram kissed her head as his gaze strayed over the village. Straighter footpaths, moving the dumpsite further away, and sturdier homes had improved the character of the village. Even Obed applauded their efforts.

Aram heaved a deep sigh. After all their work, he dearly wanted to stay put. The pains in his joints slowed him, and he would hardly be fit enough to manage a great expedition.

His gaze shifted to Eymard's dwelling, which stood silent and without the usual bustle of activity that surrounded it. Eymard was in bed with a fever, as were several other clansmen. It seemed as though a giant cloud had descended over his people.

A small hand gripped his shoulder.

Bethal, a vision of loveliness with a perfectly oval face, and deep-set brown eyes, high cheekbones, and a small red mouth patted Aram's arm. Clenching her hands into a fist, she implored him. "Mama needs you. She's sick."

Closing his eyes, Aram's heart squeezed tight. In his mind, he spoke to a dark stillness. *Oh, God, help me!* Facing his fears, he thrust Gizah up onto his shoulder, grabbed his staff, and limped after Bethal.

He had added a room to the dwelling when he learned of Namah's most recent pregnancy. Despite his crippled body, he was proud of his skilled work. Leaning his staff in the corner, he laid Gizah on a soft mat in a cool corner of the back room.

Namah lay in the room directly off the entrance.

Bethal ran to her. "Mama, here he is."

Aram smiled and laid his hand on Namah's burning forehead.

Tossing and turning, her hair disheveled, sweat beaded on her flushed face.

Swallowing back fear, Aram glanced at his daughter.

"Bethal, get your mama a drink."

Namah's eyes flashed open, and she stared at Aram. She gripped his tunic, while her voice rose in a husky whisper. "It's a killing fever. I'll be taken—"

Smoothing her brow, Aram forced a smile "You'll be fine. You're a little sick, but you'll fight this off—don't worry. You're not alone."

Closing her eyes, Namah fell back against her pillows with a deep sigh.

Bethal stepped closer. Her thin arms shook as she held out a cup of water.

Perplexed, Aram took the cup, drank deeply, and handed it back. "Thank you. You're a good girl. Your mother is resting now. She'll be better soon. Give her time—you'll see."

Bethel's eyes glimmered in the dim light, and tears spilled down her pale cheeks. Her lips quivered, but she said nothing.

Scooping her into his arms, Aram pressed her head against his chest and fought back his own tears.

A fist banged on the doorway, and a familiar voice called out cheerfully. "Aram, you home?"

Still holding Bethel, Aram shuffled forward and stepped into the sunshine.

Obed stood tall with his staff in his hand. When their eyes met, he grinned.

Flustered, Aram limped forward. "Namah's sick with fever. She just fell asleep. What's the news?"

His grin fading, Obed brushed a stray lock of hair from Bethel's tear-streaked face. "Jonas thinks that the sickness should pass when the rains come. She says this happens when the water grows stagnant. Our people have been ill too, but she says they'll recover with rest." His brows furrowed. "How is Namah then? You think her illness is serious?"

"I hope not. She fears the worst, but that's natural with a fever. Still, I feel as if I've been expecting some terrible trial for months."

Obed nodded. "I know the feeling."

Aram motioned for Obed to wait and carried Bethal inside. He laid her next to her sister. Staring at his two girls, their hair streaming out, framing their calm faces, he sighed.

After stepping back into the blazing sun, Aram motioned for Obed to follow him, and they circled around to the shady side of his dwelling. Aram sank down with a grunt of relief. "That child weighs more than she looks." He patted the ground. "Sit with me."

Obed peered over the horizon, his frown deepening. "Would you mind if I counted how many people have the fever? Knowing exactly who is sick might help." He glanced down at Aram's slumped figure. "I'll send Jonas word to look in on Namah. Being with child, she'll need more help to recover, and Jonas would want to know."

Clasping his hands over his knees, Aram nodded in silent agreement.

In officious haste, Obed turned away.

Namah cried out, and Aram rose to his feet.

Chapter Forty-Three

—River Clan—

Lud Returns

Lud's powerful, agile body bespoke his manhood. His steady blue eyes and stout heart proclaimed more confidence than men with a far greater number of years. His reddish hair had turned darker, and his lithe frame had filled in with muscles. He jogged along, leaping over obstacles when boulders or streams interrupted his stride. Pele's gentle face floated in his mind's eye, sending an equally gentle smile over his face.

Lud had found his home. To his astonished joy, his entire family had survived except for an older brother who had fallen early in the battle. When Lud had appeared, the whole clan had rejoiced at the miracle.

It was a miracle indeed that he had ever managed to find his way home again. He had run out of provisions early on, but he always managed to find ripe berries, nuts, grains and even fresh meat, which was his luck to kill with subtle skill. Though he carried a leather pouch for water, he frequently needed refills. And just when he feared that he might faint with thirst, a fresh stream or a clear lake would present itself in his path. It was as if the hand of the mighty Sky Warrior gently but persistently encouraged him forward.

Not many days later, he strode into his father's village and stood staring—weeping with joy—at the sight of his mother and other women he recognized from boyhood. In answer to his mother's call, his father, brothers, and a little sister he hardly knew came running. They rushed into his embrace.

His father called out the news as if no one had eyes to see. "My son is back! Look, look, everyone, my son is back!" The whole Earth seemed to rejoice with the reunited clan. Lud rested and reacquainted himself with his family. Stories were told and retold. The missing years were relived amid tears and laughter. But in the back of his mind, Lud remembered Pele. He trusted that Hagia would take good care of the girl. Yet fear stalked him.

A year had passed when he heard the rumor of a massive battle between clans in the south. Lud's apprehension redoubled. The image of Pele taken prisoner and treated brutally compelled him to return to the lands of his slavery and find her. He would bring her home. She would love these simple hill people, and they would welcome her happily.

He neared the river that wound to the south and knew he was only a short distance from Ishtar's clan. It took two days to cross the grassy plain to the water's edge. As he drew near, a strange smell curled about his nose. He wrinkled his face in surprise. The ground felt hard under his sore feet. When he reached the rocky shore, he saw the source of the stink that assailed him.

The river, shrunken to a meandering stream, slowed to a trickle and dead fish lay rotting on the shore. As night fell, he stumbled in the murky blackness, trying to find a clear space to get a drink, but it all tasted brackish and horrid. He forced himself to take a few sips to satiate his overwhelming thirst. No longer wanting to travel along the water's edge, he thought of the Grassland People and decided to head in their direction.

Lud gathered bits of twigs and grasses and made a fire. Crouching in front of his small blaze, he consoled himself. Pele would only be that much more relieved to see him and willing to travel to his clan in the hills where the water still flowed clear and sweet. Lying down on a cleared space, he imagined Pele's eyes when she'd first catch sight of him. A smile played over lips as he fell into a deep slumber.

After killing a tough, old rabbit and cooking it to make it

edible, he forced his weary legs to stagger on. It took three days to cross the grasslands and find Obed.

The village appeared unnaturally quiet. Few people milled about. The wheat and barley crops bent over on thin stems amid fields overgrown with weeds. The dwellings stood in shabby disrepair. No dogs barked at his arrival, and no sheep or goats ambled on the hills.

As the hot sun beat on his head, dizziness overwhelmed him and surprise warred with anxiety.

"Lud, is that you?"

Lud's head swiveled, and he nearly fell backward.

Eoban smiled, reaching out.

Relief, like cool rain, flooded Lud's exhausted body. "Eoban! I'm glad to see you! I was beginning to wonder where everyone had gone. What's happened? Where is Ishtar's clan?"

Eoban raised his hand. "Let's find a more suitable place to talk. The sun is too hot these days." Throwing his arm around Lud's shoulder, he ambled along at his side. "My questions first." He patted Lud's muscled shoulders. "I can hardly believe it is you."

Leading Lud down a well-worn path between two sturdy dwellings, he arrived at the last dwelling in the village. After ushering Lud into the welcoming shade of a front room, he pointed to a woven rug. "Sit and rest yourself.

Eoban bustled about like a worried mother. He gathered a tray of dried fruit, cheese, and bread and slid the repast before Lud. He snatched up a jug and a bowl and hurried outside. In a moment, he returned and placed the bowl and jug of water close at Lud's hand.

"Sorry we don't have the usual amenities and be careful with the water. There is precious little of it these days. The stream is all but dried up, and even the lake is showing signs of the times." He pointed to a bowl of dried fruit. "Here, take some of these. They aren't sweet, but they'll hold body and soul together."

Lud dutifully washed his fingers. After pouring a measure of water, he took a long drink. With a relieved sigh, he started on the fruit.

Eoban watched silently, a grin crinkling around his eyes. "It's good to see a healthy appetite again. I was beginning to fear I'd be the only one to outlast this fever." He tapped his fingers together. "See if you can talk and chew at the same time. Tell me where you've been and why you've come back. Give me all the details. I could use a good story."

Leaning against the reasonably cool wall, Lud told of his long search for his family and their reunion. Eoban grinned in reflected joy. When Lud mentioned Pele, Eoban's face clouded, and his gaze dropped to the ground.

Lud leaned over and tapped Eoban's knee. "I want to take Pele home with me."

Eoban lifted his head, his eyes widening. "As your wife?"

His face burning, Lud shook his head. "Not as a wife. I know what you're thinking, but it's not that way between us. Pele can't be bound to earthly love as a man would expect from a wife. I just want to offer my friendship and my family for peace and security. She should have that."

Eoban rubbed his chin. "You look so young, but you speak like a wise old man."

Rising to his knees, Lud waved his arm. "Now it's my turn. Where has Ishtar gone and where is Pele? Are they near?"

Wrapping his arms around his knees, Eoban hunched forward and averted his gaze. "After our battle with the men from the mountains, Ishtar's clan resettled between us and the great lake. It's been a good thing, for the lake has been the salvation of all three clans. I cannot imagine how we would've survived if we had not had its teeming depths. Still, as the sickness spreads, there are fewer to feed."

"When did the sickness start?"

"It's been months now. We've lost fifteen people so far, though it is often surprising who recovers and who dies. I thought that the oldest would die first, but they didn't. It's been the children and their mothers who've been most vulnerable."

Lud sat with his chin in his hands. "You still haven't told me about Pele. Has she taken ill?"

Eoban closed his eyes.

His heart pounding in panic, Lud jumped to his feet. "Tell me. I must know. What's happened?"

Eoban lifted his head and cleared his throat. "Pele died. If there is any eternal justice, then she is in a better place than she ever knew on this earth. There must be a fitting dwelling place for so noble a mind and so courageous a heart." Eoban's gaze dropped. "She died not of fever but of exhaustion, for she spent herself to save the rest of us."

Lud fell to his knees and buried his face in his hands.

Eoban gently pressed the boy's shoulder. "Listen now, for the telling of this sad tale may lessen your grief. Pele was truly an extraordinary girl. When I said she was noble, I didn't say half the truth, for words cannot speak the fullness of her measure. If she hadn't taken a special task upon her shoulders, then Ishtar wouldn't have realized that battle was approaching. She traveled all alone into the enemy's camp. After a long, weary journey, she brought a weapon of war back to Ishtar and told of their preparations. She gave her life to help the very clan that had made her a slave."

Eoban gestured, waving his finger at the door as if pointing to a hidden figure. "Hagia mourns her loss like a bereaved mother. She calls upon a nameless God to watch over Pele's spirit. I know little of such matters. But this I do know—great souls exist, and when they pass from our vision, we are brought along with them into an Unseen Land."

At a loud noise outside, they both turned their heads.

"Eoban! Come here!"

Eoban and Lud rushed outside.

Obed stood pointing to pillars of smoke rising in the sky.

Eoban jumped forward. "Fire! Everyone to the stream."

Lud stared at the dark cloud, frozen in shock.

Obed gripped Eoban's arm. "The stream can't save us. A fire this size can leap from one side to the next. We'll go to the lake." He gestured toward the village. "Help move the sick. There's not much time. Fire is swifter than men."

Suddenly his gaze caught the silent figure. "Lud? You've grown!" A smile flickered and faded in an instant. "I'd like to talk with you, but now is not the time." His gaze swept over Lud's muscular frame. "But perhaps you can help."

Nodding, Lud followed Eoban. Together they gathered frightened villagers together and directed them to the lake.

Shouting above the tumult, Eoban sent men and boys to help the sick and infirm.

For a brief moment, Lud envisioned his parents, their quiet dwelling and their simple, wholesome life. A wave of loneliness swept over him. The image of Pele's face that had so long sustained him now vanished into the grave.

A sobbing child tripped and fell in the swirling dust.

Lud trotted forward and scooped the child into his arms. He rocked and crooned to the baby boy in a soothing tone. After a moment, his gaze roamed longingly north, but he quickly returned to the child and gave him a gentle hug. The boy's heart thudded wildly. Lud smiled.

Obed hurried forward, leading a ragged line of children. "Thank you, Lud. I always knew you were a good man. These children are either separated from their families, or there's no one well enough to look after them. Lead them to the lake. I'll manage things here and meet up with you later, all right?"

Lud peered at the group of frightened, sad little charges, and he clasped the hand of the smallest child. While he cradled the boy in his arms and led the girl by the hand, he told the rest of the children to hold hands. Turning, he nodded briefly at Obed with a ridiculous grin and started forward.

Amid the grassy plain, Ishtar and three other men marched along a narrow path through the brown grass. When he saw Lud, Ishtar's face lit up but then a confused frown clouded his features. "Lud, I'd ask about you first, but your company begs a different question. What new evil has befallen us?"

"Fire at Obed's village."

"Where are you taking the children?"

"To the lake. There are many who need help, but I fear Obed chose a poor mother bird." Lud flapped his arms. "Clearly, my wings are not big enough."

Ishtar nodded. "I see what you mean." He surveyed the assembly and his frown deepened. "Obed must have been in desperate indeed. No offence, Lud, but you do not look anything like a mother bird. I'll go ahead and leave Kittim here to help you. He gestured to the tall, bronze-skinned man at his side. Take them to our village. They'll be happier with women who'll know how to care for them."

Lud nodded while patting various heads in turn so no one would start crying.

After Ishtar hurried away, Lud followed Kittim. He tapped the silent warrior on the arm and jutted his chin forward. "You might pick up that little girl. She's too tired to go much further, and if you take that one by the hand—" He tipped his head to the side. "You won't have to keep shepherding him back into the group. He likes to wander." Lud marched forward, nudging a little boy along.

Kittim marched ahead with the girl in his arm and tugging the little boy.

Lud peered into the sky. He could see Pele's face again, and she was smiling.

~~~

Ishtar sprinted into the village and frowned at the sight of so many struggling men and women leading children and old people from the smoke-filled village. He pulled his long hair away from his face and squinted, his eyes stinging.

He surveyed the scene. A single sunbeam broke through the smoke and illuminated the tip of the spear in his hand. He surveyed the scene, wishing the enemy were flesh and blood and not fire.

Obed stood in the center, calling out directions.

Ishtar jogged over to him and gripped his shoulder.

Obed turned, his smoke-filled eyes full of tears. He grinned in apparent relief at the sight of Ishtar.

Yelling above the tumult and the roar of the flames, Ishtar waved. "What can I do?"

"There's little left except check each dwelling and make sure no one is left behind."

"We can do that." Ishtar motioned to his two men and sent them off.

Obed pointed to one side. "I'll go to the north. You go south. Be quick! The fire will soon be upon us."

Making haste, Ishtar searched each room of every dwelling on the south side, even glancing in the storerooms. He shook his head at the loss of work and food. As the smoke stung his eyes, his throat constricted. Fear crept up his spine as he searched for the fastest way to get clean air.

Stumbling, his mind returned to that fateful day when he and Joash had strode into this village. The people had welcomed them, never suspecting the real intent of their visit. Now, as he pelted across the village, fresh tears sprang to his eyes.

Waving his arms, Obed beckoned to Ishtar. His two-year-old daughter, Mari, clutched his sleeve as she curled up in his arms.

Jonas, looking emaciated, lifted five-year-old Onia. She staggered.

Obed passed his daughter into Ishtar's arms. "We're too slow. You take Mari. I'll carry Jonas with Onia. Tobia can run along."

Ishtar shook his head. "We can to do better than that." He scanned the village. The sight of a sled half buried under a load of bricks caught his eye. He ran over and dumped the load.

Obed settled Jonas and Mari inside it with Tobia and Onia.

Grabbing the lead rope, the two men pulled the sled behind them. Tears streamed down their cheeks, as they coughed in choking gasps.

Jonas and the children trembled, covering their faces with their hands.

Obed struggled to speak. "It's just…a village…it can be

rebuilt."

Ishtar ducked his head and pulled harder. "Anything can be rebuilt. I should know."

~~~

Lud sighed in exhausted weariness that evening as everyone settled down for a night's rest. He sat next to Ishtar and recounted his adventures.

Lying on his back, peering up at the starry sky, Ishtar listened in silence. When Lud described his plan to bring Pele back to his family in the hills, Ishtar turned his head. "I wish I had realized her worth before she died. Hagia will tell you all about her splendid qualities. She believes in the Sky Warrior Pele professed to see."

Ishtar tapped his fingers together. "There's so much in the world that we can't see with our eyes." He sighed. "Pele may have been a slave to Neb and Joash, but her spirit was always free."

Lud squeezed back tears.

Sitting up, Ishtar let his head fall back, his gaze canvassing the heavens. "Would her Spirit Warrior come at my call?"

Lying on his stomach, propping his head on his hands, Lud frowned at Ishtar.

Ishtar shrugged. "There's no reason he shouldn't visit me as well as Pele."

Lud sniffed and jutted his chin at the horizon. "You think the fire has gone out—or changed course?"

Ishtar's gaze swept right and left. "It's gone out. There's a dry riverbed between us." He sighed. "Wish it would rain."

Silence fell as Lud rolled onto his back.

Ishtar shifted. "Perhaps the Sky Warrior will bring us rain."

Lud slapped his hand over his face. "I don't know. He might not like us asking for favors."

"Who's asking for favors? I'm simply asking for a basic element that the gods offer as it pleases them. Surely, there's no harm in asking."

Lud rolled over, covering his head with his arms. "Fine. Do what you want. Just leave me out of it."

Crossing his legs and lifting his hands, Ishtar peered up into the sky and chanted. "Sky Warrior! We need you! Hear our call."

Lud scooted like an inchworm away from Ishtar; his eyes squeezed shut.

Ishtar straightened and chanted louder. "Oh, Sky Warrior! I'm Ishtar of the River Clan, or we used to be a River Clan--"

"He doesn't need to know all that." Lud hissed through clenched teeth. "Get to the point."

Ishtar frowned at Lud with annoyance. He repositioned himself. "We have no rain. Our crops are dying. We had to move because we were attacked—"

Lud groaned, squirming. "Oh, God."

Ishtar glowered at Lud and then refocused. "Our people sicken and die. Obed's wife is sick, but he doesn't—"

Jerking bolt upright, Lud peered at Ishtar. "You'll get us all killed!" Lud stood and lifted his arms. "Please, Lord of the sky and clouds, have mercy on us! Give us rain." He plopped down, rolled to his side and clamped his hands over his ears.

Pursing his lips, Ishtar tapped his fingers. "I'm not as bold as you."

Lud raised his head, scowling.

"I merely called on the Sky Warrior. You spoke to God."

Lud curled into a ball, muttering under his breath.

Lying on his back, Ishtar pillowed his head on his hands. "Tomorrow's another day." He closed his eyes.

Both men relaxed and slept, their breathing soft and even.

Clouds rolled in, blinking out each starry light in turn. With a whoosh of gentle wind, soft rain pattered on their heads.

Chapter Forty-Four

—OldEarth—

To What Purpose?

Teal watched the falcon soar over the treetops. His gaze followed as it swooped low and then alighted on a branch. It stared down through piercing black eyes.

Ark's voice rose in the distance. "What're you doing? Planning breakfast?"

Teal's gaze dropped to the Cresta, who lumbered forward on his naked three-toed feet, swinging his tentacles in wide arches, spraying water in all directions.

"Your dip in the lake didn't satisfy?"

Chuckling, Ark plunked down on a dead log. "It was beautiful!" Gathering his gear, he wiggled one foot into the top of the boot as if to give it encouragement. "Pity you couldn't join me." With a shrug, he dismissed Teal's limitations. "Couldn't hold your breath for more than two—three minutes, could you?"

Teal turned his back on the falcon. "You forget. I can take any shape I want."

Sighing, Ark tugged at the boot helplessly. He glanced up. "I do forget. You seem so...terrestrial." His wide-eyed gaze flittering from Teal to his boot hinted at his need. "Do you suppose?"

With a smothered grunt, Teal ambled over and knelt in front of Ark. Huffing, he pulled the slippery boot over the fleshy toes. It took their combined grunts and a couple snappish comments to get the boot all the way up his long, flabby leg.

Ark wiped sweat from his forehead. "Good! Now the other."

The falcon squawked.

Teal's head jerked to one side. "By the Divide, she's laughing at us!"

Ark's gaze followed Teal's. "You mean the Bhuaci beauty?" "You know—?"

Zuri marched forward with a scowl. "I've got all my samples. I think." He waved his hand at Ark. "You couldn't bring up anything more valuable than that gooey mess you handed me?"

Gripping Ark's second boot, Teal glanced over. "Look, you've had five days to get your samples." He shoved Ark's toes into the boot. "To be honest, Ark did you a favor on that last one. I would've made you dive for it."

With a wince, Ark gripped the edges of the boot and tugged. His exertion sent swirls of water bubbling over the edge of his breathing helm. "No…prob…lem. Glad…to…help."

With a quick headshake and a smirk, Zuri stepped forward, nudged Teal aside, and yanked Ark's boot into place—lifting the Cresta a meter into the air at the same time.

Attempting to regain his balance and his portly dignity, Ark swiped the waving fronds on the top of his head into proper position.

Teal tapped him, his gaze swinging to the falcon. "You know about her?"

Zuri glanced around. "Who?"

With a grin, Ark took a tentative step forward. "Of course. I always keep a close eye on shape-shifters—except you. You're so laudable. I hardly need to *see* you at all. I can smell your honesty a hundred kilometers away." His gaze swiveled to the falcon. "She's crafty, that one."

Pounding closer, Zuri bellowed. "Who?"

The falcon leapt into the sky and soared away.

Teal turned and started up an incline. "That falcon is a Luxonian named Sienna. She's working with a Bhuaci, the clerk—"

"Who doesn't matter in the least." Ark toddled along after

Teal. He waved Zuri forward. "They work for a hidden mind, someone who wants to keep an eye on us."

Zuri flapped his arms at his side. "We're already keeping an eye on each other. Isn't that enough?"

Ark stopped and appraised the horizon. "I think we need to go south." He scowled. "All that tramping around yesterday rotated my internal compass."

Teal dragged his fingers through his hair. "What are you looking for? Water? The lake is that way." Teal pointed north.

Ark shook his head. "Not the lake. I want the grave where they buried the girl, the one who carried the spear away."

Teal's eyes widened in shock. "Pele's…grave?"

"Yes, I want to discover what really killed her."

Charging forward with his jaw clenched and his eyes flashing, Teal confronted Ark. "Why? What difference does it make? She's dead!"

Tapping his tentacles together, Ark tilted his head as if appraising a slow student. "That's my point. Either she had a weak heart and died of over exertion, or she had a strong heart and something else killed her." He shrugged. "Either way, it's a mystery. How could a child like her do what she did? It's an achievement I must understand."

Zuri chuckled. "You want to study human organs to find strength?" He clapped his hands together. "Now I've heard everything."

Ark swung around. "There is more to the human heart than muscle, Ingot. Your mechanical systems blind you. While you mine their world and Teal wring his hands over human weakness, I want to find the root of their strength."

Teal stepped closer, his gaze focused and intense. "To what purpose?"

The falcon circled overhead.

Ark grinned as he glanced up. "Theirs—and ours."

Chapter Forty-Five

—Lake Clan—

Who We Are Meant To Be

Namah opened her eyes. Her head felt heavy, but the pain was gone. She stretched, relaxed and deeply contented. The baby lay nuzzled in the crook of her arm, wrapped in a soft sand colored cloth. He wriggled as she adjusted her arm. Laying the baby on her tummy, she admired his small face and abundant locks of dark hair. Beautiful and perfectly formed.

She smiled. Just as he entered the world, gentle drops of water pattered on the roof. Soon, flashes of light and a clap of thunder announced the pounding rain, which refreshed the parched earth. The wondrous scent of fresh, clean air and crisp breezes swept through and lulled her exhausted body into a peaceful sleep.

Aram shifted on his pallet, rubbed his eyes, saw the light breaking through the doorway, and sat up. He turned to Namah.

She grinned.

Stretching, Aram ambled over and crouched at her side. He caressed Namah's face. Glancing at the baby, his eyes glimmered in the morning light. "Bar-Aram, my son! All is right with the world once again."

When Bethal trounced in from the fresh air, she squinted in the dim light and gripped her father's arm. "Is Mama all right?"

"Yes, she's fine. We'll let her have a little more rest, and soon she'll be on her feet again."

Leaning forward, Gizah tried to catch a hold of the baby's hand.

Aram pressed her hand into his own. "Not yet, little one. Give him time to grow up a bit."

Gizah tilted her head. "Tomorrow?"

Aram and Namah exchanged glances. "Not that soon but in good time."

Frowning, Gizah shrugged. "Oh, all right. But I hope he hurries up. I have a lot to teach him."

Aram laughed. Namah grinned, and they clasped hands.

Near sunset, Bethal and Gizah led Eymard to the new baby with wide, proud eyes.

Gripping Aram's shoulder, Eymard's eyes shone in the dim light. "You have a son to teach in the ways of men." He bowed to Namah, who grinned her salutation. "You're looking much better. It seems that we still have work to do, for the other world has not yet claimed us."

Namah tipped her head, her eyes closing as in a grateful prayer.

Tapping Aram, Eymard chuckled. "Have you heard? Milkan is with child." He glanced at Namah. "I can think of no better woman to instruct her in the ways of motherhood." He mocked a depreciating sigh. "Since I'm not qualified."

Her face engulfed in a wide grin, Namah sat up. "It would be my honor."

The baby squalled, his face turning red and his hand clenched as they beat the air.

Aram winked at Eymard. "He has a lusty appetite!"

Eymard gestured toward the door.

Aram squeezed his wife's hand and ushered the little girls out before him.

Free from the confined space, the two girls bounded ahead and joined a throng of children at the center of the village.

Using a staff to lean upon as he walked, Eymard shuffled beside Aram. "Eoban is set to travel again, but this time he's taking Barak with him. Milkan is not pleased." He waved a protesting hand. "Not all husbands are as attentive as you, Aram."

Ambling along the edge of the village, Aram's eyebrows rose in teasing. "True." His gaze wandered over the homes and his clansmen.

A woman perched on a rooftop wove thatch tightly into place.

Peering up, Aram called, "Where's your husband? Is he not back on his feet again?"

"Oh, yes, he is inside helping me now."

"Helping...how?"

"He tells me what to do."

"He should use his hands and not his mouth. He'd get more done."

A head poked through the doorway. "I heard that, Aram!"

"Good. Get out here and save your wife from exhaustion."

The little man jerked his thumb in her direction. "Oh, her? She likes to work. I can't keep her busy enough."

A load of loose straw fluttered down on the husband's head.

The wife smiled and dusted her hands.

Aram choked back laughter and strode on with Eymard at his side.

As they neared an old woman, Aram's smile faded. "How are you today, Nana?"

The dark, wrinkled face turned, peering at Aram. Wiping her cheek, she pointed to a silent, broken-down dwelling. A few tattered blankets hung limp on a line while an outdoor fire vainly attempted to warm the underside of a stew pot. "I'm all right." She shrugged. "Considering I am an old woman alone in the world."

Eymard tottered closer and hooted. "Compared to the years I've seen pass, you're a spring blossom."

The old woman waved Eymard away with a hint of a grin twinkling in her glimmering eyes. "Spring blossom indeed! It's an autumn harvest you're thinking of. I'll not deny that you must be as old as the mountains, but while the mountains grow taller, you seem to shrink."

Aram choked back a laugh.

Eymard grinned good-naturedly. "Ah, but at my age, wisdom is easier to carry than mountains."

Aram waved to a young woman next door as he ambled up to the old woman and pressed her shoulder. "You're never alone. I want to hear about you every day, so I am appointing—" He glanced at the young woman. "I am appointing—"

The young woman bowed, twisting her hands nervously. "Shela."

"Shela, let me know each day if Nana needs anything. Be of service to her whenever you're able. You'll do this kindness for me?"

Shela smiled. "Nana and I good friends."

Aram smiled and turned to Nana. "Though loved ones pass to the other side, we must not grieve too much. Our turn will come. We must accept loss and live the fullness of each day." He bowed to the old woman and smiled at the girl.

They stood quietly, bowing in return.

Eymard's eyebrows rose significantly.

Aram frowned. "What?"

"Nothing. Just remembering a man I once knew."

With an eye roll, Aram gestured forward. He peered over his shoulder. "It was tragic—burying so many from one family, but she's brave. She'll not let her sorrows crush her."

Eymard nodded. "Like an old tree that's weathered many storms, she may feel every buffeting wind, yet she'll still stand."

"Not so with everyone." He glanced toward a young man crouching by the doorway of his dwelling.

Aram strode ahead, his shadow falling diagonally over the hunched man. He cleared his throat. "Vitus, wake up. The sun is running across the sky, and there's plenty of work to do."

The head stirred but did not rise.

Aram nudged the man's shoulder. "Vitus! Don't give in to your grief like this."

The head lifted, his eyes wide and vacant.

Frowning, Aram offered an encouraging pat on the shoulder. "Good. Sit up. Get your blood stirring again."

The blue eyes focused like a man waking from a trance. "Aram? What time is it? Where's Ila?"

Aram's eyes dilated, his face flushing. "Ila's been gone over a month—you know that."

Vitus' eyes rolled up, and he fell back against the wall, lifeless again.

Squaring his shoulders, Aram thrust his hands on his hips, his temper cracking. "You're a man—act like one! Others have suffered as you, but they don't lie around waiting for death to carry them off. You must get up. Ila would want you to."

Hunching limply, like a rag doll, Vitus's head hung over his chest.

Drawing his foot back, Aram prepared a kick.

Leaping forward, Eymard jerked Aram aside.

"Let him be. He lived a charmed life. He's not accustomed to tragedy. Losing his parents, his wife, and his only child—it's too much for any man. Give him time. He'll recover despite himself."

Aram snorted. "He's more plant than man to wither so."

Plucking Aram's sleeve, Eymard scowled. "Your great strength ought to give you great compassion."

Heaving a long sigh, Aram shrugged and crouched by Vitus. "I'll come again, Vitus, and I expect to see you standing like a man. If not, I'll take matters into my own hands!"

As the two stepped away, Aram ran his fingers through his hair. "It's bad enough to have to bury body after body, but to watch the healthy give up—as if they were sick too!" He grunted and stopped at the edge of the cliff overlooking the lake.

A massive tree spread its green foliage against the blue sky.

Eymard sighed. "There are many kinds of sicknesses, but the most mysterious are those of a troubled mind. Vitus was unprepared for such a blow—who would be? He's hiding, or trying to—in his own way—to decide whether to live or die." Splendid rays of pink and purple highlighted the horizon. A flock of birds cawed in the distance and fluttered into the branches of the tree. The lone howl of a night predator called in the descending darkness.

Clasping his hands, Eymard turned with a lopsided grin. "Now, tell me. Do you approve of Barak going off with that wanderer, Eoban?"

Leaning against the tree and contemplating the sunset, Aram chuckled. "Yes, indeed. It's a good idea." He shifted and focused on Eymard. "Eoban might be right. It could be to our advantage if men travel and bring back news of the great world." He rubbed his arms as an evening chill settled. "And they're going to trade goods—woven cloth, beadwork, ceramic dishes, and even a few carved pieces. Perhaps someday our people can learn these skills."

Wolves howled.

Eymard surveyed the horizon. "Obed's clan is learning to use metal, forging blades and tools. Ishtar's people have discovered a new material, and they're mixing the metals. They want to fashion longer blades with sharper edges. The only problem is coming up with enough raw material."

Aram rubbed his hand across his jaw, a headache pounded behind his eyes. "Ishtar has become rather secretive of late. He was always so open and friendly before. It's strange to see this bend in his nature."

Eymard nodded in sage agreement. A sly smile rippled over his face. "If you're worried about loyalty, the best solution is to join your clans in marriage. Friendship lasts as long as friends' hearts beat true, but family creates bonds of flesh and blood, which even death cannot break."

Aram's gaze rose above the dim horizon into the star-speckled sky. "I'm no longer young. I can only hope to help arrange the alliances between my clan and our neighbors. I can't see the future. I'm not like you, Eymard. Wisdom doesn't grow on me. Why must I struggle so hard to find my purpose—just when my life nears its end?"

Eymard pointed to the falling sun. "We pass through peace and trial to learn who we are and who we are meant to be."

A single bird, a black silhouette, leapt into the air and flew from the rest, winging its way into the night sky.

"Your words are well said, but when I look at my children, I want to protect them and shape their futures. I want every sunrise fair and every sunset peaceful."

With a frown, Eymard shook an admonishing finger. "You must not allow yourself to indulge in fantasies or shrink from duties that are yours to fulfill." Eymard pointed at Aram. "You have your part to play. The more honestly you do what you must, the better off everyone will be."

Bethal and Gizah scampered toward them, calling to their father.

With a slow smile, Eymard watched the children pelting across the grass. "You're already powerful in ways you little suspect. More is achieved by the humble than the proud."

Wrapping his arms around his girls, Aram grinned at their bright faces in the evening light.

Turning, Eymard nodded. "Such beauties as these will have no trouble finding good matches."

"Not yet! They're mine for a few seasons more."

Milkan strolled toward them, her arms swinging at her sides. Eymard's eyes lit up. "Ah, here is my spring time."

With a teasing frown, Milkan wagged a finger at the girls. "I told you to wait for me." She tousled their hair, laughed and met Aram's gaze. "It's good I found you. Barak wishes to speak with you. I'll take the girls home for their evening meal." Her gaze swiveled to the old man. "Would you help me take care of these two sparrows for the night?" She sighed. "Barak's packing. He's planning to leave before sunrise."

With a mock spasm of pain, Eymard rubbed the small of his

back. "Why, you know, I can hardly take care of myself. But I trust these two will help an old man." Like a pathetic puppy with begging eyes, Eymard blinked at the two girls. "You'll take care of me, won't you?"

With wide eyes, the two girls nodded. Bethal took charge. "I'll hold him up on this side. Gizah, you take that arm."

Winking at Aram, Eymard let the girls lead him home.

Aram chuckled. "That old goat is as wise as his years are long." He turned to Milkan. "Be sure to give that old man plenty to eat. I walked him all over creation today."

Milkan smiled and nodded goodbye, then she followed the trio as they merged into the darkness.

After strolling across the village, Aram found Barak behind his dwelling with the flicker of a small fire holding back the darkness.

"Eoban's not arrived?"

Barak jerked in surprise. "Oh, it's you, Aram. No, not yet." He thrust his pack aside. "Did Milkan take the girls to Eymard's then?"

"Yes, you should see my daughters taking care of the infirmed."

"Excuse me?"

Aram shook his head. "Nothing. Just…when you married Milkan, you gained a treasure in the old man."

"Oh, Eymard. Yes, I know." Barak sniffed and rubbed his nose. "I sometimes I forget to see past Milkan."

Sitting on the edge of a bench, Aram leaned back and clasped his hands in his lap. "So, you're ready for an adventure?"

"I sincerely doubt it." Barak exhaled. "But I'll go anyway." He laced his fingers behind his head. "I can only hope my future adventures prove less dangerous than my first."

Aram snorted. "Lord, I hope so." His gaze swiveled around the dwelling. "What ever happened to those cat skins?"

"After my father passed away last year, I gave them to Milkan, but she doesn't like them—said they cost too much. But I can't part with them."

Aram nodded. "Pass them on to your sons. They'll see the valor hidden from Milkan's eyes." He rubbed his hands and sat straighter. "So, are you ready to travel with Eoban? Anything you need?"

After tossing another branch on the fire, Barak shuffled inside and came back cradling a carafe of wine and a bowl of bread, dried fruit, and nuts. He propped the two up between them. "Am I ready?" He shrugged and tossed a handful of nuts into his mouth, chewing meditatively. "I have one problem."

Holding the carafe, Aram peered over. "Only one?"

"Part of me is staying behind." He nodded in the direction of Eymard's dwelling, where the lights dimmed, and the sounds of the children's voices faded into the night. "I know that Namah and Milkan will look after one another, and you and Eymard will take care of things, but—"

His gaze flittered to the star-speckled sky. "On my last journey, I realized how close death could come." He sucked in a deep breath. "If something happens to me, will you find a suitable husband for Milkan? Someone who'd treat her well and care for our child." He hesitated. "Someone from Obed's clan—not Ishtar's."

Aram pursed his lips and stared ahead in silence.

Hunching forward, Barak hurried to explain. "Everything will be fine, and I'll return in a month or so, but just in case. You understand?"

Aram rubbed the back of his neck, a sinking feeling in his stomach. "I'm glad that you trust me enough with such a commission. But—"

Barak titled his head, waiting.

"Why not from Ishtar's clan?"

"It is hard to say." Taking a long swig of wine, he handed the carafe back to Aram. "I've never fully trusted them. They're allies, true, but I'm not sure I want to put my most prized possession into their hands."

Aram stretched his legs and sighed. "I respect your wishes—set your mind at ease. If anything happens, you can rest assured—Milkan and your child will be well looked after." He wagged his finger at Barak. "My only request—be quick about your business and return with good news. I'm not sure who will miss you more—your wife or me."

Standing, Barak kicked his pack. "I was a fool to go looking for that cat, but I'm glad I did. I learned enough about leadership to know I'd never want the job." He glanced at Aram. "I wish you'd come. We'd have fun traveling together."

"No, my job is here. I was reminded by a wise old man today—we all have our tasks to attend to." He gripped Barak's arm. "Go. Enjoy your adventure. Your family will be well looked after. I'll see to that."

Grimacing, Barak rubbed his hand over his mouth. "I have only one fear left."

Aram's head jerked around. "Good Lord. What else?"

Barak coughed and leaned closer, his voice dropping into a confidential whisper. "Will Eoban sing? I've heard he sings like a frog—loud and long about past adventures. Worst yet, he insists that his companions sing with him." Barak's arms flapped at his sides. "I can't sing!" He hissed his next words. "What if he tries to make me to sing in front of others? What'll I do?"

A great hand fell on Barak's shoulder from behind. "You'll sing as long and as loud as I do, man! Why, the frogs will envy us. You will sing of Milkan's beauty, Eymard's wisdom, and Aram's prodigious strength! We will sing, and our listeners will know our greatness!"

Barak stumbled backward. "Eoban! I didn't hear you coming."

Eoban slapped Barak on the back and swung his gaze to Aram. "Good evening, Aram. How are you on this fine night?"

"It's good to see you, Eoban." Aram glanced at Barak. "I hope you weren't offended—he's a mere youth in matters of the world."

Eoban snorted. "He just needs some time away from the softening influence of women. A month or two with me, and he'll gain a man's confidence."

He nudged Aram playfully. "He'll be ready to take over leadership—so you can take your ease." His eyebrows rose to new heights as he grinned. "How about that?"

Barak froze, his face stricken.

Like a rushing wave breaking over a damn, Aram burst out laughing.

Pounding the two men on the back, Eoban drew them back to their seats. "A repast? How convenient!"

As they sat around the fire, they shared stories, laughed, and snorted in uproarious good humor.

When the moon crested in the sky, Aram stood and rubbed his back. He sucked in a deep breath. "Namah and the baby will need me in the morning. She'd appreciate it if I was awake."

Eoban snorted. "There are many women who can help her. Someone should care for you while she's taking her rest."

Aram dropped his hand on the big man's shoulder. "You know little of a woman's love, my friend." He turned to Barak. "Remember me as you wander. And return home soon."

Barak stood and clapped hands with Aram. "Soon—and with good news."

Turning away, Aram wandered back to his dwelling.

An owl hooted in the distance.

Suddenly, Eoban's voice boomed in the darkness. "So, what do you want to sing first? I'll start!"

In the dark night, Aram grinned.

Chapter Forty-Six

—River Clan—

Our Injured Past

Ishtar, his gaze seared to the ground, was so lost in thought that he didn't move a muscle even as the sun baked his back. The lake spread before him in all its blue-white glory while a swirling wind rippled the golden grass waving on the shore. His long hair, loose from its tie, fluttered around his face. He clasped his hands over one knee and propped one foot on a boulder as he lifted his eyes and scanned the lake.

Scampering wild life hunted for food along the shore.

Turning, he marched back to his village.

Lud, his mouth in a stern line and his body beaded with sweat in the heat of the day, perched on the rooftop as he repaired a hole in Ishtar's dwelling.

Ishtar stepped forward.

Lud waved, a smile gleaming through his eyes. "Good morning. Have a nice walk? Your mother is looking for you."

Ishtar shielded his face from the glare of the sun. "I could say the same to you. Surely, your mother is wondering where you are and when you're coming home. She couldn't know that you're prolonging your visit just to fix someone else's roof."

Lud chuckled. "I'm eager to return. Have you made a decision?"

"I've decided to go with you."

His eyes rounding, Lud scrambled down the ladder. "Really? You'll come with me?"

Ishtar nodded. "I can't be gone long, but the journey will do me good. Eoban and Barak are traveling. It's only right I do as much. Aram and Obed can manage, and Hagia will help. I enjoy seeing new things, and it'll be good to travel for pleasure for once."

Lud bounced on his toes in excitement. "Let's prepare. You tell Hagia. I'll finish the roof. We'll arrange supplies quickly. It won't take long—now that I know where I'm going!" He chuckled as he scampered back up the ladder.

Ishtar called after him. "You're certain your family will welcome me? I'm the enemy remember."

Halting in the middle of his climb, Lud's face blanched. "That was all Neb's fault—not your doing. My people will realize things have changed. I told them about you. Don't worry. You'll be welcome. Now, hurry up! I can't wait to start."

Ishtar and Lud stood in the early morning light ready for their expedition.

Hagia wrung her hands as the sun broke over the eastern horizon. "You don't know what you're doing. These people won't have good memories of our clan. They'll fear you, and fear makes men blind and angry."

"Neb's raid was many years ago. Lud is a man now. Besides, I want to meet new people and establish trade. We need new ore supplies to make our metals. Don't you see? I'll help our clan advance without bloodshed!"

Hagia shifted, her gaze falling to the ground and her lips puckering.

Caressing her arm, Ishtar glanced at Lud. "You'll see. I'll bring home new treasures and perhaps I'll make an alliance and find a beautiful woman to marry." He nudged her playfully. "That'd surely make you happy."

Shaking her finger at Ishtar, Hagia glared. "Don't you dare marry a strange woman! If you must marry outside the clan, go to Obed's people. Now—go on—get this journey over with."

Wrapping his mother in an embrace, Ishtar winked at Lud. "I'll be home soon. You won't even have time to miss me."

He started away. Looking back, he saw Hagia standing before her dwelling, watching them. He waved and slung his pack higher over his shoulder.

Hagia shrugged, lifted her eyes to the sky and shuffled inside.

After snapping off a grass stem, Ishtar chewed it as he strolled at Lud's side. "This may be the beginning of great things."

Lud nodded. "I couldn't bring Pele home. I have to accept that. But at least we can bring peace to our injured past."

Both men looked to the sky.

Chapter Forty-Seven

—Lake Clan—
Haunting Melody

Barak loped along, his gaze sweeping from right to left. The sun, cresting on the western horizon, brightened a landscape of green grass and distant hills against a background of high bluish mountains.

Loping along beside Barak, Eoban sang stories of the mountain men—a race of men abandoned by the gods who created them. His voice rose with a haunting melody, underscoring their tragedy as if it might be the fate of all mankind.

Just when Barak couldn't stand the lump rising in his throat, Eoban changed his tune and sang of the hill people—a race that thrived on challenge, their hearts neither divided nor afraid.

Intoxicated by new thoughts and stories of heroic deeds, Barak grinned as he tromped along. Only when Eoban told him to join in a refrain did he falter.

When night fell and the moon rose, a haze of milky white splashed across the sky, reminding Barak of the stories of the souls of departed spirits. When they settled down after a simple repast, Eoban chanted about the moon that made her home in the sky, leaving an earthbound lover bereft. The haunting specter of longing and lost love forced Barak to close his eyes, his hands clasped tight.

Ending his chant, Eoban tapped Barak's arm. "Don't miss her so much."

Barak opened his eyes and swallowed. "I can't help it." He

peered at Eoban. "Isn't there anyone you miss?"

A wistful smile played on Eoban's lips. "Of course. That's why I sing."

Before Barak could ask another question, Eoban lay down and slung his blanket over his body. "Get some sleep. The morning light makes everything easier to bear."

Shifting into a comfortable position, Barak watched the firelight play against the night. Laying his head down, he closed his eyes.

Eoban snored in peaceful slumber.

Chapter Forty-Eight

—River Clan—

Go Our Own Way

Ishtar watched Lud leap ahead, his eyes sparkling and his mouth open ready to shout in joy. Lud's village lay just ahead. Tagging along behind, Ishtar laughed. When he jogged closer, he pulled Lud to a sudden stop and lifted an admonishing hand. "I'm glad you're so happy, but perhaps it'd be better if I didn't come upon your people too suddenly."

Like a bubbling pot unable to contain itself, Lud swept Ishtar's concern away. "Don't be absurd!"

With a frown, Ishtar stood his ground.

Shrugging, Lud sighed. "Fine. But I'm going ahead. I'll announce that you're here with me, and they'll be glad—you'll see."

Lud race ahead, calling his parents' names and waving his arms.

Leaning against a tree near a frothing stream, Ishtar watched and waited.

Like an exuberant child, Lud raced to various dwellings, laughing and calling.

As if they were sleeping dogs roused from a mid-day slumber, the village came to life.

A man shouted. "Jephite! Come see your son!"

A woman shrieked "Naomi—hurry!"

Lud's parents hurried forward, their arms out, smiling, nearly crying with excitement.

Villagers ran out of every dwelling, Lud's name on everyone's lips. Children scurried through the crowd, dancing, reaching out to be touched or picked up. Dogs yipped, and even the sun shone more brilliantly on the happy scene.

Lud galloped from person to person, embracing, patting, and grinning at everyone. Questions and exclamations flew through the air amid the shouts of happy children.

Ishtar's eyes rounded in wonder. In all his years, he had never seen anything like this. Never had he witnessed the outpouring of love for a wandering son returned home. A lump rose in his throat. His eyes stung. Straightening, he reminded himself that he was the leader of a powerful clan, and he was Lud's friend. He was the reason that Lud was free.

Lud raced toward him, one arm outstretched as if to drag him back to his family that much faster.

Following Lud into the midst of the camp, Ishtar felt the hundred pair of eyes focused on him. He attempted a smile, but his face felt wooden.

Gripping Ishtar's arm too tightly, Lud stopped before his parents. "This is Ishtar—the one I told you about. He's returned with me, and he wants to—"

Lud's parent's eyed Ishtar, their gazes raking him up and down, their smiles vanishing, replaced by disgusted frowns. Jephite folded his arms over his chest, while Naomi pulled Lud away from Ishtar, closer to her side.

Jephite squared his shoulders, his chest thrust forward. "This is the man who destroyed our homes, killed our men, and stole our women and children! He dares return here?"

Pulling away from his mother's embrace, Lud scooted in front of his father. "No, you don't understand. That was his father—Neb. He was evil. Ishtar was only a boy. He helped to stop Neb's—"

Lud's mother spat to the side.

Fury flushed through Ishtar's body. Clenching his hands, he turned and started away.

Lud circled around and stepped in Ishtar's path. Gripping

Ishtar's arm, he made him turn back. He peered at his parents and the huddled, scowling villagers and called out. "Ishtar is a man of peace. He came here seeking an alliance with us."

Jephite, thin with a sharp nose and watery blue eyes, flushed as he surveyed Ishtar from head to foot. "You not only destroy others' families, but your own as well?" He glanced at his son. "You want us to trust this man, Lud? I'll attribute your lack of judgment to your innocence and this man's deceit. An enemy of this measure can never be trusted—neither him, nor any of his kin—to the tenth generation."

Lud stood transfixed. As if trapped in a nightmare, Lud plodded over to his mother. "You understand, don't you?" He clasped her hand. "Ishtar is not his father. He's brave and valiant. He changed the course of his people. They're peaceful now. I'd never deceive you."

Naomi's eyes scanned her son's face, and her scowl softened. "I believe you, but you've always been too trusting. We've learned from cruel experience that the bees that make the sweetest honey can still sting."

Jephite wrapped his arm around his wife. "Naomi is right." He glanced from Ishtar to Lud. "Show your friend to the village edge, son, and keep him company tonight, but in the morning, he must leave. No matter what else, he carries the blood of our enemies in his veins."

Lud shook his head, his mouth open, disbelief showing through his bewildered eyes.

Naomi forced a smile. "It is time for you to find a wife, Lud. No more wandering." She glanced at Ishtar. "Say your goodbyes and know that you will each be where you were meant to be." She clasped her husband's hand and nodded to Lud. "We'll see you tomorrow—early."

Ishtar stared through cold eyes, watching as the villagers returned to their duties. Disgust tasted foul on his lips. He turned on his heel and strode away.

With dragging steps, Lud trudged at his side, his head hanging low.

When they arrived at the same tree Ishtar had stood under just a short time before, they stopped.

Ishtar grabbed Lud's shoulder. "You won't stay with me tonight, Lud. I'm leaving. Go back and do as they say. Marry and have children. Maybe your sons will have more forgiving spirits. Some day you can visit, and we'll remember old times together. But for now, it's best to go our own ways." He lifted his gaze to the sky. "I have much to ponder and decide."

Tears streamed down Lud's face. "It shouldn't have happened this way! If I could forgive, why can't they?" He choked back tears. "Even dead, Neb spreads his evil. Will it never end?"

Ishtar shook his head. "I don't know. Go to your people, Lud. They want you home, and I wish to be off." Clasping his shoulders, he stared into Lud's eyes. "Goodbye, my noble friend. We'll meet again someday."

Ishtar turned and marched away, peering back only once.

Lud watched him, his body hunched in defeat, his eyes grieved.

Ishtar stopped. "Go home, Lud."

Lud turned and traipsed away.

Ishtar climbed down a steep hill. His face burned in flushed fury. Lud's family had been wrong—but Hagia had been right. Landing on level ground, he marched with his head high and his fists clenched.

Chapter Forty-Nine

—Grassland—

Useful Talk

Barak watched Eoban trade goods. Though he had seen him do it many times, he never ceased to be amazed by his friend's cunning. The bargaining went on for some time, and Barak's eyes wandered over the scenery around him. This village bustled with many times more people than their own village. These people favored bright colors instead of the earthen shades their own clan preferred. Various dialects mixed with the cacophony of mooing, bleating, and screeching animals herded from place to place.

When Eoban made the final exchange, he smiled broadly at his benefactors. Pounding them on the back, he said that he held no hard feelings even though they were stealing food from his babies' mouths, and he and his wife would probably starve. He was pleased he'd been able to do them some small service and would be glad to bargain with them again—if he lived long enough to do so.

They nodded agreeably, stating that though they had always tried to be generous to strangers, they had outdone their usual munificence on this occasion. He was getting the better deal, but they'd not complain.

After much back thumping, they parted and Eoban sauntered back to Barak with an armful of bulky packages wrapped in cloth.

Barak grinned. "What'd you get?"

Eoban lifted his hands like a man surrendering to the crack

of doom. "What did I get? Why, I got robbed! These are the hardest hearted people in all the world." His voice rose as he glanced back. "Little do they care if my sixteen children starve!" He bounded past Barak, a smile tugging at the corners of his lips.

Barak sauntered behind. They settled in a quiet corner by a low wall, and Barak proceeded to unpack food from his bag. He passed a hard cheese and bread to Eoban, who slurped a long drink from a skin bag. The two chewed in silence while they gazed across the landscape.

After swallowing the last of his meal, Barak crossed his arms. "Robbed, eh?"

Eoban shrugged. "These people may be hard-hearted and thrifty to the bone, but they've never met me before. I did pretty well." He shuffled through the bag. "The cloth brought the best price. We'll have to bring more next time."

Barak's eyebrows rose to great heights.

Eoban uncovered his goods: knives, chisels, an ornamented tray, sharp spear heads, pipes, a set of dyes, two pounds of spices, four sets of copper clamps, a coil of copper wire, hundreds of colored beads, an assortment of wedges, and two socket hammers. He glanced at Barak. "Now, that we're out of trade goods, we can head home."

Tugging his sleeve, Barak frowned. "You don't want to look around anymore? I thought we'd stay another day—or so."

Eoban reared back, scowling. "We've been here long enough to draw attention to ourselves, and that's not a good idea. Besides, I thought you were anxious to return to Milkan."

"You're worried about Milkan?" Barak's eyes narrowed. "Why? What's happened?"

"All right, don't get so inquisitive." Eoban waved his hand and faked a hearty laugh. "You see that group of men by the well?"

Barak glanced over.

"They've had their eyes on me. I feel like the pig that's been picked out for the feast."

"Would they attack us in the open?"

"No." Eoban huffed. "They'll follow and attack us in the dark—probably while we're sleeping."

Barak's shoulders slumped and his head dropped to his chest.

"So, we're leaving today. I know a place we can go for the night. It's safe and easily defended." He tapped Barak's shoulder. "There's more to this business than just making a good bargain. You have to hold on to your valuables, or someone will relieve you of your burden—which can include your life."

"I am not completely ignorant. I've seen the world—a bit."

"Of course—a bit." Eoban smiled patronizingly.

Barak threw the water skin at him.

"Gather your things, but pretend we're going to lie down for an afternoon rest. When I stir, get up and follow me. If we get separated, head south outside the gate. Go to the copse of trees and wait for me."

Barak nodded.

~~~

Barak followed directions precisely, and after they made it safely to the trees, Eoban gestured for him to follow his lead.

The day wore into evening as they tromped through the dense woods. They marched through an old wooded glen, crossed their own path several times, and turned south into a clearing with a gentle stream that ran down from the hills toward flat land that lay ahead. The scenic view shown spectacularly in the golden light. Huge boulders lay strewn about as if a giant had thrown them into heaps to clean up the valley floor.

After sunset, Eoban gripped Barak's shoulder, signaling him to stop.

Picking a sheltered spot, they dropped their bags and settled in for the night. Barak leaned against a tree. "You think Vitus could fashion tools like the ones in your bag?"

Eoban shrugged. "It's possible. I don't know the man

personally, but I've heard he was quite skilled—once upon a time."

"It might make all the difference. If only he had a reason to live."

Eoban snorted. "Something we all need."

Curling up on his side, Barak wrapped his fingers around his knife.

Barak awoke to the sound of Eoban humming a cheerful tune. A fire flickered in a small pit, and two fish roasted on a spit.

Eoban turned as Barak rose. His eyes rounded with wonder. "I feared you were dead. I was going to dig a shallow grave and say some heartfelt words over you—after I ate my breakfast."

Barak raked his fingers through his hair, blinking in the bright morning light. "Yesterday's little jaunt through the trackless wilderness tired me—a tad. Even the most intrepid traveler needs rest. Except you, apparently." After rising and stretching, Barak sniffed appreciatively at the roasting fish. "But this little repast will help me along. There's enough for both of us?"

Eoban stared in wonder while his lips moved in silent convulsions. He bowed in servant fashion. "Why, master, I'm sure my miserable little fish—the ones I caught and cleaned early this morning—could not satisfy you. There're plenty left in the stream. I'll just eat my little morsel—if you don't mind."

Barak's lips pursed as he peered through half-lidded eyes. "It's going to be one of those days, is it?"

Eoban crouched close to the fire, watching his fish sizzle to perfection. He lifted the smaller one out of the flames.

His shoulders slumping, Barak threaded his way between the boulders, silent guardians of their camp.

Four men approached.

Swiveling on his heel, Barak ran back to camp. Sucking in

frantic breaths, his heart pounding, Barak scrambled to his bag and began stashing every weapon he owned on his body.

His eyebrows rising, Eoban turned. "What?"

"Four men—coming through the trees. Be prepared!"

"And when—exactly—were you going to share this magnificent news with me?" Eoban sprang forward and tripped, knocking his well-cooked fish directly into the flames. Reaching out, he burned his fingers and yelped. Glaring at Barak, he flung the tail he managed to save dramatically into the fire.

As Eoban tucked the last of his weapons in place, four men strode around the largest boulder. They were dressed rather nicely for men tromping through the woods.

Barak and Eoban backed up to a smaller boulder, shielding themselves.

The tallest stranger called out and offered a friendly wave. "Don't be afraid. My name is Malak. I'm from the clan of Onia. We mean no harm. We're only travelers." He lifted his hands. "You wouldn't happen to know of a leader named Obed? Onias was a relative of mine, and I wish to see his widow and know that his sons are well cared for." His open, friendly face lighted in a wide smile. "You can trust us."

Eoban and Barak glanced at each other, communicating an understanding. They stepped forward, Barak behind Eoban, who strode out stiffly as if being pushed by an unseen hand. "You say you are kindred to Onias. He was my friend, but I don't recognize you."

The young men, arrayed in long robes of soft cloth with tasseled edging, wore beaded sandals and knit caps. Their clothing, fair skin, and clipped beards signaled more style than sense.

Sizing up the assembly, Eoban relaxed.

Barak shook his head, a sneer curling his lip. These were not battle-ready men. Their soft hands and long nails fluttered like frightened birds as they picked their way over the rough terrain.

The tallest held one hand against his chest and pointed to the other three. "We're just travelers, looking for the kindred of Onias—four brothers—our mother was Onias' mother's sister." He stepped closer. "Word reached us of Onias' death." His eyes widened and his voice dropped. "We've even heard of battles against the wild men of the north."

His brothers shuffled uneasily, glancing around.

"Where are my manners?" He pointed to each brother in turn. "Achan, Zara, and Charn. They're my younger brothers, as you must have guessed." Perching on the edge of a boulder, he clasped his fine fingers together. "We enjoy trading and have done well for the clan. My father is very proud."

The three young men flashed eager smiles of practiced charm.

Eoban nodded and returned an insincere smile. He pointed to the burned-to-a-crisp remains of his breakfast. "We were about to have breakfast, but—"

"We'd be happy to eat with you."

Barak smothered a groan.

Eoban clenched his jaw and headed for the stream.

~~~

Barak sat to the side, leaving the conversation to those who wished to engage in a battle of wits.

After a breakfast of roasted fish and bread, the brothers daintily dusted their hands free of crumbs.

Malak leaned forward and tapped Eoban's knee. "We'd like to journey with you—if you don't mind." His eyebrow arched. "You're returning home, are you not?"

Eoban shrugged. "We might travel a bit more."

Malak's face fell. "Oh, I'm sorry to hear that. Imagine the gratitude of Obed and his wife when they hear of what you've done for us. I had just about given up—"

Rubbing his temple, Eoban relented. "Oh, all right. I see your point. We can travel together. You'll honor us too, I suppose."

He stepped toward the boulders. "Wait while my brother and I gather our things."

Barak raised one eyebrow, following Eoban out of earshot. As they gathered their things, Eoban hissed into Barak's ear. "They're hiding a secret. Stupidest four thieves I've ever come across. This whole situation stinks like rotten fish. I wish we were closer to home."

"But if they want to attack, why don't they do it? Surely, they can see we're outnumbered."

Eoban's brow furrowed. "These men have never fought. They're like children playing a game." He nodded sharply. "Keep your eyes open and your hand on your weapon."

Barak adjusted his bag over his shoulder, scowling as he followed Eoban back to the others. "By the way, I didn't get any fish."

"Good, keep that in mind. Remember who interrupted breakfast."

Once they were all assembled, Eoban led the way with Malak at his side. Barak took up the rear while the other three staggered in the middle. By noon, they reached an open area where the hot sun beat on their heads.

The sky arched in a wide expanse of brilliant blue without a cloud in sight. Insects and birds hummed and twittered in a chorus of exuberant nature. Bees buzzed on the sweet-smelling flowers while grasshoppers leapt from twig to stem.

Barak's stomach growled, and Eoban glanced at him sympathetically, clutching his own stomach.

Closing his eyes, Barak pictured a stroll through Ishtar's village with these villains trailing along. Glancing back, he frowned.

Eoban stared straight ahead, a scowl etched across his forehead.

The four brothers huddled shoulder-to-shoulder, whispering. Eoban's gaze rose and his steps slowed.

The birds had flown away. The open glen lay silent as a grave.

Suddenly Malak strode to Eoban's elbow. "My friend, my

brothers and I are not so strong as you. We're weary and in need of a rest. Could we beg you to stop so we can catch our breath? We'd be glad to share the last of our bread and honey." His shining, merry eyes made him look like a man holding back laughter.

Eoban glanced from the brothers to Barak.

Barak tipped his head in agreement.

Eoban's stomach clenched with hunger. He covered his middle with a nonchalant gesture. "I guess we can take a break—for your sakes."

Barak thrust his spear into the ground and plopped down beside his bag, rummaging for scraps.

Eoban stretched out in the shade of a boulder that jutted from cliff. No sooner did his head hit the ground than he found himself surrounded by six hulking forms.

Huge warriors, like the mountain men but with different clothing, hairier bodies and darker skin, pointed their spears at Barak and Eoban.

Leaping to his feet, Barak reached for his spear, but one of the brothers grabbed it and shoved him forward so that he and Eoban stood together.

Unwilling to give up so easily, Eoban kicked two of the brothers off their feet, but the giants quickly quelled his act of defiance.

Malak chattered to one of the giants in a dialect Barak only dimly understood. "Dispose of them as you wish. We'll take care of their belongings. Now, take them far away. I don't want carrion birds hovering over us."

The oldest warrior scowled. He pointed to three men striding toward them. "Master has come. He would speak with you."

Malak's eye's narrowed. "I didn't ask for him. I told him I'd come later. Why is he here?"

"Not for me to say. He will speak to you."

The largest, most muscular giant Barak had ever seen strode forward and stopped in front of Malak, his black eyes glittering. "You did not keep your word, small one. I will take the leavings this time."

Malak's brows furrowed into petulant mountains. "You have no authority here. My father has an agreement with you. If I'm displeased, you'll have to explain it to him!"

The giant's hand wrapped around Malak's throat. "Your broken body will do all the talking. Get out of my way. I want to inspect the prisoners."

Barak stepped back, involuntarily swallowing as the giant towered over him. Squaring his shoulders, he stiffened and held firm.

The giant circled Barak slowly like a man about to make a judicious purchase. Slowly, his gaze roamed over to Eoban. The two pairs of eyes locked. They stood staring at each other, stiff and unyielding.

Without warning, Eoban struck the giant across the face.

Barak groaned.

Flinging his hands on his hips, Eoban glared at the hulk. "That's for the care package you sent with me. That snake was still alive, you know!"

The entire assembly froze in stunned silence.

The giant rubbed his jaw, his gaze fixed on Eoban. Just as suddenly, he burst out laughing. "I thought you liked fresh food! It was the largest I could find that would fit in your bag."

Cocking his head back like a scolding mother, Eoban spat his words. "Large? And poisonous! It was a matter of who was going to eat who." Eoban's whole body relaxed. He chuckled, breaking the tension. "I brought it home and showed everyone. The story I told made everyone's hair stand on end. I still have his skin as a keepsake—to remember you."

The giant thumped Eoban on the back, his gaze traveling over the four brothers. "So, you're getting robbed by these thieves." His gaze fixed on Malak. "It's a good thing I came along." He swung an arm around Eoban's shoulder and pointed to the brothers. "They're ruthless. If I kill, at least I do it quickly." He made a wringing motion. "Or like this." He made a quick thrust. "But these vermin like to see their victims suffer."

He tapped his chest and spat to the side. "No heart. Only think of convenience. If your death interferes with their meal, they'll leave you tied up in the sun to die from the heat." He clapped his hands like a man wiping off dust. "I am sick of them." His scowl deepened. "They cheated me. That was a mistake."

Eoban glanced at the brothers, who were now well trussed up.

Taking a step forward, Barak peered from the giant to Eoban. "Who—?"

Clearly ready for a happy moment, Eoban opened his arms wide. "Barak, this giant of a man is from a mountain clan, but unlike our other encounters, he's the finest goat herder in the world! A friend—except when crossed." Eoban glanced at the brothers. "What he's doing with these four, I can't imagine."

With a bow, the giant warrior placed his hand over his heart. "My name is Gimesh. Eoban is long on words but short on meaning. You two are traveling companions?"

Barak nodded. "We went north to do a little—"

Eoban coughed and gripped Barak's arm. "Gimesh, keep an eye on these four. They might try to overpower your men."

The four brothers slumped in heaps on the ground, silent and limp while the other warriors hemmed them in with their spears.

A glint sparkled in Gimesh's eyes. "Trading? Well, Eoban is a cautious fellow. He knows, under different circumstances, I might like to look at what you have." He peered to the side. "But since I just acquired four new slaves—I'm in a good mood. You may go without paying tribute to my people."

The four brothers looked up, their eyes wide and their mouths open. Malak squirmed. "This means war! My clan will want vengeance. My father will see you roasting over a hot fire! I will laugh at your—"

Gimesh shoved Malak back with his heel, pressing his dirty foot on the prisoner's throat. "Enough." He pointed to one of his warriors, who soon wrapped a shaggy twine around

Malak's mouth.

Strolling aside, Barak nudged Eoban. "How did they know about Onias?"

"They may be who they say, but that hardly means they aren't thieves. Family members are sometimes the most ruthless. Remember Ishtar's father?"

Rubbing blood back into his stunned face, Barak plopped down on the edge of a boulder.

Eoban strolled next to Gimesh. He pointed back to Malak and his brothers. "So, what are you going to do with the fools?"

Raising his voice, Gimesh stared at the four men. "We'll eat them. Yes, roasted man is very good—especially with fresh herbs the way my wife cooks them. She has a special recipe handed down from her mother. Been in the family for generations."

Groans and a couple of obvious sobs issued from the defeated band.

Barak stared bug-eyed at Gimesh, motioning frantically to Eoban.

Eoban nodded his head sagely and patted Gimesh on the back in sympathetic understanding. He leaned closer and dropped his voice to a whisper Barak could barely hear. "Three months—they'll learn." He grinned. "But let it slip that my clan really does eat our enemies—so they won't be eager to find me again."

Gimesh smiled. "It's been a joy to see you again."

Eoban rubbed his neck. "Next time, I hope it'll be under better circumstances."

After a final pounding pat on the back, Gimesh started away, signaling his men to lead the brothers along. "Thank you for the meal. They'll fatten up just fine."

Eoban grinned; his hands perched on his hips like a proud papa.

Barak convulsively tugged at his friend's arm like a panicked child.

Eoban brushed Barak's hand away.

Barak and Eoban watched Gimesh and his men led Malak and his brothers away with a rope tied about their necks.

Once out of sight, Barak swiveled on his heels and confronted Eoban. "You could've stopped them. Though they were wrong, no one deserves—"

Eoban slung his bag over his arm and gripped Barak's shoulder. "You fret too much! They'll live like slaves for a few months—then they'll make a miraculous escape and think they're very clever. But they won't rob anyone again—at least not in this area."

Barak tilted his head, appraising Eoban.

"Gimesh knows—unlike you—that some men are twisted like trees blasted by the wind. They have to be broken before they'll ever grow straight—if they ever grow straight." He shrugged. "It's always a risk to even care. It'd be easier to kill them."

Barak's eyes narrowed. "But he won't…kill them?"

"Only if there's no other way to keep his people safe."

Barak blinked, his hands limp at his sides. "So everything you said—"

"Useful talk. Gimesh talks big, but he means no harm." Eoban bounded across the meadow as the sun hugged the western sky.

Barak traipsed along behind. "Was there ever a snake?"

"Oh, yeah. What a snake! About ten feet long. Deadly as they come—"

Chapter Fifty

—Lux—

Murky Waters

Teal elbowed his way through the crowd and faced Sienna. He crossed his arms, ignoring the milling throng around them.

As the hottest nightspot on Lux, Rambl'en bustled to the liveliest tunes of various worlds while hosting the biggest dance floor and the most extensive All-You-Can-Eat Buffet this side of The Divide.

Holding a strawberry-colored smoothie with pineapple-shaped spikes, Sienna turned on her charm, a grin wavering lusciously on her lips, and a sparkle in her eyes. "Oh, Teal. I didn't know you came here." She cocked her head and tapped his arm teasingly, her sculptured, white nail lingering on his hand. "You're much too…controlled…for such an unpredictable environment."

After glancing around in a wide circle, Teal refocused his gaze on Sienna. "I wouldn't say the same about you."

The briefest hint of irritation flittered over Sienna's gaze, but with a quick retreat to the bar, she sipped her drink and waved to the intoxicating beverages. "Pick your poison and have a little fun." Twirling, she waved her hips to a sensuous Bhuaci rhythm floating through the air. "Once you relax, maybe we dance—eh?"

Peering into the distance, Teal paused. He exhaled a slow breath, rolled his shoulders, and tipped his head. Strolling to the bar, he poured a shot glass of a golden liquid, tossed it back, and swallowed. The edges around his eyes soften as he resettled his gaze on Sienna.

Smoldering lust rose in Sienna's eyes, and she sashayed to

the dance floor. A strong female voice sang an ancient Bhuaci love song to the rhythm of an urgent, demanding beat. Sliding her hands from Teal's waist to his hips, Sienna pulled him close.

Teal lowered his head so it hovered just above hers and wrapped his arms around her back, tightening the embrace.

They swayed, slowly, silently, while Sienna nuzzled her head into Teal's chest. When she murmured a half groan, Teal tilted his head closer, his gaze low and intense.

Sienna purred. "I've always wanted this...from the first time I saw you. There's not a Luxonian alive who rivals you."

A slight grin wavered on Teal's lips. He caressed her back and his voice dropped, husky yet restrained. "Some would say I'm hardly Luxonian at all."

Sienna glanced up, her eyes wide, astonished. "That's why you're so fascinating. You're practically a man!" Her hand slid up, rubbing his chest. "You can be *anything* you want."

Closing his eyes, Teal leaned in, kissed her forehead—and pulled back. He peered into her eyes. "And you?"

Lifting her face, her lips waiting, Sienna whispered. "I'll be whatever you want."

With a quick shake, Teal stopped dancing. "I'm not a god. I'm just—"

Tugging him closer, Sienna's eyes burned in a hot glow. "You'll complete me. I can help you. I know people—everyone'll love you."

His shoulders squaring, Teal whisked a strand of hair from Sienna's face. "People?"

Her eyes drooping in half-lidded coyness, Sienna smirked. "I do more than assist Judge Sterling." Her tongue slithered over her lips. "I have friends—leaders and masters—who like to know what's going on in the universe."

Gripping her hand, Teal led Sienna from the dance floor to a tall table in a quiet corner. He laced their fingers together and leaned toward her. "You spy on others...as a falcon maybe?"

Sienna jerked upright. She gripped the table edge. "What do you know about it?"

"You followed us to Earth. Why?"

Folding her hands, Sienna collected her modesty. "Zuri and Ark are known throughout the region for their treacherous deceit." She glanced up, her eyes imploring, her knuckles turning white. "I trust you—but no one trusts them."

Swinging his head up, his gaze floating over the room, crowded with mingling life forms. Teal snorted. "Except me."

With a slap on the table, Sienna's colors shimmered, her gaze sharp and her chin jutted forward. "What?"

Teal lifted his hand in defense. "I don't mean I trust them with human lives—only with my own." He stared down at Sienna's glaring face. "I've traveled with them extensively...spent time chatting with them. And them with me. We have an...understanding."

Dragging breath from the deep like someone struggling for air, Sienna reached across the table and gripped Teal's hands. "A Cresta and Ingot?" She sucked in a shuddering breath. "You know what they're like. They killed those men—"

"Neither Ark nor Zuri killed them. They died of poisoning—a shared meal gone very wrong." Teal slipped his hands from under Sienna's grasp. "Ark showed us proof. That's why he did the experiments. He couldn't understand why five otherwise healthy men lay huddled in grimaced death. And when Zuri came upon them, he buried them in a shallow grave. He knew I'd blame him."

Sienna slipped her hands off the table, but Teal grabbed them and held them in his own. "Now you talk. Who's the clerk—the one you conspired with in the meeting hall?"

With a sniff, Sienna jerked away. She snorted an abrupt laugh. "You're not the man I thought you were."

"That's been said before."

Stepping away from the table, Sienna slid her gaze up and down Teal's body. "And it'll be said again—no doubt." In a flash, she disappeared.

Raking his hand through his hair, Teal exhaled a long breath. Zuri sauntered to his right side, while Ark plodded to his left.

They leaned over the table, surrounding Teal.

Zuri patted Teal's shoulder. "Can't win 'em all."

With three arching tentacles, Ark slid drinks in front of each of them. "Might as well enjoy the lubricants."

They lifted their drinks in salute.

Ark sighed. "One third of Cresta citizens dead, and we don't even know who did it."

Zuri arched an eyebrow. "We know—just not their names or where they live."

Teal's gaze traveled to where Sienna had stood. "Or what they want."

Ark plopped his drink back on the table. "We're in murky waters."

Teal, Zuri, and Ark placed their drinks on the table—untouched.

Chapter Fifty-One

—Grassland—

Exchange

Aram sat perched on the edge of a wide stool, a staff in his hand, and considered the assembly. Eoban and Barak sat next to each other as they held a council with Obed and Ishtar. The five men huddled around an open fire on a cool, cloudy afternoon. The days had been dry, but a breeze blew across the land, tossing the grass in green undulations.

Eoban laid out his treasure in a splendid semi-circle. The assembly nodded, their gazes roving over various examples of fine craftsmanship. With friendly banter, they divided up the goods based on what had been traded of equal value.

Picking up a tray, Ishtar traced the inscriptions carved around the image of a bull. "What's this meant to symbolize?"

Leaning in, Eoban peered at the etching. "That's the mark of one of the metal workers." He sneered. "He considers himself a god because he can work such strong metal. Arrogant fellow. He even has a special name for that bull. Says he's descended from a noble line of such god-bulls. Blathering idiot, if you ask me."

"But his work is quite good." Ishtar's eyes glittered. "If I could craft metal like this, I might think so myself."

Eoban waved as if to brush away an annoying insect. "Owning that tray is enough to show your importance."

Ishtar rose and strode across the circle. "Might I trade, Obed, for this tray? I know it's yours by right, but can I persuade you to take something else in exchange?"

Eoban and Aram exchanged glances.

Obed shrugged. "I have no great need for a tray. Trade as you see fit. I'm well pleased with what we've acquired. In the future, we'll send four men and double our fortune." He turned to the side. "What do you think, Aram?"

Aram studied Ishtar, a puzzled frown crushing his brows. He tore his gaze away and focused on Obed. "Yes, fine. Just be sure that Eoban goes along—so that he can meet up with old friends as need be."

Eoban grunted with a nod and turned to Ishtar. "What're you going to do with the tray?"

With a glowing smile, Ishtar stared at the distant horizon. "Trade!"

The other men exchanged glances.

Obed broke the silence. "Well, Eoban and Barak, you've done well. I never thought our goods would bring back such marvels."

Eoban shifted. "It was the cloth that did so well. You don't realize how much fine quality material is prized. The designs with reds and blues were especially popular. I could've sold more, but I ran out of goods. Next time, gather all we can spare, and I'll bring back greater treasure."

Obed grinned. "I'll spread the news." He wagged a finger as if making a pronouncement. "No idle hands from this day forth." Nudging Eoban, he dropped his voice. "Did our carved pieces attract any notice?"

"Not much. Oh, people made favorable comments but few wanted to trade for them. They were useful to seal a bargain though, and I gave some away to make friends."

Pulling his lip, Obed frowned. "Tobia has taken to carving. He thinks he can trade goods for such things. I'll have to tell him to put his efforts into something more useful. Perhaps he could ornament handles and learn to make metals like that tray."

The sun hovered over the horizon, purpling the sky and sending pink rays in long radiant fingers. Birds settled into nests and twittered languid goodnight songs.

Barak turned to Aram. "Perhaps we could invite Vitus to try his hand at copying some of these goods. Or maybe he could trade with us next time."

Aram pursed his lips. "Good idea. He needs something to pull him out of his grief." He glanced at Ishtar. "May I borrow that tray and show it to Vitus? Perhaps he'd be inspired."

A scowl darkened Ishtar's face as he clutched the platter in his arms. "I'd like to, but I'm afraid I have plans, and I need it just now."

Dropping his gaze, Aram pursed his lips.

Obed rose and stretched, reaching for the sky. "The smell of roasted meat tantalizes me. Talk as long as you want, but I'm going for food."

Eoban climbed to his feet. "A fine idea. I'm as hungry as a lion."

Barak stood and tapped Eoban's stomach with the back of his hand. "Better hurry. When Eoban has an appetite, the food disappears quickly." He tipped his head at Eoban. "Show a little mercy. Let the others go first."

Wide-eyed, Eoban thrust his hand over his heart. "I'd never consider anything else. My leader, my friends, and then myself."

"Glad to hear you say that." Barak started forward. "Perhaps I'll get something to eat this time."

Chapter Fifty-Two

—Lake Clan—
—Ten Years Later—

By All the Stars of Heaven

Aram stood along the shore, leaning on his staff, the wind blowing gray locks of his hair into his face. Waves lapped over his gnarled feet, only to withdraw, leaving them covered in sand.

Coming up from behind, Tobia sauntered to his right and shared the view. He sighed. "Its beauty never ceases to amaze me."

Glancing aside, a smile tweaked Aram's lips. "Coming from a man of your vast experience, I must agree."

Tobia dropped his head and wiggled his toes into the sand. "You tease me like I'm a child."

Reaching out, Aram gripped the young man's shoulder. "I tease you because it is one of the last joys in my life."

Tobia swiped a stone from the shore and skidded it over the water. It bounced three times before dropping below the surface. His jaw clenched. "I wish Ishtar hadn't taken over the trade routes."

Aram shook his head and leaned more heavily on his staff, shifting his weight. "I wish he'd never gotten married—at least not to that wretch."

Gathering up a handful of stones, Tobia skidded them over the water in turn. "He won't take any of my carving—says they don't serve any purpose."

"Give me one of those." Aram held out his hand.

Tobia dropped a stone onto his palm.

Bracing himself, Aram arched his arm and flung the pebble. It skipped twice and plunged under the surface. He shrugged. "He's obsessed with metalwork. Claims it's our only hope." He glanced at Tobia. "Personally, I think he still feels guilty about Neb, trying to outshine his father's evil with the promise of prosperity."

Tobia kicked the foamy surf. "Obed should do something…make him stop pushing so hard." He stared at the horizon. "But he's not going to get involved."

"Can't blame him." Aram faced Tobia. "I'm still head of my clan, and Obed still has control of his people. We just don't manage the trade—"

"As things stand now, that means Ishtar rules everyone!"

Aram scowled and lowered his voice. "Hardly. Eoban and Barak are as independent as ever."

A woman's voice called from the top of the cliff. "Tobia? Come home now."

Tobia turned, sighed, and clasped Aram's elbow. "You want help up?"

Aram grinned and ruffled Tobia's hair. "I'm still capable of getting home on my own."

The voice called again. "Tobia! Hurry up, son."

Aram chuckled. "You better hurry before she comes down here and beats me for delaying you."

Tobia smiled. "She'd never beat you. Scold your ears off, but never beat you."

"Go on then. Keep both our ears safe."

Tobia hustled up the incline.

Aram's gaze traveled over the horizon. A sudden wind flapped his cloak and sent a wet chill over his arms. With a sigh he started up the incline.

A high-pitched cry made him turn too quickly. He stumbled and fell, sprawled on his back. Closing his eyes, he muttered under his breath. "By all the stars in Heaven, I'm not—"

A soft breath wafted over his cheek. Aram stiffened. Alarm spread through his body. He opened his eyes and stared into the icy blue orbs…of a kitten.

It mewed and lifted a paw in supplication.

Dropping his head back onto the sand and staring at the golden evening sky, Aram laughed.

Chapter Fifty-Three

—Grassland—

The Heart of Our People

Jonas beat a rug against a bench and scrunched her face as dust billowed into the air. "I've never liked that woman, and I never will. She reeks like rotten fish. I wish Ishtar had never brought her here."

Leaning again the doorpost, Obed grinned. "You've wished that so many times, she ought to disappear, but she's still around." He waved the dust away with the back of his hand. "Just stay out of her way, and you won't have to think about her."

"Sounds easy! Poor Namah has to listen to her every time she comes through. She never fails to mention that—in the clan of her birth—deformed children are disposed of. She looks at Gizah as if she were made of mud!"

"Namah is quite capable of taking care of herself and her child. Gizah hardly seems to even notice Haruz. She never complains, and she is a good, obedient girl, which is all that anyone cares about. Haruz expresses her opinion wherever she goes. It's who she is."

"I wish she were someone else."

Rounding the corner of the hut, Tobia stumped forward, met his mother's gaze, and frowned. "What's the matter?"

Pushing off the post, Obed started away. "Your mother's just airing her thoughts on the merits of marrying foreign women."

Tobia's gaze rolled skyward. "Ah. Haruz? She's a viper, isn't she?" Striding to his mother, he wrapped his arm around her shoulders. "Don't worry. I won't let her plant her god here.

I have more respect for our God than anything she believes in—even if it is made of metal."

Obed stopped and turned back, his hands perched on his hips.

Jonas swiveled on her heel, tossed the rug on the bench, and stared into her son's eyes. "What do you mean? What's she done now?"

Obed shook his head. "You get along with everyone. How is it that you can't make peace with this woman?"

Her hands trembling, Jonas crossed her arms. "You don't see it, do you? She cares for no one—not as a wife or as a mother. She lords her authority over everyone. If Ishtar gives her things, he is useful. If her sons do her bidding, they are useful. In her mind, she is all that matters."

She glanced back at Tobia. "What god is she obsessed with now?"

Tobia played with the frayed edge of his sleeve. "She's building a temple…on the south end of the village. Surely you noticed. Men have been clearing the space for days, building a platform."

Jonas slapped her hands together, wringing them like she would strangle a hen. She turned to her husband. "I thought that was something you ordered, Obed. Why didn't you tell me?"

With a shrug, Obed started away. "I didn't want to upset you. It's just a place to put her god. She says it'll help the village prosper. What harm can it do?"

Her eyes widening and her shoulders rising, Jonas flung her hands into the air like a woman taking an oath. "What harm? A god's image has power! If she offers the power of her god to meet our needs, people will be beholden to her. She'll gain control over the hearts and minds of our whole clan."

Obed stopped, slapped the post of their dwelling, and turned around. He frowned, rubbing his cheek.

"Unless—" Tobia held out a small figure. "—We have a stronger God." He stepped closer, lifting a carved figure of a man with his arms outstretched.

Taking the figure and examining it from every side, a smile softened the furrows etched in Jonas' brow. "This is beautiful! How did you make his expression so peaceful? He looks like someone I'd like to meet."

"I've been working on him for a long time. Years ago, Eymard described the vision of his God, and I've kept it in my mind. He used to tell me wonderful stories about how the world came to be and how man was created." Tobia's gaze seemed to peer into a hidden distance.

Shifting his weight and shaking his head, Obed chuckled. "Eymard was a charming storyteller, no doubt. But don't forget, they were just stories."

Tobia's face clouded. "Mother is right. The God you choose makes a difference."

Rubbing his neck, Obed pointed a finger in the air. "I thought you said that there's only one God."

Jonas glared at her husband. "Some lie and pretend to be what they are not."

Obed dismissed her fury with a laconic wave. "Believe what you want. Leave me out of it." He strode off.

With a sigh, Jonas put her arm around Tobia's shoulders. "I'll share your God, if you don't mind." She placed the figure back in his hand and closed his fingers around it.

"Perhaps we'll see Him some day—like Pele used to see her Sky Warrior."

Jonas closed her eyes. "I miss Eymard." She glanced after her husband. "Nothing's been the same since he passed on."

Tobia opened his hand, stared at the figure, and sighed.

Chapter Fifty-Four

—River Clan—

Body and Soul

Hagia closed her eyes to the nasty, nasally voice in her head: *Old as the hills.*

Children's laughter warmed her cold bones. She opened her eyes and considered the state of her wrinkled, age-spotted hands.

What's worn out—should be thrown out.

She wagged her head. *Wait until your time comes, woman.*

Her two grandsons played tag with the other children.

Free as birds...wild as wolves...if only Ishtar had listened.

In a sudden turn-around, the two boys pelted toward her, throwing themselves onto her abundant, though frail, lap.

"We're hungry!"

Hagia didn't doubt it. She sighed. Hugging them, she started to rise, her arms shaking under the effort.

Each boy took an arm and helped her to her feet.

Peering down, she saw her son reflected in their eyes—not their mother. *Thank the God of Creation.* "Come, let's eat. We'll hold body and soul together once again."

~~~

Ishtar crouched in a dark corner with his hands framing his face as his shoulders hunched in fear and frustration.

His wife, Haruz, turned and sliced her hand through the air, like a mother admonishing a naughty child. "You know perfectly well that our god is angry. There'll be no metal in the soil until you do something worthy—a sacrifice of some kind. My people would offer a child or an old person. Personally, I think children are better, for the gods receive them gladly, and they're not a serious loss."

Ishtar's head ached. He grimaced as she pounded across the room, her bracelets tinkling like bells. "Would you consider one of our sons a worthy sacrifice?"

Scrunching up her face in annoyance, she waved the thought away. "Ishtar, you're such a fool. Of course, we can't offer either of them. They must support us when we grow old." She plucked a fig from a plate of fruit, popped it into her mouth, and chewed noisily. "You've been taking from the earth for years now—you must be grateful and give something back. It's simple. If you want the gods to supply you with ore, you must offer a sacrifice. Make it a girl. They're not as valuable as boys."

Ishtar squeezed his eyes shut, his body trembling.

Smoke wafted from a small central fire, filtered across the room. Haruz waved it away and swiped another fig.

Gripping the wall, Ishtar climbed to his feet and staggered to the doorway. He glanced back.

Haruz had flopped down on a pile of soft pillows and picked through the fruit tray.

"I need some air."

Haruz frowned. "At this time of night? It's black as death out there."

Stepping into the night air, Ishtar muttered under his breath. "Same in here."

Hagia jerked awake and struggled to sit up. She tilted her head to listen. When she heard a soft groan, she crawled out of bed and struggled outside. She found Ishtar seated on a boulder a little distance from the rippling stream. Placing her old crippled hand on his shoulder, she sat next to him. "What is it, my son? Tell me."

Ishtar moaned again and leaned slightly on his old mother. "Haruz, my prize wife, will be the death of me."

Slumping in exhaustion, Hagia hunched forward and held Ishtar's hand. "She's like Neb—a stony heart with a flint mind." Her eyes glimmered in the darkness. "Do you have any doubt about what you must do?" She caressed his head. "Do not pay for prosperity with your soul."

Straightening, Ishtar squared his shoulders. "From the moment I brought her home, I've had abundant good luck. I'm the leader of three clans. My word is law. We've more trade routes and more goods than ever before—and we've not had to fight one clan in battle!"

Hagia snorted. "I love you more than words could ever say, Ishtar, but you're not the man you were. Prosperity has ruined you. Your wife has plucked out your bones and ground them into dust."

Dropping his head into his hands, Ishtar moaned. "We're out of ore. Our trading days are over. Prosperity is dead."

Hagia clenched her hands so tightly, she winced.

"Don't believe what that woman tells you. You wouldn't submit to Neb. Don't submit to her."

"She says the gods are angry because I took from the earth and never offered anything back."

Hagia dropped her voice to a husky whisper. "Offered—what?"

"A sacrifice—a girl child—or something."

She jerked her head up and spat her words. "If Haruz thinks there should be a sacrifice—let her sacrifice herself. You'll find your prosperity with sweat and hard work—like other men do."

Clutching the walls for balance, Ishtar stood. "Are all my accomplishments nothing?" His eyes blazed in fiery fury. "Do you think there are no gods?"

A shaft of moonlight fell across Ishtar's face. She saw his drugged stupor. The red-rimmed eyes. The slack mouth. The mind vacant of reason.

Covering her face with her hands, Hagia's shoulders slumped till she was bent nearly double. Sobs wracked her body. After crying herself to weariness, she heaved a long breath and, despite her blurred vision, rose and hobbled back to her dwelling.

~~~

Aram awoke to a strained tone in Namah's voice.

"Wake up, Aram. We have a problem." She rubbed his arms, tugging him to sit upright.

His bleary eyes opened a slit. He groaned, his body aching, as he tried to rise. "I'm tired. Can't this wait?"

Namah shook her head with sharp decisive motions. Suddenly, a figure stood beside her. She glanced over, her eyes dilating. "Oh, Ishtar, I thought you were going to wait for me to bring him out."

Ishtar stared down at her. His pupils, mere pinpricks of their former selves, appeared as vacant as if the soul had left the man and only the shell were left to perform this task.

Namah shuddered.

"I'll speak to him alone. Now." He stepped forward and stared hard at Aram.

Aram sat up, wide-awake now. Without a word, he reached for his tunic, thrust it over his head, and motioned Ishtar to join him in the other room.

Ishtar stood motionless. "What I want to say will only take a moment. I am going to make a sacrifice tonight. I want you there."

Blinking, Aram stared at Ishtar. "I heard rumors. Jonas came with a story that she'd heard from your mother. You think you'll please the gods with a human sacrifice? Have you gone insane?"

Ishtar's red-rimmed, vacant eyes stared at the wall. He didn't move a finger.

"Don't you remember Neb? The curse? You of all people

ought to realize that any god who's pleased by death isn't a god but a devil."

Slowly, Ishtar's gaze rolled back to Aram. "God or devil—it makes little difference. The power is there. I must bow to a greater authority—or be destroyed."

Grabbing his staff, Aram slammed it against the wall. "You've made yourself a god!" He swung the staff around and waved it at Ishtar. "Who would you sacrifice?"

Turning away, Ishtar stepped out the door murmuring. "The gods will decide."

After throwing his staff against the empty doorway, it clattered to the ground. Aram dropped his head onto his chest, heaving a shuddered breath. *Oh, God.*

Wringing her hands, Namah stepped in. "Who will protect us from such madness?"

"We'll call a council and speak to the people. This can't be allowed to happen." He reached for his staff and tottered.

Namah grabbed it and placed it in his hands.

"I'll talk with Barak. Send for him please."

After she left, Aram leaned against the wall and slid to the floor, staring at his cracked staff.

~~~

Aram stood at the edge of the cliff and watched the sun descend to its place of rest.

Turmoil stirred the air. Huddled crowds hunched together, talking in muted tones. A few angry shouts rang across the village.

Vitus pounded up to Aram and stopped at his right side. "We need the ore, Aram, or we won't be able to trade anymore. We'll be at the mercy of other clans who can make better weapons. Is one life too much to ask so the whole clan can prosper?"

Aram scowled, his lips curled in disgust. "Would you offer up your child, Vitus?"

"If there was no other way, I'd have to. We can't make ore! It comes from the gods."

"Greed blinds you. I remember a man so distraught by the loss of his wife and child that he could hardly sit up. Doesn't the child matter? Or the parents?"

Folding his arms over his chest, Vitus shrugged. "You have a better solution?"

With a snort, Aram limped away.

Suddenly, young arms surrounded his waist. "Let me come with you, father." Gizah gripped his arm, steadying him as he hobbled home. Her back, slightly humped, bent lower as she watched their steps over the dusty ground.

"Where's your sister?"

"Bethal is with her beloved." A smile quirked at the corners of Gizah's lips. "They can't stay apart for even half a day."

Patting his daughter's hand, Aram glanced at her face. "Are you all right?"

"Of course. My leg is better today."

He stopped and faced her. "I need to see Barak."

"I'll take you—"

Aram sighed. "Only if you stay outside."

"Yes, father." She lowered her eyes and led him forward.

Milkan sat in the shade of her dwelling, nursing a baby while other children chased each other or sat on benches, grinding corn or weaving cloth. Milkan slapped the wall and called out. "Barak—Aram's here." She smiled from Aram to Gizah, patting the bench.

Freeing her father's arm, Gizah sat next to Milkan.

Barak arrived in the doorway and gestured for Aram to step around back.

When Aram settled on a bench, Barak strode to a pile of split wood and started to stack them by the wall. "Sorry I haven't visited, but the wife—" He gave a sidelong glance with a hint of a smile. "You know. And Ishtar wants me to—"

With a groan, Aram dropped his head onto his hands.

"What is wrong?" Barak straightened and stared at Aram, his

eyes widening. "Don't tell me the rumors are true!"

"Oh, Ishtar's mad all right." He swiveled and glanced around. His eyebrows rose.

Barak shook his head. "They've gone inside."

Aram dropped his voice. "I'm afraid."

Barak's chin jutted forward. "Of Ishtar?"

"Of him and everything he represents. I can't stop him."

"You worry needlessly. Ishtar's full of wild notions. No one takes him seriously."

Aram slammed his fist into his hand. "Ishtar means to do this, and no one will lift a finger to stop him. Some are actually in agreement with him." He warbled a weak imitation of Vitus. "'We need the ore, Aram, we need the ore.'"

Barak rubbed his chin. "I'll find Eoban and Obed, and we'll make sure that no human sacrifice is made. What insanity!"

Aram peered at Barak. "You really think so?"

"You said yourself—he's mad."

"Ishtar, yes. But not Haruz. Or rather, not the force that directs her. It's a brilliant tactic. No matter what happens, she can threaten that the gods were not pleased. Through Ishtar, she can demand whatever she wants, and if it's not your wife or child, you'll consider yourself lucky. The one who speaks with the voice of god wields the knife."

Dropping on the bench beside Aram, Barak's shoulders slumped. "Now I *am* afraid."

"You should be." Aram jerked his thumb backward. "You have a household of sacrifices in there."

Chapter Fifty-Five

—Lux—

Dark Matter

Teal curled his hands into fists as he stared out the window overlooking the brilliant Luxonian horizon.

While humans would see luminous, oversized peacocks with colorful flowing tails chasing each other across the pearl colored sky, Luxonians saw the glory of shimmering light in action.

Teal faced his mentor. "Excuse me, sir, but have you taken leave of your senses?"

Sterling's jaw tightened. He returned to a large mahogany desk overflowing with labeled artifacts from various worlds: striped Sennacheb seashells from Crestar, a five-level children's game from Ingilium, a twisted miniature evergreen from Helm, and a petrified crab with sixteen claws from Sectine. Peering down, he tapped his datapad. "I'm the most sensible Luxonian I know."

The door slid open and Sienna stepped in. She saw Teal, hesitated, and then turned around.

Sterling lifted his hand. "Not so fast. I have a game I'm just dying to try, and I need all the players in the same room." He pointed to a circular space in the center of his office. "There. Stand on the far side—leave room for the others."

After an obedient three steps, Sienna turned. "Who—?"

"Tut, tut! Curiosity killed the quadruped."

Teal rolled his shoulders. *If I spontaneously combust, it won't be my fault.*

The door slid open. No one entered.

Dutifully, Sienna perched on the rim of a red circle drawn on the floor.

Teal and Sterling stared at the open door.

Ark's disembodied voice called, "Is this where I should be?" Stomping to the doorway, Teal reached over the threshold and tugged Ark into the room. "What do you think? Judge Sterling isn't given to flights of—" He glanced at Sterling and clamped his mouth shut.

Sterling lifted his arm in welcome. "Please, come in. Take your place next to—"

Ark's golden eyes glowed as they fixed on Sienna. "Oh, you don't need to tell me. Mistress of the skies!" He slogged over to Sienna's right. "Catch any delicious prey lately?"

With a hooded gaze, Sienna sniffed and turned away.

A red orb appeared in the center of the circle, rising from the floor. Rays of colored light stretched, and, like a self-constructing web, began to zigzag across the central space, creating a three dimensional mini-universe.

A bell toned.

While Ark, Sienna, and Teal stared—absorbed by the holographic universe—Sterling clapped and rubbed his hands together like a delighted schoolboy. "Oh, good. She brought her bell."

The door slid open. The clerk stood on the threshold. "You sent for me?"

Wrapping an arm around the petite Bhuaci, Sterling led her into the room and positioned her to the right of Ark. "Yes, Kelesta, you're here to assist us with a little experiment."

Kelesta frowned and shrugged Sterling's arm away. "I'm a court reporter—not a scientist." She squinted at Ark, her lips pursed in distaste.

"Of course, you are." Sterling scurried back to his desk and tapped a console. "Where is that Ingot?"

Sienna gasped as a star exploded on the hologram. It sent out showers of sparkling lights in all directions, nearly obliterating the scene.

Teal frowned, his edges glowing.

"Oh, blast. Wrong sector." Sterling tapped his datapad.

The door slid open, and Zuri pounded into the room. "What's this all about?" Glancing from Sterling to the circle, he met Ark's and Teal's gazes.

Sterling peered up. "Perfect."

The holographic scene blurred and reformed. In the center, a large water-based planet with two moons circled a mid-sized star.

Ark sucked in a draught, nearly choking. "Crestar?" He turned, his tentacles flinging out in all directions. "What's the meaning of this?"

Stepping closer, Sterling opened his hands like the president of a college about to address the new student body. "You've been gathered here for the express purpose of solving a mystery."

Ark shook his head. "If you're trying to discover who murdered one-third of our population—"

Sterling lifted his hand, alarm widening his eyes. "Not at all." His tone dropped. "I think we all know the answer is one we'd rather not antagonize." Whirling his hand over the hologram, he turned it so that Ingilium became the focus, with Crestar now a mere dot on the far-left side. He pointed. "Helm is over here, and Sectine twirls in her own purple sphere just there." Tapping the air, each planet glowed, highlighted against the universe.

Zuri folded his arms across his chest. "And Lux?"

Sterling tapped again, and another planet glowed on the revolving scene.

"Where's Earth?" Teal's eyes narrowed as he titled his head, staring at Sterling.

"Ah! There's the mystery." He retreated to his desk and tapped the console. The glowing scene blackened and then a new scene appeared. Earth and her compatriot planets circled the brilliant sun as the Milky Way spread out into a wider universe.

"Did you know that what we see—our mutual worlds and the universe we inhabit—are growing dark? In fact, we're almost nothing more than dark matter?"

Ark's gaze jerked away from the scene, his golden orbs wide with horror. "What's this?"

Sterling lifted a finger. "Watch." He tapped the console. Their home universe reappeared while Earth and its accompanying universe disappeared.

Zuri poked the air. "I don't get it. What are you trying to say? That we have two universes has long been known—"

Kelesta whispered as she gripped Sienna's arm. "We're not in *different* universes."

Sterling nodded. "Give that Bhuaci a prize." Snapping his fingers, Earth disappeared and the room plunged into darkness.

Sienna gasped.

Ark gurgled and choked.

Zuri cursed.

"Stop playing games!"

The lights blinked back on.

Teal stood by the wall, his hand over the console trembled. He marched up to Sterling. "You mean that if humans looked for us now, we'd appear as nothing more than dark matter?"

Turning on his heel, Zuri clomped to Sterling's desk and pounded the console. Earth reappeared. "We've traveled for eons." He shook his finger at the revolving universe. "I've been to Earth! It isn't buried in blackness."

Stepping over to the little Bhuaci, Sterling took her by the arm and settled her on a couch near the back of the room.

Limply, Kelesta fell onto the cushions and buried her face in her hands. "I thought we were in control—using them. But all along—they've been using us."

"Who the hell are we talking about?" Zuri's metallic boots clicked on the stone floor as he strode to the couch. He peered down at the Bhuac.

His head dropping to his chest, Ark inhaled a deep draught

and let the foamy bubbles settle before he spoke. "They-who-shall-not-be-named, the ones who just lay Crestar in the dust of devastation—" He lifted his watery gaze. "But why?"

Sienna crouched at Kelesta's side. "You know—don't you?"

Kelesta shook her head, tears glinting in her eyes but refusing to fall. "Bhuaci have been hounded from the beginning our existence. Like animals with prized qualities, we represent what other races wished they had—but we're not prey. We're—" Her lips trembled. "For lack of a better word, we're simple—like children. Innocent." A tear slipped down her cheek. "We once knew uninhibited joy, but cruel encounters have taught us a painful lesson."

Sterling stepped closer, his hands clasped before him, and his gaze soft like a gentle but grieved father. "What did they promise you?"

"They said that if we kept our eyes open and reported back, we would never be victims again."

Ark slapped his tentacles together and wrung them into whiteness. "But why kill us?" His breather helm heaved as his bubbling breaths rose and fell faster. "Why couldn't they have just talked with us?"

"You dared them! You challenged their authority!"

"A few simple questions—"

Kelesta leapt to her feet. "There are no simple questions for Crestonians! They know your zealous, obsessed minds better than you realize. They took matters into their own hands to keep you—"

"Ignorant and afraid?" Zuri's eyes narrowed. "Not so."

His body glowing in heat, Teal stomped forward and gripped Kelesta's arm. "They murdered innocent beings on the supposition that Crestonians would use their knowledge for evil purposes." His hand tightened on her arm. "They had no right."

Sterling nudged Teal's grip off the Bhuaci with the back of his hand. "It's over now. The Ingal will deal with its own trials." He glanced around. "But we have troubles of our own."

Zuri turned back to the hologram. "So you're saying that we can see Earth, but they can't see us?" He shrugged. "They're primitives. What's the problem?"

Teal shook his head. "If a race of beings can turn the lights off for humanity, what's to say they won't—"

Sienna shuddered. "Oh, God."

Ark wrapped his tentacles around his middle. "Call on who you like, but we'll never forget—or forgive."

Sterling rubbed his eyes. "I feel rather weary. Knowing who turned off the lights doesn't really solve the mystery."

Teal turned and glared at Sterling. "What mystery would that be?"

Sterling pointed to Earth as it serenely orbited its sun. "What'll happen when the lights go back on?"

Chapter Fifty-Six

—River Clan—

Your Chosen Creed

Aram joined a large circle of men who stood encircling a massive fire in the center of Ishtar's village. Sparks rose up toward a full moon that glowed in the eastern night sky. Barak and Eoban stood at his right, while Obed stationed himself at his left. Aram peered, frowning, at a shining obsidian knife laid aside on a small table.

A murmuring, agitated crowd milled along the periphery, waiting for the spectacle while a few children scurried between the adults, chattering in nonsensical excitement. Occasional shrieks of laughter broke the tension, sending titters through the multitude.

Every now and again, a youngster skittered forward and threw dried grass and branches onto the massive flames, sending more sparks into the sky.

The moon, at its zenith, cast an eerie glow on the spectators.

Hagia sat outside her dwelling, slumped and muttering.

Tobia stepped forward and glanced at his mother as she waited, tense and alert, with the other women. He marched over to Obed's right side.

Obed glanced at him and frowned, though he gripped Tobia's shoulder as if to communicate silent strength.

In an abrupt motion, Ishtar emerged from his dwelling, pounding the butt of his spear in the dirt. Ishtar's unfocused gaze floated above the assembly. He wiped his red-rimmed eyes with the back of his hand and marched forward.

Following behind, Haruz held her chin high, her gaze

glittering in the firelight. Her hair was tied in a multitude of braids and gathered high, like a woman with snakes coming out of her head. She nudged Ishtar forward.

Ishtar raised his arm, his eyes blazing like the fire before him.

The crowd froze. Not a breath stirred.

"My people!" Ishtar waved his fist, his voice rising to a hysterical pitch. "We must appease the gods with a sacrifice...one chosen from among our own."

Eoban snorted, his arms crossed high over his chest. "Your people? Be honest, Ishtar, admit it. Your wife put you up to this. Let's stop this foolishness. Take that woman of yours and go home." He glanced to the side. "Barak, Obed, let's—"

Grasping his spear with both hands, Ishtar lunged forward and swung at Eoban. "I'll sacrifice you for interfering with the gods." His gaze swept around the circle. Several men stepped forward ready to assist. "Everything must be done properly."

Aram pushed ahead, but Jonas gripped his arm and whispered. "He'll kill you!"

Barak leapt from the crowd, flushing in fury. "If blood must be spilled tonight, it won't be from the innocent, Ishtar! Your rule is over. Aram has given leadership of his clan to me, and I claim all the trade routes." His voice dropped as he leaned in. "I have enough men to destroy you."

Squaring his shoulders and thrusting out his chest, Ishtar bellowed. "You can't destroy the forces I call upon!"

Tobia suddenly stepped into the light, holding out his carved figure. "But God can! The God of all good men—of Eymard, of Pele. The one that saves rather than destroys."

Ishtar swung around, spittle flying from his raging mouth. "There is no such God!" Staggering like a drunken man, Ishtar twirled his spear above his head. "Dark spirits haunt us all— in the hearts of men everywhere." He pointed to his wife. "But the god that put ore in the earth will reward us...if we offer one life...just one."

Suddenly, into the wavering light stepped the figure of a young man. Gasps from the crowd spread as necks craned to

312

see the newcomer.

Barak sucked in his breath. "Lud?"

Lud met Ishtar's confused gaze. "There is One stronger than your haunting spirits, Ishtar."

A shimmering light spread before the assembly and clarified into human form. A calm, young woman appeared in their midst.

Ishtar leaned forward, frowning. Suddenly, he reared back and stumbled.

Struggling to her feet, Hagia whimpered. Sobbing, she hobbled forward, her arms outstretched. "I knew you'd come back. Pele, my girl! You were always so good!"

The crowd broke into confused chatter.

Ishtar blinked, shaking his head like an angry bull. He stabbed the ground with his spear. "We buried you. I was there. You can't be here!"

Pele lifted her arms as if to embrace everyone. "You don't know what's possible, Ishtar. You are blind. Once you swore never to forsake the cause of good. But here you stand, serving evil."

Ishtar swayed, his hands holding his head as if grappling with an interior foe. He moaned and drool slid down his chin. He pointed an accusing finger at Haruz. "She made me! She brought the evil back." Falling to his knees, he doubled over on the ground.

Flinging herself between Pele and Ishtar, Haruz snatched Ishtar's spear from the ground. She swung around and spat her words at Pele. "You don't belong here! Others rule where you have no power."

Clasping her hands, Pele peered up into the night sky as if addressing an unseen host. "Tell us, Haruz, who were you going to sacrifice?"

A sly grin slithered across Haruz's face. "Bring out the child!"

A large man clumped forward, carrying the unconscious body of a young girl.

As terror shot through him, Aram howled. "Nooo!"
Namah shrieked.
Obed jumped forward. He gripped Haruz's arm. "Are you mad, woman? What have you done to her? This is Aram's child."
Throwing back her head and lifting her voice, Haruz pointed the spear at the sky. "She's been chosen by the gods since her birth for just this moment." She gestured like an accusing witness at the child. "See the withered hand, the misshapen back... She's marked—meant as an offering to please the gods." Lowering her gaze, she peered at Aram who was being held back by Barak and Eoban. "You should be honored...your daughter can finally serve a useful purpose after such a meaningless existence."
Fury blinding him, Aram broke free and leapt at Haruz. His crippled foot crumpled, and he staggered to the ground.
Haruz laughed.
As if a string pulled him from his middle, Ishtar rose and circled the shimmering figure of Pele. "This is not Pele! It's an imposture." He swung his gaze around. "You're clever, Obed! Was this your idea?"
Eoban shook his fist. "I don't know if Pele has returned from the lands beyond, but I do know—" His voice rose to fever pitch. "The only offering acceptable to me would be your head, Haruz." He waved at Barak and Obed. "Let's take the child home—"
Disbelief warred with fury as Aram staggered to his feet, his gaze searching the assembly "We can't leave now. They've drugged my child, tried to kill her—all because she has an imperfect body." His gaze swung from his child lying on a stone slab to the crowd. He ran his hand over his torso. "What about my broken body? And others yet to be born, and old women and crippled men who can't fend for themselves? Who will be sacrificed next?" Aram limped to his daughter's side.
Brightening to an intense glow, Pele's gaze locked on Haruz. "You will suffer for your chosen creed."

"Enough of this idle talk!" Haruz slammed Aram's head with the spear, knocking him out of the way and snatched the knife. She slapped it onto Ishtar's palm. "Now!"

Using both hands, Ishtar gripped the knife and towered over the sleeping child.

Aram scrambled to his feet, holding his head.

Obed, Eoban and Barak rushed forward. Confusion broke over the assembly as some men jerked aside and others struggled to stop the mad rush.

Ishtar's gaze swerved to Lud. "Your people accused me of evil even when I came in friendship. Now I do what I must—but still you condemn me!"

Leaping ahead, Lug gripped Ishtar's raised hand in his own, panting with exertion. "Pele warned me in a dream. She still cares for you—"

They both glanced to the side, but the shimmering presence had disappeared.

Ishtar's grip slackened, and Lud stepped back.

Tears streaming down his face, Aram lifted a moaning Gizah into his arms.

Plowing into Lud like a mighty wave, Haruz knocked Aram aside again and grabbed for the knife. But Ishtar tightened his grip. They struggled for control.

Eoban and Barak weaved back and forth on their feet, straining for an opening.

Haruz glanced at her men. "Help me. Ishtar has betrayed—"

Ishtar reared up and hefted all his weight down, plunging the knife deep into Haruz's bowels.

She shrieked and staggered backward, blood staining her long pale tunic. "Look what you've done! You've slain your wife!" Crumpling to the ground, she gasped and groaned, still clutching the hilt of the knife.

Ishtar stood transfixed, his mouth open, his body heaving and trembling.

Obed and Barak gripped him by the shoulders.

All eyes fixed on the gasping woman as she fell backward,

her eyes wide, staring at the sky. Her hands dropped limply at her sides and her gaze froze. A single tear slipped down the side of her face.

Leaning against the restraining hands of his friends, Ishtar's voice dropped to a husky whisper. "A curse…you share…my son." He turned, shook himself free, and staggered away.

The silent crowd stepped back, staring, struck dumb.

Returning to Aram, Obed lifted Gizah from his arms, and carried her beyond the retreating throng. Namah, Jonas, and Milkan followed.

Barak and Eoban stood shoulder-to-shoulder before the dying fire. Eoban pointed to Lud. "He always shows up at just the right time, doesn't he? If only—" His gaze turned to the blackness where Pele had appeared.

Stepping up to his friends, Lud pointed to the retreating figures. The three turned from the scene and followed their friends.

Tobia stood alone, silent, staring at the dead woman and the blood-soaked earth. He still clutched the wooden figure.

Aram stepped up and laid his hand on the boy's shoulder.

Tobia stared at the flickering flames. "Will Gizah be all right?"

Aram nodded. "She'll recover…in time"

Tobia faced Aram. "Will you?"

Turning, Aram glanced at the bloody body and shuddered. He looked up to the star-strewn sky. "Maybe…in God's time."

Chapter Fifty-Seven

—Lake Clan—

Welcome

Tobia stepped inside, studied his mother as her hands worked the colored threads on the loom, and exhaled a long breath. "Should I go?"

Leaving her colored threads, Jonas wrapped her arm around her young son's shoulders. "He doesn't have much time left, but he'll be glad to see you. Don't be afraid."

"I am not afraid, just sad. He's always been kind to me. The world's a safer place because of him. Besides, he understands…things."

"Aram's a remarkable man, no doubt. But he isn't gone yet. Now go."

After tromping out into the slanting afternoon sun, Tobia rowed a small boat across the lake, climbed the incline, and trudged through the village. The sun edged the horizon when he arrived at Aram's dwelling.

Namah ushered him into the dim back room.

Aram lay on a soft pallet covered in blankets though a sticky heat suffused the evening air.

Tobia lifted his hand in formal salute. "Mother and father send their greetings." Shuffling in place, he glanced around the room.

Aram motioned to his side. Shifting to an upright position set off a coughing fit. Once he settled, he leaned back and patted Tobia's hand. "Tell them I returned their greetings."

After slinging his bag from his shoulder, Tobia reached in and pulled out a carved figure. He held it up, so the light from the window slanted over it, bathing it in a golden aura. "I was going to make you a cat, like the big one that chased you out of the woodlands." He shrugged. "I'm thankful for that cat. If you hadn't come, we'd have died or been made into slaves." A sad smile flickered over Aram's face.

"Was it planned—did God know that we'd need help—so He pushed you in our direction?" Aram's gravelly voice dropped to a whisper as he closed his eyes. "I hardly saved you. Just helped you save yourselves."

Tobia leaned forward, his fingers clenched around the figure. "You chose a side. You fought. Your people died to help us—it changed everything. Ishtar would never have been freed from Neb if you hadn't come." Tobia bowed his head, squeezing his eyes shut. "Please, don't go."

His eyes welling with tears, Aram pressed Tobia's hand. "I'll miss you too. But, we'll see each other again—someday."

Opening Aram's hand, Tobia laid the carving on his palm. "I made it after talking with Eymard about his God. I thought—maybe I could belong to Him too. He's not human, of course, but if He were, this is how he'd look—with His arms out stretched in welcome."

Aram clasped the figure to his chest. "Thank you."

Swallowing back emotion, Tobia stepped to Namah's side, and after one backward glance, strode out the doorway.

Aram shuddered through a body-wracking sigh, lifted the figure into the beam of light, and smiled.

Chapter Fifty-Eight

—Grassland—Lake Clan—River Clan

Loved Well

Obed leaned against a wall with his arms crossed and watched Jonas throw wet clothes over a taut line. The sun shone on a brilliant new day and the clan bustled in everyday duties.

A tunic splattered onto the dusty ground, and Jonas muttered a curse under her breath.

Shoving off the wall, Obed grinned and strolled over. He carefully laid the last garment on the line. "The tunic meant no harm. No reason to wish it ill fortune."

A frown warred with a half-smile while Jonas shook her head and lifted the dripping basket. "You're hardly one to talk. You've been as antsy as a wet cat ever since—" She closed her eyes and clenched her jaws, her lips trembling. "Sorry."

Obed took the basket out of her arms, dropped it to the ground, and pulled his wife into an embrace. He caressed her head under his chin and whispered. "We'll always miss him. But we must go on."

Nuzzling against Obed's chest, Jonas murmured, "I know. But I hate losing people. I've lost so many—"

At the sound of hurrying footsteps, Obed glanced up.

Tobia jogged into sight and stopped short. "Oh. Sorry, I didn't mean to—"

Obed sighed, holding Jonas tighter, and peered over the top of her head. "Yes?"

Tobia jerked his thumb backward. "Onia has been quarrelling with the other boys, and I'm afraid he's annoyed some of Ishtar's men—"

Obed wagged a finger at Tobia. "I don't care what Ishtar's men think! Ishtar's gone, disgraced beyond redemption and—"

Jonas pulled away and retrieved her basket. "Stop—please."

Blowing air between his lips, Obed squinted at Tobia. "I thought you were helping in the field?"

Tobia lifted his hands in innocence. "I just needed to finish a figure, and Onia slipped away—"

Pounding forward, Obed clenched his hands into fists. "Not anymore! Get back to work and forget those worthless carvings, would you?"

Her eyes blazing, Jonas gripped Obed's arm. She nodded to Tobia. "Get your brother and go back to work."

Tobia's shoulders drooped, and he turned away.

Jonas called after him. "We'll talk about your carving tonight."

After Tobia disappeared around a shed, Jonas spun on her heel, and glared at her husband. "How dare you lose your temper at him! He's not his brother's keeper."

Obed shook his head. "Isn't he?" His gaze roamed over the village. "Somebody had better be." Refocusing on his wife, he clasped her by the shoulders. "We're a little lost right now—" He glanced up at the bright sky. "But we'll find our way."

Her gaze searching the sky, Jonas allowed Obed to pull her into his arms again. "We're not alone."

~~~

Eoban rowed over the lake and tromped across the grassland until he stood at the edge of Ishtar's village. Ishtar's two sons, Amin and Caleb, sat in huddled heaps against the doorway of their dwelling. Their disheveled hair and ragged clothing spoke of indifferent care. The smaller child wiped his tear-streaked face with the palm of his hand. Then Amin wrapped his arm around Caleb's slim shoulders and pat him like one would pet a beloved dog.

A throbbing ache pounding in his chest, Eoban shook his head and started forward. At the sound of a voice, he stopped short.

From across the way, Hagia hobbled forward calling. "Amin! Caleb! Come eat now. It's getting late."

The two of them looked up and scurried to her, burrowing their heads in her ample middle.

Hagia cuddled them in her embrace.

Stepping back, Eoban exhaled a long breath. *Another day.* He turned, and started home.

~~~

Barak wandered through the village offering a wave or a nod to everyone he passed, though he couldn't feel the smile plastered on his face. Stopping before Namah's dwelling, he watched Gizah prepare dinner.

The young woman moved with remarkable agility.

Namah called from inside, "Gizah? Come, help me a moment."

Gizah turned and passed over the threshold.

As Barak neared home, three children pattered forward calling, "Papa! Mama wants you home. Says you're to fix the bench or no supper."

Barak's eyes twinkled. "Oh, she did? But what if I'm busy? I'm sure one of you could manage." He tweaked his eldest son's nose.

His little girl groaned. "We'll die of hunger, papa!"

A man's voice called from another dwelling. "Barak? We need to talk about the sheep problem. We've outgrown the eastern pasture."

A woman waved and trotted forward. "Ay! Barak, is anyone going trading again soon? I've been working—"

Barak sighed and peered down at his children. "Tell mama, I'll be home soon."

The children scampered away. Stepping forward, Barak glanced into the sky. "Stop laughing."

Ishtar's hands bled as he flung a final shovel-full of dirt out of a deep hole. He wiped sweat from his beaded brow and tossed the implement aside. After climbing up, he crawled over to the wrapped figure lying by the edge. Tugging the ungainly body into position, he jumped back into the hole and pulled the feet first, nudging the corpse until it fell lengthwise. Climbing spider-like, he positioned his wife's dead body as straight as possible and clawed his way to the surface. Attacking the earth pile with the spade, he swung the dirt back into the hole, sprays and clumps landing in thudding heaps.

As the sun neared its peak, he staggered back into the village.

Amin and Caleb scampered to him, grabbing his tunic, crying and clinging to him.

Ishtar pushed them away with a feeble hand. Taking nothing, seeing nothing, he passed his sobbing mother and wandered over the grassy plain, away from his home, his family, and a history he could not change.

Namah sat beside a rounded mound of earth at the edge of the cliff overlooking the glorious blue lake and stared into the pink and purple sunset. She wrapped her hands around her knees as a cool breeze rippled her shawl.

Gizah settled at her mother's feet, and they shared the view.

Birds twittered and an owl hooted. A small animal scurried through the grass.

Gizah tilted her head, her hand passing lightly over the green grass. "He's at peace now."

Namah smiled. "Strange to say, but I think Aram was always at peace—deep down."

Gizah glanced from the mound to her mother. "How is that?" She clutched a handful of grass. "He suffered so much."

"The measure of a man's contentment is not in his

322

suffering—but in his loving." A single tear meandered down Namah's cheek. "Aram loved well." She reached out and clasped her daughter's hand. "And he always will."

Chapter Fifty-Nine

—OldEarth—

Peace, My Friend

Teal crouched by the mound as the sun rose in the eastern sky. Patting the earth, he glanced at the shimmering lake.

"Peace, my friend." He peered back at the sleeping village. "You brought them home safe."

He rubbed his jaw and peered at the last disappearing stars in the sky. "Not many have accomplished so much."

Standing, he stepped to the edge of the cliff and stared into the distance. "Ishtar wanders into a dangerous world, leaving innocent children behind. Obed, Barak, and Eoban have yet to fulfill their missions."

He clasped his hands behind his back. "I must leave again…but I'll return. One of us will always return. For humanity's future and ours are destined to intertwine."

Three figures stepped forward.

Sienna wrapped her arm around Teal and laid her head against his shoulder.

Ark twined his tentacles behind his back.

Zuri pointed to the sky. "Time to go."

All four stepped away, their silhouettes black against the sky.

Teal turned to the grave one last time and lifted his hand in salute.

A glorious golden sun crested the horizon, and brilliant rays enlightened the world.

About the Author

A. K. Frailey, an author of a historical sci-fi and science fiction series, short story collections, inspirational non-fiction books, a children's book, and a poetry collection, has been writing for over ten years and has published 17 books.

Her novels expand from the OldEarth world to the Newearth universe-where deception rules but truth prevails. Her nonfiction work focuses on the intersection of motherhood, widowhood, practicing gratitude, and rediscovering joy.

As a teacher with a degree in Elementary Education, she has taught in Milwaukee, Chicago, L. A., and WoodRiver, and was a teacher trainer in the Philippines for Peace Corps. She earned a Masters of Fine Arts Degree in Creative Writing for Entertainment from Full Sail University.

Ann homeschooled all eight of her children. She manages her rural homestead with her kids and their numerous critters. In her spare time, she serves as an election judge, a literacy tutor, and secretary/treasurer of her small town's cemetery.